Yuletide Redemption

Jill Kemerer

&

The Pastor's Christmas Courtship

Glynna Kaye

🌿
LOVE INSPIRED
INSPIRATIONAL ROMANCE

Recycling programs
for this product may
not exist in your area.

LOVE INSPIRED®
INSPIRATIONAL ROMANCE

ISBN-13: 978-1-335-42497-6

Yuletide Redemption and The Pastor's Christmas Courtship

Copyright © 2021 by Harlequin Books S.A.

Yuletide Redemption
First published in 2016. This edition published in 2021.
Copyright © 2016 by Jill Kemerer

The Pastor's Christmas Courtship
First published in 2016. This edition published in 2021.
Copyright © 2016 by Glynna Kaye Sirpless

This edition published by arrangement with Harlequin Books S.A.

For questions and comments about the quality of this book, please contact us
at CustomerService@Harlequin.com.

Love Inspired
22 Adelaide St. West, 40th Floor
Toronto, Ontario M5H 4E3, Canada
www.Harlequin.com

Printed in U.S.A.

CONTENTS

YULETIDE REDEMPTION

Jill Kemerer

To my dad, Ron Devereaux.
You always make me smile.

To my mom, Jean Devereaux.
I want to be just like you when I grow up.

To my father-in-law, Leo Kernstock.
You always treat me like your daughter.

To my mother-in-law, Sharon Kernstock.
You bless me in a million ways.

To all those with scars inside or out—you're loved.
Merry Christmas!

Special thanks to Rachel Kent and Shana Asaro
for making this book shine.

But he said to me, "My grace is sufficient for you, for my power is made perfect in weakness." Therefore I will boast all the more gladly about my weaknesses, so that Christ's power may rest on me.
—*2 Corinthians* 12:9

Chapter One

Sam Sheffield curled his fingers around the wheel-chair's hand rims and, for the first time in months, tried to fight his bitterness rather than lingering in self-pity. His prayers had gone unanswered, but his family was right. He had to accept his limitations and move forward.

But how?

The bank of windows showcased maize leaves drifting to the deck. Sunshine glinted off the blue waters of Michigan's Lake Endwell. A stunning day in late October. He still loved the lake. At least the accident hadn't taken that. Too much had been stripped away almost a year and a half ago, though. He'd yet to step foot in his auto dealership. Couldn't imagine running the business from a wheelchair.

A knock on the door made him flinch. It must be the woman his sister had mentioned last night. Claire had advised him in her gentle-but-firm tone to be on his best behavior, that Celeste needed a new start. What Claire hadn't said had come through clearly—his family was tired of doing everything for him. It was bad enough

Claire had hired a caregiver without his permission, but the bomb his brothers had thrown out yesterday? Turned his blood to ice. He wouldn't think about it. Not now, anyway.

Sam rolled across the hardwood floor. He had no need for a caregiver or personal assistant or whatever his sister wanted to call her. Sure, Claire claimed it was the only way Celeste would stay in the cabin next door for free. But whatever had happened to this girl couldn't compare to what he was going through.

Leaning forward, he winced at the tremors in his leg and opened the door. A willowy brunette stood before him, and Sam moved back for her to enter. With her face shadowed by long dark hair, she took a few tentative steps his way. He held out his hand. "Sam Sheffield."

"Celeste Monroe." Her grasp, like her entry, was elusive, as if she wanted to be as invisible as possible.

He tried to catch a glimpse of her face, but her tucked chin and curtain of hair didn't give him much to work with. Spinning the wheels around, he headed to the oak table. "Have a seat."

She obeyed, not bothering to look his way.

"I saw the moving truck earlier." He splayed his fingers on the smooth wood. "I take it Claire's cabin is working out for you?"

"It's perfect." Celeste pushed her hair behind her ear. Deep brown eyes, nervous, glanced at him.

His breath caught in his throat. *She's beautiful.* "I'm glad you like it."

She smiled, revealing slightly misaligned teeth. Only then did he notice the scars. Jagged silver lines crisscrossed her left cheek and forehead, and one slashed her chin. They in no way detracted from her unusual beauty, and he was tempted to stare, to memorize her face. She bobbed her head, her shiny hair slipping back into position.

A volley of questions flew around in his mind. How had she gotten the scars? Why did she need a new start? What had Claire left out? But the puzzle kept coming back to those eyes—they'd touched a part of him that had been buried since the accident.

He forced his attraction deep down, unreachable. What woman would want a man who couldn't do the most basic life tasks for himself? He couldn't protect her. He could barely take care of himself.

"How do you know Claire?" he asked.

"I don't. Not really. She works at the zoo with my mom's best friend, Nancy, who told your sister about my accident. A few weeks ago Nancy put the word out that I was looking for a cheap apartment. Claire said she had the perfect solution. Basically, I get to stay in her cabin for free if I help you out."

His meddling sister. He wasn't angry, though. Claire couldn't help worrying about him any more than she could control her urge to help Celeste by letting her stay in the cabin.

"You mentioned an accident," he said. "What happened to you?"

"Car accident." The words tumbled out. "My face took the brunt of it. The first five weeks were a blur in the hospital followed by a month in the rehab center. When they released me, I was in no shape to take care of myself. I ended up moving back in with my parents."

"How long were you out of work?"

"I never went back. Until this summer, some issues prevented me from working full-time, and my boss hired someone else anyhow. But I'm working again. Self-employed. Virtual assistant. I'm hoping to take on more clients now that I'll have my own place."

"The cabin's been empty since June," Sam said gruffly. An accident had ripped her life apart, too. And she didn't look much older than his twenty-seven years. "Claire and her husband moved into a new house. She hasn't had the heart to sell it. I hope she cleaned it for you."

"She did." Celeste cast a sideways peek his way. "You didn't know, did you?"

"Know what?" He itched to return to the windows, to stare past the deck and lawn out to the lake, to let the peaceful view soothe the commotion stirring inside him. Did Celeste mean he didn't know about Claire's arrangement with her? Or something else?

"My face."

The scars. If he wasn't so focused on himself, he would have put it together. It explained the fragile air about her. "Why would that matter?"

"It matters to most people," she said so softly he barely heard her.

Wanting to put her at ease, he lifted his shirt to reveal the right side of his abdomen. He had his own scars, except they'd faded to a dull red. They lashed up and down the length of his torso. "I guess we're even, then."

Her eyes widened, and a breathy "oh" escaped her mouth. "I'm sorry." The way her eyebrows dipped assured him she meant it.

"They're the least of my worries." His physical scars didn't bother him, but the collateral damage from the accident festered. Memories from the conversation yesterday returned with a vengeance. His brothers, Tommy and Bryan, had actually suggested he consider selling his dealership.

Sell his dream?

He balled his hands into fists. Maybe they were right. The accident had been over sixteen months ago, but he couldn't do even simple work tasks. The first time he'd printed out a sales report, his professional goals had seemed so out of reach he'd almost thrown up. He'd printed another one since then, but within minutes he'd broken down in tears. Tears. From him, the man who never cried. But then, he wasn't the man he used to be. He wasn't sure he would ever be more than a broken body.

Celeste's shoulders hunched as she picked at her fingernail. Sunlight spilled into the room, making the table glow.

"I'm glad you recovered enough to work again." He tapped the table lightly. "I don't know how much Claire told you, but I was in a boating accident. The propeller sliced my right side. Severed the sciatic nerve in my upper thigh. The nerve graft wasn't completely successful."

Just speaking those words riled him up. Why hadn't God listened to his prayers? Half of patients like him were able to get around on two feet again. Why couldn't he be one of them?

Well, he *had* been making progress. Before the slip in the shower a few months ago, he'd been walking on crutches, getting closer to graduating to a cane—working hard so he wouldn't need a wheelchair to resume running his dealership.

Let it go. Accept it. Move forward.

"Are you dealing with any long-term issues?" Sam asked. "Beyond the scars, I mean?"

"Some nerve damage. Headaches." Those espresso eyes met his, warming him. "Nothing I can't handle."

He envied her for only having headaches and scars. She had her legs. She could walk.

"When was the accident?" Sam asked.

"It will be a year on December 18." Her attention shifted to her hands.

"The first annual Lake Endwell Christmas parade."

"Excuse me?"

"Sorry." Being trapped in this cottage all the time must have gotten to him. His conversation skills needed work. "The date's stuck in my head. My aunt Sally has mentioned it about fifty times in the last month. December 18. She's on the planning committee."

"A parade." Her chin lifted as she gazed ahead through the windows. He couldn't tell if she liked or hated the idea of a parade. "A nice distraction. I'll be honest—I'm dreading the date."

A twinge of guilt pressed against his chest. Her accident may not have taken her legs, but it obviously had taken a lot from her, too. "I don't blame you."

"How did you get through yours?"

"Through clenched teeth. My family stayed with me all day." Reminding him how much he'd lost. His brothers and sisters went on as usual while his life had been turned upside down. They either spoke in hushed tones, or they faked chipper, everything-is-fine conversations. He ignored their furtive glances and nagging for him to go back to physical therapy. After his fall in June, he'd stopped going, knowing he might never walk unassisted on both legs. The torn ACL and resulting surgery had left his right knee unstable and both legs weak.

A cane, crutches, a wheelchair—all props reminding him he'd suffered permanent damage. He would never carry a bride over the threshold. Even if a woman could see past his disability, what did he have to offer her? Not a whole lot.

"My parents will probably insist on spending the day with me, too." Celeste rubbed her upper arm. "Your family seems nice."

"They are nice. They just don't get the fact I want to be alone."

"I get it."

She was the one person who probably did get it, and for some reason, that made him feel better.

"Yeah, well, my family is tired of me." Sam gave her a tight smile, squaring his shoulders. "You're the only one brave enough to be here right now."

"I'm sure that's not true."

"Oh, it's true. Ask any of them." His family had been taking turns checking on him, cleaning, making meals, doing his laundry and anything else he needed for months. While he appreciated everything they did, he was tired of the strings attached, the incessant hints about physical therapy being at the top of his list.

Maybe they all needed a break from each other.

"Can I get you something to drink?" He wheeled away from the table in the direction of the kitchen, which was part of one wide open area along with the dining and living rooms.

"No, thank you. I'm fine."

He opened the fridge and swiped a bottle of water. Celeste seemed quiet—easy to be around. Not too talkative or demanding. But before he let her into his world, he needed to set some boundaries. After taking a drink, he returned to the table.

"Well, we should discuss the arrangement," he said. "Regardless of what my family thinks, I don't need or want a nurse."

"No one said anything to me about nursing."

"Good. If you wouldn't mind picking up a few groceries for me, doing some light cleaning and helping with my laundry, I think everyone will be happy."

"Oh, no." Celeste faced him, her brown eyes wide. Once more he was struck by her pretty features. "Claire wouldn't be happy at all. When I talked to her a few days ago, she was quite specific."

He squeezed the arms of the wheelchair. "What exactly did she say?"

"Physical therapy at least three times a week. I'm to drive you there and back. And…"

"And what?" He forced himself not to growl. He was going to have a long chat with his sister later.

"I'm not to take no for an answer."

"No."

Celeste expected the negative response, but she didn't expect to sympathize with him. From the minute she stepped into this grand, lakefront cottage—completely wheelchair-accessible, according to Claire—she'd been fighting a losing battle. She'd agreed to be Sam's assistant, because it felt like a God-given gift dropped in her lap. Celeste would get a rent-free home away from the whispers and all the darted looks at her disfigured face. The cabin would make it possible for her to expand her business, take on a few more clients. After all, she had other things to consider now.

She needed to convince Sam to go to physical therapy.

Sam had wheeled his chair in front of the patio door. The wall held floor-to-ceiling windows with magnificent views of mature trees, a rambling lawn and the sapphire water of the lake dancing in the sunlight. An incredible room. And the man with dark blond hair and piercing blue eyes wasn't bad, either. The fact Sam had his own scars to heal made him less intimidating than most of the people she encountered.

Sort of.

But whether he was gorgeous or not wasn't the issue. If she wanted to live in Claire's cabin, she had to follow Claire's rules. "What's wrong with physical therapy?"

"It didn't work." His profile could have been etched in marble.

She thought back to what Claire told her, and something wasn't adding up. "What do you mean?"

"All my progress was for nothing."

"But you were making progress?"

"I'll always need a wheelchair." His lips drew into a thin line.

Should she continue this obviously touchy subject? If she didn't, he might refuse physical therapy. Claire's cabin meant a life of her own. Privacy. A reprieve from what her life had become. She couldn't depend on her parents forever.

The plastic surgeon would reevaluate her at the follow-up appointment on December 16. Then she'd have another operation to reduce her scars. Who cared that he had already warned her he didn't recommend fur-

ther surgery? The appointment would prove him wrong.
It had to.

This handsome, hurting man in front of her—the one
who'd been given a crummy deal the same way she'd
been—only made Celeste want her old face back more.
She'd never been a supermodel, but men used to notice
her and little kids didn't ask awkward questions. She
couldn't imagine a romantic relationship in her current
skin. It had been hard enough in her old one. More surgery was vital. Living here, away from unwanted attention, was, too.

She squared her shoulders. "You're not paralyzed,
correct?"

"No. Not paralyzed." He flexed his hands. "I slipped
in the shower back in June. Tore ligaments in my right
knee. Had to have surgery on it."

Her heart tightened at all he'd been through. *Lord,
I'm sorry for all the ways I pity myself. Please help Sam.*

"Claire mentioned the possibility of using a cane." It
had been a while since she engaged in conversation this
long with a stranger. She clasped her hands in her lap.

"My doctor didn't make any promises."

"Doctors can't really make promises," she said quietly. Hers certainly hadn't. "What did yours say?"

"With enough physical therapy, I *might* be able to get
around with a cane eventually. I'll need a wheelchair or
crutches to give my leg a break when the pain gets bad."

"I'm sorry. I take it you can't walk at all?"

"For short periods. With crutches."

"That's good." She nodded.

"I haven't used them much since I fell."

"Oh. Does the doctor want you off your leg so it
can heal?"

He didn't meet her eyes, but his right shoulder lifted in a shrug. "It's less painful this way."

Not exactly the answer to her question. "But how will you get better if you stay in the wheelchair?"

"There's no getting better. I won't be able to do the things I used to do. I'll never run, ski or slam-dunk a basketball again."

Heat climbed her neck. It wasn't her business. She was here to help him in exchange for the cabin. Nothing more. But she really couldn't follow his way of thinking. He refused to go to physical therapy, but without it he'd always be in a wheelchair. *Hmm...*

"I don't know much about it," she murmured.

"I don't want to be confined to this chair, but I can't risk permanent damage."

"So let me take you to physical therapy."

"No."

"But you just said—"

"I'd give anything to walk again. Hobbling around with a cane isn't walking. It's a rotten consolation prize."

"I'm really confused. You have a chance to improve your life." She let the rest of her thought go unspoken. *But you're too proud to see a cane as an improvement.*

He jerked his head to the side. "I don't want this life."

And there it was.

Now Celeste understood why Claire had offered an empty cabin in exchange for help with Sam. Until this moment Celeste had worried the offer was only made out of pity. But if pity played a part, Claire's concern for her brother was clearly the bigger factor. This man had been through so much, and he hadn't reconciled his past to move on to the future.

"What do you want?"

He didn't answer right away, but he sighed. "I was the CEO of Sheffield Auto, our family business. Making decisions for five auto dealerships, including one of my own. Everything was going great. Then one day I go fishing with my friend, and nothing has been the same since."

Celeste nodded in sympathy. He'd had big goals. Unlike her. Until last December, she'd been drifting along, working for an insurance agency and living in a dinky apartment. Her degree in history had been filed away in a box, unused. Lately she'd been thinking of dusting it off to become a teacher. Be the woman she could have been.

But not with these scars. She'd be the laughingstock of the school.

"My life isn't the same, either. I don't think it ever will be." She focused on a chickadee perched on the deck railing outside. Another joined it and they flew off together. Escaping. Lake Endwell was her escape.

"I haven't figured out how to move forward." With his elbow propped on the table, his chin rested on his fist.

"Do you still want to run your dealership? And be CEO?"

"Not from a wheelchair."

Her gut told her this man needed physical therapy as badly as she needed more surgery on her face. But how could she convince him?

"What about returning to work with a cane? You have options." She tipped her head. "Try physical therapy again. Claire won't let me live in her cabin unless you do."

"My sister?" He scoffed. "She wouldn't kick you out."

"She would. She's determined to get you back to PT."

"I'll find you another place to stay."

"I don't want another place." She didn't know why this man was touching such a nerve in her. She could live somewhere else. But the dark circles under his eyes shot compassion through her heart. She wanted him to smile. Wanted him to have hope. And her approach clearly wasn't working. "Look, I need this."

"Why?"

What was the saying about desperate times and desperate measures?

"I'll show you." She prayed this didn't backfire as she walked out the door.

Sam rubbed his forehead as the door clicked behind Celeste. For a soft-spoken person, she sure knew how to say things that barbed right to his soul. He wasn't angry. Wasn't even upset. For months he'd carried a Dumpster full of excuses on why he should give up. Why physical therapy wasn't for him.

And for what? He kicked the table leg with his good foot. This was no way to live.

If he didn't return to work after Christmas, there would be no work to return to. His brothers had told him they couldn't continue to help run his dealership. They each had two of their own, and they'd given up most of their free time to keep his profitable.

He would be forced to sell the dealership. They would name a new person to step in as CEO. Succeeding in this business took a hands-on approach and a special personality—one Sam used to have.

Maybe that was the real problem. He'd lost his courage. Lost his identity. Maybe it *was* time to try physical therapy again. His bones ached thinking about it. Getting around in the wheelchair wasn't ideal, but it kept him from the relentless aching and stiffness PT brought on.

Besides, his weak knee could very well cause him to fall, putting him at risk of tearing open the healing sciatic nerve. He'd fought hard to regain feeling in his foot and lower leg. Portions of it were still numb. He might not be moving forward, but at least he wasn't in danger of a permanent setback—paralysis.

The door opened with a creak. Sam sat up straighter, not believing what he was seeing.

Celeste held a dark-haired child in her arms. The baby rubbed his eyes and let his head fall back against her shoulder. He wore little navy pants and a lime-green shirt. A diaper stuck out from the top of the elastic, and his feet were strapped into tiny running shoes.

Sam's heartbeat paused at the picture they presented.

She had a baby.

Longing for a child of his own slammed in his gut. He closed his eyes briefly, willing the futile emotion away.

No wonder she needed a new start. It all made sense now.

Celeste padded forward. "Is it okay if I sit on the couch?"

"Of course." He followed her to the leather couch and chairs. A sweet smile graced her face as she stroked the sleeping child's hair from his forehead.

"This is my nephew, Parker. His mom was killed in the accident."

Sam's mouth dropped open. Wasn't expecting those words. A nephew. The accident. Had Celeste's sister been killed?

"Brandy and I were best friends ever since we sat next to each other in first grade. My big brother, Josh, started dating her after we graduated from high school. They got married four years ago—Josh was deployed off and on throughout their marriage—and then they found out about this little bundle of joy."

"I don't know what to say. I'm sorry." His mind reeled. Here he'd been having a pity party about his leg, not realizing Celeste had lost her best friend. Her sister-in-law.

"I am, too. It breaks my heart every day knowing Brandy and Josh are missing Parker's life."

"Josh? Was he in the car as well?"

She shook her head. "No. He was killed overseas a few weeks after finding out Brandy was pregnant. Roadside bomb in Afghanistan. After he died, Brandy got really depressed. She was obsessed with making up a will. Of course I agreed to be Parker's guardian, although I thought she was a little too intense about it. But here I am. Raising Parker. Permanently."

He could barely take it in. "So your brother never got to see his baby?"

Celeste kissed Parker's head. He slept soundly on her lap, his cheek still resting on her shoulder. "No, and it breaks my heart. I wish he could have. He would have loved his baby. I miss him."

"Don't you have family who could raise him?" He couldn't imagine taking on such a big responsibility so soon after an accident.

"*I* want to raise him. I promised Brandy. My brother

and I were close, and I consider it an honor. Besides, my parents both work full-time. They're getting older, and they don't have the energy I have."

Sam hesitated. "Why is it so important for you to live in Claire's cabin? Why here?"

Her pretty brown eyes dimmed. "I need to create a life of my own." She wrapped her arms tightly around Parker. "I guess I need some time away from it all. Losing my brother and my best friend. Getting used to this face. It's hard when people see the new me but mourn the old me with their eyes."

He understood what she was saying. It was why he hadn't left the cottage in a long time. People expected to see the Sam with a quick joke who could stand tall and play volleyball at a picnic. Seeing him in a wheelchair made them uncomfortable. Or maybe it made him uncomfortable. Maybe both.

"Yes, that's a good way to put it," Sam said. "I guess neither of us got what we wanted out of life."

"I guess not." She tugged Parker's shirt down over his back. "But I'm going to be the best parent Parker could have in this situation. I'm going to make sure he knows everything about his mommy and daddy. Brandy would have done the same for me. And Josh—well, I'd do anything for him."

Sam thought of his four siblings. He'd do anything for them, too.

He'd been selfish. It was time to start thinking about someone other than himself. He had an opportunity to help Celeste. And the baby in her arms.

"Okay, I'll go to physical therapy."

"Really?" Celeste blinked, then beamed.

Man, she was pretty. "Yeah."

"Good. I hope you don't mind Parker riding with us. I'm kind of all he has."

"I like kids." The desire for one of his own hit him again. "How old is he, anyway?"

"Just turned a year. He's almost walking. Claire told me there are plenty of babysitters she can recommend if you don't want him underfoot when I'm cleaning or helping you."

"Save your money. He's welcome anytime. It will be easier for all of us. Why don't you give me your phone number, get settled next door and come back in a few days. We'll work out a schedule then."

Celeste stood, jostling Parker, and rattled off her cell phone number. He typed it into his phone. She carried the baby to the door. "Sam?"

"What?" He followed her, waiting as she stood in the open doorway.

"Thank you."

"For what?"

A blush rose up to her cheeks. "For understanding."

Once she left, he stared at the closed door for a long time. If she had the courage to raise a little boy and continue with her life after being in a terrible accident and losing her best friend, maybe he could find it in himself to try again.

Because he didn't want to spend the rest of his days in a wheelchair.

Chapter Two

"Well, that was unexpected." Celeste breezed past her mother through the hall to lower Parker, still sleeping, into the portable crib she'd set up in the second bedroom. Their new home. Her first step of independence in a long time. How she wished she could call Brandy and tell her every last detail about Sam and the cabin and… She choked down the lump forming in her throat. Brandy was gone, and Celeste was to blame. Living without her best friend didn't get easier. She suspected it never would.

For now, though, she needed to get the house in order. Start fresh. Put the past year behind her.

After kissing her fingers and pressing them against Parker's forehead, she returned to the living room, dodging a pair of burly guys who carried boxes to the kitchen.

"It didn't go well?" Her mom cleaned the inside of a cupboard with a disinfectant wipe.

In black yoga pants and a hot-pink sweatshirt, Shelly Monroe looked younger than fifty-five, but then, she'd always been a believer in drugstore hair color, mascara and fuchsia lipstick.

"Was he unfriendly or something?" Mom sat on the recliner, which was swathed in clear plastic, as Celeste collapsed on the matching couch.

"No. He was…" Celeste didn't know how to describe him. Wasn't sure what her impression was yet. The only thing she knew for certain? She anticipated seeing him again. "Well, for one, he's really good-looking."

"Ooh." Mom's face lit up. She pretended to lick her index finger and made an imaginary mark in the air. "A point in his favor. Bonus. What else?"

"He's in a wheelchair, but he's not paralyzed." Celeste twisted her hair back and secured it with an elastic band. "But it sounds as though physical therapy won't cure him, at least not entirely. I think he's been depressed. You know how it is."

"I do." Mom's brown eyes filled with sympathy. "You'll be good for him."

"We'll see." She shrugged. "I got him to agree to physical therapy, so I don't have to worry about losing this place."

"His family will be relieved. And it will get you out more, which makes me relieved."

Celeste didn't respond. How could she admit she only planned on driving him to and from the rehab center? She wasn't stepping foot in the place—or any place, for that matter. All the shopping Sam needed she'd do as early as possible to avoid people staring at her.

"I know that look." Mom drew her eyebrows together, pursing her lips. "I'm still not thrilled about you moving here, but since you have, I hope you'll try harder to get out and about. Your scars have faded so much. You don't need to be self-conscious."

She wanted to yell, *"You go out there with slashes across your face and tell me I don't need to be self-conscious. You don't know!"* but she held her tongue. She loved her parents. She'd probably say the same thing if she were in their shoes. "I'll try."

Mom reached over and patted her knee. "I know it's hard on you. I hope you'll go to the church Claire mentioned. It might help."

"I have my Bible, Mom. I pray. I'm closer to Him than ever."

"I know. It's just…well, studying on your own isn't the same as having fellowship with other believers."

Not this again. "One thing at a time, okay?" Celeste missed going to church. Another reason she desperately wanted more plastic surgery. Maybe next year would bring the new life she craved. The one where she could go out in public without feeling like an exotic creature at the zoo.

Sam's pinched face came to mind when she'd asked him about his injury. She couldn't really blame him for being upset at the way his life had turned out. If he'd never be able to walk on his own and do all the things he must have loved, why would he be excited to go through the hard work of physical therapy?

Both of their lives were on hold. And they had taken a far different turn from what either of them had expected. She got it. She did. She felt a special bond with him because of it. Had he felt it, too?

"Does Sam have a girlfriend?"

"I don't know." And she wasn't going to find out. Between her disfigurement and her nephew, she couldn't imagine dating anyone. Especially not the cute guy next door. She lacked flirting skills, anyhow. The feminine gifts women seemed to be born with had escaped her. Too often, she was tongue-tied and awkward on a date. No, she didn't see a boyfriend in her future. But, hypothetically, if she did picture one, he looked exactly like Sam Sheffield. "I'm here to help him out. Nothing more."

"You never know," Mom said in a lilting voice. The set of her chin meant she was ready to dig into the topic.

"I do know." Celeste stood and began peeling the plastic off the couch. "Dating, romance—I can't deal with any of that right now. I have enough on my plate as it is."

"When the right guy comes along, you'll be ready." Mom helped her yank the plastic off. "Maybe he's next door."

She fought the urge to roll her eyes, even if the idea made her heart beat faster. "I'm his personal assistant, driver, shopper—whatever he needs. That's it. In the meantime, I need to get at least two more clients for my virtual assistant business."

Her mother made a face, so Celeste jumped in before she could speak. "And I've decided to look into teaching history."

"Really?" Her mom's eyes widened, looking suspiciously moist. "That's wonderful!"

"But first I'm waiting to see what Dr. Smith says."

Mom clamped her mouth shut, arching her eyebrows. "He's already told you. You need to let it go."

She pivoted and marched to the kitchen, shoving the wad of plastic in the trash before returning. "And everything I've read said to wait twelve months, get reevaluated and make decisions then. My condition might change."

"What if it doesn't?"

"It will."

"Celeste—"

"Let's drop it."

"I don't want you getting your hopes up only to be devastated." She stepped forward and cupped Celeste's chin with both hands. "You're beautiful."

Celeste jerked away. Beautiful? Only a mother could say that.

She had a mirror. She was not beautiful.

Mom continued. "Josh's benefits should be enough to cover your basic expenses, especially since you don't have to pay rent. Dad and I have your medical bills almost paid off, so don't worry about money."

Celeste hugged her mom. "Thank you."

"You don't have to thank us. We're blessed your insurance covered as much as it did."

"But still… I want to pay you back."

Mom shook her head and patted Celeste's cheek. "Dad and I can afford it. We both have good jobs. You worry about yourself and the baby."

When she had enough clients to support herself, she planned on setting aside money for Parker's college fund. In the meantime, she'd research what it would take to get certified as a teacher.

Mom pushed up her sleeves. "It might take Parker some time to get used to this change, too."

"Yeah, I know." She was new at this parenting thing. She'd been caring for Parker while living with her parents, but they'd helped her when they got home from work. Would she be able to do this all by herself?

"We're only half an hour away. Call if you need anything. Dad and I will come by a few nights a week, and we'll take him anytime you need a break."

The sliding door leading to the deck opened, and her father, Bill Monroe, stepped inside. "Is your mother giving you a hard time?" He kissed the top of Celeste's head and squeezed her arm. "You doing okay, kiddo?"

The tension in her neck dissolved. Dad had always been her champion, the one she ran to when life got her down. Since Josh's death and the accident, worry lines had dug deep around his eyes, but his tall, trim figure and thick gray hair still gave him a vital appearance.

"I'm fine, Dad. Just got back from Sam's. He's the first person I've met in a long time who has as many, if not more, problems than me."

"I'm sorry to hear he's struggling. Sounds like he needs your help."

"Thanks, Dad." She wiggled one arm around his waist and leaned her head against him.

"Nice yard you've got back there. You'll have to watch Parker with the ornamental pond, though. It's wider and deeper than it looks. It only takes a few inches for a child to drown."

"Do you think we could fence it off?"

"We have to do something. I'll run over to the hardware store." He patted his back pocket to check for his wallet, then pulled out his keys. "Be back in a few."

Mom returned to the kitchen and unpacked glasses. "Are you sure you can handle Parker? If it's too much for you, say the word and we'll move you home with us."

She grimaced, shaking her head. "I need this, Mom."

"But—" Concern glinted in Mom's eyes.

"Don't worry. If my headaches get bad again, I'll

consider it, but I don't think it will be an issue. They've been much better since summer."

"Okay, okay." Mom stretched on her tiptoes to place a glass on the upper shelf.

Celeste stripped packing tape off a box in the kitchen and stacked plates in a cupboard. This cabin felt like home already. And knowing she wouldn't run into anyone from her past took a layer of pressure off. All the rumors about the accident had gotten back to her over the previous months. Variations on the same theme— she'd been either texting or negligent or intoxicated before the car jumped the ditch and wrapped around a telephone pole.

A shiver rippled over her skin. No, she hadn't been texting or drinking. But if she'd paid more attention to the weather conditions, she would have realized the pavement was covered in black ice. She would have driven slower.

And Brandy would be alive.

The plate in her hand slipped. She tightened her grip.

When she got the surgery and no one could see the scars anymore, they would forget about the accident. She'd be able to face herself in the mirror. She could look at Parker and not want to crush him to her, crying out, "It was my fault! I killed your mommy!"

She'd lived with the visual reminders for too long. They'd forced her into hiding, away from the options that used to be available to her. Her mind flipped to Sam, his comment about not wanting his life.

She didn't want hers, either.

The life she wanted depended on more surgery.

Sam wiped the sweat off his forehead with a towel Saturday morning. The clock read 9:20, which meant he needed to get ready. Celeste would be here in ten minutes to work out a schedule. *Schedule.* The word brought a bad taste to his mouth. It was impersonal, reminding him he was a duty, nothing more. It had been three days since Celeste moved in, and he hadn't been able to get her or Parker off his mind.

He tightened his hold on the crutches as he clip-clopped to the kitchen. Regardless of what his family thought, he hadn't completely given up on himself. Every morning he spent an hour performing range-of-motion exercises and working his upper body with weights. The effort always exhausted him, and the pain in his legs? Excruciating. He dreaded returning to physical therapy next week.

Maybe he should cancel.

And break his promise to Celeste? If he was that much of a coward, he might as well give up on life now.

He'd go to PT. He was a fighter.

Was being the key word.

When was the last time he'd fought for anything other than to maneuver his body out of bed without aggravating his leg? Lately he'd played the role of invalid a little too well.

Fumbling with the cupboard door, he almost dropped his crutch. It had been a long time since he used them to get around the cottage. Both arms and legs already ached. Whenever he put weight on his bad leg, his ankle rolled and knee caved. Balancing on his left leg and crutch, he pulled a glass out of the cupboard and flipped on the faucet, letting the water stream until it ran cold.

In some ways he'd been fortunate. Within six months of his first surgery, he'd regained feeling in his foot. Most of his leg followed. He'd used crutches until June, when one slip in the shower had thrown him back to square one. The ligaments in his right knee had torn and the healing nerve graft had been strained. Another surgery had repaired the knee, but three weeks with his leg immobilized had set his progress back considerably. The physical therapist made home visits for two weeks, but when the home visits stopped, so did Sam's motivation. The flexibility and strength he'd fought so hard for had declined.

What if physical therapy didn't work? Why do it if he'd be stuck in this state forever?

You promised her, Sheffield.

Now and then he'd caught glimpses of Celeste carrying Parker across the lawn to the edge of the lake. Her hair was usually pulled back, and her face would glow as she held both Parker's hands so he could toddle in front of her. He wished he could join her and toss Parker up in the air and catch him the way Tommy did with his youngest, Emily, who would giggle nonstop.

Sam frowned, thinking of Parker's dad. The kid didn't have a father, and Celeste appeared to be single. He hadn't seen any cars besides her parents' pull up.

He changed into a clean T-shirt and checked his appearance in the bathroom mirror. Too thin and pale with dark smudges under his eyes. In other words, a train wreck. The sensation of pins and needles spread across his right knee as a faint knock came from the kitchen.

Crutches or wheelchair? Experience said to settle his leg on the footrest of the wheelchair or he'd be in for a world of hurt, but vanity won. He thunked his way down the hall and hollered, "Come in."

Celeste stepped inside with Parker on her hip and her head lowered. When she glanced up, Sam's lungs froze. Maybe it was the shyness in her brown eyes or the slight imperfection in her smile—whatever it was, she affected him. If his life was different, he'd be tempted to ask her on a date.

The muscles in his stomach tightened. His life wasn't different. He couldn't even handle leaving the cottage. How could he fantasize about dating?

"You're up and about." Celeste sounded surprised. The day was sunny but cool, and she wore a beige cardigan over dark jeans and matching beige slip-on canvas shoes. "You look pale."

Yeah, a mere hour of exercises left me limp.

"Come in and sit down." He led the way to the living room and sat on a chair. He made a conscious effort not to hiss as he lifted his bad leg onto the ottoman. *Sweet relief.* The aching lessened but the tingling sensation increased.

She perched on the edge of the couch and bounced Parker on her knees. Sam peered more closely at him. His eyes were lighter brown than hers, and he had chubby cheeks and a happy air about him. Sam had the craziest urge to take the boy in his arms and set him on his lap.

"Cute kid." He smiled at him, then studied Celeste from her shiny hair to her slim frame.

"Thanks." She seemed to be aware of his scrutiny and shrank into herself. She nodded to his leg. "How are you? Are you feeling okay?"

"I'm fine."

"Are you sure? You're not in pain?"

Here he'd been trying to appear somewhat normal, and he'd obviously failed. She viewed him as a patient. Not as a man.

"Did you bring your calendar?" he said. "Let's figure out a schedule."

"I keep everything in here." She held up her phone.

Phone. His was in the bedroom. As much as he wanted to get it himself, the sensations in his leg screamed not to. "Mine is in my room. Would you mind getting it for me?"

"Sure." She rose, taking Parker with her. The boy watched him over her shoulder. Sam almost waved at the little guy.

"First door to your right. It's on the table." Next to his hospital bed. A further reminder he was an invalid. Real men didn't sleep in beds with railings.

Why was his pride flaring up now? She'd see the entire house when she cleaned. Would he feel the same if Celeste were older, unattractive, unavailable? Probably not.

If he could go back in time, back to when he was whole...

"Here you go." She handed him the phone, her slender fingers brushing his.

"Thank you." Ignoring the way his adrenaline kicked in at her simple touch, he swiped the screen and clicked through to his calendar. "Why don't we start with cleaning?"

For the next ten minutes, they hashed out a schedule. Toward the end, he struggled to concentrate. His leg had been growing stiff as they talked.

"Could you grab me an ice pack from the freezer?" He grimaced, shifting to ease his discomfort. "It slips into a wrap." Beads of sweat broke out on his forehead. When would this get easier?

She set Parker on the area rug a few feet in front of

him, went to the kitchen and returned, handing Sam the ice pack. "Is there anything I can do? You look like you're hurting."

He was. Every day brought pain. "The ice wrap will help. I overdid my exercises this morning."

She helped him fasten the wrap on, and he leaned back in the chair, closing his eyes and counting to five. If she said anything, he didn't hear it. When the worst of the pain passed, he opened his eyes.

Parker still sat on the rug, but his little legs pumped back and forth as he laughed, both fists full of the fluffy material. Sam's discomfort faded at the sight of such delight.

"You do exercises?" She resumed her spot on the couch, leaving Parker where he was to enjoy the rug.

"I did physical therapy nearly every day for the first year after the accident. I was making decent progress until I fell almost at the year mark. Ever since the operation in June, my knee's been weak and stiff. I still do a sequence of exercises each morning." It wasn't enough. He knew it. Had known it for months. But the longer he stayed away from therapy, the more daunting it became.

"I had to learn how to eat again. A few spots are painful to touch." She pointed to the scar on her cheekbone then to her chin. "It's hard." Her tone softened. "What you're doing is hard."

It was hard. No one understood how hard.

Except maybe her. Which made him like her even more.

"Can you drive me to the rehab center next week?" he asked gruffly. "I have appointments scheduled Monday, Wednesday and Friday. Ten o'clock each morning."

"Sure." She typed the information into her phone. "Anything else?"

"Not right now." He wasn't ready for her to go, though. She distracted him from the monotony his life had become. "Tell me about your life before the accident."

"There's not much to tell." Celeste rummaged through the diaper bag and handed Parker a small stuffed dog. He promptly shoved the ear in his mouth. "I answered phones for an insurance agency. My major didn't exactly help my job prospects."

"What was your major?"

"History."

"You don't want to teach?" His muscles loosened as the ice worked.

"Actually, I've been thinking about getting certified." She gave him a shy glance. "It depends. A lot has changed."

Parker squealed and the floppy dog flew through the air. He crawled after it. Sam grinned. Yes, he could see how things had changed. She had a baby to care for.

"What about you?" she asked. "Do you think you'll work again?"

The thought of not working again horrified him almost as much as the thought of living out his days in a wheelchair. "Yes."

"The dealership?"

"Uh-huh." He tightened the wrap. As much as he'd tried to deny it, he craved his job. He'd been toying with the idea of printing off last month's profit-and-loss statement again. Maybe this time he could get through it without vomiting. "I oversaw Sheffield Auto. My brothers and I had meetings every Friday morning at the closest dealership—one of Tommy's—to go over quotas, employees, budgets, you name it."

And he'd been in charge. Finally a respected part of the family business instead of the pesky little brother. Man, he missed it.

"Do you miss it?"

It was as if she'd read his mind.

"Yeah."

"You should go to one of the meetings."

"I don't know." He frowned as the view of his propped leg greeted him. He'd gone from annoying little brother to respected member of the company to cripple. He was afraid of breaking down in front of his brothers and dad. Could he return to the job he'd thrived on?

Parker hauled himself up to a standing position, then fell back on his bottom. He chewed on the toy again.

"Would they come here?" she asked.

They probably would. But he wanted out of this cottage. Wanted to be the CEO, not the victim.

Was he capable, though? The accident had injured him in ways he didn't want anyone to know. "I'll see how I'm feeling after a couple of weeks."

Her sweet smile made him want to declare he would be at those meetings, but he knew better than to make promises he couldn't keep. The only thing worse than being pitied would be for Bryan, Tommy and Dad to witness him having an emotional breakdown.

The last thing he wanted was another devastating setback. He had to be careful, which meant playing it safe and taking things slow with his leg—and with his life.

Monday morning Celeste craned her neck to peer over the counter. Parker sat on his play mat and grunted

as he gripped a toy airplane over his head. When he shook it, music played and lights flashed. She had five minutes before she had to buckle him into his car seat. Today was Sam's first day of physical therapy, and she'd promised she'd get him there early. A thrill of excitement sped through her veins at the thought of seeing him again. He had a kind heart. It matched his face, which kept flashing before her when she closed her eyes at night.

He was way out of her league. Too handsome, too next-door, too everything.

She frowned at the drizzle outside. Sam had already told her he would be in the wheelchair since he couldn't take the chance of hurting his leg using the crutches. What if he slipped getting into her minivan? And would she be able to help him in and out without hurting him?

After a final swipe of the dishcloth over the counter, she hustled to the front hall closet for her jacket. Then she nestled Parker into the car seat, ignoring his protests at being separated from the toy. He arched his back and fussed as she clicked the straps into place.

"I know, baby." Grabbing the diaper bag and her purse, she tensed at his increasing cries and lifted the carrier as her cell phone rang.

"Hello?"

"Celeste? This is Sue Roper from Rock of Ages church."

Brandy's old church. Dread pooled in Celeste's stomach.

"Yes, hello, Sue."

"I know you're raising Parker now, and I wasn't sure if you were aware that Brandy's grandmother, Pearl, recently moved to an assisted living facility."

"Yes, I know. I've been meaning to visit." Grandma Pearl. The woman had hosted countless tea parties in her parlor for Celeste and Brandy when they were little girls. Rheumatoid arthritis and weak bones had forced her into an apartment in assisted living. Guilt pinched Celeste. She hadn't visited the endearing lady in a while. At least her parents had brought Parker to see her a few times.

"She would love that," Sue said. "But that's not why I'm calling. We're preparing the children's Christmas Eve program, and we have a favor to ask."

Parker's cries became wails. A favor? She rocked the carrier. "Is there any way I can call you back?"

"It will only take a minute."

"Okay, just give me a second." Celeste suppressed a sigh and took Parker out of the car seat, settling him in her arms. His cries stopped instantly. "Okay, I'm ready."

"Well, Pearl is very near and dear to us, so the ladies and I have been discussing it, and we want to give her a Christmas surprise. Since Brandy died, she's been really down. Still comes to church, thankfully. Lou Bonner brings her each Sunday. The one thing that brightens her up is Parker. She always talks about him and shows us the pictures you send her."

Celeste's chest tightened. She should be doing more for Grandma Pearl than sending a few pictures now and then.

Sue continued. "Wouldn't she love it if Parker was baby Jesus in the program? I can't think of another gift that would make her happier. I know he's a bit old for the part, but we'd love to have him for Pearl's sake."

In her head, Celeste instantly ticked off problems with the scenario. Parker wasn't walking, but he was at a stage where he hated to be constrained. Having him in a Christmas program seemed overly ambitious. Then there was the fact Grandma Pearl went to Brandy's old church.

There would be questions. And attention. The kind she avoided.

Sure, Sue was friendly on the phone, but what about Brandy's other friends from church? Did they consider Celeste responsible for Brandy's death?

Why wouldn't they? She was the one who'd been driving.

"Um, he doesn't sit all that well right now."

"If he won't sit still, he can be a sheep."

She longed to decline, but this was for Grandma Pearl, and the woman was alone and, most likely, sad. Not to mention Brandy would have wanted Parker in the Christmas Eve program—she'd climb Mount Everest for her beloved grandmother.

"What would I have to do?" Parker tried to wriggle out of her grasp, but she held tight, pretending to blow him kisses. Anything to avoid a meltdown.

"Practices are Thursday nights starting after Thanksgiving. We'll walk the children through their parts and fit them for their costumes. I know it's a lot to ask, but we don't know how many Christmases Pearl has left. Would you do this for her?"

"Of course."

"Thank you. We'll see you in a few weeks."

Celeste hung up with mixed feelings. Maybe Mom and Dad would take Parker to the practices. If not, she would act like an adult, drive him there herself and deal with it.

Wait. The church was on the same road as the accident site. If she drove Parker, she would have to pass the ditch, field and telephone pole where she'd lost so much.

The moments before the car spun out came back. The loud Christmas music, the laughter—what had they been laughing about?—the happy, girls'-night-out feeling she always got when she was with Brandy.

She would never have it again.

Her stomach felt hollow. Mom and Dad would have to drive Parker, because she wasn't ready to confront her past.

There wasn't time to think about it now. She was late. Once again, she strapped Parker into the carrier. He whimpered, rubbing his eyes. She rushed down the porch steps into the rain, slid open the side door of her red minivan and locked Parker's seat into the base before driving the short distance to Sam's. Tossing her hood up to protect her head from the rain, she ascended the kitchen steps and knocked.

"I'll meet you at the bottom of the ramp," Sam yelled.

"Okay." She hurried down the staircase and wiped her palms on her jeans, holding her breath when he rolled her way. "Do you need me to help?"

"No. Got it."

As soon as he reached the passenger side, she held out her hand to help him into the van. He kept his weight on his left leg and got into the seat slowly and with concentrated effort. Parker had finally stopped crying. *So far, so good.*

"Let me put this in the trunk, and we'll be on our way." She clutched the hood together under her chin before awkwardly loading the chair in the back. Once inside the van, she checked on Parker, whose eyelids were heavy, and buckled her seat belt. "Sorry I'm late. Something unexpected came up."

"For a minute, I thought you stood me up."

Stand him up? Not in a million years.

"No, nothing like that. A lady from Brandy's church called."

"Is everything okay?"

"Yeah…well, no. Not really." She shook her head, swallowing the knot in her throat. "Never mind. I don't know what to think. They want to surprise Brandy's grandma by having Parker be baby Jesus in the Christmas Eve service."

"Why do you sound upset? Don't you like her grandma?"

"I love her. She's sweetness personified. In fact, I feel guilty I haven't visited her in a while. She adores Parker."

"Don't feel guilty. You're doing the best you can."

The road wound through trees. The wipers swished rapidly as she sneaked a peek over at Sam's profile. She guessed he smiled a lot—or used to, anyway—by the faint creases around his blue eyes. Did her heart just flutter? He was so handsome, even if he was worried. The lines in his forehead and slight bulge in the vein near his temple didn't lie.

"Are you nervous about today?" she asked.

"Yeah." Sam faced her, and her stomach dipped. *My, oh my.*

She turned and continued along the two-lane road. The forest gave way to farm fields, some with faded yellow cornstalks standing limp in the rain, others with dried stumps of harvested crops. The trees in the distance looked like a watercolor painting of fall colors.

"What else is going on?" The way he said it gave her the impression he'd welcome a distraction.

"I'm still not sure about this baby Jesus thing in the Christmas Eve program."

"He's pretty young." Sam frowned, looking back at Parker. She checked her rearview. He'd fallen asleep.

"Yes, but if he won't cooperate, they'll let him be a sheep."

"Cute." The corner of his mouth kicked up in a grin, and his eyes twinkled. "I'd like to see that."

"Yeah."

"Don't sound so excited."

"I'm not a hundred percent sold on the idea."

"Why not?"

"Well, like you said, he's pretty young. Not even walking yet. And I would have to take him to practices."

"What's so bad about that?" He shifted, watching her.

Everything. Brandy's friends might blame me. And then there's my face. She tilted her chin up. "The church is a mile north of where my car spun out last December. I would have to pass it to get to the practices."

He didn't say anything for a while, just stared at the rain splashing on the window. "If it would make it easier, I could go with you."

Celeste sucked in a breath. His offer burrowed into her heart. All her reasons for not taking Parker seemed petty. But reality set in. Then doubt. Sam would see other people's reactions. She didn't want him to think less of her.

"Thank you, but I can always ask my parents to take him."

She could feel his stare but didn't bother looking

over. He didn't understand, and she wasn't explaining. She wished she could take him up on his offer. Wished she had met him before her accident, when things were different. When even a tongue-tied girl like her might have had a chance at dating a guy like him.

"You've been working on your upper body strength."

"Every morning your voice echoes in my head, chiding me about working hard and pushing through." Sam's left leg trembled at the exertion of the last hour. His right hip was ready to explode. The pain differed from what he'd been feeling at home, though. He recognized it from all those months he'd worked with Dr. Rachel Stepmeyer. The pain of exertion brought a rush. And hope.

Last time he'd hoped, he'd been let down. How many times had he prayed for complete healing? He'd believed God would heal him, too. He'd memorized the Bible verse about being able to move a mountain with enough faith. His faith hadn't lacked. God hadn't listened to him.

God didn't care.

"The good news is your muscles haven't atrophied. You're weaker, obviously, and you've lost some range of motion, but commit to your sessions and you'll get it back. We have a new muscle stimulation system. It could help with your pain." Dr. Stepmeyer typed something into her tablet. "I want you out of the wheelchair more. I know it's hard, but the crutches will force you to build muscle in your legs."

"Yes, ma'am."

That brought a hint of a smile to her face. She handed

him a brochure about muscle stimulation. "Read this over and let me know if you want to try it."

"I will." He tucked it between his thigh and the side of the wheelchair.

"See you on Wednesday."

"Thanks."

"Oh, and Sam?"

He waited.

"It's good to have you back."

Nodding, he spun the chair and wheeled away. Rain still pounded against the glass door. He didn't see Celeste's minivan, so he waited near the entrance. Ever since his last doctor's appointment a few months ago, he'd pushed aside the nagging worry that the fall in the shower had killed his chances at ever walking unassisted. After the last surgery, Dr. Curtis had warned him it might take two more years for him to heal. If he healed…

But today Dr. Stepmeyer had assured him he just needed to keep working at it.

His thoughts turned to the conversation earlier in the car. Sam had made the offer to accompany Celeste to the practices because he thought she needed a friend. And, if he was honest, because he'd been thinking about her more and more each day. He wanted to spend time with her. Enjoyed talking to her. She didn't put pressure on him the way his family did.

The fact she was avoiding the site of her accident didn't surprise him. What did? How quickly she turned him down.

He wasn't used to women turning him down.

Celeste's red minivan stopped at the sidewalk. He pressed the button for the doors to automatically open.

The handicap buttons were getting old. His life was getting old.

Would Celeste have said yes if he wasn't in a wheelchair?

He didn't know. He wasn't sure he wanted to find out.

Chapter Three

Celeste pushed the dust mop across Sam's living room floor while Parker stood, knees bouncing as he held on to the wooden coffee table. For three weeks she and Sam had been settling into a comfortable routine, one with clear expectations. She took Sam to and from physical therapy three days a week, shopped for his groceries at the crack of dawn on Tuesday mornings and cleaned on Fridays after his physical therapy session. Sometimes she wished their relationship wasn't so businesslike.

Her mind wandered to her clients' long to-do list waiting at home. She was a virtual assistant to busy, successful people, and working while raising Parker was proving more challenging than she'd expected. To fit in all the projects—from emails and phone calls to invoicing—she got up at six, worked a few hours and did the bulk of her duties when Parker napped or after he went to bed.

Then there was her main charge, Sam. At least she'd managed to nip her growing attraction to him in the bud by telling herself over and over that he was off-limits.

Sam treated her for what she was—the caregiver who lived next door.

She sighed. One more room and she'd be finished with the light cleaning he required. This place needed some music, preferably upbeat Christmas songs. Hard to believe next week was Thanksgiving already.

"You think today will be the day Parker makes his big move?" Sam swung into the room on his crutches. After his therapy session, he'd disappeared to his bedroom to shower and change. His damp hair looked darker than usual, and his smile made her stop sweeping midstroke.

Look away! He can't help he's gorgeous.

Now that she was around more, she'd taken to studying him—to make sure he was okay. While around six feet tall, he wasn't large. He had muscular arms, but his legs were lean from lack of use. Some days his face faded white and his lips tightened to a thin line. Those days she knew he was in a lot of pain. But today he had a relaxed air about him. He settled into his chair, setting the crutches down as he carefully straightened his leg on the ottoman.

He waved to Parker. "I think he'll start walking on his own this week."

"I hope so. Everything I've read said babies usually walk unassisted by twelve months. His pediatrician told me not to worry, but I can't help it."

Parker made a goo-goo noise and zoomed around the table, not taking his hands off it. He tripped, toppling over on his side.

"Oh!" She lurched forward, but Sam held his hand out.

"Let him be. He'll figure it out."

She paused, waiting for a cry, but Parker pushed himself back up and held on to the table once more. He stared at Sam with a big grin, then took a wobbly step toward him.

"Look at that! He's doing it!" Sam held his arms open wide, reaching as far as his extended leg would allow him. "Come on over, buddy."

Celeste whipped her phone out of her back pocket, fumbling to enter the passcode. She pressed Video and directed it Parker's way. He stood immobile with his hands in the air, but he hadn't taken a step yet. *Come on, come on, you can do it, little man!*

Parker lifted his chunky leg and promptly fell on his bottom. She exhaled the breath she'd been holding. "Oh, well. He'll do it one of these days."

"Maybe today. You never know." Sam made funny faces at Parker, who laughed and crawled to him, pulling himself to the edge of Sam's chair. Sam picked him up.

At the sight of Parker on Sam's lap, Celeste's heart swelled. He always had a smile for her nephew, often shaking his tiny hand or ruffling the hair on his head, but this was the first time he'd held the boy. The picture they presented? Priceless. But unwanted thoughts surged through her mind. *Josh should be here cradling his son. What if Parker never has a daddy?*

What if she ended up raising Parker alone forever? It was a scenario she knew could come true. What guy would want to raise her nephew and wake up to her scars every morning?

Celeste was it for Parker. Part of her loved being his mom, but the other part worried she'd never be enough.

The baby had lost his mom and dad, and he was stuck with his aunt who'd basically become a recluse.

She grabbed the dust mop with more force than necessary and swept the rest of the floor while Sam made funny explosion noises and tickled Parker, who giggled loudly. Outside, the wind blew a few straggling brown leaves across the deck. Winter had arrived. Snow would be coming soon.

"Why don't you take a break, Celeste?"

With a few taps she emptied the dishpan in the trash. She never lingered after cleaning, but then, Sam never asked her to stay, either. What would it hurt? Parker looked so content on his lap she didn't have the heart to tear him away. "Okay."

She took a seat on the leather couch. Crossed one leg over the other. Had no clue what to do next. Parker yawned.

"I noticed you running the other day." Sam tucked him under his arm. Be still her heart. There was something very appealing about Sam holding a child. "Your parents still helping out?"

"Yes. They miss him. They swing by after work a few days a week. They'll be here Sunday, too."

"Good." He didn't seem to know what to say, either. His eyes darted around the room. "I didn't know you ran."

"I haven't as much lately. The days are getting shorter, so my long runs are numbered."

"Oh?" He adjusted his leg, holding Parker firmly. Parker's eyes had grown heavy, and he let out another big yawn.

"It's kind of hard with Parker. I have a jogging stroller, but for me, running is a solitary sport. It's not the same pushing a stroller. I'd rather have my arms moving."

"What about a treadmill?"

She twisted her face, sticking her tongue out. "Yuck. Boring. I'm best outside."

"I take it you've been doing it a long time?"

"Running used to be a big part of my life."

"How's that?"

"Well, let's see." She tapped her finger against her chin and flinched, suddenly remembering the tender spot. "I started running cross-country in seventh grade. I ran varsity all four years of high school. Got a partial college scholarship out of it, too."

"Impressive."

She diverted her attention to her lap. "Running kept me focused, but I didn't give enough thought to life after college. It's probably why I have a degree I'm not using." She let out a self-deprecating laugh.

"Well, that makes two of us. I'm not using mine, either." He frowned. "I think I need to change that." She waited for him to say more on the subject, but he shook his head. "I take it you didn't have dreams of marathons?"

"Oh, I had those, all right. I saw myself as the next Joan Benoit."

"Who is she?" He gave her a pointed stare, his eyes playful.

"An amazing American runner."

He looked suitably impressed. "So what happened?"

She shrugged, brushing a piece of lint from her jeans. "No matter how hard I trained, I wasn't as fast as the top runners. I got injured my junior year of college. I'd had tendinitis and other problems off and on, but the stress fracture took a long time to heal. My college career was a disappointment. I did end up running in a few marathons after college."

"Not anymore?"

"No." Memories flitted to her. The feel of packed earth beneath her feet at all those high school races. Sweat dripping down her back as she pushed herself to stay conditioned on lonely roads during the summer. Lifting weights to get an edge. Being top ten in her district, but not good enough to take the state title. She missed those days.

"You don't mind holding him?" She nodded at Parker, who had fallen asleep in Sam's arms. What would it be like to have a man in her life, a husband to help raise Parker?

"Not at all. My niece Emily used to sleep on my lap, before…well, before I had the second surgery. The family doesn't meet here for Tuesday dinners anymore. In fact, no one comes around as much. I didn't want them to."

"I get it. I pushed people away, too." *And some of them pushed me away.*

The clock on the wall ticked as silence stretched.

"You never told me if your parents are taking Parker to the Christmas program practices."

Celeste wrapped her arms around her waist. "I haven't asked them."

"Why not?" He sounded skeptical.

"It slipped my mind." It hadn't slipped her mind, but every time she considered calling Mom to ask, she balked. Something about the request reeked of desperation.

"Well, I should probably go back." She rose. "Is there anything else you need before I leave?"

"Yes, actually." Sam shifted in his seat, his face distorting as he did. "There is something you can do for me. I want to get out of here."

"Oh, okay." Celeste blinked. "Right now? It's kind of cold out."

Sam groaned. That wasn't what he meant. He didn't exactly know what he was asking.

"No." He inhaled Parker's baby shampoo, fighting the frustration bulging inside him. The accident had taken the use of his leg, but sometimes he thought it had taken his speech, too. Conversation had been easy—his strong suit—before the accident. And now? He might as well be a caveman, grunting and gesturing. "I mean in general. I was wondering if I could go grocery shopping with you."

"Oh." Her face fell as she sat back down. "Sure. No problem."

But the way she slumped said it was a problem. "I don't want to go out in the wheelchair. I don't like being stared at, and I need to build strength in my legs. I'm just… Forget it." He jerked his head to the side. Why did he have to be so dependent?

"Well, if you're trying to avoid stares, I'm probably not the best person to be out with." Her hair had fallen in front of her face, the way it had the first few times he saw her.

"Look, I know I'm asking a lot from you, but I've been hiding away for a long time. If I'm going to have any shot at a somewhat normal life, I have to go back to work. I thought if I start getting used to my crutches in public places, maybe it would be easier. I'm just asking to go with you when you have errands to run. Like when you stop in town for coffee or go to the library—that sort of thing."

"I think that's wonderful, Sam." She tucked her hair behind her ear. "But your family is better suited to take you out."

"They all work. I would have to go with them at the busiest times, and everyone in town would stop and ask a million questions. My legs hurt the worst at night." His forehead tightened, and he could feel his pulse hammering in his temple. He hated begging, but he'd given it a lot of thought over the last couple of weeks. Since he was back in physical therapy, he could see how much he'd been missing. It was as though he'd spent the last months under a dark tent, and the flap had opened, revealing a sunny meadow.

Frown lines deepened above the bridge of Celeste's nose. "I'll have to think about it."

"What's there to think about?" He massaged the back of his neck with his free hand. "I understand I would slow you down, but it can't be that big of an imposition."

"You wouldn't slow me down, and you're no imposition." She wrung her hands together. "It's just… well, I don't go to the coffee shop or the library. I do the grocery shopping as soon as it opens, and I practically sprint through the aisles to get it done as quickly as possible."

Some of the things puzzling him about Celeste finally added up. "You don't want people to see your scars."

Her throat worked as she swallowed. Was that a tear glistening in her eye?

"But you're beautiful."

She gasped, staring wide-eyed at him.

He shrugged. "I barely notice them."

"You're the only one, then. I have a follow-up appointment in December. I want more surgery."

Something in her tone made him pause. In his experience, the doctors told him when he needed more surgery, not the other way around. He didn't want to push the issue, though. He'd already brought a tear.

"Celeste?"

"Yes," she whispered.

"Where do you miss going? You know, the places you took for granted before the accident?"

She gazed at the wall, a faraway look in her eyes. "Well, like I said, running. I'd run for miles whenever I wasn't working. And we had a café I loved going to. I'd buy the latest David McCullough biography and just sit and read, sipping a latte. No one would bother me."

She glowed as she spoke, and he wanted to give it to her—her old life—but he could no more fix hers than he could fix his own.

"With the weather getting colder, you won't run outside anyhow, will you?" He couldn't imagine running when it snowed. He'd never been an exercise fanatic. Played basketball now and then, and that was about it.

"Are you kidding? Of course I run in the winter. Ice and negative windchill are the only things stopping me." She waved. "Well, until Parker came along, that is."

Her words gave him an idea. He didn't know if it would work, but he wasn't about to overanalyze it at this point. "What if I watch Parker for you so you can run?"

"What?" She shook her head. "No. I couldn't ask you to do that."

"I realize I'm not the best babysitter material. But if you brought him over here, there's really not anywhere he could go. It's a big open space for him. And I've got a television. We can watch cartoons."

"But your cabinets aren't babyproofed." She stood, crossing her arms over her chest. "What if he falls or something and you can't get to him?"

"I'm not paralyzed. I get in and out of my wheelchair fine, and you know I've been using my crutches longer each day for the past couple of weeks."

Regret shone in her eyes. "I'm sorry. I didn't mean—"

"No offense taken. I understand. If you're worried about babyproofing, we can empty the cupboards. I never use them." He tightened his hold on Parker, so warm against his chest. He wouldn't mind taking care of the little guy for her, not at all. "How long do your runs last?"

"Thirty minutes to an hour. When I trained for marathons, I did longer runs, but I'm not training now." She began to pace. He liked watching her graceful movements.

"Do you want to?" he asked.

She stopped, turning to him. "Do I want to what?"

"Train for a marathon."

"I don't know. I haven't considered it."

"Why not?"

"Well…" She returned to the couch and gave him a frank look. "My life revolves around Parker. And I'm having a hard time fitting everyday activities and work around him. Even taking a shower has gotten complicated."

He didn't doubt that was true, but he guessed her insecurity about her scars was the bigger problem.

"Let me take him off your hands a few mornings a week so you can fit your runs in."

He could see in her face how tempted she was to take him up on his offer.

"You can drop him off first thing Tuesday morning, and afterward we'll go grocery shopping together. Look, you miss running. I miss work. I want to go to the Friday meetings. I want to inspect the cars on my dealership lot, talk to my employees and sell vehicles to my customers. I miss the reports, the quotas, the rush of meeting our sales goals. I need to get back. I might never walk on both feet again, but I can work. I want to work. But I need to do this, first."

Celeste clasped her hands tightly. She had to say yes. She knew it. How could she deny Sam this? But how could she agree?

He didn't know what he was asking.

"I want to help you, Sam, but there's a reason I don't go to the coffee shop and read anymore, and it has nothing to do with Parker. People don't just stare. They ask questions, and sometimes it hurts."

If she took him with her, he'd see how other people viewed her. He'd said she was beautiful—of all the wonderful things he could say!—but he'd see for himself no one else thought she was pretty.

"Maybe you're wrong. They don't know you, but they know me. If you take me with you, the people we run into might not notice you because it's been so long since *I've* been out."

She hadn't thought of that. "Yeah, and then a mom

will stroll by with her young kids and one will say, 'Mommy, why does she have all those marks on her face?' It's embarrassing, Sam."

His lips lifted in a grin. "I can handle that if you can handle, 'Look, Marge, isn't that the Sheffield boy? What a shame it's been this long and he's still not walking.'"

She giggled. She didn't mean to, but it came out. "Do people actually say that?"

"I don't know." He waved, his eyes twinkling. "It's been months since I've left the cottage. Come on, Celeste. I've got to get out of here. You take me out of this place a few times each week, and I'll watch Parker on the mornings you want to run. In fact, I'm going to put the cherry on top of this deal. You said your accident anniversary is December 18, right? Let's go to the Christmas parade together. You won't have to be alone, and everyone in Lake Endwell can gawk at both of us. We'll make goofy faces back at them."

She'd never seen this side of him, and she liked it. He was charming, funny, and— Wait. Had he just asked her to go with him to the Christmas parade?

For a split second she felt normal.

How she missed feeling normal.

If she accepted Sam's offer, she wouldn't have to dread the anniversary. She'd been fighting off memories of Brandy nonstop. They'd been having a great time that night. The trunk had been full of Christmas gifts for Parker and her parents. If she had known it would be the last time she'd see Brandy, she would have...

"Come on, say yes." The gleam in Sam's eye reminded her of Brandy's—the way she'd rope Celeste into her schemes. Brandy had been so much fun, and

Celeste could almost hear her urging, *"What are you waiting for? He's so cute. Say yes already!"*

"Don't say I didn't warn you," she said. "It might not be fun when you see what I have to deal with."

"You'll be too busy trying to make sure I don't slip and fall on my face to notice what anyone else is doing. I haven't walked with crutches anywhere but here."

"You get around good on those, but we should probably take the wheelchair with us, just in case."

"So is that a yes?" His eyes shone with intensity. A warm, excited feeling spread over her body.

"You meant it about the Christmas parade?"

"I meant it."

"Okay, then. You have a deal."

Chapter Four

Snowflakes chased and teased each other outside Celeste's picture window early Tuesday morning. Steam spiraled from the mug of coffee warming her hand. All weekend she'd coaxed Parker, but he still hadn't taken more than one step on his own.

Today would be a day of baby steps for them all.

Her first early morning run since moving to Lake Endwell.

Sam's first attempt at babysitting Parker.

Their first public outing. To the grocery store.

She took another sip and padded in her fuzzy black slippers to the bedroom. She dug around in her dresser to find leggings, a long-sleeve air-wicking T and the rest of the layers. Why had she agreed to this again?

Anticipation revved her nerves at the thought of jogging in the crisp air under the gentle snowfall, but imagining the rest of the day made her stomach heave. What if Sam took his eyes off Parker, and he got into something dangerous? Choked on a toy, or worse, fell?

Would Sam be able to take care of him?

She tossed all the clothes on the bed and shook her

head. She'd watched Sam's strong arms scoop Parker onto his lap and knew firsthand his agility getting in and out of the wheelchair. His right leg didn't bend all the way, but he functioned pretty well. His family had cleared out the bottom cupboards over the weekend, and yesterday, she'd installed a portable baby gate with a swinging door to block the hallway leading to his bathroom and bedrooms. Parker would be safe and sound in the huge open living area.

But…

Dear Father, give Sam everything he needs to protect Parker.

As for her promise to take Parker's new babysitter to the grocery store, maybe it would be better for Sam to see people's reactions now—before she let her attraction bloom. Because every time she thought about him, her heart did a little flip. It wasn't just his looks, although his chiseled jawline had made her forget her whereabouts on more than one occasion. It was how he cared about her nephew, the grit he showed going to physical therapy and the fact he'd asked her to the Christmas parade.

A date!

Well, kind of a date.

Once they got through grocery shopping, who knew what she would call it. Would Sam view her differently after he saw how people reacted to her scars? Would he pity her? Pity, she could probably deal with, but the worst would be disgust—she'd seen it a few times around her hometown before she stopped going out.

Half an hour later, she'd fed Parker and changed him into a pair of jeans and an orange sweatshirt sporting a tiger face. Celeste laced her running shoes, pulled

her purple fleece headband over her ears and bundled
Parker up in his stocking cap and puffy blue coat. She
hoisted him on her hip and slung the diaper bag over
her shoulder.

Out in the fresh air, Parker raised his face to the
sky and squinted as snowflakes tickled his cheeks. He
clapped his hands and laughed.

"It's snow. You like it, don't you?" Celeste hugged
him close to her. "Guess what? You get to play with
Sam today while I go running."

"Mama!" He looked at her and pointed to the flakes.

Had he just called her Mama? Her heart practically
thumped out of her chest as a sinking sensation slid
down her throat. Could he call her that? Could he call
her Mama?

She wasn't his mama. Brandy was. And Brandy
would be here if it wasn't for her.

Celeste had been the one who insisted they go out,
that Brandy needed a break, needed some fun. She'd
been worried about how listless Brandy had become.

I don't have time to think about it now.

After taking a deep breath to calm her nerves, she
kissed Parker's cheek and hurried up the steps leading to Sam's kitchen. She knocked, waited for the go-
ahead and entered. Swiping Parker's hat off his head,
she stomped her feet free of snow, then quickly took off
his coat and set him on the floor. He instantly crawled
toward the living room. Sam waited on the couch, his
right knee in a black brace under his basketball shorts.
The skin on his leg held thick purple scars and rivets
where he'd lost tissue. She hadn't seen him with his
leg uncovered, and the shock of his injuries took her
breath away.

"Hey, buddy, you're hanging out with me this morning." Sam held his arms wide as Parker approached. Using the edge of the couch, Parker stood and bounced until Sam picked him up. Sam grinned at Celeste. "What did you feed him this morning? He's excited."

"Apple-and-cinnamon oatmeal. Breakfast of champions." She dragged her toe back and forth in front of her. Maybe this was a bad idea. She forced herself not to stare at his leg. No wonder he dealt with so much pain.

"What's wrong?" He narrowed his eyes at her. "You worried about me watching the little guy? We'll be fine. I've got you and my aunt Sally on speed dial."

"I know. It's just… I've never left him with anyone but my parents, so I'm a little nervous." She bit the corner of her lip. "Plus, my head's kind of messed up right now. A minute ago, Parker called me Mama."

"And that's a problem?"

She shrugged. "I don't know. I wasn't prepared for it. I guess I thought he'd call me Auntie or something."

"But you're his mom."

"I could never replace Brandy."

"That's not the point." He tightened his hold around a wiggly Parker. "You're going to raise him as your son, and you're the only mother he'll ever know. He should call you Mom."

Put in those terms, her reservations didn't make sense. But they still bothered her.

"I just don't want to take this away from her." She'd already taken enough.

"You wouldn't be. You *are* planning on telling him about his mom and dad, right?"

"Of course!"

"Then what's the problem? He'll know he had parents who loved him but who couldn't raise him, much as they would have liked to. And he'll have a mom who loves him and *can* raise him."

She didn't know how to explain. It felt like a betrayal to Brandy and to Josh.

But Parker couldn't call Brandy Mama. She'd never hear that word from his lips.

Maybe Sam had a point.

"I'll think about it." She avoided eye contact until she cleared her throat. "I'd better take off. Do you need anything? His diaper bag is right there by the couch. He shouldn't need a change. Just watch him. He's been putting things in his mouth, and I don't want him to choke."

"We'll be fine." He grinned, playing peekaboo with Parker. "Take your time."

They would be fine. Wouldn't they?

Once she reached the bottom of his porch steps, she inhaled the brisk air, tipped her chin up, pushed through a few light stretches and surged forward.

She had enough on her mind today without adding the whole mama issue. As her feet hit the gravel, she tried to forget about Brandy and what was happening after the run. The less she thought about the upcoming grocery-shopping trip, the better. Yes, a nice long run would help her forget.

Passing tall, stark trees, she rounded a bend. What were Sam and Parker doing now? She'd forgotten to mention Parker had a tooth coming in. Maybe she should go back and grab the teething ring in the fridge, just to be safe.

Her pace slowed.

They'll be fine.

But the worries kept coming. Something told her

nothing could clear her muddy mind, not even a long run through snow-topped pines.

Exactly one hour later, Sam waited next to Celeste's minivan while she took Parker out of his car seat to strap him into the shopping cart. Looking around the packed parking lot of Lake Endwell Grocery and the steady stream of people bustling in and out of the automatic doors, Sam didn't care this was step one toward a more mobile life. He wanted one thing. To go home to the privacy of his cottage.

The snow still fell, but it was melting as soon as it contacted the blacktop, so slush wasn't a factor to worry about. He'd still have to be careful on the crutches, though.

Babysitting—all twenty-four minutes of it—had been fun. After a session of tickling Parker until he howled with laughter, Sam had found a fuzzy stuffed elephant in the diaper bag and, with a low voice, pretended to make it talk to Parker. Celeste had chosen that moment to return. Her flushed cheeks had done something funny to his brain, causing him to drop the elephant. Parker had flopped forward trying to get it, forcing Sam to clutch Parker to prevent him from falling. It had been difficult to keep his hold on the baby.

For the first time, he'd seriously doubted his abilities to take care of the boy.

Celeste must not have noticed he'd almost let Parker slip from his hands. All the way here, she'd been chattering nonstop about how great it felt to get outside and clear her head. He couldn't admit he was nervous about watching Parker, not after seeing how happy running made her.

"Are you ready?" Worry lines dug between Celeste's eyebrows. Her hands were encased with black suede gloves, but he guessed her knuckles were white under them. He didn't want to stress her out more by admitting he was nervous. She looked nervous, too.

"Yep." He swung forward. *Watch the puddle. You've got this.*

"It looks busy. We can come back another time if you want."

"Nope. Let's go in."

With a loud breath, she pushed the cart to the entrance. He stayed by her side, carefully placing each crutch before swinging forward. What would it be like to be shopping as a couple, instead of as the result of an agreement? He liked the idea of cooking with Celeste and picking out cookies and snacks for Parker.

He *really* liked the idea of being able to push the cart.

Where was his head at? Had he gotten a concussion recently and not known it? They weren't a couple. Never would be. And Celeste would see why in roughly six seconds, because he recognized almost every person inside this buzzing beehive. They entered the produce section, and Sam girded himself.

The bright, spacious store felt like a football field compared to his cottage, and Christmas music— "Rockin' Around the Christmas Tree"—played over the sound system. He smelled pumpkin pie and fried chicken. Both made him hungry.

"Well, I'll be." Alma Dartman, a woman in her eighties from church, nudged her husband. "Look, Irv, it's little Sam."

"Who?" Irv's hunched back and thick glasses prevented him from seeing far. His hearing aid buzzed, and he yanked it out of his ear. "Blasted nuisance."

"The youngest Sheffield boy." Her voice carried, and she spoke louder. "The one in the accident. Sam."

Sam closed his eyes for a split second. Why didn't she just announce it over the loudspeaker? Then everyone would know he was here, and that, yes, he'd been in an accident. A few people turned to see what Alma was talking about, and before he knew what was happening, Sam had four people in line to ask him questions. His first instinct was to look for Celeste. She hung back.

"You're walking." Ms. James, Lake Endwell High's retired gym teacher, stopped in front of him. After more than thirty years, she still looked like a gym teacher in her black tracksuit and short gray hair. The only thing missing was a whistle hanging from her neck. "Haven't seen you out in a long time, Sheffield. How've you been?"

"Hanging in there."

Ms. James noticed Celeste and nodded at her. "You in the accident, too?"

Celeste ducked her chin and shook her head. A surge of protectiveness had him taking a clumsy step closer to her.

"Oh, sorry. I assumed…the scars…but that's right. Jeremy was in the boat with you. I heard he made a full recovery and is back in Cheboygan." Ms. James hefted the bag of potatoes in her hand. "Well, I've got to motor. Before you get back at it, there's a run on stuffing mix, so if you're here for Thanksgiving staples, you might want to hit aisle five first." She gave him a knowing look, then walked away.

For a moment he thought the questions were over,

but he'd forgotten about Alma and Irv. "How are you doing, dear? We haven't seen you in a while, have we, Irv? Why are you still on those crutches?"

If there was ever a time he wished he could disappear, now was the time. "Hi, Mr. and Mrs. Dartman." He wanted to rub the back of his neck, but he didn't dare let go of the crutch. "I've been back in the wheelchair for a few months. Hurt my knee." He tried to smile, but his face felt crumbly, as did his noodle legs. Coming here was a mistake.

"We're praying for you, honey." Alma patted his cheek. "We'll keep praying. And who is this young woman and baby?" Alma clapped her hands and stood in front of Parker, making kissy faces. "Hello, baby."

"This is Celeste Monroe, my new neighbor, and her son, Parker." He smiled at Celeste, but her hair hid half her face from view, and the side he could see was paler than the white bakery bags he could just make out from the corner of his eye. "It was nice to see you, Mrs. Dartman, but we're going to have to keep going. Parker's due for a nap soon."

"Oh, yes, dear. I remember how cranky babies get without a nap." She wiggled two knobby fingers at Parker, smiled and joined Irv, shouting, "He hurt his knee."

"What?"

"His knee…"

Sam moved next to Celeste. "Are you okay? I'm sorry about that."

"I'm fine," she said in a strained voice. "Nothing to be sorry about. How are you holding up? It's nice of her to pray for you."

He hobbled in the direction of the grapes. "It *is*

nice of her to pray. Alma Dartman is sweet. Loud, but sweet." He flashed a grin to Celeste, but she glanced away. "What's wrong?"

"Um, I guess being out. It's kind of new for me." She paused to place a bunch of bananas in the cart.

"If it makes you feel better, it's new for me, too."

"It does." The gratitude shining in her eyes slammed into his chest. He'd felt so useless, his life had seemed so pointless until she'd come along. And she was the one who was grateful?

They slowly gathered fruits and vegetables. Sam had to fight his irritation at not being able to select and bag everything himself. If he tried, he would drop a crutch. He couldn't take that chance. So he told Celeste which tomato he wanted and how many apples to buy. As they made their way to the bakery, he sensed her relaxing.

"Should we get something decadent?" He stopped in front of the row of desserts. A line of shoppers waited in front of the bakery counter. Boy, this place was crowded.

"You should definitely get something decadent." She pointed to a Black Forest cake.

The pumpkin pie aroma from earlier hit him full blast. "What are you doing for Thanksgiving, by the way?"

"Parker and I are having dinner with my parents. What about you?"

"Aunt Sally's. It's a tradition. I probably won't stay long."

A cart bumped into Sam's crutch, flipping it out of his hand. His right foot came down hard on the floor. He sucked in a breath at the pain shooting up his leg.

"Oh, no! Sam, are you all right?" Celeste grabbed his arm to steady him.

"Sorry!" A harried-looking mom stopped with a toddler girl by her side and a baby in the cart. "I didn't see you. I'm so sorry."

"It's okay," he said through gritted teeth.

Celeste bent to pick up his crutch and handed it to him. The little girl pointed at Celeste. "What's on her face, Mommy?"

"Shh!" The mom tugged her hand and pushed the cart ahead. "That's not polite."

"But what are those lines?"

The mom's cheeks turned brick red, and she disappeared around the corner, practically dragging the little girl by the hand.

At the stricken expression on Celeste's face, Sam forgot all about the pain in his leg. This trip was turning out to be the disaster they'd both feared.

"Come on." He couldn't help that his tone was harder than a slab of concrete. "We're getting out of here."

Celeste didn't move. The girl's question and the mom's escape defeated her in ways she hadn't anticipated. It was as if she had driven them away by the way she looked.

Sam's pulse throbbed in his neck, and his eyes had turned slate blue. Sharp, like his jawline.

"We're taking a break. Wheel the cart over here." He swung stiffly toward the floral department. She followed him. A small coffee shop with three round tables hid behind the flower displays. She'd never noticed the area before, probably because she hadn't taken the time to look around. Sam carefully took a seat and propped his crutches against the wall.

"I didn't know this was here." Celeste pushed the cart out of the way and hoisted Parker into her arms.

"Would you mind ordering coffees for us? Cream for me, no sugar. I'll hold Parker."

She handed Parker to Sam and ordered the coffees. Minutes later, she set his on the table and popped the cover off her cappuccino. Sam didn't touch his drink, though. Instead, he covered her hand with his. "I'm sorry about back there."

Emotion pressed against the backs of her eyes, but she swallowed her embarrassment. "Don't be. I'm used to it."

"Well, you shouldn't have to be used to it. I'm not. I'm about ready to make a sign that says, 'My leg is not up for conversation.' Why is it the first thing people comment on?"

She blew across the top of her drink. "I don't know. I guess it's human nature."

"It shouldn't be." Sam rapped his knuckles on the table. Parker started fussing and reaching for Sam's coffee. "Sorry, bud, you're too young for this." He gestured to the diaper bag. "Did you bring anything for him?"

She found a baggie of crackers and a sippy cup. Sam handed them to Parker, who took the cup in both hands and leaned back into Sam's chest. Longing pinched her heart. Sam's support tempted her to count on him. But how could she? The past five minutes revealed her new reality. People were uncomfortable around her because of her scars.

Was she partly to blame?

"I wish I handled things better." She took a tentative sip of her drink. Still too hot. "I never know what to say, and I get so self-conscious."

"I'm no help there. The last thing I want to discuss at the grocery store is my leg. It's hard enough getting around on it."

The tension in her neck melted. He felt self-conscious, too. It wasn't just her.

"How is your leg, by the way? Maybe I should take you home."

"Nah, she nailed the crutch, not my leg. I lost my balance, came down hard on my foot. It hurt at first, but it's leveled off." The strain around his mouth told her otherwise.

"Do you need an aspirin or anything?"

"I'll take one at home."

Grocery shopping shouldn't be this complicated. And they'd gotten through only a quarter of the list. She sighed and took another sip of the coffee.

"Well, I think we hit everything we discussed last Friday. The awkward questions. Me almost falling flat on my face. What more can happen? Did we forget something?"

Celeste chuckled. She couldn't help it. "You're right. If someone had been listening in on our conversation, they might have thought we were being melodramatic. But clearly, we knew what we were talking about."

"You can say that again." Sam lifted the cup to his lips, and Celeste let out a teeny sigh. What was it about this man that had her heart tying itself up into knots? He leaned back. "Since we've survived produce—and I use the term *survived* loosely—are you up for heading back to the bakery?"

"I think so, but will it bother you if people stop us

and ask more questions?" She couldn't ask what she really worried about. Did it bother him when people pointed out her ugly scars?

"I guess I'll have to get used to it." He tilted his head. "I can't change the fact my leg doesn't work right."

"No, I didn't mean about your leg…" She twisted a napkin, darting her eyes to the side.

"Hey." He reached forward and lifted her chin with his finger. "You're the most beautiful woman here. You can't help that people notice you."

His words seeped into her soul, leaving a splendid emptiness where she'd been storing a full supply of insecurities.

"You're a terrible, wonderful liar, Sam Sheffield. And I love you for it. Thank you."

His face went blank.

"We'd better get back out there before the bakery sells out." Celeste forced a teasing quality to her tone. "There's a Black Forest cake with your name all over it."

Maybe she shouldn't have mentioned love. She'd meant it casually. He obviously didn't realize she'd said it as a joke.

Or had he guessed the truth? It would take all of three seconds for her to mean it for real.

Chapter Five

"Were you expecting the football team or something, Aunt Sal?" Sam handed the heaping platter of turkey to his sister Libby. Even though he'd had his misgivings about the holiday with his family, it felt good to be back. Getting around Aunt Sally's house on crutches was a welcome change from being alone at home. The best part? His siblings were treating him less as a trauma patient and more as their brother. Maybe he'd stay longer than he'd originally planned.

"What are you talking about, Sam?" Aunt Sally's blond hair was pulled back with an orange headband, and glittery pumpkin earrings dangled from her ears. "Football ended two weeks ago. Too bad varsity didn't make it to the play-offs. Do you need a dinner roll, hon?"

"Already have one."

She widened her eyes at the butter dish in her hand. He nodded, and she passed it over. Aunt Sally had been like a mother to him. He had no memories of his own mom, who died giving birth to Libby when he was two.

But between Aunt Sally and his older sister, Claire, he figured he had the mom thing covered.

"So I heard you were at the grocery store this week, Sam." The twinkle in Libby's eye sent warning flags soaring. "And I heard Celeste and Parker were with you."

Since it wasn't a question, he saw no reason to reply. He shoveled a mound of mashed potatoes into his mouth. He was just glad his foot was okay from the impact of that lady's cart hitting his crutch. He'd iced the leg when he got home, and so far, he suffered no lingering side effects.

"You went to the grocery store?" Claire set her fork down. She sat across the table and to the right of him. "I don't remember the last time you went anywhere other than a doctor's appointment."

Again, no need to reply. He bit into his roll.

"I also heard you weren't in the wheelchair." Libby rested her chin on her fist, and her blue eyes twinkled. "Celeste is clearly a genius."

He fantasized about throwing his napkin on the plate and leaving the table in a huff, but it would take too long to get up with his crutches. Besides, the food was really good.

"Or maybe *you're* the genius," Claire said softly. "Celeste has had a rough time of it. Her mom's friend Nancy told me how difficult it's been for her to go out in public."

"Right. Let's change the subject." He looked to his brothers, Tommy and Bryan, for some backup.

"Who's Celeste?" Tommy asked. His daughter Macy sat next to him, and little Emily was on the lap of his wife, Stephanie.

"Really, Tom?" Stephanie sounded exasperated. "I told you she moved next door."

"The one living in Claire's cottage," Bryan added, giving his wife, Jade, the basket of rolls.

"Oh, that's right," Tommy said. "She's taking care of her nephew. Didn't you say something about her being in an accident, too?"

"Car accident," Claire said.

Sam took a drink of his water as his blood pressure rose. The way they were discussing Celeste irritated him on all levels. "Why is the fact she was in an accident so important? It shouldn't define her." *Or me.*

The table went quiet until Dad spoke up. "Tell us more about her."

He wanted to switch topics, but he'd gotten himself into this. "Celeste ran cross-country in college. She has a degree in history, but since she's raising her nephew, Parker, she prefers to work from home. Her brother died overseas. She's doing a good job as a mom." He stabbed a yam. "Now can we talk about something else?"

She sees more than my injuries. She's nice. She joked the other day that she loved me, and all I could think was I wish it could be true. I wish I could date again and have a future with a woman like Celeste.

"Done." Reed, Claire's husband, stood. "Should we tell them?"

Claire blushed, nodding.

"Sam, you made this easy on me." Reed grinned. "We didn't know how to announce this, so here goes. We're having a baby."

Aunt Sally squealed. Libby's mouth dropped open. Macy started clapping, which caused Emily to start clapping, too. Everyone talked at once.

"Congratulations…"

"When are you due?"

"Boy or girl?"

"How long have you known? Do you have morning sickness?"

Sam wiped his mouth with his napkin. While he was happy for Claire and Reed—they'd been trying for a long time to have a baby—his ribs seemed to be closing in on him. He took a moment to study his huge family around the table, and he couldn't help wondering when it would be his turn. When would something great happen to him?

They all had the ingredients for the life he wanted.

Closing his eyes, he could picture Celeste sitting here and Parker on his lap.

Reality crashed down.

He hadn't worked in over a year. Could barely walk. He'd watched Parker for twenty-four minutes and almost dropped him. He couldn't protect Celeste from insensitive questions. Couldn't protect her from anything. Until he got his life together—if he got his life together—his fantasies would remain unreachable.

Could he get his life together?

The doctors had never wanted him back in the wheelchair after the last surgery, but…

He'd blamed it on the constant pain. Refusing to use the crutches hadn't just been due to pain, though.

He'd given up. On walking, on healing, on working, on living.

Maybe it was time.

Time to take another step.

Thinking about dating again was futile at this point. What was left?

Work. Work he could do. His dealership had been everything to him, and he'd let it slip between his fingers.

Sam caught Bryan's eye and motioned for him to come over.

"What's up?" Bryan knelt next to him.

"After dinner, can we talk about Sheffield Auto?"

"Of course, man."

"I'm going back to work in January." Sam had no idea how, but he had to try. "I'll be at the meeting next Friday."

"That's great." Bryan grinned, clapping him on the back.

The old Sam wouldn't have let anything keep him from making the dealership a success. And he would have asked Celeste out—he'd enjoyed a healthy dating life even if he'd never fallen in love. He might not be ready to date, but he could spend time with Celeste without feeling like an invalid.

Before he lost his courage, he sent Celeste a quick text.

If you're not busy Saturday morning, will you stop by?

"Where did Dad go?" Celeste cleared the final plate from the table. "He's usually first in line for pumpkin pie."

"He's picking up Grandma Pearl. We invited her for dinner, too, but her nephew is eating with her. She sounded excited to come here for dessert, though."

Celeste's emotions played tug-of-war. She wanted to spend time with Grandma Pearl, and in the past, they'd avoided discussing Brandy, but what if the conversation took a bad turn? What if Grandma Pearl asked questions about the accident, questions Celeste didn't know how to answer?

"You didn't tell me how the shopping trip with Sam went. Your first time out together, right?" Mom snapped a lid on the plastic container full of gravy and stacked it on top of the leftover stuffing.

"Yes, it was our first attempt." She tossed the old coffee filter in the trash and filled the pot with fresh water. "It was interesting." She filled her mother in on the stares, the inappropriate questions, the little girl whose face was seared into her brain.

The only thing she wasn't revealing? Sam's words after. The ones she'd memorized and kept coming back to. *You're the most beautiful woman here. They can't help but notice you.* But his reaction to her stupid comment about loving him kept her feet on the ground, where they belonged. She'd spent two days trying to decipher the look on his face.

Horror?

Too dramatic.

Fear?

Maybe.

He might be worried that she was falling for him.

He probably had a right to be worried.

"I'm sorry." Mom hugged her, then stepped back, looking her in the eye. "What did you say to the little girl?"

"Nothing. I froze. I…just don't know how to handle those situations."

"Hmm…"

The coffeemaker made gurgling noises as the pot began to fill.

"Would you feel better if you had a reply ready when someone asks about your face?"

"Oh, I have a reply ready, all right." Celeste crossed her arms over her chest and jutted her chin out.

Mom laughed. "I'm sure you do, but I was thinking more along the lines of something nice."

"You got me there." She grinned. "I have no idea how to respond. It's so embarrassing."

They went back to the living room.

"Kids say the first thing in their heads. They don't realize they're hurting your feelings."

"I know." Celeste sat on the couch and hugged a throw pillow to her chest. "The mom's face said it all— she was probably more mortified than I was."

"Exactly. And you're most likely going to have to deal with this again."

"Undoubtedly."

"How would you feel if you said something simple like, 'I was in a bad car accident'?"

The familiar sensation of floundering churned her insides. "Would I have to give details?" Because the details were there, and they haunted her. One minute happy. The next minute waking up after surgery, unable to see because both eyes had puffed shut. She couldn't talk. Her tongue had swollen, she'd lost a tooth, and her nose had been broken.

Blind, mute and confused.

She hadn't known where she was or what had happened. When the nurses told her she'd been in an accident, all she could think was she had to see Brandy.

Mom had broken the news to her.

And if she could have wept, she would have. But she'd lain there, immobile, hooked to a million tubes, afraid she'd never see again. She'd wanted to die. She'd already lost Josh that year. Life without Brandy hadn't seemed possible. Still didn't seem possible.

"Honey, are you okay?" Mom asked.

"Yeah." She shook her head free of the memories. "Why?"

"You didn't answer my question."

"Sorry, got lost in my own little world." She propped her elbow on the arm of the couch and let her cheek rest against her palm. "What did you ask?"

"I asked what you would feel comfortable telling a stranger."

"The truth. Like you said, I was in a bad car accident." It seemed easy…if it worked. "What if they ask more questions?"

"Just because they ask doesn't mean you have to answer. You could say you're thankful to be alive and leave it at that."

The front door opened and Dad hollered, "Hope you have the pie cut because we're ready for dessert."

Celeste's nerve endings prickled. She hadn't seen Grandma Pearl in a long time. She stood to greet her as she emerged from the hall. Grandma Pearl still had silver hair and the kindest eyes in the world, but she walked with a stoop, and her thin face looked sallow.

"Celeste!"

Celeste gave her a big hug. "Happy Thanksgiving. We're so glad you came."

"Got my hair done yesterday." Grandma Pearl pretended to fluff the back. "It's not every day I have dessert with my great-grandbaby."

"Want me to wake him? He's taking a nap. The excitement wore him out."

"Let him sleep a bit more." Grandma Pearl sat at the dining table, and Celeste helped her mom get out plates and mugs. After pouring coffee, they all dug into pumpkin pie.

"How have you been feeling?" Celeste asked.

"Tired and creaky, but I'm doing well." Grandma Pearl's coffee cup trembled as she lifted it to her mouth. "Tell me about your new home. Your dad said you're living over in Lake Endwell now."

"Yes. Parker and I have a beautiful view of the lake. He's almost walking on his own. We keep waiting for him to take more than one step."

"We?"

Celeste's cheeks flamed. "My neighbor Sam and me. He's the one I'm helping out in exchange for the cabin. He was in a bad accident, too."

Grandma Pearl cut a bite of pie with her fork. "I'm sorry to hear that. It broke my heart the day I got the call about you and Brandy. She shouldn't have died so young." She pulled a handkerchief from her pocket and dabbed under her eyes. "Tragic. But I hope you know I'm thankful every day you survived, dear."

Celeste bowed her head. *It should have been me. Brandy should be here eating pie with her grandma.*

"What would we have done without both you girls? And what would have happened to sweet Parker." She smiled at Mom and Dad. "I know you two would have raised him, but it's better for him to have a young mom like our Celeste."

Celeste clutched her hands together tightly. *Brandy had a son who needed her—still needs her. I need her. And I'm single. Why her? Why not me? The world could have gone on fine without me.*

Parker yelled "Mama" from the bedroom. Another thing Celeste was torn about.

"I'll be right back." She hurried down the hall. Parker stood in his portable crib and lifted his arms. "Mama!"

She picked him up, pressing him close to her. He smelled so baby fresh. She took a minute to savor his warm, cuddly arms around her neck. Was it wrong to love this child so much? "Guess what? Grandma Pearl is here. She can't wait to see you."

He scrunched his nose and patted her cheeks.

"I love you, Parker Monroe."

"La!"

She kissed him and carried him back to the table.

"There he is!" Grandma Pearl clapped her hands and held her arms wide. Parker wiggled to get out of Celeste's grasp. She set him on his feet. He grinned and laughed. Took one step. Two steps. Three…and he was in Grandma Pearl's arms.

"He did it! He walked!" Mom jumped out of her chair and clapped. "Good job, Parker."

Celeste ran to the kitchen to get her phone, but by the time she got back, Grandma Pearl had already set him on her lap and was feeding him a bite of pie.

"We didn't get it on video." Dad sounded disappointed.

"We'll get the next one." Celeste winked. She noticed a text from Sam.

He wanted her to stop by on Saturday? A warm feeling radiated all the way up from her toes to her head. She quickly texted back that she'd stop by around nine Saturday morning.

"This is the best Thanksgiving I could have asked for." Grandma Pearl beamed.

It seemed fitting Parker would take his first steps into Grandma Pearl's arms. A gift to her when she'd lost so much. God was good. Even in the hardest parts of life, God was good.

Grandma Pearl deserved some good in her life.

Celeste would have to keep reminding herself how much Parker meant to the woman. Because the Christmas program practices started in exactly one week. And she was not ready to drive past the accident site.

She wasn't ready to discuss the accident with Brandy's church friends, either. Mom made a good point about having an answer ready for curious strangers. But for the people who knew Brandy? The ones who might have questioned Celeste's driving that night?

She had no answers for them. None at all.

Mom and Dad had assured her over and over it was an accident and how thankful they were she'd made it out alive. But it didn't change the fact that Celeste was here eating pie with Brandy's grandma and raising Brandy's son when Brandy should be the one doing both.

I'm sorry, God. I'm sorry I love Parker so much and I'm happy he's mine. I shouldn't be happy about it, should I? How can I let him call me Mama? It's selfish. I'm selfish.

The emotional turmoil swirled inside her. Only one person came to mind who might understand.

Sam.

The startled look on his face when she jokingly said she loved him crashed back.

Her current strategy of staying silent on the subject of Brandy's death seemed wise, but her heart ached to spill everything to Sam.

* * *

Sam zipped his winter jacket Saturday morning and hoped this outing would help him feel less like an invalid and more like a man. He was glad Celeste had agreed to join him. The weather was cooperating. Clear sky and sunshine.

"You're bundled up." Celeste entered by the kitchen door, followed by a chilly breeze.

She and Parker wore winter coats and matching green-and-white knit hats. She looked young and free, less somber than she often did. Sam stared a moment too long. Had the craziest urge to take her hand in his. Yeah, that would go great. Instead, he shoved a black hat on his head.

"Hey, buddy." Keeping hold of his crutches, he gave Parker a little wave. "Ready for a walk?"

Celeste's mouth dropped open.

Sam quickly added, "Outside. The three of us."

"Are you sure?" The look she gave him screamed, *You're crazy, right?*

"Do you know how long it's been since I've spent any time outside? I'm just talking about a short walk by the lake." He waited, ready to argue whatever problem she dished out. It had taken him thirty minutes to layer jeans over his knee brace and don the rest of his outdoor gear along with running shoes. He was not backing out now.

"I'll go get the stroller."

He nodded. "I'll meet you in the driveway."

Holding Parker, she left with a soft click of the door behind her.

That went better than he'd expected. His sisters would have lectured him about not taking chances, and

he would have argued with them until his face turned as blue as the sky above.

He positioned himself in the wheelchair and wedged his crutches upright between his legs as he wheeled out to the patio, down the ramp to the driveway. The air smelled crisp, the way only a forty-degree day on the lake could smell. It hadn't frozen yet, and the water looked turquoise. Sam sucked in a deep breath, lifting his face at the pleasure of it.

He'd just gotten to his feet when Celeste returned. The jogging stroller crushed the gravel as Parker pounded his hands on the bar.

"I'll put the wheelchair under the deck to protect it." She jammed her foot on the stroller brake, moved the wheelchair and was back in a flash. "Where are we going?"

"This way." He jerked his head to the lake. "Let's take the path."

They fell in beside each other as geese honked overhead. Trees rustled in the breeze, and a quiet peace spread over the lake. Sam soaked it all in. He'd missed this aspect of life—the simple pleasure of a stroll outdoors on a winter day. "I forgot how quiet this time of year is when you're outside."

"I never thought about it, but you're right. No bugs buzzing about, I guess."

"And the trees lost most of their leaves, so they're quieter, too."

They continued past her cottage.

"How was your Thanksgiving?" they asked simultaneously. Sam grinned, and Celeste laughed.

"You first," he said.

"Really good. Dad deep-fried the turkey. It was delicious. Brandy's grandma came over for dessert— Oh! I forgot to tell you! Parker finally walked—right into her arms. It was amazing."

"He did? And here I'd been hoping I'd get to see it. Well, good for you, buddy." He stretched his neck to make a funny face at Parker. He had been hoping to see his first steps. Could he be getting too emotionally invested in his neighbors?

He looked around at the grass starting to yellow, at the evergreens and the glints of light sparking from the water. Maybe it was okay to be emotionally invested. He wouldn't be out here today enjoying this beauty if it wasn't for Celeste moving in next door.

"What about your Thanksgiving? Your aunt's house, right?"

"It was good. Really good. My family treated me like a normal human being for the first time in a long time. Oh, and Claire and Reed are having a baby, so I'll be an uncle again." He grinned, but his heart fell. He loved being an uncle, but would he ever be a father?

"That's wonderful!" Celeste beamed.

"Ga! Ga!" Parker pulled himself forward and pointed. Sam stared in the direction he was pointing.

"Look, he found a cat."

A fat orange cat sat facing the lake. Its fur was fluffed up, making it look like a puffball.

"Do you think it's cold?" Celeste asked.

"Doubt it. Looks pretty happy to me. It's definitely being fed."

"You can say that again." She chuckled. "It's got to be twenty pounds. Someone may be feeding it too much."

"Like my aunt Sally. She had enough food at Thanksgiving to feed a small country. Not that I'm complaining. She's a fantastic cook."

"Well, congratulations about Claire having a baby. They must be excited."

"Yeah, it's taken them a while to get pregnant, so they're happy."

They passed the cat, and Parker twisted to try to see it before giving up and settling back in the stroller.

"I remember when Brandy found out she was having Parker." Celeste smiled, a faraway look in her brown eyes. Sam forced his gaze back on the path. He'd never felt this comfortable around a woman he was attracted to, but Celeste was easy to be with. She shook her head. "She flipped out. Took four tests. We jumped up and down in her tiny living room, laughing and screaming. Then we got ice cream."

"You must miss her."

Celeste nodded, the light in her eyes dimming. "I've been struggling with it more lately. I'd begun to make peace with losing Josh and then…"

"You lost *her*."

"Yeah." She slowed the stroller and turned to him. "It's not just missing her. This is probably going to sound stupid, but sometimes I feel like an impostor, like I shouldn't be raising Parker. She should be here raising him."

Sam frowned, trying to take in what she was saying. "But she's not here. Who else would love him the way you do?"

"True. Is it wrong to love him so much, though? I'm fighting these weird feelings. I don't know what's wrong with me."

He paused, resting on the crutches. "Nothing is

wrong with you. You're raising a kid, and it's not as if you have any experience. Plus, you miss your friend, and you don't have a husband to help you. I'd be wrestling with a lot of thoughts, too."

She blinked, her lips twisting. "So you don't think I'm betraying her memory or anything?"

"You'd be betraying her memory if you didn't love Parker as your own son. Isn't that what she would want? For him to be raised in a home full of love?"

She nodded.

"I never knew my mom. I was two when she died giving birth to Libby." He gestured for them to continue forward. "My dad raised me."

"I didn't know that. I'm so sorry." They reached a section canopied by trees.

"Don't be. My aunt Sally and my sister Claire were all the motherly figures I needed in my life. Do I wish I'd had my mom? Of course. But I turned out fine, and I'm grateful for the family I have. They annoy me at times, but I still love 'em."

"I understand." She grew serious. "I've never seen you out here. Why did you decide to come out today?"

It was his turn to grow serious. "I told Bryan I'm returning to work in January."

"That's wonderful, Sam. When did you decide this?"

"Thanksgiving. I guess I'm reclaiming my life little by little."

"Are you nervous about the pain? I know you didn't want to use your wheelchair at work, but if you're going back so soon, I guess you'll have to, huh?"

No way was he working in the wheelchair. "My physical therapist wants me on crutches."

"Oh." The wind blew her hair across the front of her

face and neck. "I hope you'll take it slow. Don't want you aching and miserable."

She didn't think he could handle it. Would she always see him as the patient next door?

The temptation to pray—to ask God for help—hit him.

Like God would waste time helping him now, when He'd ignored Sam's pleas all last year.

Sam would do this on his own.

So far, the longest he'd been on his feet with the crutches was two hours, and his knee had felt as if a fireworks display was exploding inside it afterward. Eight to ten hours on crutches were sure to be grueling. Or impossible.

He increased his pace, flinching when his crutch hit a stone. *Slow down. Do you want your knee to blow out again?*

"Well, I'll be happy to drive you Friday," Celeste said.

"You don't mind?"

"Of course not." She frowned.

"What's wrong?"

"I just remembered Thursday night is the Christmas Eve program practice."

"That's right." From the look on her face, he'd say she dreaded it. "I'm going with you."

"You don't have to—"

"I'm going. I know you're worried about it. You've done a lot for me. Let me do this for you."

Her shy smile sent a zip of pride down to his toes. Maybe she was starting to see him as more than a patient. He wanted to be there for her, to be the friend she needed. Most of all, he didn't want to let her down.

Chapter Six

"I can't go back to the cottage. Not yet," Sam said, eyeing Celeste's parked van as they came out of the diner on Main Street Monday afternoon. His physical therapy session that morning had gone so well he'd asked Celeste and Parker to join him for lunch—his treat. Although the place had been packed with customers, only a handful of people had stopped by their table asking him how he was. The waitress stared overly long at Celeste, but mostly, they'd eaten in peace. He didn't want the peace to end. Not yet. "What a perfect winter day."

"Where do you want to go?" Celeste carried Parker, who clapped his mittened hands, his face full of joy at being outside.

Snow had fallen the night before, giving the lampposts and trees a frosted look. The sun made everything sparkle, and the Christmas decorations throughout town added to the season's cheer.

"How about a little window-shopping?" He spied the town Christmas tree a few blocks down. He'd skipped Christmas last year. And before that? He'd taken it for granted. "I know you have to get back to work, but it's been a long time since I've hung out down here."

"I don't mind. Should I get the stroller?"

"How wiggly is he?"

Parker bounced in her arms. She chuckled. "I'll get the stroller."

A few minutes later, Sam led the way down the sidewalk, pointing out stores as they passed. "My best friend, Jeremy, and I used to spend all our allowances in there." He stopped before a drugstore/gift shop. "They had a huge selection of candy. You could buy caramels, chocolates, taffy and hard candies in bulk."

"Do they still sell bulk candy?" Celeste stretched her neck to see inside the window.

"I don't think so."

"Want to find out?"

He was taken aback, surprised she suggested it. But she hadn't flinched at eating lunch with him earlier, so maybe she was getting used to being out in public the same way he was.

"Yeah. Let's go in. If they still have the candy, I'm buying a bag."

"Fair enough." She bent to lift Parker from the stroller. He babbled all the way inside. An employee barely glanced up from behind the checkout counter, and a pair of women perused the greeting cards.

"The candy bins used to be here." He went to the back wall where shelves of cough syrups and allergy medicines were placed. "There was a hanging scale, too, so you could weigh your candy before buying it."

"You bought a lot of sweets, didn't you?" She set Parker on the floor, keeping a tight hold on his little hand.

"You have no idea." He leaned against his crutches and smiled at the memories of running in here as a kid to blow his allowance. "I'm pretty sure I single-handedly kept our dentist in business."

She chuckled. "Brandy and I rode bikes all summer from the time we were twelve until we could drive. We ate our fair share of candy, too. And ice cream." Parker reached for a small stuffed bunny. "No, sweetie, that's not for you to touch." She steered him away from the display, and his light brown eyes filled with tears.

"I'll buy it for him." Sam smiled at Parker.

Celeste's eyes shone but she shook her head. "I appreciate it, Sam, but I don't want him expecting a toy every time we go to a store."

He almost argued, but Parker had already forgotten about the stuffed animal and was pulling Celeste to the colorful candy bars in his sight. "So you have a sweet tooth, too, huh?"

"Mine is more of a salty tooth. I can pack away a bag of chips. But I won't turn down a candy bar, either."

"Chips should be their own food group." After Sam purchased three candy bars and a pack of gum, they exited the store, and once Celeste strapped Parker back into the stroller, they continued down the sidewalk. They stopped in a few more stores before strolling to the town Christmas tree. It stood at the entrance to City Park with the white pillars of the gazebo visible behind it. Snow dripped from the branches, which were covered in lights.

"It's so pretty." Celeste stretched her neck back to see the star on top. "Look, Parker, isn't it the biggest Christmas tree you've ever seen?" He held his arms up for her to unstrap him. She glanced at Sam. "Do you want to stay a minute or head back?"

"Stay." He lowered himself onto one of the benches facing the tree as she set Parker on his feet, adjusting his hat and mittens. Parker giggled, slapping the bench seat over and over with both hands. "Doesn't take much for you to have fun, does it, buddy?"

"Mind if I take a picture?" Celeste's brown eyes waited for an answer, but she was so pretty he forgot the question. She cocked her head to the side. "Sam?"

"What?" He tore his gaze away and held out his hand for Parker to take. Parker patted it.

"I want to take a picture. He looks so cute in his snow boots."

"Sure." Sam got Parker's attention, pointing for him to smile at Celeste. "Hey, there, look that way."

The boy laughed, his eyes glued to Sam, and placed both hands on Sam's thigh.

"Guess I'll have to be in it, too." Sam turned Parker to face Celeste. "Say 'cheese.'"

Parker squealed in delight as Celeste snapped the photo.

"Why don't you let me take a picture of you with him?"

"That's okay." She ducked her chin. "I should probably get back. I have a long list of work to do."

"Come on, let's get a photo of you two." He wanted to hold on to today. It had been so long since he'd enjoyed being out. He'd like to look back at this moment and remember Celeste's smile and Parker's happiness. Capture the joy of the moment. Didn't Celeste feel it, too?

"No." Her clipped voice set him back.

"Okay." He got to his feet as she took care of Parker.

Why did he keep forgetting about her scars? "Do you ever take pictures of you two together?"

She didn't answer, but her nose twitched.

"Celeste, don't you think he'll want to look back at you and him?"

"Not like this."

They headed back to her van in silence, and he couldn't help feeling he'd messed up their friendship. If she could see herself the way he did—glowing, smiling—a person he wanted to spend time with. But she clearly didn't see herself that way.

He didn't know how to fix it. He didn't even know how to try.

Celeste's fingertips tapped against the keyboard as she finished typing an ad for a new client. She needed to cram three hours of work into the twenty minutes she had left before driving Parker to the Christmas program practice. What she wouldn't do to call Sue Roper and cancel tonight. The sour taste on her tongue grew positively pungent. She popped a peppermint candy in her mouth.

They were counting on her. A Christmas surprise for Grandma Pearl.

She'd floor it past the accident site if she had to, but she would get Parker to the rehearsal.

The calendar hanging on the bulletin board above her desk caught her eye. Bright green X's showed the countdown. Today was December 2, just two weeks—a mere fourteen days—until her follow-up appointment. An appointment that could free her of these chains. Too ashamed to have her picture taken, even with sweet Parker. How sad was that? And what did Sam think about it? His comment Monday about Parker wanting to look back at pictures of them had dented her ironclad stance about not drawing attention to her face.

Earlier, she'd forced herself to do a little research about becoming a teacher. She glanced at the blue folder with the information she'd gathered. All the steps she needed to pursue a career teaching history. Right in there. She'd have to take almost a dozen college courses, which she could do online, and once done, she could sign up for student teaching and begin the process of getting state-certified. It would take at least two years, maybe more, before she could even think about teaching.

But could she really consider it?

It depended on her plastic surgeon.

Was she wrong to pause her life until she got the outcome she longed for?

Focus. She didn't have time for dreaming.

After a quick scan of the ad, she printed a copy to proofread later. Then she marked the item off her checklist and went to the next one.

Six in the evening and already pitch-black out. Maybe the darkness would make it easier… She wouldn't have to see the crash site when she drove past. But she'd still have to interact with the people from Brandy's church, many of whom had known Brandy and also had small children.

Celeste had no idea how she'd be received by them.

At least Sam was driving with her tonight. They'd survived another round of grocery shopping Tuesday, this time with only two locals stopping Sam about his leg, and, thankfully, nobody said a word about her scars. She'd actually enjoyed the trip. It helped that since Monday, Sam had gone out of his way to keep things light. She was learning more about him.

He ate mostly healthy foods, and he knew all kinds of fun facts. He'd explained how to figure out if a pineapple was ripe by plucking an inner leaf out of the top. If it came out easily, the pineapple was ready. Who would have known? Most of the food he bought was portable and easy to grab. Single-sized yogurts, sliced cheese, lunch meat, crackers, granola bars. He explained that with both hands on the crutches, it was difficult to carry anything. That was why he kept a bag he could sling over his shoulder at all times to carry things between rooms.

She learned more than his food preferences, though. He was funny, kind. He treated her like a trusted friend. What a gift to have his friendship.

A text came through from Sam. We'd better leave early. It's starting to snow.

Tiny white pellets blew past the window. With a frustrated exhalation, she saved her work, got up from the desk and stretched both arms over her head.

Lord, You've gotten me through some big changes lately. I need Your help tonight. Give me the strength to drive to church and the words to say when we arrive.

She'd put more thought into her mom's suggestion. She'd keep any replies to questions about her face simple and direct. No lengthy explanations—assuming she could will her mouth to open and speak at all.

Ten minutes later Parker was babbling quietly in his car seat while Celeste helped Sam into the passenger side of her van.

"You ready for this?" Sam asked as she pulled away.

"As ready as I'm ever going to be." She licked her

chapped lips and headed north. The church was twenty-five minutes away. That left about twenty-four minutes before they passed the dreaded spot. In the meantime, she needed a distraction. Sam. "What about you? Ready for the big meeting tomorrow?"

She peeked over to catch his reaction. His hair was expertly gelled on top, and although it was dark, she could make out the twinkle in his eyes as he nodded.

Yep, he was a good distraction. A good, gorgeous distraction.

"I'm ready, thanks to you. I'm not as worried about slipping and falling with the crutches, and I forced myself to walk around the house with them for three hours."

"You won't be marching around on those through the dealership tomorrow, will you?"

"No. But come January, I will be. I've got to be prepared. My job has never really been a desk job. I spend a lot of time checking the different departments, talking to customers and inspecting the lot."

"It's great to hear you excited." Celeste flipped on the wipers as the snowfall increased.

"Do I sound excited?" he joked. "I'm nervous."

"Why?" She glanced at him. "You'll be fine."

He rubbed his chin and shrugged. "Been a long time."

"It'll all come back to you."

"That's what I'm afraid of."

She chewed on the comment a minute. She understood. She was afraid of it all coming back, too, and it would be shortly. "I know, Sam. I'm afraid, too."

"What are you afraid of, Celeste?" The words were a caress, low and soothing.

Could she tell him everything on her mind? She worried about remembering the crash. Had her memory left out a detail that would prove her negligent? "I just want to get there and not think."

"I want to go back to work and not be bombarded with the former me."

The former him? She frowned, keeping her eyes on the road. "You lost me."

"I'm starting to get used to this being my life. The last time I was in my office, I had no clue I would come close to dying. The memories of who I was, what I could do—those are what worry me. I'm not sure about the mental side of going back to work."

That, she got. "It's the same reason why I'm a jittery mess right now. The mental aspect. Seeing Brandy's church friends, driving past the site. It's scary. I don't blame you for having doubts."

He reached over and put his hand on her shoulder. The touch surprised her, made her want to bend her head and rest her cheek on his hand. "I'm here if you need me for anything. We'll get through it."

We? What a relief to have him to rely on. She sniffed, nodding. He turned the radio to a station playing Christmas music.

"So are you and Parker up for helping me decorate my Christmas tree Saturday afternoon? And by help, I mean you'll basically have to put all the decorations up. Unless I can juggle the crutches somehow."

Celeste laughed. She pictured him smiling, placing candy canes on the tree. "Of course. We'd love to help. I need to decorate my cabin, too, but with Parker walking, I have to be careful."

They discussed her setting up a small tree on a table

out of his reach, and before she knew it, she was turning down the road where she and Brandy had spun out. Her breathing quickened, and her palms grew sweaty. She swallowed. Twice.

"This is it, isn't it?" Sam asked. "Do you need to pull over or anything?"

Everything flooded back. Them laughing and singing "A Holly Jolly Christmas." That was the song she'd forgotten. A split second later the wheels had taken a life of their own and the car had spun sideways, sliding, turning. It had hit the ditch with a thud, jerking them around in their seat belts, and the car launched up— they'd both screamed…

And that was when she remembered. She'd reached for Brandy and held on to her arm the instant before she blacked out.

"Celeste?"

She inhaled and saw the pole. The one her car wrapped around. The one that left her scarred and alone.

It loomed gray and tall and lonely from the field.

You took her from me. You stupid piece of wood.

Her hands clenched the steering wheel as tears began to pour down her cheeks, and a minute later, she drove into the brightly lit church parking lot and cut the engine. Her forehead dropped to her palms, and she shook as she cried.

Sam must have unbuckled because he moved close, putting his arm around her and drawing her to him. She turned, wrapping her arms around his neck.

"I don't understand why, Sam. Why Brandy? Why that night?" *Why not me?*

"Shh…" He brushed her hair from her face. "I don't know. Why don't you tell me about it?"

"We were coming home from shopping. The trunk was full of gifts and wrapping paper. We ate at a Mexican restaurant, and we were having so much fun. Laughing, singing. Brandy had been so tired from the late nights with Parker, and she'd been quiet, depressed since Josh died. She needed a night out. I kept insisting she come with me. And there we were, on our way back to her apartment when the car hit the ice and spun out. The air bags didn't deploy. The officer told my parents it was because of the angle we hit—no sensors were tripped. And I lost her. I lost her."

She let out another cry and held Sam tightly. He rubbed his hand up and down her back, murmuring in the hair against her cheek, "It's okay. It's okay."

When she got her breathing under control, she gazed into his eyes. She could see it—he wanted to take her pain from her.

The truth had to be told.

"It should have been me." There. She'd said it out loud.

"What?" His eyebrows drew together.

"Why did I get to live and she was taken away? She had a baby, a job as a nurse's aide. The world could have gone on fine without me, but here I am." She wiped the tears from her face with the backs of her hands.

"You're wrong." He stroked her hair. "The world couldn't have gone on fine without you. I don't know why she died, but I know why you lived. The world needs you, Celeste."

She shook her head violently. "Don't say that."

"I will say it." He nudged her chin to look at him. "I'll say it over and over until it gets through that pretty head of yours."

Pretty?

"We should go," she said. "It's almost time for practice."

"Not yet." He shifted closer so their noses were almost touching. "The accident wasn't your fault. Okay?"

Hearing him say those words was like a dose of calming oil on her nerves. The steel keeping her spine rigid dissolved. She knew in her heart it wasn't her fault—it could have happened to anyone—but the aftermath was hard to digest.

"It might not have been my fault, but the results are the same. My best friend is gone, and my nephew—her son—will never know her."

"You told me yourself you're going to make sure Parker knows everything about her."

"It's not the same."

"No, it's not." He took her hand in his. "Being together after this life will have to be enough."

She didn't trust herself to speak. He was right—they'd be together someday. Why wasn't it enough? "I guess I'm selfish. I want her here now." She gave him a halfhearted smile.

"I don't blame you." He ran his hand over his cheek. "I guess I'm selfish, too. I'm glad you're here. I didn't know Brandy, but I'm glad you survived the crash. You've made my life bearable."

She blinked, stunned.

"We'd better go inside." He opened his door, prompting her in motion.

She hurried around the van and got his crutches out of the trunk. When she handed them to him, she covered his hand with hers. "Thanks."

"I meant it. And I mean this—let it go. You can't bring her back."

Maybe she'd been living with too many regrets. She couldn't bring Brandy back. But was it dishonoring her memory to embrace the future?

Sam swung through the church entrance as Celeste held the door open for him. Holding her in his arms moments ago had felt right. More right than he'd felt in a long time. And the fact she'd opened up to him, confided in him, made him feel invincible. Even the fact he was on crutches couldn't dampen his mood.

Did a guy have to be physically whole to consider having a future with a woman? He used to think so, but now he wondered.

"Hello." A frazzled-looking woman appeared in the coat area. She held a clipboard and wore a red-and-white Christmas sweater with kittens on it. She blew a piece of curly brown hair from her eyes. "Are you Celeste?"

"Yes. This is Parker." Celeste took off his stocking cap. He rubbed his eyes and dropped his head to her shoulder. "Are you Mrs. Roper?"

"No. Sue got the flu. I'm Donna Flack. I understand you're raising Brandy's little boy." She didn't make eye contact with Celeste. Her gaze ran up and down the paper attached to the clipboard. Something about her raised Sam's hackles. "If you'll wait in the fellowship hall with the other parents, we'll get started in a few."

Celeste unzipped Parker's coat. "I'm not sure if he'll do what you need."

"Well, let's hope he can sit on our Mary's lap and act like a baby." She clicked her pen and made a tsk-tsk noise.

"He is a baby." Sam moved next to Celeste. The lady's annoyed tone was rubbing him the wrong way.

"This is Sam Sheffield, Mrs. Flack."

"It's Miss Flack." Her tight smile held no joy. "Well, you know what I mean. If he can sit still, we'll be fine."

Celeste's face fell. "He just started walking, so I'm not sure."

"Shelby Dean is wonderful with babies. She's our Mary, and I have full confidence she'll get him to mind." She pivoted and strode down the hallway to the fellowship hall.

"Get him to mind?" he said. "What did she mean by that?"

"I don't know." She hung up their coats, and they headed in *Miss* Flack's direction. "I'm not sure I want to find out."

"Hey," he said. She stopped and turned to him. "You don't have to do this. It's been a hard night already. We can take off if—"

She shook her head. "No. It's for Grandma Pearl. I'll be okay."

He wasn't so sure, but he had to trust her. They emerged into a large room with groups of parents talking in clusters and kids running around. Laughter and random piano notes filled the air.

"What now?" he whispered. This was out of his element. He'd let Celeste take the lead.

"I have no idea," she whispered back. She set Parker on his feet, but he whirled and held his arms up for her to hold him, which she did.

"May I have your attention?" Miss Flack clapped her hands. "Thank you all for coming. Your children were given their parts in Sunday school last week. I hope they've had a chance to review them. We're going through the recitations tonight and measuring the children for their costumes."

A little girl with braids ran past Miss Flack and chased a towheaded boy.

"Molly, that's enough of that. Both of you stand with your teachers." With a loud sigh, she pointed to a group of kids. "Now, where's Shelby? Matt?"

A pretty dark-haired woman with a wide smile raised her hand. She looked to be in her early twenties. A tall, husky guy joined her. They made a striking couple.

"Everyone meet in the front of the church, and we'll get started." Miss Flack pointed to the doors. "Shelby, Matt, come and meet our baby Jesus."

"I'll be there in a minute," Matt said. "I'm helping Frank get the sets out of the shed."

Sam stood straighter as Shelby and Miss Flack approached, and he sensed Celeste stiffen. He wanted to reassure her, but how? He glanced at her. Sure enough, she'd lowered her face.

She didn't need to do that. She had nothing to be ashamed of. He hitched his chin, ready to defend or help her. Whatever she needed.

"Shelby, this is Celeste and Parker. She's raising Brandy's little boy."

"We were all sad about what happened." Shelby's brown eyes oozed sincerity. She ran her hand down Parker's back. "It's terrible, this sweet baby losing his mama."

Celeste lifted her face and nodded. Sam ground his teeth together. This Shelby lady seemed nice and all, but did she have any idea how her words were affecting Celeste?

Shelby's eyes widened. "I forgot you were driving."

Sam forced himself to keep his eyes trained on Celeste. He recognized the panic rising, the way her eyes darted. Steadying himself, he placed his hand on her lower back.

"How are you doing?" Shelby continued, her voice comforting. "I'm sure this must have been awful for you."

"Having Parker makes it easier."

"May I?" Shelby smiled and held her hands out.

Celeste nodded, and Shelby took Parker in her arms. "How are you, sweet one?"

Not making a sound, Parker stared into her eyes. He seemed to be studying her. She gave him a little hug and laughed. Sam had to give it to Shelby—she was good with him.

Four young kids ran up to Shelby. "Hi, Miss Shelby. Is that your baby?"

"No, Luke." She grinned at the preschoolers. "This is Parker. He's our baby Jesus this year."

Two girls stared up at Celeste. The one with freckles asked, "What happened to your face?"

Shelby started to reprimand her, but Celeste smiled, shaking her head. "It's fine." She addressed the girl. "I was in a car accident."

"Oh. I'm sorry. It must've hurt pretty bad."

"It did."

Shelby shifted Parker to her hip. "Melissa, do you remember Mrs. Monroe? Brandy? Your aunt Jackie was friends with her."

"The one who died?" The girl's face fell, freckles and all.

Sam wanted to put an end to the conversation. Celeste appeared to be handling it okay, though, so he kept his mouth shut.

"Yes. This is Parker, her baby," Shelby said. "And this is his new mommy."

Celeste cleared her throat and crouched to talk to the kids. "My last name is Monroe, too. Brandy was married to my brother, Josh. She was my best friend in the whole world."

"Is that his daddy?" The blonde girl pointed to Sam.

The question landed in his gut like a brick. If the boat hadn't almost killed him, would he be married by now? With a child of his own?

"He's my neighbor and my friend. Mr. Sheffield."

"Were you in the accident, too?"

Sam belatedly realized the kids expected him to say something.

"No," he said. "I was in a different accident."

"Is your leg broke?" One of the boys eyeballed the crutches.

"Kind of."

"Did it hurt?" Freckles asked.

"Yes. It still does."

"You should get an ice pack." The blonde girl pointed to him, and he tried not to smile at her serious tone. "My daddy always puts an ice pack on his neck when he gets home from work."

"I'll do that."

The sound of hands clapping interrupted them. "We're waiting for you. Come on, children."

Shelby, still holding Parker, led the way, and the preschoolers lined up behind her like they were following the Pied Piper.

"I think Parker is in good hands." Sam waited for

Celeste to slip into the back pew and sat beside her, laying his crutches on the floor.

"I do, too."

"You handled that well." He stretched his arm out behind her along the back of the pew.

"You think so?" The tightness in her face disappeared, making her appear younger.

"I know so. You did the right thing letting Parker be in the program." The opening strains of "Joy to the World" blared through the organ. "I want to come with you on Christmas Eve."

She did a double take. "Really? Don't you want to be with your family?"

He loved his family. Always went to church on Christmas Eve with them. But Celeste needed support, and he wanted to give it to her.

"I want to see Parker as baby Jesus. If you don't mind?" He watched her reaction.

She smiled. "I don't mind."

He caught sight of Shelby up there bouncing Parker in her arms and singing.

Before the accident, he hadn't put much thought into having a wife or family. Earlier he'd questioned if he'd be married now, but he knew better. He'd be opening his second dealership, married to his job.

Sam clenched his jaw. His job had been fulfilling, but something had been missing even then. There was more to life than success. And he wanted more. Could he have it?

Celeste dropped Sam off at his brother's dealership the next morning and drove through Lake Endwell. The town was adorable. Walking around with Sam earlier in the week had opened her eyes to its charm. Brick storefronts, pretty awnings, benches on the sidewalks. Everything was decorated for Christmas. Wreaths hung on doors, snowflakes were painted on store windows, Christmas lights were wrapped around trees. Sam had assured her Bryan would take him home, so she and Parker were going to explore on their own.

She stopped at City Park. Taking a drink of coffee from her travel mug, she took in the view of the lake. Last night had changed her. Sam had changed her. She'd never come here before because she'd been too self-conscious. She had even worried about someone staring at her through her van window.

She shook her head. How foolish. She could see that now. Their outings had loosened her up, and the success of being around the kids last night gave her the courage to break out of the cabin on her own.

Anticipation filled her with energy. The snow from earlier in the week had melted. It was a great day to get out.

"What are we waiting for? Let's walk around the park." She turned to grin at Parker, but her grin slid away at the sight of his closed eyes. Sleeping. So much for that.

She started the minivan back up. Should she go home? The blue sky and bluer water in the distance beckoned. No, she wasn't going home. She could sit here and relax awhile. She settled back in the seat and sipped her coffee.

Last night when the little girl had asked her if Sam was Parker's daddy, Celeste hadn't been prepared for her internal reaction. She'd wanted to tell the girl yes, he was his daddy. Spending all this time together, doing the mundane daily stuff, had spoiled her. She relied on Sam. Hadn't understood how lonely she'd been until she moved in next door to him.

What would it be like to come home to a husband? To raise Parker with someone who treated her the way Sam did? To be a family?

She let the glow of possibility wash over her, remembered how strong his arms had felt last night as he'd comforted her. The pressure of his hand against her back when she met Shelby had reassured her. He had the touch. To have those arms around her every day?

She sighed.

She wasn't being realistic. They lived in a bubble. When the real world interrupted—and it would soon—things would change. He'd go back to work. He wouldn't be just hers anymore. It would be good for him to see how important he was again. He'd realize he could have any woman. He'd want a family of his own—not her and her nephew.

She just wished she could stay in the bubble longer.

Sam adjusted his leg in the conference room of Tommy's dealership. A circus had performed in his stomach all morning, and it was all he could do not to stand and pace the room on his crutches. Dad and Bryan hadn't arrived, and Tommy was talking with a customer. What if Sam flipped out the way he had the last time he'd printed out the sales report? If he started crying or had to throw up…

He might as well kiss his career goodbye, because he wouldn't do either in front of the men he respected most. *Get it together, already. If you can't look at a piece of paper without blubbering like a baby, you don't deserve this job.*

He wanted to pray.

I can't pray. I haven't prayed in forever.

God didn't listen, anyhow.

But what if God did? Today?

No, I'm not doing it. I'm not. I can handle this.

"Hey, Sam." Dad charged into the room, jangling his key ring around his finger. "You are a sight for sore eyes, son. I've wanted to see you right there for so long."

Sam's throat tightened. He was going to cry! Right here. Right now.

God, I need Your help. Don't let me fall apart. Not in front of Dad. Don't humiliate me.

He inhaled deeply and began to calm down.

When he trusted himself to speak, Sam said, "I've wanted to be here. It's good to be back."

"You want some coffee?" Dad zoomed straight to the small counter with the coffee supplies.

"Yes." Maybe coffee would scorch his throat free from any inconvenient emotions.

Tommy and Bryan entered the room, laughing about something, and closed the door behind them.

"Look who made it," Tommy teased. "I hope you have a good excuse for missing the last seventy-five meetings."

Sam's stomach did the tango. He wasn't going to throw up, was he? He pressed his hand to his gut.

Bryan winked. "We'll let it slide. As long as you take over the cost-reduction program. I don't know how you did it, man. It's been driving me crazy."

"I cross-referenced all five dealerships' advertising fees, employee salaries and…" He rattled off the specifics, surprised he remembered the details after all this time. Cost reduction was one of his favorite aspects of the job.

Wait—he didn't feel sick. He didn't want to cry.

"See?" Tommy tapped his temple. "This is why we need you back so bad, Sam. Bryan and I hate that stuff."

Dad slurped his coffee. "I got tired of it, too, boys. The only one who really loved it was my dad. And, apparently, Sam here."

Sam waved two fingers for Bryan to pass him a folder. "Let's see what you've done with this place while I was gone."

As he scanned the first sheet of the report, excitement built.

He wanted to make phone calls and check spreadsheets.

He wanted to joke around with the Sheffield Auto employees again.

Could coming to a meeting really be this easy?

Thank You, God.

This was a gift from the Lord.

Maybe he needed to take his faith one day at a time, too.

Chapter Seven

Sitting in the wheelchair in his bathroom the next afternoon, Sam toweled off his hair and patted aftershave on his neck and face. The loose-fitting jeans weren't his favorite, but they covered his knee brace and allowed him to wear somewhat normal clothes. He'd put on a casual button-down shirt for the occasion. Much better than his usual T and athletic pants. They were decorating the Christmas tree soon.

He wanted today to be special, to repay Celeste for all her kindness. Generosity wasn't his only motive—he enjoyed being with her. He could tell her things he didn't tell other people, including his family. She saw his struggles and didn't seem to think less of him. Lately he'd been thinking about her as more than a friend. And definitely more than the woman next door.

Which brought him to the question: What kind of man did Celeste need?

He was wired to protect and support a woman. If anyone deserved protection and support, it was Celeste. Support he could do once he returned to work. But protect? Might take months or years before he could walk unaided on his own two feet.

The fact he defined himself by his legs was starting to bother him. Could insecurity be a form of pride? *Pride?* In his weak legs? Hardly.

He raked the comb through his hair. The urge to pray pricked at his conscience. For what?

For a future.

What if he started praying regularly? For healing? What if God ignored him again?

Too much was riding on his recovery.

He'd just keep working hard at physical therapy. The harder he worked, the sooner he'd be off these crutches for good. Then he'd be ready for the future he'd been dreaming about. His store numbers were average, which gave him the kick in the pants necessary to build his sales back up, but the company overall was thriving.

If Celeste would drive Sam to their main office twice a week, he could resume his duties as CEO. Or was he getting too ahead of himself? It had been so long that he'd been pumped up about anything. He wanted to rush in and take life by both hands.

He went back to the living room. The artificial tree stood tall and bare in front of the bank of windows. He'd asked Dad to buy it for him. Bryan had set it up this morning. Bryan had also offered to bring Sam's ornaments from his storage unit, but he couldn't remember the combination to the lock, so Bryan ended up poking around in the cottage's basement, unearthing boxes of ornaments, which now sat unopened in the living room. Aunt Sally had dropped an apple pie off earlier.

Surprising himself, he'd told Dad, Bryan and Sally they were welcome to stop by later and see the finished decorations. He wanted to introduce the family to Celeste and Parker. Seeing how well she'd handled being out with strangers the other night, he guessed she was ready for it.

He clip-clopped to the stereo and carefully lowered himself to the ottoman to find a Christmas music station.

Knocks at the door threw his pulse into gear. "Come in."

"Hi. I hope we aren't too early." Celeste shook snowflakes out of her hair and set Parker down. He toddled to Sam as fast as his chubby legs would take him. Once again, Sam regretted not being able to swoop him up and toss him in the air. Parker wrapped his arms around Sam's leg.

"Let's sit down, and I'll hold you." Sam laughed, trying to walk backward with his crutches.

"What smells so good?" Celeste hung her coat over the back of a dining chair.

"Apple pie. Aunt Sally brought it over."

"I see you got the tree up. It's tall, isn't it?" Her hair fell softly over her shoulders. He had to force himself to look away.

"Yeah. Bryan put it up for me." Sam backed to the couch and sat down. Then he picked Parker up and blew raspberries on his tummy. Parker squealed and laughed.

Celeste poked around the boxes. Fat snowflakes meandered down outside. The cinnamon aroma, Christmas music and snow blended together for an enticing effect.

"What should I do first?" Celeste held up a tray of silver bulbs. "Are the lights strung?"

"The tree is pre-lit." He put Parker on the floor and hauled himself up with the crutches. Parker immediately fussed and held his arms in the air for Sam to take him. A pang of regret ricocheted through his heart. He wanted to carry Parker to the tree, put the star in his hands and hoist him up to place it on the tippy-top. But he couldn't. "Sorry, buddy."

Parker plopped on his bottom and started to cry. Sam tried to bend, but his knee felt as though it was going to give way. A flash of heat rippled over his skin. His heartbeat pounded. He forced himself to stay upright and be still a moment. Why couldn't he just bend down and pick the kid up?

"All right, that's enough, Parker." Celeste gave him a stern look, and he sniffled, then crawled to Sam and stared up at him through watery brown eyes. "He'll have to learn you can't carry him around."

The words ripped down his heart. If Sam had kept up with his physical therapy after the last surgery, would his legs be strong enough for a cane?

What did it matter? He couldn't hold Parker *and* use a cane. He needed the balance of both legs.

Parker tugged on Sam's pant legs, tears dripping down his cheeks. Sam clenched his jaw. As much as he didn't want to use his wheelchair in front of Celeste unless absolutely necessary, it would allow him to hold Parker.

Was it worth it?

Whimpering, Parker pulled on Sam's pant leg, and Sam sighed. Yes, Parker was worth it.

"I'll be right back." As soon as he swung the crutches away, Parker began wailing. Sam lowered himself into the chair, balanced the crutches on his lap and wheeled back to the living room. He rolled right to Parker.

"Come on up, buddy."

With watery eyes and a huge grin, Parker stood and held his arms out, and Sam picked him up, settling him on his lap. Parker sighed and snuggled into his chest, sucking his thumb.

Celeste met Sam's eyes, and he forgot to breathe. Instead of pity in her expression, he saw admiration. Attraction, even.

She was attracted to him? Even in the chair?

Every muscle fiber ached to stand up, to drag her in his arms, to run his fingers through her silky brown hair, to press his lips against hers. To kiss her.

But Parker's warm body had melded into his side, and Sam could no more pluck the child from his lap than he could act on his fantasies. So he wheeled to the nearest box and, with his free hand, grabbed a sealed plastic bag full of ornaments.

"Let's get this decorated." He sounded like a drill sergeant, but what else could he do? *God, I know I'm out of line here. It's been a long time since I've prayed on a regular basis, but I don't know how to handle this—how to handle these feelings for Celeste. Will You help me?*

Celeste was hanging bulbs around the tree. She moved near Sam and stretched to place one close to the top. Her slender waist was right there in front of him. Within reach. The urge to hold her grew stronger.

Great. That's not helping.

Parker's little body radiated heat through Sam's shirt, and soon his even breathing assured Sam he'd fallen asleep. He better get his mind off Celeste and onto the task at hand. He ripped the bag open and pulled out a Mrs. Claus felt ornament.

Who had spent money on this thing?

"This is the ugliest ornament I've ever seen." He gave it a skeptical stare. "It looks like a cat toy."

She tipped her head to the side to see it. Her sparkly eyes did something to his pulse. "It's not so bad."

"How can you say that? This gal looks like she hasn't seen daylight since 1954." He drew out a matching Santa. "It gets worse. They're a pair."

Celeste laughed, loud and tinkling. "Well, be thankful there aren't matching reindeer."

"Wrong." Sam held the clear bag up. Several brown felt reindeer with gold cording winding around them were visible.

"Oh, my." She tucked her lips under in an attempt not to laugh. "Aren't these your decorations?"

"No. They're Granddad's."

Celeste smiled and lifted her knuckle under her chin. "When do you think they were last on a tree?"

"Like I said, 1954." He blew dust off a small brown box.

"How sweet. Think of all the memories here. I wonder if your grandparents bought or made them. Maybe they were gifts. I can imagine a young couple, newly married, decorating a tree with all of these. Can you?"

"I do remember an old picture. Grandma had a blond beehive, and Granddad's hair was slicked back. He had his arm slung around her, and they both were laughing."

"I'd love to see it." Celeste dug through a paper bag. "Where did they live?"

He thought back to what he knew of his grandparents. "They built a small brick ranch in town when they were first married. A few years later, after Granddad made his first dealership profitable, they built a larger house in the country."

Celeste held up a painted glass ornament shaped like a cone. "Were they happy?"

"Yeah. They were. They built this cabin before I was born. Grandma died when I was young, though, so I don't remember much about her. But Granddad was great. Lived here as long as I can remember."

"These boxes are like a time capsule. I wish your grandparents were still around so we could ask them about their first Christmases." She carefully threaded a hook through a pink felt ballerina. "Sam?"

"Hmm?" He untangled the reindeer. Something in her posture made him think she had more than his grandparents on her mind.

"What do you want your memories to look like?"

He stretched Rudolph apart from Dancer and Prancer. "I'm not sure. Everything kind of got divided pre and post accident for me. Before? I planned on getting my dealership to the point it was consistently making enough money so I could build another one in the next county. My life revolved around my ambition. I really wasn't looking for anything else."

"But now?" she asked quietly as she placed the ballerina next to a ceramic kitten on the tree.

He glanced at Parker snuggled into his side, then met Celeste's rich eyes, full of expectation. How honest should he be?

"More has been on my mind. Family."

She blinked, a smile lighting up her face.

Sam patted Parker's head and untangled the final reindeer. "When I'm out of this chair and off these crutches, I'll put more thought into it. I do know this guy has me wrapped around his pinkie."

"Did you hear something from your doctor?"

"No, but I'm counting on it." He was no longer willing to accept a lifelong disability. He'd made considerable strides over the last month. But what if something happened? Another accident? Another slip? "I'll figure the rest out when I'm on both feet again."

Furrows dipped in her forehead and the light in her eyes faded.

"What about you?" he asked.

She selected beaded candy canes and disappeared behind the tree. "Today will be a good memory."

Why did he have the feeling he'd just let her down?

An hour later the Christmas tree was crammed with a combination of painted glass ornaments and a huge assortment of felt reindeer as well as Mr. and Mrs. Claus—or the Ugly Couple, as Sam called them. Celeste admired the view before slipping into the kitchen to start the coffeemaker. The white lights cast a charming glow, their reflections bouncing off the windows. She didn't want today to end. She enjoyed existing in this snow globe where Sam looked at her as if she was special. How long would it last?

They'd set Parker, still sleeping, on a folded blanket on the fluffy area rug in the living room. He'd be able to finish his nap safely there. The late afternoon sky was growing darker, and the snow that had fallen all day coated the ground by at least an inch. She peeked out the kitchen window. Maybe two inches. She hoped so.

From the minute Sam rolled into the living room in the wheelchair to accommodate Parker, Celeste had been losing the battle warring in her heart. She was getting too attached to Sam. Dare she admit, even to herself, she was halfway in love with him? And the flirty mood earlier hadn't helped—not one bit. How could she protect herself from getting hurt when Sam stared at her *that* way? Or when he casually mentioned he'd been thinking of families?

Did he have any idea how many times she'd caught herself wishing they were a family? That Parker had him as a dad and that she had Sam as a husband?

But then he'd iced the atmosphere with his comment about walking on two feet before thinking about having more. She'd watched enough of Sam's physical therapy sessions since she'd met him to know he had no guarantees he'd walk unassisted again.

Would he let his physical limitations decide his future?

Like she was one to talk. Her mirror revealed the truth every time she glanced its way. Her life was on hold for the same reasons.

Maybe they were both being selfish.

Nonsense.

Falling in love with him was all wrong, and she was the one who would lose. She knew he was terrific, and it was only a few weeks before he'd be back out and about in Lake Endwell every day. He'd see other women, reminding him he had options. Ones that didn't include a scarred single mom.

Christmas music still played in the background, and the apple pie beckoned. She rummaged through drawers until she found a knife and serving utensils.

"Ready for a break?" She held up the pie as Sam approached on his crutches.

"Definitely. Is that coffee I smell?" His blue eyes twinkled with something she couldn't decipher, but whatever it was, it overrode her admonitions to keep her feelings in check. He stopped close to her. Closer than usual. He smelled fantastic, all spicy and manly and…

"Coffee. Yes." She took a tiny step back, but Sam leaned toward her.

"I'd offer to carry it but…"

Was he teasing? She searched his face. He sure was. She forced a lighthearted laugh. "Oh, no. Your hands are full, and we don't want to lose this pie."

"True." He nodded, faking concern with an insincere frown. "Aunt Sally's pie should never be wasted."

"Exactly." She could feel the warmth of his body near hers. He seemed taller. But that might be because she wasn't usually inches away from him. She had to tilt her chin up to meet his eyes. Which was probably a mistake, considering her mouth dried like tissue paper as soon as she did. Those cheekbones. That face. His bottom lip was fuller than the top lip. But why was she thinking about that?

And the way he looked at her? Made her think he had feelings for her, too.

Shrugging slightly, she sidestepped around him and carried the dessert in her jittery hands to the table. Then she returned to the kitchen for plates and silverware. Her fingers trembled as she opened cupboards. Finally, she wiped her hands down her jeans. "Do you want a slice of pie now or do you want to wait until the coffee is ready?"

"Let's wait. Come here a minute." He swung the crutches to the living room, and she followed. He took a seat on the couch and patted the spot next to him. She raised her eyebrows, her skin tingling—what was he up to?—and sat down, hands folded primly in her lap.

Taking something off the end table, he turned and faced her. "Look what I found."

Oh, my.

He lifted his hand above her head, and she looked up. Mistletoe.

Mistletoe? Her heartbeat was tripping over itself.

"You know the tradition, right?" he asked, huskily.

She had no words. Just a million and one impressions. Her mouth opened before she had time to think. "It represented peace to the Romans, protection from death to the Nordic people, and in Victorian England, it was a big deal if a girl refused a kiss. She wouldn't find a suitor the next year."

His face blanked, and then he grinned. "Well, I have my own rules about it."

"What rules?"

"The mistletoe rules." He leaned in, smiling, his blue eyes intent. His right hand caressed her hair before settling behind her neck. He drew her closer to him. Firm hands, the smell of his skin, warm breath all collided as his lips brushed hers.

Before she could process the sensation, his lips pressed more insistently, but not demanding. She relaxed into his arms and followed his lead. Her arms wound round his neck, and she reveled in the softness of the hair at his nape. Kissing him felt so right, even better than her dreams. If they could freeze this moment—she could live right here, right now, forever.

Sam's kiss tapered off, and he searched her eyes, his lips spreading into a satisfied smile. Their faces were almost touching. The slightest movement and he'd be kissing her again.

"What were the rules?" she whispered.

"Rule number one. I've wanted to—"

"Yoo-hoo!" The door opened and a gust of snowy air blew in, bringing with it a noisy group of people led by a short blonde older lady wearing fake reindeer antlers on her head.

Sam rolled his eyes, muttering, "Perfect timing."

She squinted. Was Claire behind the antler lady?

Let the earth swallow her now.

Celeste kept her spine as straight as the flagpole in front of the cottage. Laughter and conversation spilled inside with the rest of the crowd. Two of the tall men were clearly Sam's brothers, but the other two? She had no idea. As the adults shrugged out of their coats, a little dark-haired girl, six or seven, ran straight to Sam and fell into his arms.

"Uncle Sam, I got you something." The beautiful child kissed his nose. "Want to see?"

"Of course I do, Macy."

She ran back to the kitchen, disappearing in a sea of legs.

"Sam," Claire yelled, her face glowing. "Where did you find Granddad's old ornaments? These bring me back." With her hand on her tiny belly, she shook her head in wonder and stepped back to survey the tree.

Celeste swallowed her mortification and stood. She hadn't talked to Claire since moving next door. She needed to congratulate her.

"And what a great surprise to see you here, Celeste." Claire rushed forward, taking Celeste's hands in hers. Claire kissed her on the cheek, and Celeste was so surprised she couldn't find a single word to say. "Did Sam rope you into decorating for him? I hope he hasn't been a slave driver with this tree."

"Congratulations. I hear you're expecting." Celeste nodded to Claire's tummy.

"Thank you," she said, her eyes growing damp. "We had a hard time getting pregnant."

A commotion made them both turn.

"Hey, watch the baby." Sam glared at two of the men and wielded his right crutch to point at Parker. "And for crying out loud, don't wake him up." His eyes met Celeste's, and he tilted his head to the side. "Come on, I'll introduce you to everyone."

"Let me move Parker first."

The next fifteen minutes were spent meeting an endless supply of Sheffield siblings, wives, husbands, nieces, his aunt Sally and uncle Joe and, finally, his dad.

"Glad to meet you," Dale Sheffield said. He wasn't as tall as his sons, but he seemed energetic. He had a thick head of silver hair and the kindest blue eyes she'd ever seen. "I see you got the tree decorated. Reminds me when I was a kid. I didn't know the old man saved all those decorations."

Aunt Sally scampered over, antlers jiggling. "Look, Dale, I haven't seen those reindeer in years. Remember how Ma made us put them up every Christmas?"

"They were ugly then, and they're ugly now." Dale crossed his arms over his chest. "But she sure loved them."

"Well, you know why, don't you?" Sally shifted her weight to the side, putting a hand on her hip. "She and Dad didn't have any money those first two years they were married."

"I know, I know."

Sally glared at him, then turned to Celeste. "Our mother hated the idea of a bare tree, so she and her sister made all these ornaments out of felt. Hours of cutting, embroidering, sewing and stuffing. She was so proud of them she put them up every year, even when they had enough money to decorate with crystal."

Dale chuckled. "Dad said the same thing each time they lugged them out. 'If it wasn't for your mother's resourcefulness, Sheffield Auto never would have survived the first years.' I think he might have been prouder of those homemade decorations than she was."

Sally nodded, a soft gleam in her eyes. "Yeah, they appreciated each other, that's for sure."

A couple approached. Celeste tried to remember the man's name. Tom? He looked like an older, darker, more mischievous version of Sam. "It was good to have you back yesterday."

Sam grinned. "It was good to be back."

Tom pointed at Sam. "Now you have no excuse. Macy's singing in church with her Sunday school class Wednesday night. It would make us happy if you came and watched her."

"Why Wednesday?"

"Did you forget about that thing called Advent?"

"Oh, right."

Parker's cry alerted Celeste he'd finally woken. She excused herself and picked him up. His cheeks were flushed from sleep, and he rubbed his eyes with one fist and clung to her neck with the other.

She took him to the spare bedroom and changed his diaper. When she returned, cheerful chatter filled the room, and one of the women approached. Tom's wife, Stephanie? Sam had introduced them only minutes ago—she hoped she got the name right.

"Your little boy is so cute." She held a toddler girl

with dark brown curls. "I know we can be overwhelming. I'm Stephanie, and this is Emily. How old is he?"

Celeste caught a glimpse of the other men. The dark blond who seemed quieter than the others was Bryan. The other two men were Claire's and Libby's husbands, Reed and Jake, and they happened to be brothers.

"Parker turned a year in October. What about Emily?"

"She'll be eighteen months in a few weeks." The girl wriggled for Stephanie to put her down. As soon as her feet hit the floor, she took off running to Claire. Stephanie shook her head, grinning. "She is a handful. Everyone calls her Sweetpea, but trust me, she's less sweet and more tart."

Celeste laughed. "Yeah, Parker's been starting to cry more when he doesn't get his way. He's kind of obsessed with Sam."

"Well, Sam's good with kids."

A petite, stylish woman with green eyes materialized next to them.

"How are the Christmas products selling, Jade?" Stephanie asked. She shook her head, addressing Celeste. "Where are my manners? Have you two met? Celeste, this is Jade, Bryan's wife."

Jade grinned, her eyes sparkling brighter than the lights on the tree. "We were introduced a little bit ago, but I'm terrible with names, so if you ever forget mine, I won't be offended."

Celeste smiled, and Jade turned to Stephanie. "Libby and I ordered handmade ornaments. Metal, wood, glass. They are gorgeous. You should stop by and check them out. Bring the girls."

"Did I hear my name?" A stunning blonde, the

youngest of Sam's siblings, approached Stephanie and Jade, putting an arm around each of their shoulders.

"I was just telling Stephanie and Celeste about the ornaments." Jade practically wiggled in excitement. "Celeste, have you met Libby?"

Celeste nodded, fascinated by the interaction.

"We're so thankful for you," Libby said. She glanced over her shoulder at the men. "Sam's himself again. Because of you."

"I didn't really…" Celeste wasn't sure what to say.

"Yes, you did, but I'll drop it for now." Libby winked. "So, I went to the Ann Arbor art fair this summer and met the most amazing artists…"

"Do you two work together?" Celeste asked when Libby finished telling them about the hand-stamped metal ornaments.

"Yes! Jade opened a T-shirt shop almost two years ago, wasn't it?" Libby asked. Jade nodded, so she continued. "After she married Bryan—thank you a million times over for making him happy—we decided to join forces and expand the store. Shine Gifts is now double the size. You might have seen it downtown Lake Endwell. We have a purple—"

"Eggplant," Jade interjected.

"Excuse me, eggplant—" Libby grinned, scrunching her nose "—awning over the front door. Stop in anytime."

"I design and make the custom shirts and bags and such." Jade waved her hands as if to say "ta-da."

"And I find the jewelry, books, art and gifts." Libby drew Jade in for a one-armed hug. "We make a great team."

"I heard you run your own virtual assistant business, Celeste," Stephanie said. "I know at least four businesses who would jump at the chance to hire you part-time."

"Really?" Celeste let the possibility wash over her. More work meant more money, which she needed, but she already had a hard time fitting in the clients she had. She wouldn't need to hustle for more work if she went through with her teacher certification. She could raise Parker on a modest teacher's wage. Until then, though, she'd have to consider new business contacts. "Feel free to give them my number. I'll leave a business card with Sam next time I come over." Parker started getting antsy in her arms, so she set him down, keeping an eye on him as he headed toward Macy. The little girl crouched as he approached and ruffled his hair as she smiled.

"Macy loves babies," Stephanie said as Macy took Parker's hand. "You might never get him back."

"She's darling." Celeste watched Macy slowly walk with Parker to the tree. She pointed out ornaments, and he stared at her, mesmerized. Sam chatted with his brothers and uncle a few feet from the tree.

Celeste met Sam's eyes across the room. They shimmered with appreciation. Heat flashed up her neck, and instantly, she thought of their kiss. The pressure of his lips against hers. The strength and tenderness of his hands. The feeling of being cherished.

As much as she enjoyed the interaction with his family, she wouldn't mind if they all disappeared, leaving her and Sam alone. To have him explain the mistletoe rules a little more in depth.

But she shook the ungracious thought away. His family was wonderful. None of them had asked about her face. They all treated her as if she didn't have scars. For a few moments, she'd forgotten about them.

A burst of laughter filled the air from the men. She closed her eyes, savoring this—a house full of fun people on a winter day surrounded by Christmas scents, twinkly lights and laughter.

If things were different…

But they weren't. Maybe she and Sam were both indulging in wishful thinking. She kept pretending life would change with more surgery, and he pretended his legs would somehow spontaneously heal.

She'd have to hold on to the memory of today forever, because her gut told her the snow globe they were in was about to shatter.

Chapter Eight

"What am I going to do with all this?" Sam leaned against the kitchen counter and shook his head in amazement at the plastic containers full of sugar cookies, bowls of frosting in pastel colors and every type of sprinkle imaginable. He and Celeste had just returned from his Monday therapy session. For two days he hadn't stopped thinking about their kiss. In fact, he couldn't get Celeste off his mind. And he needed to. Soon.

"Um, wow." Celeste crossed her arms over her chest and bit her lower lip, but her eyes danced with laughter. Parker played with a toy car on the floor.

"Aunt Sally's finally lost it."

"Did she mention anything about this to you?"

"Nope. No, she did not." He lifted his eyes to the ceiling. "Aunt Sally texted me she was dropping something off, but what was she thinking? There's enough sugar here to give someone diabetes."

"Is that a note?" Celeste pointed to a sheet of paper wedged under a package of plastic pastry bags. He scanned the note.

*I made too many cookies and thought that darling
baby might enjoy decorating them with his pretty
mama and you. Love, Aunt Sally.*

Uneasiness prickled over his skin. As much as he
wanted to spend the day decorating cookies with Celeste and Parker, he knew it wasn't wise. He had to stop
thinking about himself and start thinking about what
was best for her. Which wasn't him.

She plucked the paper from his hand. "Isn't that
sweet? Thinking of Parker."

Thinking of setting him up with Celeste was more
like it. His aunt had a history of matchmaking. Didn't
his aunt realize Celeste was special? That she needed
a guy who could be there for her in ways he couldn't?
Her slender arms carried too much every day as it was.
He would not be another burden on her.

"Why don't you change, and I'll get everything
ready?" Her clear brown eyes held no questions or concerns. Just anticipation.

What was he supposed to do now? Tell her to hit the
road? That she couldn't stay because his heart was getting in way too deep? Yeah, that would go over well.

"Okay."

When he'd changed, he paused a moment in the doorway. Celeste had laid the cookies out on wax paper at
the dining table. Parker was strapped into his portable booster seat. He nibbled on one cookie and banged
another against the table. She was spooning the icing
into the pastry bags. The Christmas tree twinkled beside them.

What had been an empty cottage had become a
warm, inviting home.

What would it hurt if he simply enjoyed being with them today?

He took a seat next to Parker and pretended to take a bite from his cookie. Parker squealed, snatching the cookie back. Then he thrust it back to Sam, and Sam laughed, pretending to take another bite. The boy laughed harder. Sam made gobbling noises, egging him on.

Celeste set the bags of frosting on the table, and he almost caught his breath. She looked happy. Beautiful.

He cleared his throat. "What do you do with this?" Picking up a squishy bag full of baby blue frosting, he tried to shake his head of all the warm fuzzy feelings invading him.

Her fingers brushed his as she demonstrated how to pipe the icing onto the cookie. "Easy, huh?"

"Yeah." It was. Easy. All of this was too easy.

And it wouldn't last.

He knew better than to count on it. It was one thing to be friends, another to kiss her, and still another to fall in love. He'd never been in love before. He'd liked casual dating, enjoyed dinner and a movie. This…this doing regular everyday stuff with Celeste and Parker compelled him. He'd rather hang out and decorate cookies with them than anything else. But it wasn't fair to her.

Parker stared up at him through big hopeful eyes, the cookie stretched toward Sam's mouth. Once more he pretended to gobble the cookie.

"Are you going to help or do I have to crack the whip?" Celeste popped her hand on her hip in mock anger.

"Okay, I'll get at it, boss." He frosted a snowman cookie and sifted colored sugar on top. Celeste sat across from him, and she carefully decorated the cutout cookies. After a while, Parker got antsy, so she took him out of the high chair and let him play with his car again.

Contentment crept up on him. He watched Celeste's lips curve into a slight smile as she put the finishing touches on a cookie shaped like a snowflake. Simple pleasures. Ones he craved. The only way he could justify spending all this time together was if he knew for sure he'd be walking on his own soon.

Maybe it was time to ask Dr. Stepmeyer about his progress. How long would it be before he could have a real life?

Another Wednesday at physical therapy, another round of torture.

With his right leg, Sam lifted the exercise table's torque arm, straining to get it high enough. His thigh muscles protested, but not as much as his stiff knee. Sweat dripped down both sides of his forehead. At least his hour was almost up.

He ground out the remaining sets and slumped, reaching for the towel and water he kept nearby. After a long drink, he sucked in another breath and willed his legs to stop twitching and shooting fire.

Dr. Stepmeyer returned. He stretched his neck from side to side. "Can I ask you something?"

"Of course."

"Do you think it's working?"

"Yes. Don't you? I thought your progress was obvious." She handed him his crutches and strolled to the treatment table. When he was ready, she hooked up the electrodes and started the machine.

"You came in here five weeks ago in a wheelchair.

You could barely stand on your left leg and couldn't put any weight on your right. Your left leg is strong now. Much stronger than it was. The right knee still can't take much pressure, but yes, your time and effort are paying off."

"I need to go back to work."

"I figured." She sat on the stool next to him, her clipboard in her lap. "Have you looked at your leg lately, Sam?"

He glanced down. Purple scars spiraled around it, and parts of his thigh and knee appeared to have been carved out, chunks missing. "Yeah. What about it?"

"We see the outside, but we don't know what's going on inside. When is your next doctor appointment?"

His leg may be ugly, but it was whole. He'd purposely tried not to think about what was going on inside it. The nerve was supposed to reconnect. That was the whole point of the nerve graft. "Dr. Curtis warned me healing would be slow."

"He was right," she said, nodding. "But these surgeries don't always restore full function. Dr. Curtis warned you about that, too."

"What are you saying?" he snapped. The odors of the room assaulted him—sweat, sweat and more sweat.

"I'm saying, keep working hard. Make an appointment with him before you go back to work."

"I'm going back in January."

"Okay. But be careful. And protect your leg as much as possible." She set the clipboard down and swiped her tablet. Clicking her tongue, she read whatever was on the screen. "During our initial interview, you told me you spent seventy-five percent of the workday on your feet before the accident. Will you modify that?"

He sighed. "I'll try."

"You're going to have to do more than try, Sam. Don't expect work to be the same."

"Nothing is the same, is it?" He grabbed the water bottle and took another drink. If only she'd hook the electrodes up to his flaming emotions. Release the tension every word she said brought on. "I'm going to be using a cane soon. I have to."

"You're not ready." Her mouth twisted in disapproval.

"I am ready. Ready to move on with my life. The crutches are impossible. I can't use my hands for anything, and I'm tired of having to wear a man-purse to carry something from one room to another. How can I shake a customer's hand if I'm worried my crutches will fall?"

"That's why you need to talk to Dr. Curtis before returning to work."

"So what are you saying? If he doesn't clear me, I'm stuck at home?"

"I don't know. That's your call. You might be better off using the wheelchair at work. You can keep coming here three times a week and use the crutches at home."

"I'm not going to work in a wheelchair." He stared at the wall. All this work and for what? Nothing?

"Hey, normally I'd agree with you. I want you out of the wheelchair as much as possible. But I don't want you collapsing on the floor with a muscle strain. Or worse. Think about it."

Dr. Stepmeyer shut off the machine, carefully detached the electrodes and told him to go down the hall.

If this place had a punching bag, he was ready to go nine rounds with it. Instead, he made his way to the hall. All the prayers he'd pleaded last year roared back. How many times had he begged to be blessed with the ability to walk on his own?

The urge to ask again hit him hard, but he shook it away.

He didn't care that God ignored him or that Dr. Stepmeyer thought he should wait. He was tired of waiting for his life to turn around.

He'd go back to work. He'd stay on his crutches. Soon, he'd walk with a cane.

He'd show them all.

"How did it go?" Celeste drove out of the physical rehab center's parking lot after Sam buckled himself in. They'd decided to make their first appearance at Lake Endwell Library today to pick up Christmas picture books for Parker. It had been over a year since Celeste had been in a library or bookstore, and she couldn't wait.

"It went fine." Sam kept his head turned away, staring out his window. The way he said it told her it was not fine.

"Did something happen?" She turned left at the stoplight on their way out of the city. The air had a bite to it, and the snow from the weekend still covered the ground. Had it been only four days since he'd kissed her? She'd mentally relived it about four hundred times since then, but who was counting? He'd been so wonderful with Parker when they'd decorated the cookies, but she'd been a wee bit disappointed that he'd kept his distance from her. He certainly hadn't attempted to kiss her again.

"No," he barked. "Let's drop it."

She sat up straighter. *Well, then.*

Tempted to ask, to push him for details, she gritted her teeth and cranked the country music louder.

He flicked the radio off.

"What is wrong with you?" She didn't even try to keep the exasperation out of her tone.

"Nothing."

"Do you still want to go to the library?" *Please say yes.*

"Why wouldn't I?" He crossed his arms over his chest, not looking at her.

"You tell me."

He didn't respond.

Wonderful.

She'd gone into full-blown dreamy schoolgirl mode, unable to contain her enthusiasm about seeing Sam again. And Sam? Seemed as enthusiastic as an angry raccoon.

But why?

The miles sped by without conversation. Bare trees and evergreens lined the side of the road. As they neared Lake Endwell, her irritation mounted.

She hated the silent treatment. Didn't she have enough to worry about right now? Like the upcoming evaluation by her plastic surgeon? And what about her home life? She was regularly staying up past midnight to meet her clients' needs and was so tired in the afternoon she'd taken to napping with Parker. She'd gotten an email this morning from her top client. They wanted to double her hours after the holidays. How was she going to keep up?

With one hand on the steering wheel, she rubbed her left temple. The work didn't fulfill her. Sure, she was organized and good at her job, but she found it boring. She wanted to share her love of history with others as a teacher. If she was this busy trying to raise Parker and make ends meet, how would she find time to take the online courses she needed to get certified?

Lake Endwell Library came into view. She found a spot, and minutes later, with Parker in her arms, she held the door open for Sam and followed him inside.

It smelled like books. She closed her eyes and smiled. Books—the best smell in the world.

"Mama! Mama!" Parker bounced in her arms. She set him down, keeping a firm hold on his hand.

"Stay with me, Parker. Let's go find the children's section." She didn't bother looking Sam's way as she led Parker to the corner with hot-air balloons painted on the walls. Miniature hot-air balloons in assorted primary colors hung from the ceiling, too. Very cute.

Parker toddled to a table with wooden puzzles. Celeste helped him sit in a tiny chair. She browsed the picture books while he played. An adorable Christmas book with a big brown bear on the cover caught her eye. She flipped through, smiling at the beautiful illustrations. How did artists do it? Create such imaginative pages conveying different moods?

Within minutes she'd collected a pile of picture books. Parker was still happily clanging the big wooden puzzle pieces against the forms. Someone had left a stack of magazines and books on the table, so she sat in one of the tiny chairs and eyed the titles.

A celebrity magazine, a Southern cookbook, two mystery novels and a nonfiction book. The nonfiction piqued her interest. Something about being okay after life falling apart.

She itched to pick it up and read the back cover, but what if the person who'd selected it came back? Would they think she was poaching their book?

With a turn of her head to the left then the right, she tried to locate who might be checking out this pile. A librarian stood behind a counter. An older man near the fireplace read a newspaper with one ankle on his knee. Sam stood in front of the shelves with the DVDs. Her gaze lingered on his broad shoulders.

What had put him in such a bad mood? She nibbled her fingernail. Was it something she'd said?

She snatched the book. It was written from a Christian viewpoint. She sighed. It probably was going to drone on about how life will be perfect if you just trust in God enough.

Life wasn't perfect. No matter how much she trusted God.

After flipping it over, she read the opening line of the back cover. *Life isn't perfect for Christians or anyone.*

Huh. Maybe she should give this one a try.

The bullet points reiterated the theme: *God will help you survive any circumstances.* It promised the secrets of having peace regardless of your trials and recognizing how something good can come from something bad.

She needed this book.

Opening to the first chapter, she began reading. And she didn't look up until Sam stood next to her. She sensed his presence before he cleared his throat. "Are you ready?"

"Sure." She rose, checking on Parker. He still sat at the table, but now he was flipping the pages of a board book with a caterpillar on the cover. "Did you get what you wanted?"

"Yeah." His posture wasn't as stiff as earlier.

"Would you watch him for me while I check out?" Celeste hauled the picture books into her arms, and she set the nonfiction back on the other pile.

"Of course."

She walked in the direction of the front desk, but on a whim, she turned to the computer. Maybe the library had more than one copy of the book she'd left on the table. If not, she could put a hold on it. She typed in a search of the title, and when she saw they had another one available, she almost raised her hand for a fist pump. It took only a minute to find the book.

At the checkout desk, the librarian blinked when she registered her scars, but Celeste just smiled. Books made everything better. She didn't have the energy to be self-conscious, not when she couldn't wait to carve out a few hours to read.

She wanted to find out how God could make something good come out of something so bad. Was it even possible?

"I'm all set." She approached Sam and Parker. With one hand full of books, she attempted to pick Parker up. She almost lost her balance, but on the second try, she settled him on her hip. Kissed his soft cheek. "You ready to go home?"

He wrapped his arms around her neck.

They left the warmth of the library for the cold wind outdoors. Strange, but having the book in her possession made her not care if Sam was grumpy or mad at her. She didn't want to analyze his mood.

"Do you need anything else?" She started the van. "Want me to stop anywhere?"

"No. I'm ready to go home."

Disappointed, she nodded. He didn't want to be with her. *Good.* She had a book to read. Work to do. Her life to figure out.

The problem? It was all easier with Sam by her side.

Even if she shoved her romantic feelings underground, she couldn't imagine forging forward with her new life if Sam wasn't a part of it.

She glanced at his profile. Serious. Reflective.

Unfortunately, she had no guarantees their friendship would last.

Chapter Nine

Sam followed Bryan and Jade into the pew later that night. He hadn't been to church in a year and a half. Was he ready to trust God again? He wasn't sure, but if not, why was he here?

For Macy. And Tom and Stephanie. He loved his niece, and it was time to support her the way his family had been supporting him. And he felt guilty about being short with Celeste earlier, but there was only so much bad news he could take.

Soft strains of "Angels We Have Heard on High" filled the room along with the smell of freshly lit candles. The stained glass windows appeared dark, the scenes difficult to see at night. Kind of like his mental state. Difficult to discern. Sam opened the program. Five hymns. From the looks of it, the service would be long. He stretched his leg out.

The pastor welcomed everyone, and the opening hymn played on the organ. He shouldn't have taken his annoyance out on Celeste. She understood him without judging him. He liked their small talk, the ease of being with her.

It would be simple to have that ease back, but how could he lead Celeste on?

If he went to the doctor and found out he wasn't cleared for work, he didn't know what he'd do. The facts were there—out of work, couldn't drive, couldn't walk—basically helpless. What woman wanted that combination in a man?

Maybe he hadn't been leading her on. Maybe the doctor would clear him for work.

The pastor motioned for everyone to rise. Sam gripped the back of the pew in front of him and hauled himself to his feet, careful not to put too much weight on his right leg. He joined in a responsive reading and soon was sitting again.

Sam relaxed as the pastor read the sermon text, then preached about Jesus's birth from Mary's perspective.

"Picture a young woman, thrust into a drama she hadn't expected. First, she's visited by an angel and finds out she's going to be the mother of the promised Savior. Then she almost loses her fiancé because of the baby, and instead of enjoying the pregnancy in familiar surroundings, she's forced on a long, strenuous trip to Bethlehem, where she gives birth in lowly circumstances."

Sam folded his hands in his lap. He hadn't put much thought into Mary at Christmas.

The pastor continued, "And what about Joseph? Here's a man who was shocked to find out his bride-to-be was carrying a child. A visit from an angel explained the baby was from the Holy Spirit, but I'm guessing it was a lot to take in. On top of that, they're forced to travel to Bethlehem at a time Joseph would most want to protect Mary. The town was so crowded.

Joseph couldn't even provide proper lodging for them. They had to use a manger for a crib. Most husbands don't want their pregnant wives making a difficult journey, and they certainly don't want their baby to sleep in a feeding trough."

Joseph's issues? Sam understood. Of course Joseph wanted to protect Mary. If it was Sam, he would have knocked on every innkeeper's door and demanded a room, which, now that he thought about it, Joseph probably did.

Why hadn't God given them a room? He'd sent angels to Mary and Joseph, explaining what was happening, but He wouldn't give them a comfortable bed?

"Sometimes God's ways don't fit in with our expectations," the pastor said. "We expect God's Son to be born in luxury, not his humble beginnings in the small town of Bethlehem. All-powerful but with no earthly kingdom. It's almost incomprehensible God would send His beloved Son to earth to die for our sins."

Sam frowned. If he had a son, he'd protect him and not let anything bad happen to him.

"But Jesus didn't stay dead. He conquered death. This Christmas season I hope you focus on this—God loves you so much He sent His son to live a perfect life, to die for you, and to rise again so that you can have eternal life. This is the real Christmas gift. The gift of salvation by grace alone."

"Amen," the congregation said.

Piano chords filled the church, and Sam shifted to watch two rows of children march up the aisle. Macy's ringlets bounced above her dark purple dress. When they were lined up, they began to sing "O Little Town of Bethlehem."

He bowed his head, surprised at the emotion pressing against his chest. Jesus never had it easy. Born poor. Tempted by the devil. His friends betrayed Him. And He was crucified even though He'd never done a wrong thing.

Sam swallowed to loosen his tight throat. Jesus's entire life had been filled with struggles—and He not only *was* God but was loved by God. Jesus could have led an easy life. He could have hopped right off the cross, but He refused.

Maybe Sam had been wrong all this time.

Maybe God did care about him.

Could God have plans for him that he didn't understand? He glanced sideways at Bryan, who had his arm draped over Jade's shoulders. Sam hoped so.

He wanted a family of his own. Mary and Joseph had made it work, and they had a lot of obstacles to overcome.

He needed to apologize to Celeste. Make an effort with her. Be the friend to her that she'd been to him. Their friendship was growing into more, and maybe he didn't need to fight it. Maybe it was time to do something together just the two of them.

After the service ended, he gathered with the rest of his family in the large entryway.

"Nice singing up there, Sunshine." Sam winked at Macy.

"Thanks for coming, Uncle Sam." She hugged him. Her pretty blue eyes sparkled. "Are you coming over for cocoa?"

"Umm…"

"Are you up for it?" Bryan asked him as he helped Jade into her coat. "We'll drive you."

"I think I am." Sam nodded as Macy jumped up and down, clapping.

"I'm going to tell Mommy!" She ran to where Tom and Stephanie chatted with a few other parents.

So simple to make Macy happy. Showing up really wasn't hard. Why had he convinced himself it was? Asking Celeste on a date might not be hard, either.

"How do you two feel about kids?" Sam asked Bryan and Jade.

A look of terror crossed Bryan's face, but Jade grinned. "We love kids, don't we, Bryan?"

His brother visibly gulped.

"I'm going to ask Celeste out this Friday. Would you consider babysitting Parker?"

"Of course!" Jade said. "We'd love to. We are so glad you met her."

He was, too. He'd survived weeks of physical therapy, attended a Sheffield Auto meeting with his dad and brothers. He'd even gone back to church. Going on a date couldn't be that big of a deal.

Anxiety knotted his gut. Dating. Did he even remember how to date anymore? And what if Celeste said no?

Celeste massaged the back of her neck and collapsed on the couch later that night. She'd finally finished her to-do list. She checked the clock. After nine. *Not bad.* It was the first time this week she'd finished before eleven. She hadn't had time to open the book she'd gotten from the library earlier, so reading tonight was her reward for wrapping up early.

She hoped this book would help her get her head on straight. It was time to overcome her infatuation with

Sam, because having him act distant sliced her worse than any knife could.

The hot tea she'd brewed earlier had cooled, but she sipped it anyhow. Covering her legs with a plush cream blanket, she enjoyed the silence. Parker slept in his bedroom, and she'd tossed all his toys in a bin after putting him to bed, so the living room was neat, tidy. Home. Her home—and it felt like home more than her old apartment. She'd been aimless there, just going with the flow of life, not following her dreams. Her dreams finally felt close, almost possible, living here in this pretty cabin on the lake.

Yawning, she reached for the book. *Lord, please open my heart to what I need to hear tonight.*

Two pages in, she hopped up and scurried to her small desk for a notebook. She wanted to remember the words, save them for when she had doubts. She returned, jotting notes as she studied the chapter. When she finished, she flipped back to review what she'd written.

When life doesn't pan out the way we imagined, we often blame ourselves. Life is full of surprises, some good, some bad. Accept them. Give thanks for them. Embrace the good surprises, and pray through the bad ones.

Pray through the bad? Did that imply the bad surprises would eventually end? She closed the notebook and clutched it to her chest.

God, please get me through the next week until my appointment. These scars were a bad surprise. Please change the doctor's mind. I want my old face back.

Her stomach coiled as she stared at the multicolored lights twinkling from the small tree she'd decorated and set up out of Parker's reach. Christmas—the time of hope.

Prayers were full of hope, too, so why didn't her prayer make her feel hopeful?

Random impressions flitted through her mind. Her mom's smile when she'd tucked Celeste's hair behind her ear on Thanksgiving. Dad's big hugs, the way he supported her decisions. The look in Sam's eyes when he called her beautiful.

Something niggled, and she didn't want to delve any deeper, but she couldn't deny reality—her prayer about having her old face back didn't leave her reassured. Maybe she needed to pray harder.

Her cell phone rang, shaking her out of her thoughts. She checked the caller, answering as soon as she saw Sam's name pop up.

"Hey, sorry to call so late." His voice reminded her of warm chocolate sauce, rich and decadent.

"I wasn't sleeping." Why did she sound like a chipmunk? She cleared her throat. "What's up?"

"I wanted to apologize for the bad mood I've been in. I shouldn't have taken it out on you."

He wasn't mad at her. She didn't fight the smile spreading across her face.

"Also I was wondering if you're free Friday night," he asked. "I want to take you out. On a date. We could get something to eat, go Christmas shopping or to a movie—whatever you want. Bryan and Jade will watch Parker for us, if you're okay with that."

He was asking her on a date—a real date!

"I would love to go. How about a toy store? I need to buy Parker's presents. I know what I want to get him, but I haven't had a chance to get out and purchase them."

"Sounds good. I'd say I would pick you up around six thirty, but you'll have to pick me up instead."

She laughed. "No problem. Six thirty it is."

That niggling doubt from earlier was nothing. She'd wanted a hopeful feeling, and Sam's call had more than accomplished it. She'd keep praying. The appointment would be a good surprise. It had to be.

Chapter Ten

Sam couldn't take his eyes off Celeste Friday night. She looked incredible in a deep red sweater, dark jeans and stylish boots. Her dark brown hair hung straight and shiny over her shoulders, and she wore eye makeup and red lipstick. They'd decided on an Italian restaurant, and after waiting thirty minutes for a table, they were finally sitting across from each other. With the exception of a few crying children, festive conversations filled the air. The right atmosphere to explore their relationship. Find out how she felt about some of the things on his mind.

The orders had been placed, and the salads had arrived. And his nerves were tighter than the compression sleeve he'd worn on his leg for months.

"How did Parker do last night?" Sam asked. "Are they still using him as baby Jesus?"

Celeste's smile took his breath away. Literally. An oxygen tank might be necessary.

"He did great. He was pretty tired, so Shelby kept him on her lap, and he didn't make a peep."

"Think he'll sit still on Christmas Eve?"

She shrugged, swirling her water with the straw. "I

don't know. I hope so for Grandma Pearl's sake. I want her to be surprised, not embarrassed. I also don't want everyone thinking I'm a bad mom."

"You're a great mom." He wouldn't get a better lead-in than that. He leaned in. "Ever think about having more kids?"

She blinked, startled. "Sometimes."

"What do you mean?"

She fidgeted with her napkin. "I feel as if I'm in a grace period. This time in Lake Endwell—in Claire's cabin—has been wonderful, but it can't last forever."

"Why not?" He wasn't fool enough to believe it could, either, but why did she feel that way?

"It's not reality. A lot of my life is up in the air."

"I'm not following you." He pulled his shoulders back. Up in the air? Was she making plans he didn't know about?

"Well, a lot depends on my appointment this Thursday. If I hear good news, I'd like to start the process to get certified as a history teacher."

"What does your appointment have to do with that?"

Her chin dipped and her hair slid forward. "Everything. If I don't have scar reduction surgery, I don't see teaching in my future."

"You'd let that get in the way of your dream?"

"Well, *that* is a big deal to me." She straightened, one eyebrow raised. "I'm not up for the scrutiny. I can already guess the nickname the students would make up. 'Hey, there goes Scarface.'"

"They'll have a nickname for you no matter what. Kids always do. They would probably call me Limpy McGee."

"Yeah, well, I'll pass." She tossed the crumpled napkin on the table. "No, thank you."

"So, you'll keep doing your virtual assisting. No need for everything to change."

"Everything is changing soon, Sam. You know it. I know it."

He frowned. He did know it. Felt the change coming—couldn't deny it. The four walls of his life were shrinking in on him.

"You and I—we don't have to change." He waved his hand between them.

The corner of her mouth tweaked up. "I hope not, but you'll be back at work, and you'll see everything you missed. Life will be normal for you again."

"That's what I'm afraid of."

"What? You'll see everything you missed? Or life will be normal again?"

"Both. I *will* see everything I missed, and it will remind me I'll always miss some of it. Life doesn't really go back to normal. Not for me."

"Me, neither."

They didn't speak for a while. The waiter delivered steaming plates of pasta and a basket of bread, but they didn't dig in.

"Celeste? What kind of dad would Josh have been?"

"That's a tough question. He never met Parker. Never was around little kids that I can remember. I think he would have been wonderful. Maybe not the guy who volunteers to change a diaper, but he would have taught Parker how to ride a bike, and he would have played catch with him." Celeste twirled her fork in her pasta.

Her words didn't reassure him. Sam might not ever

be able to teach a kid how to ride a bike or play catch with him.

"Do you ever worry about Parker not having a man in his life? I mean, you're the one raising him. You're the biggest impact on his upbringing."

"I do worry. In fact, I feel terrible about it. I want him to have a father." She sighed. "My two best friends. Gone. Neither will know their son."

"That's why, when the time comes, Parker needs a dad who loves him." He selected a bread stick.

"I'm not thinking about any of that right now." Celeste blinked rapidly, her face stricken. "It's not as if I can pick up a dad in aisle six of the grocery store."

She wasn't thinking about any of that? "It's none of my business."

"I'm doing the best I can. Besides, no one is knocking down my door, desperate to be Parker's father."

What if someone did start knocking down her door? Someone other than him? "I'm not trying to make you mad. It's just, well, he's going to need a man in his life."

Celeste's jaw tightened. "I'm not going to date someone so Parker can have a father. I can't. I won't. I want more from marriage. And Parker has a grandpa who loves him very much. Until I find a man who loves both Parker and me with his whole heart, my dad will have to do." She shoved her chair back and marched in the direction of the restrooms.

Real smooth, Sheffield.

Why had he even brought the subject up? It wasn't as if he was in a position to be the man Parker or Celeste needed. Had he given her the impression he wanted her to find someone else?

He'd go after her, but the crutches...

Same old excuses. He hoisted himself to his feet and swung his way to the restroom hall. Felt stupid as a mom and two little girls passed him.

He waited.

Finally, Celeste opened the door.

"I'm sorry." Propping the right crutch against the wall, he took her hand and pulled her into a hug. She set her cheek on his shoulder. Her hair smelled flowery. He didn't care that they were in a restroom hallway in a crowded restaurant or that he was balancing on one foot.

She was in his arms. He stroked her hair with his free hand.

Celeste looked up at him. "Ever since our kiss last weekend, you've been giving me mixed signals."

"I know. I'm sorry. Let's talk about this at the table." They returned to their seats, and Sam waited for her to get comfortable. "I care about Parker. I want him to have a great life."

"I feel the same. I'm trying to give him one."

"I know. You're a terrific mother." The appreciation glowing in her face made him forget what he was going to say next.

Celeste tilted her head, watching his reaction. "You want kids, don't you?"

"Yeah, I do."

"You'll be a great dad."

Her confidence touched him. "Maybe someday. I can barely sign my name when I stand with these things—certainly can't change a diaper or carry a baby in my condition."

"You handle Parker pretty good now."

"Yeah, well, it's not the same. I mean, he's at my

house. I want to take my kids to the soccer fields, throw them up in the air, put them on my shoulders."

"You can be a good dad and not do any of those things. I'd rather have a dad who loves me and never carries me on his shoulders than one who doesn't care."

He inwardly frowned. Yes, he could be a dad from a wheelchair or crutches, but was that fair to Parker? Or Celeste? Not really. Celeste had so many problems. He wanted to provide solutions for her, not be one more problem. Maybe he'd been asking the wrong questions.

Trouble was, he wasn't ready to ask the right ones.

Later that evening, Celeste drove the minivan out of the mall parking lot and headed south to Lake Endwell. Stars dotted the black sky. What a beautiful night. Nothing could ruin this time with Sam. Thankfully, it wasn't snowing. "I still can't believe how many gifts you bought."

"What can I say? Big family." Even in the dim light, his smile sent sugarplums and Christmas wishes down to her boots.

The night had surprised and confused her, but after toy shopping for Parker, she and Sam were back to comfortable. She still wasn't completely sure why Sam had hounded her about dads during dinner, but at least they were talking again. And the darted glances Sam sent her all evening gave her the impression he liked her as much as she liked him.

He turned the radio on, flipping through the channels twice. "I guess we can't avoid Christmas music."

"Do you want to?"

"Nah. I love Christmas. What's your favorite song?"

She bit her lip as she thought about it. "Fast or slow?"

"Give me both."

"I love 'O Holy Night.' Gives me goose bumps every time I hear it. I've also always really liked 'Baby, It's Cold Outside.'"

He sang the opening line. She added the next one. They both laughed.

"What about you?" she asked. "What are your faves?"

"When I was a kid, I thought 'Grandma Got Run Over by a Reindeer' was the funniest thing I'd ever heard. Drove my family nuts singing it all the time. I still like it."

"Me, too." She grinned.

"Would it be too cliché to admit 'Silent Night! Holy Night!' is another of my favorites?" He shifted to face her, and she had to fight to keep her eyes on the road.

"Of course not. It's beautiful. Classic. Everything Christmas should be."

The opening strains of "Grandma Got Run Over by a Reindeer" played on the radio. Sam began belting out the lyrics. "Come on, Celeste, join in."

He sang off-key and loud, but his exuberance infected her, so she sang, too. When the song ended, she laughed, breathless.

"A Holly Jolly Christmas" came on, and Sam sang in a ridiculously low voice.

Her mind blanked. Brandy's goofy face as they sang in the car last December swirled before her.

A night like this. With Christmas presents in the trunk.

Joy-filled hearts.

Silly Christmas songs.

Taken from her, ripped from her.

Celeste's hands shook, her throat constricting, and she slowed, stopping the minivan on the side of the deserted country road. Her limbs felt ice-cold.

"What's wrong?" Sam craned his neck to see out her window, then his. "Is it the van?"

All she could do was give her head a tiny shake. A heavy sensation weighed her down like she'd been filled with concrete and it was hardening up.

"Celeste?" Sam's voice sounded far away...and worried. He shook her arm. "What's wrong? Are you okay?" He turned off the radio and grabbed his cell phone.

As soon as the music was cut, she snapped out of it. Sucked in a huge breath. Faced Sam.

"I don't know what happened, Sam. I'm sorry. I just... I heard the song and my whole body changed. I can't explain it. It was the same song we were singing when my car crashed last year." Her teeth chattered as a shiver overtook her. "This...this feels familiar in a terrible way."

"Hey..." He unbuckled his seat belt and scooted to her. Sneaked his hand behind her back and awkwardly pulled her to him with the armrests between them. He kissed her temple. "We're safe. Nothing is going to happen right now."

"You don't know that." She sniffed, easing back, but not far enough for him to drop his hand.

"We're safe."

"Brandy and I thought we were safe last year. We weren't. We're never safe. Never."

Sam inhaled, straightening his spine. "You're right. That was a stupid thing to say."

Regret at her outburst made her sit back. She didn't

know what to think, what to do. She couldn't really say she was afraid to drive or that she believed she and Sam would be in a crash tonight. Something else had forced her to the side of the road.

Fear. But not fear of dying.

Fear of losing...again.

She couldn't handle the thought of losing Sam. She'd lost Brandy. And Josh.

Celeste exhaled loudly, avoiding looking at Sam. "Let's go home."

"Wait." He touched the back of her hand. "Stay here a minute. I'm not in a hurry."

Her throat felt as if she'd swallowed acid. She brought her hands to her face, closing her eyes. She was acting like an idiot—a drama queen. Why was she so worked up? She'd driven hundreds of times since the accident. This wasn't her first go-round in a vehicle with Sam, either.

And he wasn't hers to lose.

God, I need You. I don't know what to pray for, but I need You.

"You've faced your fears, Celeste. Moved. Figured out a new job. Driven past the crash site. I haven't even gone back to my dealership." Sam's voice soothed her agitation. "How do you do it? Like tonight, you're driving. It's almost the anniversary of the accident, but you got the courage to go out there."

"Courage?" She barked a dry laugh. "This isn't courageous. My hands are still shaking."

"But you're here." He faced her again, his face intense in the dim light.

Why was she here? How could she answer him?

"I guess I didn't consider the similarities between tonight and last year. Maybe I should have."

"You still would have come," he said. "You're a fighter."

"I'm no fighter. I'm more of a drifter. Responding to what life gives me."

"That's not true."

She wanted to believe him, but her track record showed the truth. She'd never had the courage—even before the accident—to even decide what her dreams were, let alone pursue them. If she had, she'd have been teaching history all this time instead of working at dead-end jobs.

So what did she want now?

She covered Sam's hand with hers. *I don't want to lose you, Sam. But I don't know what to do about it.*

His thumb brushed hers. He pulled her into a hug, and she rested her cheek on his shoulder. A strong man to lean on—her dream guy come true.

Love. Commitment. A family.

But what if he wasn't ready for all that?

Fighting wasn't her strong suit, and right now her energy was drained. Empty. It was easier to drift along, taking what life gave.

She hoped she wouldn't have to fight for all the things she still wanted, most of all, him.

She didn't know if she had enough fight in her. She needed something easy right now.

Chapter Eleven

Sunday morning after church, Sam shoveled a forkful of hash browns into his mouth at Pat's Diner. Dad, chugging coffee and eyeing a piece of bacon, sat across from him. The sermon this morning had brought up some questions. About work. About Celeste. About his faith.

Maybe Dad could help.

"I'm starting to see why you haven't been out much." Dad clunked his coffee cup on the table. "Is everyone always this bad?"

Sam finished chewing and grinned. "Worse. This is actually light compared to what Celeste and I deal with at the grocery store."

Dad shook his head. "It's not like you were abducted by aliens. You were in an accident. And why did the Swanson kid ask if you saw a bright light?"

Sam shrugged, slurping his coffee. "You know his mom. Probably took him to see one of those I-died-and-went-to-heaven movies. It's all right. No harm done."

"It's annoying."

"I've gotten used to it." Sam soaked in the atmosphere. It was good to be back here. Pat's Diner had been a staple in his life for as long as he could remember. The red vinyl seats of the booth squeaked with each movement. Conversation hummed around them. Outside the large window, snow fell in big flakes over the sidewalk. Trees had been strung with lights for the big parade Saturday.

"Dr. Stepmeyer wants me to talk to Dr. Curtis before I go back to work." Sam flexed his right knee slightly.

"I figured that was a given."

"Yeah, well, I hadn't been planning on it."

"You should." Dad bit into the bacon.

"Nah, I'm ready."

Dad paused midchew and gave him the look, the one only his dad could give.

Twenty-seven and Sam still squirmed at that look. He diverted his attention to the stack of pancakes in front of him. After Celeste had dropped him off Friday night, he'd spent hours sitting in the living room with just the Christmas tree lights on. He'd been thinking. About Celeste and how brave she was. About how he'd been avoiding life instead of meeting it face-on the way she did.

He was ready. Ready for work. Ready for more.

And he needed to figure out today's sermon.

"Dad, did you ever feel that God didn't care about you?" Sam focused on Dad's reaction.

He set his mug down gently this time. Rubbed his chin. "I'm not going to lie. Yes. I felt that way for a long time."

"After Mom died?"

"No—before."

Sam sputtered, not expecting those words. "What? Why?"

Dad slid his plate to the side and clasped his hands to rest on the table. "I'm not proud of this, so I hope you don't judge me too hard."

His dad? Less than perfect? Not possible.

"I won't. I couldn't. You're… Just tell me."

"Your mom and I married pretty young. I was going to college to be an architect. Before either of us knew it, she was pregnant with Tom."

Sam nodded, sipping his coffee.

"I couldn't support her and a family *and* go to college for two more years, so I dropped out. Went to work for my dad."

Sam had always known Dad hadn't finished college, but he'd never really thought about the circumstances.

"I hated it at first. Loved Tom and your mother, but I resented that my dreams had to die. I stopped going to church. I told myself God didn't care or He would have made a way for me to finish school."

"What changed your mind? What brought you back to church?"

Dad smiled. "Your mother. She was something." He stared out the window, a faraway look in his eyes. "When Tom started walking, I decided enough was enough. I was going back to college and finishing my degree. It's not that I hated working for my dad—I didn't mind, not really—but I wanted my way. Wanted life to be my way. So I gathered my courage and marched into our little brick house after work one night, ready to tell your mother I was quitting my job and finishing school."

"Did she get mad or something?" Sam tried to picture them, but he couldn't. The only memories he had of his mom weren't his—just stories and photographs passed down from his siblings.

"No. She was standing over the stove, crying her eyes out." His face fell. "She seemed so devastated. I forgot everything, just rushed over and took her into my arms. I was scared, I'll tell you that."

"Why was she crying?"

The most tender expression Sam had ever seen spread across Dad's face. "She handed me a pregnancy test. We were having another baby."

Sam was taken aback. "Didn't she want one?"

"Let me finish the story." Dad lifted his finger. "When she calmed down enough to speak, she told me she knew I was miserable. She'd been scrimping on groceries and expenses so I could go back to school. She opened a cupboard and pulled down a coffee can. Handed it to me, saying, 'There's sixty-seven dollars in here. I thought we could get by if you went back to school, but with another baby on the way…'"

Sam's heart tugged at his mom's generosity. She must have loved Dad very much.

"In that moment, I changed. I completely changed. I'd been thinking about me and what I wanted, not realizing how blessed I was to have her love and her children. I silently asked God to forgive me. Wrapped her in my arms and told her I was opening my own dealership—my dad had wanted me to anyhow—and she wouldn't have to worry about money. It took some convincing, but she eventually believed me."

"Should she have?" The words were out before Sam could think about them. But he wanted to know—had Dad meant those words?

"Yes." He leveled an honest stare at Sam. "She absolutely should have believed me, because I meant it. Sheffield Auto wasn't my dream, at least not then, but *she* was. And I knew I had to embrace her and our growing family or we'd both be miserable. I'm proud of my years with our company, and God gave me a second chance at a career of my choosing when he sent Reed to Lake Endwell. I love being his superintendent. Building houses is even better than designing them."

Sam hadn't realized Dad had sacrificed so much for them.

"I've been mad at God for not healing me." Just saying those words twisted Sam's gut.

"We're all thankful you're alive. You don't know how bad it was for all of us the night of your accident. I've never been more scared in my life."

There was truth in those words, Sam knew it. But…

"You're my son, Sam. I love you. I couldn't handle losing you. I still can't. So you can be mad at whomever you want, including God, but every day I praise Him for keeping you here. If you can't praise Him for saving you, maybe you can thank Him for answering *my* prayer. Because I'd be a shell of a man if I'd have lost you, too."

Emotion welled in Sam's chest, and he had to bow his head. "I never really thought about how my accident affected you."

"It's okay. I didn't think about how my resentment affected your mom. But when I did…" Dad sipped his coffee.

"You put her first."

"Love will do that to you."

"Thanks for telling me this, Dad."

"I love you. Never forget it."

He wouldn't. Couldn't. He'd taken his family for granted, been caught up in his own problems.

"I love you, too, Dad."

Well, God, I'm doing like Dad said—Thank You for answering his prayer and saving me. I'm not thrilled about my disabilities, but I'm thankful to be here.

Another thought came uninvited.

Maybe Sam was too focused on wanting his way, just like Dad had been too focused years ago.

A wave of guilt hit him. He kept thinking about himself. He'd taken Celeste out the other night, made her uncomfortable with his intrusive comments about Parker needing a dad and hadn't put two and two together about her accident until it was too late and she was crying at the side of the road. He counted on his leg healing, but even then he might not be the guy she needed.

If he could just tell that to his heart...

"This blanket is so soft, dear." Grandma Pearl beamed. A quiet Sunday afternoon, perfect for Celeste to visit the assisted living complex and drop off an early Christmas present. "How did you know I can never get warm enough?"

"I'm glad you like it. It's hard to stay warm this time of year." Celeste turned the page of the storybook for Parker, sitting on her lap. Her heart broke a little at how frail Grandma Pearl looked lately. "Are you feeling okay? Want me to get you some tea?"

"I'm better. Had a cold last week. I'm happy watching Parker. He's a smart one, isn't he?"

"He is. Takes after Brandy."

"He's got a good mama teaching him."

Celeste didn't respond. She'd made her peace with Parker calling her Mama but she still wished his real mama was here. Grandma Pearl wouldn't be around forever, either. Why did people have to die?

"One of my friends from church stopped by yesterday." Grandma Pearl unfolded the blanket and smoothed it over her lap. "She told me she saw you with a young man. Tell me about him."

Here we go. What could she say? "Um, yes, Sam is the man I mentioned on Thanksgiving. The one who lives next door."

"Sam. That's a lovely name. I knew a Sam way back when."

She nodded, hoping Grandma Pearl would hop right back on memory lane so Celeste wouldn't have to talk about him.

"Is he a keeper?"

"Um, well…"

"Is he a Christian?"

"Yes."

"For years my Stanley never wanted to go to church with me. I could barely get him to the Christmas service, even when our Joanie—that's Brandy's mom, you know—sang with her Sunday school class. One year—Joanie must have been seven or eight—she looked at me and told me she wasn't going to church anymore."

Celeste fought back a smile.

"Well, I didn't know what to do. Joanie had always been such a good girl. I told her she most certainly was going to church, and she said, 'Daddy never goes, so I'm not going, either.'"

She bit her lower lip.

"I didn't have time to pray on it, because Stanley

stormed into the room and said we were all going to church. And he did. From then on, we went as a family. He might not have ever showed it much, but he was a God-fearing man. I was blessed to be married to him."

Parker climbed off Celeste's lap and toddled over to Grandma Pearl's. "If your legs hurt, you don't have to hold him..."

"Nonsense. I want nothing more than to hold this precious baby in my arms. We're the last ones of the family. Joanie died when Brandy was a teenager. Stanley passed a few years later. And Brandy..." Her eyes welled with tears. She gently brushed them away. "Well, I'm thankful this sweet boy will carry on. A little part of me, a little part of Stanley. Joanie and Brandy. He's got a bit of all of us."

It was true. Celeste saw glimpses of Brandy in the way he held his head when deep in thought. And she saw Josh in Parker's big smile.

"Grandma Pearl?"

"What, dear?"

"Do you ever worry about Parker? I mean, do you worry about me raising him?"

Grandma Pearl's papery cheeks lifted as she smiled. "No. I'm thankful you're raising him. I know you'll love him the way Brandy would. The only time I fret is when I think of his father."

"Josh?"

"No. The man you'll marry someday. I worry he won't love Parker the way he would his own child. But whenever I worry, I give it to God. He's gotten me through a lot of losses. I trust He'll lead you to the right man."

"You pray for me?" Celeste was touched.

"Of course I do. I pray for Parker and for you and for the man who will complete your family. I love you."

"I love you, too." Celeste looked away, emotional at her thoughtfulness.

"Tell me more about this Sam who lives next door. Think he might be the one?"

Heat climbed her neck. "I'd like him to be, but I don't know."

"What don't you know?"

"He's not ready for a family."

Her face fell. "That's too bad, dear. I was hoping for your sake and mine he would like Parker."

"I think he loves Parker. It's just…well, he was in a bad accident, and his leg might never heal all the way."

"Does that bother you?"

"No. Not at all. He's wonderful with Parker, and I like him a lot."

"So he's nervous about his leg."

That about summed it up.

Celeste shrugged. "I'm nervous, too." Parker had relaxed on Grandma Pearl's lap and rubbed his eyes. Celeste handed him a sippy cup.

"What are you nervous about?"

Celeste pointed at her forehead and her cheek.

"The scars? They could never take away from your beauty. Your soul shines through. That's the real beauty, you know."

She wished the sweet woman was right. She stood and bent over Grandma Pearl to give her a hug. "I love you."

"I love you, too, dear." She kissed the top of Parker's head. "The right man for you will never think less of you because of your scars. He'll see the best in you. Always."

Sam had never acted like her scars were an issue. He'd even called her beautiful. But maybe he'd been trying to make her comfortable. He might not have really meant it.

Four more days and she'd have a verdict about her face.

Maybe it wouldn't matter if Sam meant it or not. With more surgery, she'd be the girl she used to be. Except better. After her face healed, she was going to be the woman she should have been all along.

Chapter Twelve

"Are you sure you don't want us to come with you?" Sam stood next to Celeste as she set the diaper bag on his table Thursday morning. He wanted to ease her worry about today's doctor's appointment, but how could he? Celeste's pale face looked exhausted. Had she gotten any sleep last night?

"No, thank you." She smoothed her hair behind her ear. "Don't take this personally, but I'd rather go alone."

He propped a crutch against the table and took her hand. Cold. She must be nervous. "I understand."

"It's just a consultation."

With most of his weight on his left leg, Sam drew her closer and touched her chin directly below her lips. She flinched. Was it him? "I'm sorry."

"It's not you… It's the nerve ending there. Whenever I touch that spot, it stings."

He dropped his hand to his side and his attention to the floor. He'd seen her smart at times when she touched her face. He should have remembered.

"Are you sure you can handle him for a few hours?"

Celeste searched the room, settling her gaze on Parker banging a plastic hammer against Sam's coffee table.

Sam had asked himself the same thing. But he'd never had a problem watching Parker while Celeste ran, and what was another hour? He could always use the wheelchair if he needed both hands to change a diaper or pick Parker up.

"I've got this. And Aunt Sally is home." Sam had talked to his aunt last night, and she'd assured him she'd be home if he needed her. "She lives two miles away. If I have any trouble, she'll be here at the snap of my fingers."

"Okay. I'd better get going." Celeste pivoted to leave. "Don't want to be late."

"Celeste?" He prepared to follow her. He had so many things he wanted to say. She didn't need to worry. Surgery or no surgery, she was stunning, breathtaking. The woman who had made him want to live again. The one he owed so much to, the only woman he had eyes for. The one he'd told himself was off-limits. Who deserved more in a man than he could give. But the words dried up before he could say them. "Call me when the appointment is over."

She nodded and left.

Sunshine spilled to the deck. The weatherman had announced a high of thirty-four degrees Fahrenheit today. Fitting, since Christmas was next week. He hoped the parade on Saturday would be warmer.

He'd been anticipating the parade ever since the day he'd offered to take Celeste. And it was almost here. He wouldn't even need a wheelchair for the event. For some reason getting around town on crutches didn't bother him the way the wheelchair did. She'd told him her parents were babysitting Parker for the day, so it would be just the two of them.

"Dada." Parker pointed at Sam.

His heart stopped beating. Had Parker called him...?

"Dada." Parker ran to Sam and stretched his arms up.

Emotion swelled, puffing Sam's chest out at the wonder of those two syllables.

What if he was Parker's daddy?

That would mean... He gulped. Taking his relationship with Celeste to a level he'd refused to consider up to this point.

If he'd never been in the accident, he would have pursued Celeste from day one. With or without Parker. He liked how he felt when he was with her. He liked her smile and the way she made him want to be a better person. He liked the kisses she showered on Parker's cheeks. He liked her courage and tenacity. She worked hard and expected little.

And that was exactly what she would get if he pursued her now. Hard work and little to show for it.

He wasn't husband material. He wasn't father material, either.

But, oh, how he wanted it. All of it. Celeste and Parker were the family he wanted.

Had he fallen in love with her?

"Dada."

"Hey, little buddy, I'll pick you up, but I have to sit first." Sam headed to the couch. After he settled in, he patted his lap for Parker to join him. Parker toddled over, and Sam picked him up, hugging him tightly, breathing in his baby smell, and tucked him onto his lap. "What should we do while your mommy is at her appointment? Want me to read you a story?"

Sam stretched to grab the pile of picture books Stephanie had dropped off a few days ago. He opened one about a bunny all alone at Christmas. Parker helped turn the pages. Good thing they were made of heavy coated cardboard, otherwise the kid might have ripped them. After the first book, Sam read another. Parker got bored, so he helped him off his lap. He ran straight for the plastic hammer, and once more, he banged it on the coffee table.

Maybe Parker would build houses when he grew up. Sam's brother-in-law Reed could hire him. Sam smiled at the thought.

He turned the television to a cartoon and swung over to the table to find a snack for Parker. The diaper bag revealed wipes, half a dozen diapers, baby pain reliever, a thermometer, several plastic toys, a sealed bag with animal crackers, containers of baby food—no prunes, thankfully—and three changes of clothes. Celeste had left two sippy cups in the fridge. She certainly was prepared. He slung a tote bag over his shoulder, put the crackers in it and walked to the kitchen. He kept his crutch secure as he slipped one of the cups in his bag. Then he returned to the living room.

A quick once-over didn't reveal Parker. Sam frowned, searching for him.

There, behind the Christmas tree. Parker crawled around under the tree, snagging the tree skirt.

"No, Parker!" All he could envision was the tree toppling on the baby. "Come here."

Parker paused, staring at Sam through startled eyes that began to fill with tears. "Waah!"

As his wail picked up volume, Sam debated his next move. He needed to get him out from under the Christmas tree to keep him safe. But if he took the time to get into the wheelchair, Parker could try to pull himself up by a branch or break a glass bulb and get cut or…

What should he do? His brain froze. His body did, too.

Parker rocked back and forth on all fours, crying loudly.

"Come out here," he said in what he hoped was a soothing tone. Sam hopped as close as he could with the crutches and tried to bend. "Let's get a snack, buddy. I've got crackers."

Parker didn't crawl out. Instead, he shifted backward, his head hitting the bottom branches of the artificial tree in the process. Two felt reindeer, a candy cane and a glass bulb hit the ground. His cries grew even louder.

Sam heaved a sigh of relief that the bulb didn't break. He turned quickly, knowing he needed to get into his wheelchair so he could salvage this. But as soon as he took two steps, Parker crawled out, howling at the top of his lungs. The boy stood, stumbled toward Sam and tripped, hitting his forehead on the edge of the wooden dining chair near the tree.

Sam watched in horror as Parker bounced off the edge of the chair, falling backward and smacking the back of his skull on the hardwood floor. Sam lunged forward, dropping his right crutch and instinctively trying to bear weight on his right leg so he could pick up Parker. But the knee wasn't strong enough, and his right leg collapsed beneath him, sending him sprawling on his side.

Pain ripped up his thigh. He clutched the leg as he inched his way to Parker. An angry purple goose egg had already formed on the baby's forehead. His cries were hysterical. Waves of helplessness crashed over Sam as he writhed in pain, wanting more than anything to take Parker in his arms and assess how badly the child was hurt.

Sam pushed himself to his elbows, dragging himself to the end table where he'd left his phone. He speed-dialed his aunt.

The paper crinkled as Celeste shifted on the examination table. Dr. Smith typed notes on the laptop. He hadn't said much as he examined her. The questions had all been expected. No surprises there.

The only surprise would be his verdict.

Yes?

No?

She wanted yes.

How she wanted yes.

Dr. Smith swiveled on the stool. "You've healed remarkably well. The scars are flat, with the exception of the slightly raised one above your left temple. They've faded nicely."

Celeste's pulse raced, ticking as furiously as a bomb about to detonate.

"So what does that mean?" She wrung her hands together, daring to hope. And trying not to hope. "I can get more surgery?"

He frowned, shaking his head. "You don't need more surgery."

Didn't need more surgery? The ocean roared in her head, and a tidal wave drowned out all thoughts.

She *did* need more surgery.

Didn't he understand? Didn't he get it?

"The nerve endings are too damaged for two of your

scars, but the other ones could benefit from…" The doctor droned on but he might as well have been speaking gibberish.

She'd have to look like this the rest of her life. Have to face the reminders of that night every time she glanced in the mirror.

"…the treatment I recommend…" His voice sounded far away, in another county, another life.

She wanted to laugh—let out a high-pitched scream. She'd applied the silicone gel sheets for months. Massaged the prescribed ointment into the scars for as long as the doctor ordered. Still lathered on vitamin E cream before bed. Whatever *treatment* he recommended was not going to make these lines disappear.

"Why?" She cut him off. "Why can't I have more surgery?"

He took a deep breath. "Celeste, more surgery wouldn't help. I don't think you understand what I'm saying."

Wouldn't help? Did this guy have any idea how much this meant to her?

Her cell phone rang. She set it to silence. It vibrated over and over, and frustrated, she yanked it to see who was calling.

Sally.

"Hello?"

"Celeste, hon, I don't want to worry you, but Parker took a little tumble, and Sam did, too, so I'm at the ER to make sure they're okay. Parker has an ugly bump on his forehead, but he's sipping some milk and I've got him calmed down."

Her heart stopped beating. "And Sam?"

"I'm not sure."

Oh, no. Oh, no.

Parker. Sam.

"I'll be right there." She clicked End, sliding off the examination table, ripping the paper she'd been sitting on in the process. Parker needed her. Sam needed her. "I've got to go. My son…"

"I hope everything is all right."

"Me, too." She clutched her purse and opened the door.

"Wait. Take these pamphlets about the laser treatment I just outlined."

She wasn't interested in anything except her guys right now. She swiped the pamphlets Dr. Smith held and marched out of the room, down the hall and outside to the parking lot.

Forcing herself not to freak out about Parker, Sam or her diagnosis, she sped all the way to the hospital. Maybe if she drove fast enough, the pain stabbing her heart would vanish. If she could, she'd drive all the way back to last year, before the accident. She'd cancel her and Brandy's plans. Reschedule their shopping date. Then Brandy would still be here, and Celeste wouldn't have to worry about living with her scars, Parker being hurt or Sam not walking.

She'd gotten too close. She couldn't bear it if Sam was badly injured. And what about Parker? What could the side effects of bumping his head lead to?

God, take care of them.

"The good news is you don't need surgery." Dr. Curtis refastened the ice pack wrap around Sam's knee, which had swollen considerably. "Your quads weren't strong enough to support your weight and that's why your leg buckled. The ligaments aren't torn. The X-rays show no broken bones, and other than some muscle strain, your knee should be fine."

Sam could barely think about his leg right now. Aunt Sally had texted Sam and told him she thought Parker would be okay. Just a bump on the head. She couldn't come up yet, because she was waiting for Celeste to arrive. The hospital needed Celeste's authorization to treat Parker. And, yes, Sally had called her.

Sam ground his teeth together. Aunt Sally wasn't a doctor. She might think it was a bump, but what did she know? Why wouldn't the doctors look at the kid? Why did they have to wait for Celeste? Parker could have a concussion. Bleeding on the brain.

What if Sam's negligence caused Parker long-term damage?

"The test results were promising. You still have good reactivation in your leg muscles, but the electrical signals passing through the nerve don't have the speed we're hoping for. There is also mild inflammation in there." Dr. Curtis folded his hands.

"What does that mean?" Sam tried to sit up. Dr. Curtis pressed the button for the bed to rise.

"It means your mobility depends on continuing physical therapy and protecting your leg at all costs. When you tore the ACL in June, it set you back. In my professional opinion, it's unlikely you'll restore full range of motion in your right knee. My guess is seventy-five degrees. That doesn't mean you won't have a functional leg. You're young and healthy. The more therapy you do, the more strength you'll regain."

"What does 'functional' mean? You're saying I won't walk normally, is that it?"

"Your chances weren't good after the boating accident. A torn ACL didn't improve them. Do I think it's possible you'll need to use a cane when you leave the house? Yes. If you're diligent about strength training and PT. Who knows? Another year from now, you might surprise me by walking in on both feet unassisted."

"Why am I sensing a *but*?" Dread dropped in his gut.

"The knee injury compromised your recovery. It's hard to make a knee stable. You were already at a disadvantage to begin with. Healthy patients with torn ACLs struggle to completely heal. Protecting your leg—your knee especially—must be your top priority. I'm not talking weeks. I'm talking months. Years."

Sam tried to take it all in. He knew he couldn't reinjure the leg or knee again. It might permanently disable him, and he couldn't face the not knowing, the uncertainty of another operation. Another fall could put an end to his dream of walking unassisted. But what about his other dreams?

"It's been almost eighteen months since I've worked. I planned on returning in January."

"Remind me again what you do." The doctor took a seat in the chair next to the bed, his white lab coat spilling to the sides.

"I own an auto dealership." Sam shifted his jaw. "I'm on my feet a lot."

Dr. Curtis locked eyes with Sam's. "Last time I saw you, you weren't walking at all due to the pain."

"I'm still in pain. But I've been using crutches for over a month now."

"Yes." He clicked a pen. "And here we are."

Frustrated, Sam let his head fall back to the pillow.

"You and Dr. Stepmeyer are the ones who wanted me out of the wheelchair."

"We still do. But we also want you to be smart. You weren't wearing your brace when you arrived. I know you can bear a limited amount of weight on your right leg, but until your quads can bear your full weight, you need the brace."

"So can I go to work or not?" He sounded annoyed. He knew it. Couldn't help it. He *was* annoyed. Desperate, even.

"It depends." Dr. Curtis pulled his laptop to him. "I think returning to work is possible, but only if you take it easy. Consider part-time for the first couple of months. Expect it to be exhausting, and don't be a hero. Crutches are unstable under ideal conditions. An oil-soaked shop floor and an outdoor car lot during a Michigan winter are not ideal. My advice is to use your wheelchair in the shop and outdoors when it's snowing, raining or icy. Only use crutches on non-slippery surfaces. I'm sure I don't need to tell you this, but if you overuse your leg, it will swell. Keep an ice wrap on site. Most of all, remember what I said—protect the knee."

The advice hit home, but Sam didn't want to acknowledge the truth. He glanced at his swollen leg encased in a hefty black brace. He'd better tell the doctor everything. "I wasn't planning on bringing the wheelchair to work."

The doctor looked up from typing on his laptop and sighed. "Do you want to schedule the knee surgery now? Because one more slip with the crutches and you'll be bedridden. Again. I don't think you realize how fortunate you were to avoid tearing anything today. We could be in surgery right this minute."

Sam let it sink in.

Unrealistic—that was what he'd been. The doctor was right. Why had he thought he'd go back to working a full shift on crutches when he could only put a fraction of his weight on his bad leg? And the shop floor *was* slippery. It would be stupid to attempt hobbling around on crutches through it.

"Do you have any other questions?" Dr. Curtis stood.

Sam shook his head. The doctor nodded and said goodbye.

It was sheer arrogance to think he could resume life on his terms just because he wanted to. Forget returning to work. He'd told himself over and over he wouldn't go back there in a wheelchair. And he'd been wrong to babysit Parker today. He couldn't handle a toddler. He cringed remembering how the little guy had crawled under the Christmas tree when Sam turned his back. The way he'd run after Sam. Hitting his head.

My fault.

Sam closed his eyes, his heart burning.

He wasn't fit for work. He certainly wasn't fit for taking care of a child.

And now Celeste would know it, too. The huge purple bump on Parker's forehead was proof enough. Sam wouldn't blame her for seeing him for what he really was—incapable. He'd been right all along. Celeste deserved someone who could take care of her, someone who would shoulder the care of their children, who could carry groceries for her and drive a car.

He was not that man. It was time to put her needs first, which meant stepping away. Even if it destroyed him.

Chapter Thirteen

Celeste raced through the sliding doors of the hospital, halting at the information desk. Her mind hadn't stopped spitting out nightmare scenarios since Sally called. What if Parker had gotten worse? What if Sam had broken his leg?

After being directed to the waiting room, she scurried down the hallway and spotted Sally rocking Parker. Celeste slowed to catch her breath. "How is he?"

Sally looked up and smiled. "Almost asleep. He took a hard hit to the noggin. The nurse gave me an ice pack." She held up a round gel pack shaped like a frog. "I'll hold him while you check him in."

"Thank you. I'll be right back." Celeste pushed her hair back behind her ear. The waiting room looked inviting with sage-green chairs, a television and a large fish tank. It was also surprisingly quiet. Only a handful of chairs were occupied. Maybe she wouldn't have to wait long for them to treat Parker. After talking to a nurse, she filled out paperwork and returned. She lifted Parker out of Sally's arms, kissing the purple bump on his forehead.

"Mama," he murmured, wrapping his arms around her neck.

"You poor thing. Looks like you got an owie." A double-chocolate, frosted brownie couldn't be sweeter than this boy. She hugged him tight and met Sally's eyes. "Have you heard from Sam?"

"He was waiting to get test results last I heard."

"Do you think he tore anything? Broke anything?" Celeste moved Parker so he was sitting on her lap. She gently felt around his skull, finding a bump on the back of his head, too. Parker seemed okay. They'd find out for sure as soon as a doctor could see him. But Sam? Fear twisted in her abdomen.

"I don't know." Sally's kind eyes dimmed. "I hope not. He's been through enough."

Celeste agreed. He'd been through so much. Why did he have to fall? Today of all days. They were supposed to be going to the Christmas parade Saturday. It was all she'd looked forward to since he'd asked her to go with him. It was unlikely he'd be able to go now.

"Thank you for taking care of Parker until I could get here."

Sally patted Celeste's hand. "I'm glad I could, hon. I love babies. Parker is a sweetheart, and I'd do anything for Sam."

She would do anything for Sam, too. She loved him. And it was eating her alive not knowing if he'd seriously hurt his leg. He'd made so much progress since she'd met him.

Dear Lord, please let Sam be okay. Keep his leg safe. Heal him. Comfort him.

"What are your Christmas plans?" Sally asked.

"Parker is going to be baby Jesus in a children's

service at his mom's old church." Celeste frowned. "I should call the director and tell her Parker won't be at practice tonight. I'm sure he's had enough excitement today."

Sally gestured to her. "Go ahead. If you're like me, you'll forget to do it later."

Celeste called Sue Roper and told her Parker wouldn't be there. Then, as she chatted with Sally about the Sheffield Christmas traditions, Lake Endwell and the big parade, she began to calm down. Parker rested on her lap, and before they knew it, an hour had passed.

"Parker Monroe," a nurse called.

Celeste gave Sally a shaky smile. "We'll be back. Please let me know as soon as you hear anything from Sam."

"I'm not going anywhere. I'll shoot you a text if I get any news."

"Thank you."

She and Parker followed a nurse to an examination room. Forty-five minutes later, Parker was given the all clear, and Celeste held instructions about warning signs after a head injury. He started fussing, so she bought a package of crackers from a vending machine before returning to where Sally sat.

"He's being released." Sally slid her phone into her purse as Celeste approached. "He'll be right down."

Overcome with relief, Celeste fell into a chair, ripped open the crackers and handed the bag to Parker. "He must be okay if they're releasing him."

"Praise the good Lord." Sally closed her eyes a moment. "That boy will be the death of me. I've never worried about anyone as much as I have him the last eighteen months."

"I know what you mean. He's pretty special."

"He is." Sally pushed herself up from the chair, her eyes suspiciously watery. "I'm going to find a pop machine and get my sugar and caffeine on. Be right back."

Celeste smoothed Parker's hair from his forehead as Sally disappeared. What a day. She still hadn't processed her own doctor's visit, and here she was, dealing with Parker's and wondering how Sam had fared.

She glanced down the hall. Someone in scrubs pushed Sam in a wheelchair. Her heart did a backflip. The grim expression on his face worried her, though. Had he gotten terrible news? Was he in pain?

She carried Parker, munching on his snack, toward him. Sam said something to the man pushing him, and the man patted his shoulder then left. Sam wheeled himself the rest of the way.

"Dada!" Parker squirmed, twisting so both arms reached for Sam. She caught her breath. Had Parker just called Sam Dad? It sounded so right.

But Sam didn't look happy. He didn't take Parker in his arms. In fact, his face drained of color.

"Did they run tests?" Sam asked. "Is Parker going to be okay?"

"He'll be fine." She patted her purse. "I have a list of things to watch for, but I'm more worried about you. Are you all right?"

He nodded curtly.

"What did the doctor say?" She gestured to his leg, but he didn't meet her eyes.

"Nothing I didn't already know."

His dead tone and the way his gaze locked to the wall raised the hair on her arms.

"Tell me what's wrong." She touched his hand. He flinched, snatching it back.

"Nothing's wrong. How did your appointment go?" His question had no feeling behind it.

She wanted to lie, to tell him it went great, that a few months from now he'd see her at her best, scar-free. But this was Sam. He'd become her safe place. The man she could be honest with, the one who made her feel comfortable, happy again.

"The doctor won't do more surgery." All her hopes leaked out at each word. *Please let this not change anything. Let me be wrong. Maybe living with my scars isn't as bad as I thought.*

The muscle in his cheek ticked. "So, lousy news all around."

He still wouldn't make eye contact. And his reaction? Confusing.

What had she expected? *Comfort. A hug. Maybe even, in my wildest dreams, for him to say, "It doesn't matter. You're flawless in my eyes."*

But she wasn't flawless. Would never be flawless.

Sam rubbed his thigh where the brace ended. "I shouldn't have babysat Parker. I won't make that mistake again. And don't worry—I'll find someone else to drive me to my appointments."

Her head reeled. Find someone else? Why? Had he been banking on her being scar-free, too? Before her head exploded with worries, she inhaled. No sense guessing. She'd ask him instead.

"Why would you find someone else to drive you?"

"I was forcing something."

"What are you talking about?"

"I wanted my life to be different." He put his fist to

his lips, turning his head to the side. "I was wrong. I accept that."

Was he speaking in some weird code? She tried to decipher his words, his attitude. "Is this about my scars or your leg?"

He shrugged. "Both, I guess. We want to erase our accidents, but we can't."

Both. Her scars *were* a factor.

"What aren't you saying?" Her voice rose, sounded screechy to her ears. "Why now? You reinjured your leg, didn't you? Is it permanent?"

"This isn't about my leg." He finally met her eyes. "It's about you. And me. And reality."

If it wasn't his leg, it must be her scars. She had the sensation ice was freezing her body from her toes up her torso to her neck and head. "What changed?"

"Nothing. And that's the problem. I thought my situation had changed, but it didn't. If we don't put an end to this now, we'll end up hurt."

Too late. She was in too deep.

"I don't understand," she said. "I thought we had something…"

"I'm sorry if I led you on."

Led her on? Her throat was closing in. She fought for breath. Jostled Parker as she willed her legs to support her.

"I see," she said. "So you don't want me around at all, is that it? You don't need my help. What about the parade?"

He shook his head, his lips drawing together tightly, virtually disappearing. "It's for the best."

The words were a verbal slap to the face. Her heartbeat slowed, her blood turning to sludge. He'd obviously made up his mind. They—whatever *they* were—no longer existed. He didn't want her.

There was nothing left to do but leave.

"I suppose you heard all that?" Sam yanked the wheels to get through the hospital hallway as quickly as possible. Aunt Sally half jogged at his side. He'd done the right thing. Let Celeste go. She could find someone worthy of her, someone who would protect her and Parker.

Given his limitations, it was a crime to chain her to him. He would just bring more problems to her life. Celeste's life was full of problems already.

If he could get his heart to listen… It was clenching, bleeding, wringing itself into a tiny ball of nothing.

He'd had it all for a brief moment. Hope. The hope of the life he wanted. But reality collided with fantasy, and it was over.

"I tried to give you two some privacy, but your body language said it all." Aunt Sally made a clucking sound. "I don't know what is going on with you, but I don't like this."

"You don't know anything about it."

"I know Celeste has the patience of Mother Teresa. She's good for you. She was worried, and from the look on her face when she hightailed it out of here, I'd say you just broke her heart."

"I did her a favor." The cold air smacked his cheeks as he rolled onto the sidewalk. He stopped near the side of the entrance where he could wait for Aunt Sally to drive the car around. "I want to go home."

"Well, too bad, Sam." Flames shot from her eyes as she planted her hands on her hips directly in front of him. "You've gotten your way ever since the accident, and you know what? Today you don't get to have your way. You're going to listen to me."

"Gotten my way? Are you crazy?" He clenched his hands into fists. "Nothing in the last eighteen months has been my choice."

"Yes, it has." She bent over, jabbing her index finger into his chest. "Your recovery has been all your way. We've let you be, only stopping by when you let us, trying to make it as easy as possible for you to get back to life—"

"I don't have a life!"

Her mouth dropped open, and she drew back, shaking her head. "You have a life. If you can't see it, there's no hope for you. What happened in here, Sam?" She pointed to her heart, her eyes glistening. "Why won't you let anyone in?"

"I did!" He searched her eyes. Tried to stuff down his emotions and failed. "I let her down. I wanted to be the man she needed, and instead, I put Parker in danger."

"Pshaw." She gave a dismissive wave of her hand. "Parker tripped and fell. He'll have many more falls in his life, with or without you watching him."

"You don't understand." He pinched the bridge of his nose. "I couldn't get to him. He crawled under the Christmas tree. I couldn't reach in and grab him. I couldn't keep him safe."

"Sam, when your cousin Braedon was two, I was helping Joe fix the sink. Braedon was sitting on the couch, watching *Sesame Street*, and I turned my back for a minute. I didn't hear him and got worried. I found him on his bedroom floor, choking on something. I put him over my knees and whacked his back to try to dislodge it. Nothing came out. Fear buzzed through me, and I prayed, frantically begging God to save him. I yelled for Joe, and he raced in there, took one look at Braedon and stuck his finger down his little throat. Braedon threw up, and there in the middle was a quarter. I couldn't keep my baby safe, either. But it didn't stop me from trying."

"It's not the same."

"Sure it is."

"He was your son. Of course you kept trying. What choice did you have?"

"The same one you could have, Sam." She patted his cheek. "I have the feeling Celeste cares for you. And if I'm not mistaken, you feel the same about her and Parker. You're not in control of the universe. God is. Let Him protect your loved ones. Don't let Celeste slip away."

He not only was letting her slip away, he'd been the one to push her out the door.

"God hasn't done a very good job of protecting." The instant it was out of his mouth, shame filled him. And anger—at himself. He was tired of bottling so much anger.

"Still blaming God?" She inclined her head. "If He's not good at protecting, why is Parker on his way home with his mom as we speak? Why are you still here, for that matter? Do you know how close you were to death when the boat hit you?" She sighed. "I'm going to get the car. While I'm gone, you'd best think about the worm chewing a hole in your heart. Slay it soon, or it'll steal the best part of you."

She spun on her heel and marched her tight jeans

and purple running shoes down the sidewalk and out of his sight.

Every word she said came back to him, stabbing like ice picks. He blew out a breath, watching it puff in front of his face before disappearing. He shivered under his sweater.

There *was* a worm eating his heart. But he didn't know how to slay it. Ever since meeting Celeste, he'd been able to keep it at bay, but today it had won.

How could he slay what he couldn't define?

Fear.

Fear? Fear of what?

I need her. I'm afraid of needing her. I can survive without walking, but if I give her my heart, if I trust God the way Aunt Sally said, I might not survive another blow. What if God takes her from me?

The fear he lived with now was easier than the fear he'd take on if he committed to Celeste and Parker. The earth would keep spinning if anything happened to him, but his world would collapse into a pile of rubble if he married Celeste and lost her or Parker.

The only way to deal with the worm was to give it a corner to live in.

And to keep those closest to him out.

Chapter Fourteen

Celeste wrapped her hands around a mug of hot cocoa and drew her legs under her body later that evening. After leaving the hospital, she'd driven to the cabin, packed a bag of clothes and headed to her parents' house. Times like this called for the warmth of her childhood home. She stared out the large window next to the couch. Stars blinked beyond the outline of tree branches. An old Christmas movie was on TV. What used to be the most wonderful time of the year had officially become an annual contest for the most devastating events in her life.

And, yes, Sam's rejection was devastating.

Whipped cream melted on top of the cocoa, and she took a sip, barely noticing the sweet liquid. She'd put on her favorite flannel red-and-white pajamas and covered her lap with a fuzzy throw, but neither comforted her the way they should.

She'd been wrestling with her thoughts for hours. Strange she hadn't cried—not once—since he'd dismissed her.

Maybe her tear ducts had dried up. She felt lost. Empty.

Numb.

"Parker fell asleep. It was a treat to tuck him in again." Mom carried her own mug of cocoa into the living room and sat in the recliner. "Aah, feels like old times. I miss you. I miss Parker. I miss us all living together. I'm not going in to work tomorrow, so you just relax here as long as you'd like, and I'll take care of Parker."

Celeste tried to smile.

"I know you'll tell me what's on your mind when you're ready, but will you at least fill me in on what the doctor said?" If the crinkles above her nose didn't reveal her concern, the nervous tapping of her finger-nail against the mug did.

"What we thought. No more surgery." Saying those words rubbed her throat raw. She took another drink of her cocoa, but it didn't ease the ache.

Mom set her cup down and shifted to face her. "Tell me everything. Did he give you an explanation? Alternative?"

Who cared? Her face could be a mangled mess and it wouldn't matter, because Sam didn't want her, he'd kicked her out of his life and she had to somehow go on without him.

Celeste lifted a shoulder in a shrug. "He said surgery wouldn't help. I pretty much tuned out after that. Sally called about Parker, and I left."

"That's it?" Mom crossed one leg over the other. "I knew I should have gone with you."

"I'm a big girl. I handled it, Mom."

"Obviously that's not true or you would have listened to what he said. Did he mention laser treatments?"

The warmth of her childhood home suddenly stifled her. Was she twelve again, getting lectured for not listening in class? Didn't she have enough to deal with?

"He handed me a bunch of pamphlets." She absentmindedly waved backward and resumed staring out the window.

"And you didn't look at them?" The way she said it made it sound as if Celeste had thrown away the Hope Diamond.

"Look, Mom, I have bigger problems, okay?" She swung her legs over the side of the couch, tossed the throw off her and marched out of the room. *Great.* Not only was she being treated like a twelve-year-old, she was acting like one, too.

Her mother followed her to the kitchen. "I'm sorry. I know how much this appointment meant to you. Give it a few days and look over the material. We can figure out your options then." She wrapped her arms around Celeste, and Celeste puddled into them, not realizing how much she craved her mother's embrace.

A few minutes later, she stepped back. "I think I'll turn in."

"It's only eight." The worry lines returned to Mom's forehead.

What did it matter? She wouldn't sleep. She had so much to think about.

So much to *avoid* thinking about.

After kissing Mom's cheek, she padded to her old room, shut the door and slid under the covers.

Ironically, hearing she wouldn't be having more surgery was the least of her problems. In fact, for the first time since the accident she really didn't care. What did it matter if her face looked the way it did? Since moving to Lake Endwell, she'd been getting through life okay. She could go to the grocery store now. She'd been to the library. Awkward questions? She had answers. Stares? She was used to them. She was even ready to attend church again.

The scars no longer mattered. She'd be raising Parker alone, anyhow. She couldn't imagine—didn't want to imagine—a life with anyone but Sam. And he'd been shockingly clear he didn't want her in his.

But why?

She didn't think it was her face. He'd been grim before she told him the verdict. Whatever changed him had happened before she told him about the results of her appointment.

So what was it?

She searched her thoughts for any clue. He'd been so sweet this morning, asking if she wanted Parker and him to come with her. And she'd said no, she wanted to go alone.

Was that it? Had he felt rejected by her?

And then the hospital and Parker falling… Maybe he blamed Parker for causing him to fall. Sam had acted strange when Parker reached for him.

She shook her head. That couldn't be it. Sam adored Parker. He not only said it, he acted like it, too.

Which brought her back to her. Sam must have realized she wasn't the right woman for him.

Did he think she'd hurt him?

She would *never* hurt him.

But that might not be the kind of hurt he was talking about. He'd told her he wanted to carry a child on his shoulders. That he wasn't having a family until he could walk on his own. What if the doctor had told him he'd never walk again? Was that why he rejected her?

Acid turned her stomach into a battlefield. She clutched the covers to her neck, squeezing her eyes shut.

She might never know why he changed his mind.

And in the meantime, she'd try to forget the brilliant blue of Sam's eyes, the funny things he said, the way he made her feel at ease, the strength of his arms around her, his kiss…

Stop it! Just stop!

If she could fall asleep for two or three weeks, sleep right through this heartache…

Her brother was dead. Her best friend was dead. And she was the one who had to go on without them. Two giant holes in her life.

Losing Josh had been like losing her childhood.

Losing Brandy had been like losing her twin.

Losing Sam was like losing a lung.

She didn't know how she'd survive without him.

He hated it here.

Sam didn't turn on the Christmas tree lights or any other light, for that matter. The glow of a hockey game from the television was the only brightness in the dark room. His swollen leg throbbed even with it wrapped in ice and propped on the couch. This cottage felt like a prison.

Would he always live like this?

Alone.

Helpless.

Miserable.

And why? It was his fault.

Aunt Sally's lecture kept going around in his head, and every time he tried to shush it, it grew louder. *Still blaming God?*

Yeah. He was. And he was tired of it.

Granddad kept a Bible in the end-table drawer. Sam had never been a big Bible reader. He'd gone to Sunday school for years, attended church his entire life, and it had been enough. But ever since the accident, he'd closed his heart to God. Refused church, prayer and the Bible. Until recently.

The more he tried to shut God out, the deeper his emptiness grew.

He was tired of blaming God.

Sam opened the drawer and strained to reach the Bible. Finally, he grasped it and hauled it on his lap.

For a long time he stared at it. He didn't know where to begin.

Lord, I'm here. I'm desperate. You know that. I can't go on like this. I'm tired of being angry. I'm tired of being afraid. I'm really tired of shutting You out. I don't know if You care anymore. I don't deserve it. I mean, I've blamed You for all my problems.

Maybe he should forget this.

He set the Bible next to him on the couch. He'd pushed God away too long. How could he expect God to forgive him with a snap of the fingers?

Shouldn't he be on his knees, repenting?

Even if he could get on his knees, he didn't have the energy to repent.

Frustration mounted, and he snatched the Bible and opened it. Ecclesiastes. *Everything is meaningless?* Terrific. Not exactly the words he'd been hoping for.

He flipped through, landing on the second book of

Corinthians. He skimmed a section about the apostle Paul, stopping short when he read a verse. He double-checked it. Paul had been given a thorn in his flesh, and he begged God to take it from him, but God refused. Why?

Why did God refuse Paul?

Why did You refuse me?

Sam read the rest of the chapter and frowned. God didn't say He refused because He didn't love Paul or because Paul deserved the thorn. The scripture gave a different reason—that God's grace was sufficient and His strength was made perfect in weakness.

God's grace was sufficient? His strength was made perfect in weakness?

It didn't make sense. How could strength be made perfect in weakness?

Because it will force me to rely on God instead of myself.

He didn't want to. He didn't want to put all his trust in God. He wanted some of the power, some way of controlling his destiny—wasn't that natural?

How was that working out for him, though?

Lord, I don't know if I can give it all up to You. I just don't know if I can.

He wanted some say in his life.

Yeah, and he was doing so much with it. He ground his teeth together.

Okay, You win. What do You want me to do? What is Your will?

He waited, hoping for an answer to hit him upside the head. It didn't.

His phone vibrated. He checked the text. Bryan

wanted to know if he should pick Sam up for tomorrow's meeting at Tommy's dealership.

The doctor hadn't told him he couldn't return to work. He'd told him to take it slow, use the wheelchair. But could he? ·

Maybe it was time to pay *his* dealership a visit. He texted Bryan back.

Celeste slept until noon, shocked she'd gotten to sleep at all. When was the last time she'd slept in? Before the accident, that was for sure. She changed into a pair of worn jeans and a soft oversize black sweater, then padded into the kitchen to see how Mom and Parker fared. The kitchen was empty except for a note on the counter from her mom saying she was taking Parker out for an adventure and they'd be back later that afternoon.

After fixing a bowl of cereal, Celeste sat at the dining table and tried to keep her mind blank. Impossible.

What was Sam doing now? Did he miss her? Did he regret pushing her away?

Tomorrow was the parade. Sally had told her all about the food vendors and festivities they'd lined up at City Park. It had sounded like so much fun. Mostly because she'd be with Sam. Just the two of them.

And now there was no two of them. No clutching take-out coffee as Shriners drove down the street in miniature cars and the marching band played. No distraction from her memories, from the anniversary of the accident.

Dread filled her at the thought of getting through tomorrow. She'd missed Brandy's funeral because she'd still been in the hospital. Maybe that was part of the reason she felt so low.

She'd never said goodbye to Brandy.

The distraction of the parade had been a lifeline so she wouldn't have to face tomorrow and what was taken from her.

How could she distract herself now?

What if she didn't distract herself? What if she faced the anniversary head-on?

Today.

Right now.

Celeste set the empty bowl in the sink and slipped her feet into boots. As much as she didn't want to, her inner being shouted she needed this. She needed to go back to the accident site and face the doubts and fears swirling in her gut. Get some closure. If closure was possible.

Fifteen minutes later she parked her minivan on the side of the road. It really was a barren stretch of blacktop. No houses nearby. A field with a fresh buzz cut from the fall crop harvest—corn from the looks of it—stood in washed-out gold shades to her right. The telephone pole her car hit last year rose tall and menacing against the colorless sky. The ditch was deep and full of overgrown yellow grass and weeds. The opposite side of the road held the same view.

Celeste stepped outside, burrowing deep into her winter coat. Hands in her pockets, she stood next to the ditch. Cold wind blew her hair around her neck and bit at her face. She barely noticed. Just stared at the pole.

An ordinary thing. A tall piece of wood. Once a tree.

It had taken Brandy from her.

It had taken more.

So much more.

Something drew her to that telephone pole. She couldn't name it. She needed to cross over and touch it.

Taking a few steps back, she ran and leaped across the ditch, falling to one knee as she landed. She rose, brushing off her jeans, and trudged to the pole. Craned her neck back. A pair of birds perched on the wire. And the pole grew taller, reaching higher than before.

"I hate you," she whispered, wishing she had a chain saw or an ax. Anything to chop it down.

The words opened a cavity she'd hidden inside, and without warning, a flock of thoughts, feelings and impressions flew out.

"You were set in the ground right here." She didn't care she was shouting at an inanimate object. "Not five feet over there. Here. And if you had been there—" she pointed "—my car wouldn't have hit you. We probably would have walked away shaken up with a few scrapes. But that's not what happened. All because of you."

"I hate you," she yelled, kicking at the clump of weeds surrounding it. "I hate you!"

A gust of wind stung her cheeks.

She'd never be able to tell Brandy how much she loved her. How much she meant to her.

"Give her back!" She dropped to her knees. "I want her back."

With her hands covering her face, she wept. Shoulders shaking, the smell of earth in her nose—she didn't try to control her cries. Minutes ticked by as she released every drop of sorrow.

When she had nothing left, she dropped back and sat on the ground.

"I'm sorry, Brandy. I'm so sorry. I should have paid attention. I shouldn't have sung so loudly. I shouldn't have made you come with me. I should have…"

What? What could she possibly have done differently?

It was an accident.

An accident. She hadn't been texting or drinking or driving like a maniac. She'd been going the speed limit.

There was nothing she could have done differently. It seemed so senseless.

Why? Why had it happened? Why?

She wiped her nose and gazed up at the telephone pole.

And it was as if a lightning bolt went through her chest.

He knows. He knows how I feel. He knows why. And He doesn't want me to feel it anymore.

Jesus had been nailed to a cross. A piece of wood. Planted in the ground. Similar to this pole that took Brandy.

Both had been taken by trees.

He gave His life for me. He died on the cross for me. God knows how broken I feel, because He lost His Son.

"You get it, don't You, God?" Celeste scooted to the pole, sitting at its base with her back to it. "You lost the One most important to You, too. You understand. You know how I feel. I don't know why I didn't realize it until now."

A wave of peace crested over her body.

God had given His Son to save her, to save Brandy and Josh and everyone else who believed. He knew what it was like to grieve.

The pole at her back wasn't the enemy.

I need to let go. I've been blaming myself for the accident, but that's what it was—an accident. I will prob-

ably never know why it happened, but I can go on. God, help me let go.

She shifted, pressing her cheek against the smooth, cold wood. Just a telephone pole. A tree at one time.

For the first time in a year, she felt inner peace. Not on edge. She wasn't holding back a hundred anxieties.

She felt open.

Free.

And she let herself remember all the things that had been too hard to reflect on all year. The precious memories she'd never let go. Two little girls meant to be best friends. Jumping rope at recess, riding bikes all summer long, singing to the radio, watching movies, the countless sleepovers. Giggling, gossiping, crying, just being together. Holding Brandy's bouquet on her wedding day. Holding her hand at Josh's funeral. And laughing and singing with her the night she died.

Celeste sat there until the cold seeped through her clothes and she couldn't control her shivers.

Brandy and Josh were in heaven. Not coming back. She would see them again, eventually. She had no choice but to go on without them in her life.

But she had a choice about Sam. And whether he wanted her in his life or not, she needed to tell him how much he meant to her. She didn't want to regret *not* telling him.

How could she convince him there were no guarantees? That getting hurt could happen. That random events shattered lives sometimes, and no one knew why.

Wasn't the thought of a forever love worth the risk?

It was worth it to her. She was going to try.

Friday night at eight, Sam stared at the dark glass entryway of his dealership. Could he find the answers he was looking for here? The employees had all gone home for the night. Bryan typed in the alarm code and opened the door so Sam could wheel inside. As Sam waited, Bryan flicked the lights on. Several impressions slammed into his mind.

Pride. This was the building and business he was responsible for. He'd built it. He'd planned it. And it was still here, waiting for him.

Relief. His brothers and employees were taking good care of it. Not a speck of dirt or a desk out of place.

Memories. Strolling through it the day before the grand opening. Confident, excited and nervous. On his two strong legs. On both feet.

He blew out a breath.

"It looks exactly the same." He rolled through the showroom, slowly moving past the shiny cars displayed inside. "Well, the vehicles are different. I like this one. Who chose it?"

"I did." Bryan slipped the keys in his pocket and stayed close to Sam. "Did the doctor say you could still come back to work?"

"I can come back." He didn't add that he'd been able to come back for months—in a wheelchair.

"Good. You still want to?"

"I've always wanted to." *Just not like this.* "I'm going to check out my office."

Bryan studied him a minute, most likely seeing way more than Sam wanted him to. "I'll wait here. Holler if you need me."

He didn't linger. Spinning forward, he passed the customer waiting room and a row of cubicles for the sales staff. He rolled down a hallway. Faced a door with a shiny nameplate. *Sam Sheffield.*

His office.

In another life.

He jiggled the handle, but it was locked. He'd forgotten his keys. "Hey, Bryan, do you have the key to my office?"

Bryan's footsteps grew louder. "What do you need?"

"The key." He pointed to the handle. "Do you have it?"

"I have them all." Bryan grinned, pulling out a ring full of keys. After unlocking it, he returned to the showroom while Sam moved through the doorway.

Framed degrees and certificates hung on the walls the way he remembered. A picture of him cutting the ribbon at the grand opening sat on the desk. A smiling photo of the Sheffields taken a few Christmases ago was centered between bookshelves. His office smelled like new carpet and stale air.

The leather chair behind the mahogany desk reminded him of poring over reports, signing checks, making deals.

He wanted to sit in it again.

After setting the brake on the wheelchair, he pushed himself up to a standing position and let his left leg bear his weight. Using the desktop to keep his balance, he circled around and sat in the chair.

It felt the same.

Felt like success.

His lips lifted into the briefest smile. Then the reality of his situation choked it away. Emotions churned, but he didn't want them. Couldn't deal with them on top of everything else. He opened the top desk drawer. A slim stack of papers greeted him.

He took them out and scanned the first sheet. Dated

the day before his accident. A request from a local youth volleyball team to sponsor their season. *Sorry, ladies. Missed responding to that one.* Setting it aside, he read the next. His handwriting. Notes about a possible dealership location forty-five minutes away. A wrinkled map with highlights. He'd forgotten he'd driven out to it a few days before his life changed permanently.

He kept his eyes fixed on the wall, but he didn't see anything. The plans he'd had trickled back. The Realtor taking him to a possible site for the next phase of his business plan. Scanning the area, mentally building on the field. Shielding his eyes, trying to figure out if the two-lane road would help or hurt traffic flow.

Sam put the papers back in the drawer and shut it. Propping his elbows on the desk, he let his forehead fall into his hands.

I don't know if I can do this. I'm not the same man.

The past eighteen months—in the hospital, the physical rehab center, the cottage—flashed before him. Alone. Bored. In pain.

This dealership, this office was his. If he wanted it.

Next to the desk, the wheelchair mocked him. And the urge to yell, to beat his fists, to protest his situation consumed him.

His jaw clenched. He was so tired of clinging to this anger, this rage.

What would it take for him to let it go?

Words pressed against his heart.

No. I can't. Not those words.

If he let them out, they would either release him or destroy him. He wasn't sure which. He'd been avoiding them for months, afraid of their power.

But he had no fight left.

Only surrender.

Fear congealed in his throat. The dreaded words formed in his head.

I'm sorry, God. For blaming You. For expecting You to do whatever I wanted. For telling You the terms. I need You. I can't do this on my own anymore.

The dam inside him broke, and he couldn't control it. His eyes ached as tears spilled out, and his shoulders shook as he began to cry. For the man he used to be. For the man he was now. For the lost months, the pain, the dreams he'd clung to, the ones he'd given up on.

When he'd emptied everything out, he straightened, wiping his face with his sleeve.

Bryan stood in the doorway. Compassion glowed from his pale blue eyes. Three strides and he was at Sam's side. Bryan set his hand on Sam's shoulder and bent to hug him.

"I'm sorry. I hate that this happened to you."

Sam cleared his throat, shaking his head.

"You're not ready." Bryan rounded the desk and sat in one of the chairs facing Sam. "I'll run it. Don't worry. It will be here. Take your time."

Peace settled over Sam's soul.

The accident took full use of my legs, but it didn't take all of me.

Strangely, he felt stronger than he had in months.

He could handle this. He could do it.

"This is mine." Sam spread his palms over the desk. "I'm coming back."

"You're not ready."

"I *am* ready. I could have come back months ago, but I didn't want to work in a wheelchair. I still don't want to, but you know what? I'm going to. Who cares if I can't walk? I can still run this place."

"Are you sure?" Bryan looked like he was chewing on a tough strip of beef jerky. "You don't have to."

"Yes, I do. If I don't, I might never come back. I need this. Need my job. Need something to occupy my time."

And he needed Celeste. And Parker.

He needed them more than he needed the dealership.

They were the best part of him. And he'd thrown them out.

"Bry?"

Bryan raised his eyebrows.

"I probably won't ever walk without a cane or a limp. I might always need this wheelchair to some extent."

"Yeah, so?"

Heat climbed his neck. He loosened his collar. "Can a guy like me, with my limitations, be a good husband? A good father?"

Bryan's face contorted in confusion. "Why wouldn't you be?"

He didn't want to explain. He shouldn't have brought it up.

"You don't need to walk to love someone." Now it was Bryan's turn to look embarrassed. "To cherish them."

"And when a baby cries in the night? I might not be able to get it out of the crib."

"Your wife would."

"What if she's sick?"

Bryan rubbed his chin and stared into space. "You can always call one of us. Or you could hire a nanny at night. There might be special cribs you could buy."

True. But maybe Bryan was missing the point.

"Okay, but when all the dads are lifting a toddler on their shoulders and my kid wants to sit on mine, what am I going to do? I'll let him down."

"Buy him a balloon or something. He'll get over it."

True again. But was Bryan still missing the point?

Bryan leaned back, crossing his arms. "I think you're scared. I know scared. The worst scare of my life—the thought of losing you—prompted me to get over my biggest fear. You helped me give my heart to Jade. The night of your accident, I left your hospital room and felt destroyed. And she came to me like a gift from God."

"I didn't know that."

"If you're afraid of taking a chance on Celeste—and don't deny it, we all know you like her—don't be. I had a lot of excuses why it wouldn't work between Jade and me, too. But that was fear feeding me a bunch of lies." Bryan leaned forward. "Tommy told me something when I was being a thickheaded dolt about Jade. He asked, 'Do you believe you're divinely guided?' You'll have to ask yourself the same thing."

"I shut God out for a long time."

"He was still there. He's always there." Bryan flourished his hand. "When you trust God, He will always lead you to the right turn in the road."

The right turn in the road.

"You're right." Sam could see it all—God's hand in his life. The accident had happened, but God had allowed him to live. God had saved him, saved his leg, protected him and sent Celeste when he needed her most. "So I should fight for Celeste and Parker?"

"I wouldn't let anything keep me from Jade." Bryan grinned. "Does Celeste feel the same?"

Sam blew out a breath and shrugged. "I was a jerk

yesterday. I honestly don't know. Wouldn't blame her if she hated me."

"Get ready to grovel." Bryan laughed.

"Real funny." Even if Sam groveled, could he convince Celeste they were right for each other?

Maybe.

If he did it right...

Chapter Fifteen

Celeste had to tell Sam she loved him. Today.

Or tomorrow.

No, today.

Down by the lake on Saturday morning, she wrapped her arms around herself as the sun rose. Mom and Dad had agreed to watch Parker the rest of the weekend, so she'd driven back to the cabin late last night to strategize. To plan. To pretend she wasn't taking the biggest risk of her life.

She needed to gather her courage and march up to Sam's door.

She wasn't ready yet.

The sun's glow lit the sky above the tree line behind the lake. Darkness faded little by little. One year ago, she'd put in eight hours at the most boring job in the world, gone back to her apartment, thrown on her cutest outfit and driven straight to Brandy's.

Today could end up as traumatic as a year ago, or it could be the best day ever.

Either way, she had a feeling she'd be okay.

God was with her. Guiding her. Supporting her.

She was ready for this.

She reviewed her plan. Since she'd slept all of forty-seven minutes last night, she'd had plenty of time to get ready. She wore her favorite jeans, warm boots and a red sweater. She'd straightened her already straight hair.

Her makeup was light. It didn't cover her scars, and she didn't want it to. Either she was good enough for Sam with her scars or she wasn't. And if she wasn't, well, he wasn't right for her, either.

Stop procrastinating. Go over there, already.

Celeste headed back up the lawn. When she reached the driveway between her cabin and Sam's cottage, she stopped short. On her porch steps, Sam leaned against his crutches. Their gazes locked. She couldn't move. Couldn't think.

What was he doing there? Out of his wheelchair? On her steps?

"Hey," he said, extending his neck in greeting.

"Hey." *Brilliant response.*

"We need to talk." The words brought mixed feelings—hope, yes, but fear and disappointment over their last encounter, too.

"Now?" She hated that her head and heart were clashing right now. Her plan to tell him she loved him fled out the back door, and all that was left was uncertainty. "What if I don't want to?"

He hung his head. "Look, I'm sorry. And I don't blame you, but we need to talk."

She nodded, wishing his apology could wipe away all their problems, but it couldn't. They *did* need to talk. She could invite him in, but she wanted all her memories in the cabin to be good. If he was going to break her heart, she preferred he do it somewhere else. "Not here."

"Let's go to town, then."

"I'll get my keys." Celeste went inside and grabbed her purse, refusing to get her hopes up. He could have any number of things to say. Maybe he wanted her to move out. Since he didn't need her to drive him around, he didn't want her living there. Could that be it?

He would never be that cruel.

They drove in silence until Sam told her to park in a lot behind the most picture-perfect church she'd ever seen. Huge wreaths with big red bows hung from the double doors, and holly bushes were planted around the front porch.

"Here we are." He waited for her to bring his wheelchair around and then wheeled himself to a bench in front of the church. "Looks like it's getting ready to snow again."

As if on cue, snowflakes started falling. He sat on the bench and held his hand out. "Come here."

She obeyed, shivering at the cold seeping under her jeans. This wasn't how she'd planned it. She was supposed to go to him, tell him what was in her heart—when she was ready.

She was not ready.

"I'm sorry, Celeste."

The block party raging in her veins lowered a notch. Another apology wasn't what she wanted. She wanted a declaration.

"No, I mean it. I was stupid. I hurt your feelings, and I'm sorry."

"Apology accepted." Why did her voice sound as if it was six miles away? Because his feelings didn't match hers.

He wiped a finger across his eyebrow. Seemed nervous.

Well, join the club, buddy.

"Celeste, I was in a bad place when we met." He faced her. "Bitter. Angry. Sorry for myself. You changed all that."

She did?

"I saw how you rebounded from your accident. Raising Parker. Starting over in a new town. I admired that. And you gave me the courage to start living again. And I mean, really living. Like leaving the cottage and thinking about work. I even went back to church. This is my church, by the way."

Her throat felt fuzzy. Thoughts jammed in her mind, but she couldn't make sense of them. "It's really pretty."

He nodded. "It is. But that's not important. The more progress I made with my leg, the more hope I felt. Until Thursday. Everything kind of fell apart on Thursday. It wasn't your fault. It was mine. My breakdown had been brewing for a long time."

She winced. Usually when a woman heard the words *it's not your fault, it's mine*, it meant a guy was blowing her off. Was Sam here to blow her off? Or wait—hadn't he already done that?

"I blamed God for not healing me. I let my pride get in the way of going back to work. I pushed away my family and friends. And then you came along."

She met his eyes then—those stunning blue eyes— and a glimmer of hope lit in her chest. He looked at her with such intensity, such need.

"I tried to push you out of my life because I was scared. I thought you needed a man who could protect you, take care of you and help you. I'm not going to pretend I'm that man. I can't carry a baby around on these legs. This week, I couldn't even keep Parker safe for more than an hour. Watching him fall and hit his head because I couldn't pick him up just about broke me, Celeste. I love him."

"I know you do." She did know. What she didn't know was how he felt about her. "You lost a lot in your accident. You had every right to be angry, Sam."

"I shouldn't have blamed God."

"Well, I blamed myself for Brandy dying. I told myself I'd been driving too fast, enjoying our night out too much. Yesterday I even blamed the telephone pole. I wanted it to make sense, but I'll never know why it happened. I had to accept it. Finally, I do. Do you still blame God?"

He shook his head. "No. Like you, I may never understand why I went through this, but God knows why. He loves me and that has to be good enough."

"I'm glad you got right with Him."

"Me, too."

The words she'd been getting up the nerve to say sat on the tip of her tongue.

"Celeste, I need to get right with you, too." He took her hands in his. "I think you're the most beautiful woman I've ever seen. I'm sorry your appointment didn't go the way you hoped, but I've never noticed your scars. I see your big brown eyes and your long, shiny hair. You have a slightly crooked tooth that drives me wild. I see your heart. The way you love Parker with a love so big it can't be contained. I see more than you know, and I love it. I love everything I see. Everything about you. I love you."

He loved her?

But what about his words at the hospital? She had to know for sure if he really meant what he was saying. "At the hospital you said my scars mattered."

His eyes darkened. "Not the way you think. I was afraid of letting you down. I know you'd been let down by the accident and then by not hearing what you wanted from the doctor. Your scars only mattered because I convinced myself I would be one more let-down in your life."

"You could never let me down."

"I could, Celeste. And I probably will."

Sam watched Celeste's expression as his words sank in. Her throat moved as she swallowed, and her hair slipped over her face. He wanted to run his fingers through the silky strands. But he wasn't selling himself as anything more than what he was. If they were going to have a future together, he had to lay out exactly what life with him would be like.

What if he did and she rejected him?

At least he wouldn't have any regrets.

He caressed the back of her hand with his thumb. "Ever since you walked through my door in October, I've been trying to convince myself that this—" he gestured to his right leg "—isn't forever. That I could make it better. Be who I wanted to be. And I wanted to be a man who could carry a bride over the threshold, who could hold a baby during late-night feedings, who wouldn't limp but would be on both feet protecting his loved ones."

Her face, pink from the cold air, oozed sympathy. She squeezed his hand.

"You've had a hard life," he said. "I don't want to make it harder. I'm being selfish."

"You make it easier," she blurted. "I don't need a guy to carry me over the threshold or carry a baby or any of that. I need someone who loves me, scars and all. Someone who will be my partner and love Parker like he's his own son."

"What if you change your mind five years from now?" he asked.

"I've learned we have no guarantees. I might not be here five years from now. You might not be. But I don't want to go through those years without my best friend."

He scratched his chin. "But Brandy's gone."

She laughed. "I'm talking about you. You're my best friend. You're my safe place. I tell you everything, and I love you, Sam. I love you, too."

His heartbeat pounded, and his chest felt ready to burst. Could it be this easy? When everything else for the past eighteen months had been so hard?

Who cared? He was taking it. Grabbing it.

Sam wrapped his arms around her and drew her to him. Her lips were close, and he kissed her. Drank in their softness. Tasted a hint of coffee and vanilla. Was filled with the sensation of rightness, of his future, of forever.

Before he got carried away, he owed it to both of them to say everything on his mind. He ended the kiss and brushed her cheek with his lips.

"I may always need the wheelchair, Celeste. I'll probably always have a limp. I've lived with chronic pain every day since my accident. It might never go away. I can't carry groceries indoors or play volleyball with you at a picnic. I can't even drive anywhere, although

I hope that will change soon. Are you sure you can accept that?"

She cupped his face with her hands. A smile full of joy lit her face. "I'll bring the groceries in, and you can help put them away. I hate volleyball. I like driving. And you're acting like you bring nothing to a relationship. You support me. You brought me out of my shell. You allowed me to run again. You make Parker laugh. You're so good with him."

"I'm worried about watching him. Worried he'll get hurt, and it will be my fault."

"Don't worry. You're great with him. He's going to get hurt sometimes. That's how life is."

He nodded.

"I think he's been trying to call you Daddy. If you want me to stop him, I will…" Worry dimmed her eyes.

"I don't want him to stop. I don't want any of this to stop. I feel like I'm in a dream—a good dream, finally. I don't want to wake up."

"It had better not be a dream. If it is, it's the best one I've ever had."

He leaned in, kissing her again. She twined her arm around him, sinking her fingers in the hair at his nape. Her gentle touch undid him, made him forget why he had ever doubted they should be together. He kissed her slowly, savoring this woman who'd saved him from the pit he'd sunk into.

Thank You, God. Thank You for sending her here, for giving us both another chance at life. For leading us to each other.

Celeste broke free with a shy smile. They stared at each other for a long moment.

"Are you still up for the parade?" He pushed her soft hair away from her face.

"Are you?" Her nose scrunched in concern.

"I am. The doc told me I have to protect my leg at all costs, though, so I'm stuck in the wheelchair today."

A smile bigger than Lake Endwell spread across her face. "Fine with me. Besides, you promised."

"I did. And it's officially a date." He grinned. "Let's get breakfast, then head up to Main Street. I know just the spot on the parade route."

Celeste smoothed her skirt over her knees and peeked back at the church entrance for the twelfth time in two minutes. Why was she so nervous? Parker would be a great baby Jesus.

"Are you as nervous as I am?" Sam squeezed her arm.

"More." They sat in the second row of Brandy's church Christmas Eve night. The children's service would be starting soon. Celeste, Sam and Parker had stopped by her parents' house earlier, and the introductions had gone better than she could have hoped for. When they got to the church, Parker happily went to Shelby.

The days since the parade had flown by in a blur of shopping, wrapping gifts and watching Christmas movies—all with Sam, of course. The parade had been wonderful. She and Sam had sipped coffee and joined his siblings and their families on the sidewalk of Main Street. The marching band played "Deck the Halls" as dancers spun and leaped down the street. Miss Lake Endwell had waved from the back of a silver convertible, and Shriners drove miniature cars. The best part? Sam had held her hand the entire parade.

As he'd held it every day since.

"Here comes Grandma Pearl." She sucked in a breath and exchanged a charged look with Sam. "I hope Parker does okay."

They rose to let Grandma Pearl sit with them, and after she settled in, she turned to Celeste. "It was so nice of you to join me for the service. I know you have your own church to go to. Where's Parker?"

Celeste had talked to Sue Roper earlier, and they'd agreed not to say anything. To let Grandma Pearl realize that Parker was baby Jesus on her own. After the service they would reveal why they wanted to surprise her.

"You'll see."

A hymn began to play and the congregation stood. Dressed up in costumes, the excited children strode to the front of the church, stopping where they'd been directed. Shelby, dressed as Mary, held Parker—who was wrapped in a beige cloth—as she walked to the manger set. Matt, dressed as Joseph, stood beside her, a staff in his hand.

Grandma Pearl pressed her hand against her chest. "Oh!"

"Are you okay?" Celeste asked.

"Parker," she said breathlessly. "He's baby Jesus!" Her eyes glistened with tears and she searched Celeste's face. Celeste nodded, grinning at the wonder in her expression. Grandma Pearl dug through her enormous black purse and found a handkerchief, wiping her eyes. When she pulled herself together, she took Celeste's hand in both of hers and held tightly. "I never thought I'd see the day… You've made me so happy."

The service continued with recitations and hymns. Parker sat quietly in the fake manger, and Shelby kept a hand on him, brushing the hair from his forehead. The moment came for the shepherds to arrive. One of the sheep ran crying down the aisle to his mother. The movement startled Parker, and he sat up, spotting Celeste and Sam.

"Mama! Dada!" He held his arms out. Muffled laughter spread throughout the church. Celeste covered her mouth and glanced at Sam. He grinned, winking at her. Shelby soothed Parker, and he quieted down. The rest of the service flew by in a blur, and before they knew it, they were in the fellowship hall with Sue Roper, a swarm of parents and hyper kids.

As Sue and several women explained their surprise to Grandma Pearl, Celeste noticed Sam approaching her dad. Dad clapped him on the shoulder and nodded. *Hmm...*

Sam returned to her. "Your parents are taking Parker home for the night. I have a surprise for you."

"What kind of surprise?" This was getting strange.

"It's an early Christmas present."

"Are you sure about this?"

"Never been so sure about anything in my life."

Thirty minutes later, Celeste sat on Sam's couch, wondering what on earth she was doing there. Sam had disappeared to his bedroom. He'd refused to say anything about the surprise on the ride over. Instead, he talked about the presents he'd bought his sisters and the Christmas movie he'd watched late last night. Stalling and evading. She had to admit he was good at it. The lights from the tree they'd decorated together sparkled, casting a Christmas glow.

And then there he was.

She stopped breathing.

Absolutely gorgeous.

His blue eyes radiated love. A dark gray sweater perfectly showcased his broad shoulders. Dress pants hid the brace she could just make out beneath the fabric. Something was in his hand in addition to his crutches. He approached, carefully lowering himself to the couch next to her.

"I didn't know where or how to do this, but when I think of you, I know God sent you here to me. You helped me get right with Him again. So this, where we met, is perfect."

"For what?" Nervous anticipation made her words rush out, but she wasn't scared.

"This cottage is where you helped set me free." He looked serious. "Give me your hands."

She held out her hands. He massaged them with his. The intensity in his eyes made her gulp.

"Celeste, I love you. We both know life can change in an instant. That's why I'm doing this now. I already spoke with your dad." He held a small black box. "You're the only woman for me. I love you. I love Parker. I want to be your husband. I want to be his daddy. I want forever with you. Will you marry me?"

"Yes, oh, Sam, yes! I love you. I want to be your wife. I want you to be Parker's daddy. And, God willing, we'll have more babies, too, if that's okay with you."

He slid a ring on her finger. A dazzling diamond winked at her.

"I definitely want more babies." His husky tone

matched the gleam in his eyes. And he kissed her, thoroughly. "Thank you. Thank you for saying yes."

"Thank you for being my yes."

He kissed her temple. "You'll always be my yes."

Epilogue

Ten months later, Sam stood gripping his cane at the front of the church. He closed his eyes and took a deep breath. Today was the day. He'd met Celeste exactly one year ago, and now she would finally be his wife. *Thank You, Lord.*

"Are you ready?" Bryan, his best man, whispered, nudging him.

"I'm ready." Sam adjusted his tux. The doors were opened and the bridesmaids—his sisters and sisters-in-law—slowly walked up the aisle in matching red dresses. Macy followed, spreading flowers from her basket. Emily, wearing a white dress, and Parker, in a tiny tuxedo, held hands as they ran top speed up the aisle. Laughter erupted from the pews. And then Celeste appeared on her dad's arm.

Breathtaking.

If his knee hadn't been in the brace, it probably would have collapsed at the beauty coming toward him. Her white satin dress had short sleeves, lace and beading. He barely noticed it. It was the woman behind the veil that held him captive. Moments later her dad lifted the veil, put Celeste's hand in Sam's, and together they walked the few steps to the front.

"You're beautiful," he whispered. "I don't have words. You're the most stunning woman I've ever seen."

"I'll never get tired of hearing it," she whispered back.

The pastor opened the Bible. They listened to the scripture. Exchanged vows and rings.

"I now pronounce you man and wife."

He grinned, and she grinned back. When they'd walked all the way back to the entryway where everyone would greet them, Sam propped his cane against the wall, cupped her face in his hands and kissed her.

"Oh, my!" She looked dazed. She rested her palm against his chest. "Just think—one year ago was the day we met. I never would have imagined then that we'd be married now."

"I couldn't walk."

"And my scars were much worse."

"They were never bad." He touched her cheek. Celeste had tried a laser treatment, which had reduced the appearance of her scars. Only two were visible. Not that she could ever be less than exquisitely beautiful in his eyes, but he was glad she'd gotten the results she'd hoped for.

"A lot has changed since then." He kept her close to him as the bridal party approached.

Sam had gone back to work in January—and he was thriving. He no longer had to use his wheelchair at the dealership, but he still needed crutches sometimes. Mostly, he relied on the cane. He was fine with that. And Celeste had been taking online classes to become a teacher. It would be another year until she'd meet the requirements, but in the meantime, the high school cross-country coach had asked her to be an assistant coach.

After the obligatory hug-fest in the receiving line, where Celeste and her mom hugged for so long they had to be broken up and Aunt Sally jumped back in line three times, Sam tapped Bryan's shoulder. "Can we escape?"

"Absolutely." Bryan and Tommy rounded up the bridal party, including Claire and Reed's baby, Robert, for pictures. Then they headed to the reception at Uncle Joe's Restaurant.

Sam didn't smash cake in Celeste's face, but he could tell how tempted she was to smear cake in his. Thankfully, she refrained. The night wore on, and when they'd talked to everyone, Sam pulled Celeste to him, kissed her and said, "It's time."

Her eyes sparkled as she nodded.

"Goodbye, Parker! Have fun with Grandma and Grandpa!" Celeste kissed Parker's cheek one more time and waved as her mom and dad carried him away.

"'Bye, Mama! 'Bye, Dada!" He blew them kisses.

Sam blew them right back. He'd miss the little guy while they were on their honeymoon in Hawaii. Sam leaned on his cane and kept his other hand wrapped around Celeste's waist. He leaned close to her ear. "Let's get out of here. I have a surprise for you."

She twined her arms around his neck. "Last time you said that, we got engaged."

"I know." He tugged her close and kissed her.

"Whew." She fanned herself. "Is it hot in here?"

"Yes. Way too hot. Let's go." He moved toward the door. "I'm not going to convince you to let me drive, am I?" Earlier in the summer, he'd finally been cleared to drive. The freedom meant more to him than words could express.

"No way—I'm driving." She tapped her chin. "I told you I've always wondered what it would be like to drive a truck in a wedding gown."

He laughed. "I think you should wear it every day. You're beautiful in it. Well, you're always beautiful."

They headed out into the cold October air and shivered in Sam's truck as Celeste let it warm up a minute. "So where are we going?"

"The cottage."

"Really? I thought you'd want to go to a hotel or something."

"Nope. I have something I need to do."

"I'll take your word for it."

It didn't take long to get there.

"Wait right there a minute and meet me at the patio door." He raised a finger and got out of the truck, carefully walking up the ramp with his cane. He switched on the little white Christmas lights strung across the porch rail. Then he brought out the wheelchair and turned it so the back would be facing her.

He'd been imagining this moment for months.

A minute later, she ran up the ramp to him, holding her pretty wedding gown in her hands. As soon as she saw the wheelchair, she burst out laughing. It had white balloons attached to the handles and a Just Married sign stuck to the back.

"I've always wanted to carry a bride over the threshold." He sat in the chair and patted his lap. "Hop on. I'm carrying you over."

"I'll hurt your leg." She tentatively stepped in front of him.

"No, you won't." He pulled her down onto his lap. Her full white satin skirt trailed over the edge, and she wrapped her arms around his neck. He held her tightly. He'd never let her go.

"Are you ready?" he asked.

"I'm ready."

And he rolled the chair through the patio and into the cottage.

"Now it's official. Welcome home, Mrs. Sheffield."

* * * * *

THE PASTOR'S
CHRISTMAS COURTSHIP

Glynna Kaye

To Natasha Kern—
my agent, encourager and sister in Christ.

And without faith it is impossible to please God, because anyone who comes to him must believe that he exists and that he rewards those who earnestly seek him.
—*Hebrews* 11:6

Let the morning bring me word of your unfailing love, for I have put my trust in you. Show me the way I should go, for to you I entrust my life.
—*Psalms* 143:8

Let us draw near to God with a sincere heart and with the full assurance that faith brings, having our hearts sprinkled to cleanse us from a guilty conscience and having our bodies washed with pure water. Let us hold unswervingly to the hope we profess, for he who promised is faithful.
—*Hebrews* 10:22–23

Chapter One

"Could you use some help there, ma'am?"

Ma'am? Her hooded head jerking up, Jodi Thorpe grimaced at the sound of a male voice carrying over the rumble of a big diesel pickup. Headlights illuminating the lingering remnants of twilight, the truck idled alongside her on the snow-covered dirt road. The passenger-side window had been rolled down, but the driver calling out from the far side of the interior was cloaked in shadow, behind a veil of steadily falling snow.

Exactly what she didn't need—a small-town Good Samaritan.

"Thanks for the offer," she responded at a volume she hoped could be heard as she gave the tow rope attached to a four-foot-long, molded plastic toboggan another tug, "but I'm fine, thanks."

She waved the man off with a mittened hand and trudged on, grateful for the snow glow reflecting off the lowered clouds. Without it, it would be impossible to keep her footing on the rutted shoulder of a ponderosa pine–lined road.

Maybe a December getaway to her family's soon-to-be-sold mountain cabin in Hunter Ridge, Arizona, wasn't such a good idea after all. But with her parents out of the country, the opportunity for a quiet retreat seemed ideal. Not only for soul-searching time alone—Decembers were always a bittersweet reminder of the precious life she'd once carried inside her—but to spare her two Phoenix-based sisters from having to host her for the holidays. Why put a damper on their and their children's Christmas festivities?

"Ma'am?"

The man sounded as if he were addressing someone twice her age. But bundled in an oversize insulated coat and clunky boots she'd found in the cabin—and burdened by a backpack—she probably did look like a hunched-over crone of fairy-tale fame.

"I can throw that stuff in the back of my truck," the voice came again as the pickup crept along beside her. "And take you to wherever it is you're headed."

She stiffened. Like she was going to climb into a vehicle with someone she didn't know? The trusting brown eyes of Anton Garcia flashed through her mind. If only years ago she'd overcome her fear of telling him the truth, had accepted his marriage proposal. And if only he hadn't volunteered to hitchhike for help on that deserted Mexican road.

Why, God?

Taking a steadying breath, she yelled over the rumbling engine. "Thanks, but I'm almost there."

She could see the cabin's porch light not too far in the distance as she dragged behind her the bright red toboggan she'd often ridden as a kid. Its load of groceries and other supplies hadn't seemed cumbersome when she'd started back to the cabin, nor the journey ahead of her long. Growing up, she and her younger sisters had often traversed this route to run errands for their grandmother. But now her fingers had stiffened with cold and her arm strained at the bulky weight.

"You're going to hurt yourself, ma'am."

Enough of the "ma'am" business. Wanting to get away from the self-proclaimed Boy Scout—*or was he only pretending to be a holiday helper?*—she gave the tow rope an extra-hearty tug. The toboggan held fast to whatever abruptly anchored it under the frosty mantle and tipped sideways, spilling its load and jerking the rope from her hand. Thrown off balance, she toppled into the snow.

The sound of a truck door slamming tipped her off that the driver had exited his vehicle. Trying not to panic, she struggled to sit upright, but the weight of the backpack rendered her as helpless as a turtle on its back.

"Let me help you up." Through the falling snow, she detected the man reaching out his gloved hand. What choice did she have but to accept his assistance?

Please God, let him be a good guy. After all, it's only two weeks until Christmas. And despite what You may have heard my sisters say, I'm not a Grinch, a Scrooge or anything of the kind.

Not much, anyway.

Reluctantly, she grasped the hand that stretched out to steady her as she staggered ungracefully to her feet. Her hood fell back, snowflakes pelting her face and the cold wind penetrating her long hair.

"Jodi?" The man's voice held an incredulous note. "Jodi Thorpe?"

She blinked, trying to focus through the falling snow.

"Garrett?" In a community of under two thousand

residents, why did Garrett McCrae have to be her rescuer tonight? And what was he doing in a town he vowed never to return to once he could make his escape?

"Yeah, it's me, Jodi."

A familiar grin lit his face, and for a horrifying moment she thought he was going to hug her. But something in her eyes as she mentally flew back through time must have halted him. He plunged his hands into the pockets of his navy down jacket and took a step back, his eyes searching her face as intently as hers searched his.

Even though she and Garrett had been the best of friends as kids when she and her two younger sisters visited their grandparents' vacation home in the mountains, she hadn't seen or spoken to him in a dozen years. Not since that last ill-fated night when he'd crushed her teenage dream of them ever being more than friends.

But time had treated him well. Gone was the ponytailed hair that as a teen had nearly splintered his relationship with his dad, replaced by a conservative cut. Lines etched the corners of his eyes, evidence his sense of humor and love of the sunny outdoors had prevailed. His shoulders were impossibly broad. And those eyes... the same deep gray she too-well remembered.

"What are you doing in Hunter Ridge?" they said in unison. Apparently he was as thunderstruck by her presence in town as she was his.

"I'm working here. For a while at least." His brows raised. "And you?"

"I'm helping my folks get my grandparents' cabin ready to sell." At least that was the excuse she intended to use for camping out here until after the holidays. Nobody needed to know the mixed-up mess of the rest of it.

"So, you've been living—where? Married, with a houseful of kids, I suppose."

Her smile threatened to falter, but she held it steady. "None of the above. I'm living in Philadelphia, actually, where I'm a project manager for an athletic apparel company. SmithSmith. And yourself? Still river-running?"

It was a wild guess. Becoming a river guide was all he'd talked about after his first Colorado River rafting trip when he was sixteen, and her grandma had said he'd taken off for training right after high school graduation. So why should she be surprised to find him here in December? Most rafting companies operated with a full crew only in the summer. He probably worked at the family business in the off-season.

"It was the adventure of a lifetime while it lasted." A fleeting shadow flickered through his eyes, then he shrugged. "But I gave it up a while back."

At two years her senior, he would have recently turned thirty, an age that at one time appalled them both as prehistoric. Had a domestically inclined wife lured him away from his youthful obsession? "In other words, old man that you are now, you've turned river-running over to the younger generation?"

"Ouch!" His yelp was accompanied by an exaggerated flinch. Then he laughed that familiar laugh, and her heart inexplicably leaped. Why had she so easily fallen into teasing him just as she'd once done as his tomboy sidekick? They'd long ago left those days behind.

He openly studied her, and despite the chill air, her face warmed. Did he remember that night, too? She motioned briskly to the groceries strewn in the snow. "You're responsible for this. If you hadn't been stalking me, I—"

"Stalking you? I was trying to help you. 'Tis the season. You know, ho ho ho?" Before she could stop him, he snagged the toboggan in one hand and one of her grandma's now partially filled grocery tote bags in another and slung them into the back of his pickup with what looked to be a dwindling load of firewood.

"What are you doing?"

"What's it look like? Getting you and your stuff out of the cold." He squatted to gather the scattered contents back into the other bags. Lifting a cereal box, he waggled it at her. "Still into Cheerios, I see."

With a laugh, she snatched it out of his hand, recalling the afternoon that as an elementary schooler she'd been dared to sneak a family-size cereal box from Grandma's pantry and devour the whole thing herself. Garrett couldn't stop snickering when Grandma insisted she still clean her plate at suppertime.

"You don't need to do this, Garrett. I'm almost there."

"So indulge me." He held out his hand for the cereal box.

What would be the point in arguing? Used to getting his own way, the high-spirited Garrett had long marched to the beat of his own drummer. She'd once foolishly hoped they were marching to the same beat... but learned a hard, humiliating lesson. Except for that out-of-the-blue instance that he made no secret of immediately regretting, he'd never considered her as more than a pal. A buddy.

As soon as he'd stowed the last of her bags, he helped her off with her backpack and opened the passenger-side door. But before she could hoist herself up, a vehicle coming from the opposite direction pinned them in its lights, then pulled parallel to Garrett's truck.

A ball-capped male poked his head out an open pickup window. "I should have figured I'd find you out here rescuing a pretty damsel in distress. Way to go, Preacher."

Jodi turned toward Garrett, catching his deer-in-the-headlights look of alarm.

Preacher?

Uncomfortably conscious of Jodi's questioning gaze, Garrett raised his voice over the rumble of the two vehicles. "Do me a favor, cuz, and keep this to yourself."

"You can count on it." The other man chuckled, then offered a parting wave as he guided his vehicle on down the snowy road.

Garrett didn't meet Jodi's eyes as he held out his hand to assist her into the truck, taking note of the curtain of straight red-blond hair now lightly dusted with snow. It would be too much to hope that she hadn't caught Grady's preacher remark. Nothing much ever got past Jodi, but she'd probably think it was a joke. Some days he wasn't sure if that might be the case. God's little joke, anyway.

As she settled herself in to secure her seat belt, he wedged the backpack at her feet. Then he shut the door and jogged around the front of the vehicle to climb aboard.

"Which cousin was that?"

She'd remembered he had a bunch. "Grady Hunter, the twins' next-to-oldest brother. Luke, Claire and

Bekka are all married, and Grady's getting hitched in February. Rio's still single."

She nodded thoughtfully, as if placing long-forgotten faces to the names, maybe recalling that his mother was a sister to the dad of those cousins. He started the truck slowly down the road, its windshield wipers working overtime against the descending snow.

Thankfully, Garrett could trust his cousin to keep his mouth shut. He sure didn't need questions raised about his personal conduct because he'd stopped to assist an old friend. This past year he'd toed a fine line as interim pastor of Christ's Church of Hunter Ridge—as a *single* interim pastor, to be exact.

That was a slippery slope in a place used to family men. He couldn't afford to leave doors open for criticism of his actions if he hoped to qualify for a spot on a highly-thought-of missions team. He was *so* close and needed a positive recommendation from church leadership to seal the deal.

But this was *Jodi.*

He couldn't leave her stranded on a night like this because someone might not think it acceptable for him to escort her home alone. After all, they'd grown up like brother and sister, right?

Nevertheless, his ears warmed as he shoved away a memory he hoped she had no recollection of—although, from the look on her face when she'd recognized him, the odds of that were slim to none. He was pretty sure her grandma, rest her soul, hadn't forgotten. He'd certainly received a well-deserved earful when she'd walked in on them that Christmas Eve. Thankfully, things hadn't gotten beyond hot and heavy kissing. But he probably still owed Jodi a long-overdue apology.

He adjusted the windshield wiper speed. "What are you doing out here in the dark pulling that sled? Where's your car?"

"I use public transportation—and I didn't want to mess with renting a car." Her words came almost reluctantly, as if uncertain how much to share with him. "The forecast showed flurries the next few weeks, so I thought I could get around on one of the bikes at the cabin. I caught a shuttle from the Phoenix airport this afternoon."

Assuming they still lived in the Valley of the Sun, why hadn't she spent the night with her folks or one of her sisters?

"When I got here," she continued, "I made a mistake of stretching out for an intended quick nap. Only I woke up not long before sunset to several inches of snow. Who knows what it will be like tomorrow? So off I went."

He glanced at her, hoping she'd elaborate on what she'd been doing with her life. But she didn't. Incredibly, she wasn't married, but were her sisters? Did her university professor folks still take short-term mission trips during semester breaks? It saddened him that the cabin was to be sold, although to his knowledge the family hadn't gathered there as a whole since her grandma's health abruptly deteriorated and she eventually passed away.

Jodi's mitten-clad hand patted the dashboard. "What's with the monster truck?"

"A loaner from Hunter's Hideaway." That was the family business that had catered to outdoor enthusiasts since early in the last century. "With this cold snap,

Grady and I've been delivering firewood to those in need."

She laughed. "So you *are* a do-gooder now."

Did she have to sound so surprised? Admittedly, growing up he'd been forever into mischief. Always pushing boundaries and looking for a good time wherever he could find it. Not a whole lot into thinking of others. But still...

"You even took time from your do-gooder efforts," she noted, "to help this poor old lady stumbling along the side of the road."

"You gotta admit you looked the part." But she sure didn't right now, with that silky hair cascading around her shoulders and a smile lighting her brown eyes. Those very assets had been his downfall the night a transformed sixteen-year-old Jodi showed up in town after a few years' absence, leaving him stupefied and devoid of common sense.

Sort of how he was feeling at this very moment.

Not good.

After his most recent disappointment in the romance department, he'd steered clear of serious involvements. And for an interim pastor, this wasn't a good time to start rethinking that choice. So why had it popped into his head that her arrival in town might be the answer to a prayer he'd uttered but twenty minutes ago?

His office assistant Melody Lenter—an energetic lady about his mom's age—had called around lunchtime, informing him her father in Texas had a heart attack and she and her husband were on their way out of town. She'd have to bail out on overseeing the annual Christmas project she'd single-handedly spearheaded for the past twenty years. Between wood deliveries, he'd spent the afternoon phoning church members, trying to find someone to fill her shoes—but to no avail. He'd barely called out to God that *someone* had to cover for Melody—he sure couldn't take on one more thing— when the capable and ever-dependable Jodi appeared on his doorstep.

Answered prayer? Or a desperate, not-too-bright idea?

"So where's the motorcycle? And—" She peeked at the back of his head. "What happened to the ponytail?"

Although still waiting for her to zero in on Grady's "preacher" comment, he managed a laugh. "The tail's a thing of the past. I have an SUV now, but a motorcycle's stashed for the winter in a Hunter's Hideaway barn."

The motorcycle made some in his congregation uneasy, which wasn't surprising considering the noisy nuisance he'd made with one as a teenager. No doubt he hadn't been high on the church's interviewee preferences list for a few members. But his Grandma Jo, a force to be reckoned with, convinced them—and him— that his filling in while they searched for a permanent ministerial replacement would benefit all involved.

Coming back, though, hadn't been easy. Nobody in town had a clue what it took to regularly face his old friend Drew Everton and the accusing stares of those who held him responsible for Drew's debilitating injuries. While Drew insisted he wasn't to blame, others weren't so forgiving.

But his year's commitment at Christ's Church would be up at the end of the month, and he was more than ready to move on. Ready to live the dream Drew had been forced to abandon.

"Here we are." He turned the truck into a pine-lined

lane leading up to the Thorpe cabin, a wave of nostalgia washing through him as it often did when he drove by. While the porch light lent a cheery note this evening, in broad daylight the place always struck him as melancholy. Lifeless. Although a guy at the church kept an eye on it, that didn't make up for the absence of the warm hospitality and sound of laughter he remembered. Or for missing familiar faces peeping from the dormered attic windows and the sight of his and Jodi's grandmas relaxing on the broad front porch.

He turned to Jodi. "I felt really bad when I heard your grandma passed away." He couldn't imagine not having his Grandma Jo or Grandma McCrae around. That was one of the blessings of Hunter Ridge he'd sorely miss when he left.

"It's funny," Jodi said as she unbuckled her seat belt, "but even though I haven't been here since high school, when I arrived I almost expected to see her step out on the porch to give me a big hug."

"Smelling of freshly baked cupcakes and that honeysuckle hand lotion she always used."

Surprise lit her eyes. "You remember that?"

"I remember a lot of happy times at this cabin."

While his younger sister and Jodi's siblings gravitated to each other to do girlie things, he and Jodi had teamed up to shoot baskets, climb trees and build woodland forts. It was difficult to reconcile memories of the somewhat stout, rough-and-tumble freckle-faced tomboy of his youth with the sixteen-year-old beauty who'd blindsided his eighteen-year-old self—and with the woman who sat beside him now.

"What do you say we get your stuff inside?"

But *should* he ask her if she could spare time for

a project her grandma had at one time helped with—providing Christmas cheer for unwed mothers in the region?

Still undecided, he watched as she retrieved the backpack at her feet. Then just as he gave up on the idea and reached for the door handle, her gentle hand settled on his forearm, her eyes sparkling with mischief.

"Thank you—*Preacher.*"

Chapter Two

It was all Jodi could do to get those words out with a straight face. Garrett would be the last man on earth to be mistaken for minister material. But there it was again—that same caught-in-the-act look she'd seen earlier. What on earth had Garrett been up to that his cousin would mockingly call him "preacher"?

He released his grasp on the door handle, his expression uncharacteristically ill at ease. "You caught that, did you?"

"I take it your cousin has a good sense of humor."

"Grady," Garrett said, as he slowly rubbed the back of his neck, "has a good sense of humor, all right."

Obviously he didn't want to explain. While as a youngster she'd have kept at him, pushed until she all but choked out the whole story, that wasn't appropriate now. They were two adult strangers whose lives had moved on from each other. People were entitled to their privacy. Goodness only knew, she hoped he'd respect hers.

"I don't think I want to hear about it," she said with

a teasing lilt, letting him off the hook as she opened the door and climbed out.

In a twinkling he was at the side of the truck, probably grateful for the reprieve, and lifting out the toboggan. He set it on the ground, then snagged several bags and placed them atop it. Pulling two more from the bed of the truck, he handed her one and gripped the heavier of the two in his own hand.

"Ready?" Garrett grabbed the toboggan's tow rope. "Lead on."

With the side porch light illuminating the way, they progressed through the snow and up to the porch itself. Garrett held open the screen door as she fumbled with the keys to unlock the dead bolt. Then she stepped inside the dimly lit mudroom.

Ah, the infamous mudroom. Scene of the crime. Or rather the not-so-romantic setting of their first—and only—kiss.

The tiny space had been dark that night, too, an unexpected cocoon of privacy in a cabin teeming with family and friends readying for the Christmas Eve service. Now she self-consciously set the bag and backpack on a counter—the same counter she'd leaned against for support when her legs threatened to give way as Garrett's lips tentatively touched hers. Or tentatively at first, anyway.

Taking a quick breath, she flipped on the light switch, the bare bulb overhead banishing both the shadows and too-vivid memory. Avoiding meeting Garrett's gaze—afraid his own memories might have followed hers—she returned to the door and took the proffered bag.

He quickly transferred the remaining ones to the

mudroom floor, then propped up the toboggan outside the door. "Looks like that about does it."

"Thanks, Garrett. I'll put the sled in the shed later." She slipped out of the old coat and hung it on a peg of the knotty pine–walled room. "Would you like to come in for a cup of cocoa? Or I could fix coffee."

In all honesty, she didn't want to invite him in. The less she saw of Garrett or any other old acquaintances during her brief stay here, the better. She needed time alone to work through things—the aching loss of Anton's recent death—and to make decisions for her professional future. Time to privately commemorate the loss of an unborn life. This use-it-or-lose-it vacation forced on her at the end of the year couldn't be better timed. But the introspective hours she craved could too easily be aborted if she didn't guard them closely.

"Thanks for the invitation, but I have to get back to…" His uncertain gaze darted to hers as his voice trailed off.

What was with him tonight? Garrett in his youth had never been one to act unsure of himself or beat around the bush. "Get back to what? Your female fan club?"

Everything used to come easy to him. Athletics, schoolwork, making friends—and *girlfriends*. She used to give him a hard time about the latter, masking her own supersized crush.

His mouth twitched. "Believe me, no fan club these days. Actually, I need to get back to the church."

"Picking up another load of wood for delivery?"

"Not exactly." He cast a look upward as if appealing to the Heavenly realms. "I have to finish my sermon for tomorrow."

"Sermon?" She laughed, Grady's remark finally

making sense. "You got roped into delivering a message at the old family church, didn't you? Garrett, whatever were you thinking?"

He ducked his head slightly, then looked up at her with one eye squinted. "I'm thinking that as the pastor of Christ's Church of Hunter Ridge, that's one of my responsibilities."

What? "Come on, tell me another one."

A smile tugged at the corners of his mouth. "As impossible as it may sound—and believe me, some days it probably seems more impossible to me than it does to you—I'm degreed in church ministry and have been interim pastor here for the past year."

She stared. He wasn't joking. His cousin hadn't been joking.

"Wow, Garrett."

He chuckled, no doubt in reaction to the stunned look on her face. "Yeah, wow."

"This is…is quite a stretch. I mean," she quickly amended, "a turnaround."

As they'd progressed from Sunday school days to youth group teen years, he'd become increasingly restless, adventurous, more prone to risk-taking. A party boy who'd enthusiastically indulged a wild streak, he'd certainly never anchored himself to anything spiritual, let alone God.

But then, she couldn't exactly point fingers…

"Which goes to prove—" his smile widened "—that God's still in the business of transforming lives."

"When did— How?" She never would have expected anything like this. Not in a million years.

He shrugged. "Looking back, God's been dogging me at least since my first rafting trip on the Colorado when He really opened my eyes to the beauty and intricacy of His creation. Unfortunately, I wasn't willing to listen until about five years ago."

He was serious. This was for real.

"I'm sorry I laughed, Garrett. I was just so—"

"Shocked? Don't feel bad. My family, except for Mom and Grandma Jo, still isn't quite sure what to make of it. Some church members who knew 'the me that was' haven't bought into it, either."

She couldn't help but continue to stare at him. "This is amazing."

"That it is." He took a step back. "As usual, though, time's gotten away from me this week and my Sunday message awaits. But maybe we could get together while you're in town. Catch up."

She didn't want to catch *anybody* up on her life outside Hunter Ridge. Things she wasn't proud of. Wounds that had yet to heal. A faith that was currently so wobbly it wasn't funny. "Let's see how it goes, okay? There's lots to do to get this place ready to sell."

"You'll be at the worship service tomorrow?"

Not eager to interact with those who might remember her—or to see young mothers with their precious little ones—she hadn't planned to go. But having laughed at him, expressed such blatant disbelief, might Garrett take a refusal the wrong way?

"You can count on it."

"See you there then." Eyes smiling, he lifted his hand in a parting wave as he stepped off the side porch. "Ten thirty."

A few strides away, he halted in his tracks as if he'd thought of something he'd forgotten to say. Maybe he wanted to offer her a ride to church? Then apparently changing his mind, he tramped on through the falling snow.

Almost dazed, she stood at the door watching as he disappeared into the darkness. *Garrett McCrae. A pastor.* A heavy weight settled into the region of her heart as she closed and bolted the door.

Sorry to point this out, Lord, but your timing stinks.

She'd barely turned off the porch light and entered the kitchen when the door rattled from a firm pounding knock.

When she turned on the light and reopened the door, there stood Garrett once again.

"What did you forget?"

"Actually…" He paused as though undecided as to how to proceed. Totally un-Garrett-like. Then he plunged on. "I need to ask you something."

Oh, please, don't say anything about that night. The night he'd made it clear his little tomboy pal didn't meet his standards for female companionship.

"I know you have to get this place cleaned up, but what if I helped? Recruited others to help?" His gaze now met hers in open appeal. "Do you think, then, that you might have time to oversee a church Christmas project while you're here?"

Was he kidding?

"I don't think there's much left to do," he hurried on, "but my office assistant who stays on top of it all year had a family emergency and can't follow through. All afternoon I beat the bushes to find a replacement, but came up empty-handed. Unless things have changed, though, you have more organizational ability in your little finger than most have in their whole body."

He gazed at her with hopeful eyes as she tried to make sense of what he was saying.

"You want me to take on a church project while I'm here?"

"Oversee it. You wouldn't have to do *all* the work. I imagine Melody has it well in hand. But none of the other volunteers feel confident in assuming the responsibility."

"To be honest, Garrett, I don't think I would either." No way did she want to be sucked into something like that, even for a good cause. Getting through church tomorrow would be about as much socializing as she could manage.

"You sell yourself short, Jodi." Garrett's words lilted persuasively, too reminiscent of times he'd conned her as a kid into doing things she'd later come to regret. "Remember how you turned around your Grandma's floundering yard sale? And you were only what— eleven? Twelve?"

"Thirteen." Grandma hadn't a clue about grouping similar items and showing them off to best advantage. Or about negotiation. Despite a clearly stickered, more-than-fair price, she would accept the first ridiculously low offer without batting an eye. In addition to rearranging the merchandise, Jodi had put a stop to that.

She couldn't help but smile at the memory.

"See?" Garrett almost gloated. "You *do* remember. You have a gift, Jodi, and maybe God's called you to be in town right now so you can use it for His glory."

She folded her arms. "I'm not falling for the 'God loves you and Garrett McCrae has a wonderful plan for your life' stuff."

Eyes twinkling, he shrugged. "Figured it was worth

a try. So how about it? It won't take that much time, and I can round up some high schoolers to help whip your cabin into shape. Even if I have to get my own hands dirty, I'll see that you have extra time for the Christmas project. It's one that is near and dear to my Grandma Jo's heart—and was to your grandma's as well."

While help cleaning out the place would be welcome, no fair bringing Grandma into the equation.

"What exactly will this entail?" Why was she even asking, allowing Garrett to sway her after all these years? But maybe she *was* letting her personal problems turn her into a Grinch as her sisters had accused. Becoming selfish. *All about me.* "I'd be organizing the distribution of canned goods? Clothing? Toys?"

"All of the above. Behind-the-scenes work."

Would it really kill her to help out? To make a little room in her own plans during the next two weeks? She might not be able to boil water, but she did have a knack for project management, a talent she was paid well for in the corporate world. How hard could it be if this Melody person had been keeping on top of the project since early in the year as Garrett claimed? And maybe it would be a means of honoring her grandmother's memory.

"I guess…I can take this on."

Garrett grinned. "You won't regret it, Jodi, I promise. Melody says this project is the highlight of her whole year—that there's nothing better for the soul than making the holiday season brighter for unwed mothers."

A blast of cold air from the open door swirled in around Jodi's ankles, sending a shiver rippling through her.

Unwed mothers?

* * *

"You'd better get moving, Garrett. You don't want to be late again."

Cutting off his hummed rendition of "O Holy Night," he glanced at the rail-thin gray-haired woman standing in the doorway to his room on Sunday morning. Seventy-year-old Dolly Lovell and her husband had taken him in as a boarder a year ago when he'd been cautioned that as a single pastor it might not be advisable to get a place of his own and he hadn't want to bunk back with his folks. As it turned out, this lodging arrangement not only came with meals and occasional help with laundry, but also built-in chaperones.

"I'm heading out right now." He reached to the top of an antique dresser for his Bible and an iPad filled with sermon notes, then gave his part-time church receptionist a kiss on the cheek. "I don't know what I'd do without you and Al to keep me on the straight and narrow."

Dressed for church herself, a smiling Dolly shook her head as he slipped by her. "It's a dirty job, Pastor McCrae, but somebody has to do it."

There was probably more truth in her humorous comment than he cared to think about. Born with—and long indulging—an independent streak made coming under the authority of the church leadership a never-ending challenge. Both for him *and* them.

It wasn't far to the church, a distance he most often enjoyed walking, but this morning he jumped in his old Ford Explorer to make better time. Although he didn't have a Sunday school class to teach this quarter—he'd used the extra hour this morning to shovel out the Lovells' driveway and polish up his sermon—he'd caught his mind wandering one too many times. If he was late, it would be Jodi Thorpe's fault.

He could still hear her laughter when she thought Grady's preacher comment was a joke. Could see the shock in her eyes at his admission that he was an official God's man. He wasn't unaccustomed to that reaction since returning to Hunter Ridge, of course. With the exception of Drew, he'd taken a lot of ribbing from his high school buddies—and even was shunned by a few. Many adults who'd known him when he was growing up eyed him with skepticism. No surprise. But for some reason Jodi's disbelief pierced him to the core.

Admittedly, it *was* a stretch to accept the changes in his life. Especially when Jodi was standing in the mudroom where as a hormone-driven teen he'd once attempted to put the moves on her right under her family's nose. But deep down he'd hoped to hear the friend of his youth confess she'd seen something in his early years that foreshadowed this turn of events. Or that her grandmother had admitted to glimpsing a nugget of promise in him.

More likely, though, all her grandma saw was an undisciplined young rascal who couldn't keep his hands to himself.

Nevertheless, Jodi had agreed to take on this year's Christmas project. A load off his shoulders, for which he was grateful.

As always, his spirits rose at the sight of the church building. This morning the weathered brick edifice, built in the 1930s, looked like something out of a magazine with snow coating the roof and the surrounding ponderosa pines. Some noble soul had shoveled the walkways and bladed the parking lot, the sun now pitching in to do its part.

There were good people here at Christ's Church. He was more than fortunate to land a ministry opportunity with a congregation like this one as he prepared for a future in missions work. But did they consider themselves equally blessed to have been saddled with him? They'd been pretty desperate when he'd come along. Following the departure of their third minister in as many years, they'd been without one for six months when Grandma Jo took a hand in things.

And now they'd be looking for a replacement once again.

"Garrett!"

His cousin Luke Hunter—Grady's older brother—waved him over as he approached the front of the church. A newlywed of only a few months, he looked happier than he had in years. The high-spirited former Delaney Marks had certainly impacted the widower and father of three in a big way. He was much more relaxed now, less hardheaded, and occasionally could even pass for laid-back. While Garrett hadn't heard anything official, if Grandma Jo's suspicions were correct, child number four might be putting in an appearance not too far into next summer.

When he reached his relative's side, the men shook hands, and his cousin lowered his voice. "I want to give you a heads-up. Old Man Moppert isn't happy that you've rearranged things at the front of the church."

Randall Moppert. Again. The guy had never forgiven him for TP-ing his trees when, in the pitch dark and slightly inebriated, a teenage Garrett had mistaken Moppert's place for that of a friend next door.

"I didn't rearrange. I shifted the lectern and the Lord's Supper table slightly off-center so there's room for the kids' choir. They're kicking off our service with 'Away in a Manger.'"

"Well, he doesn't like it. I overheard him telling one of the board members that you're taking liberties in God's house."

"I'll talk to him."

"Better you than me." Luke grimaced, then glanced with interest toward the parking lot. "Who's that with the Palmers?"

Following the trajectory of his cousin's gaze, Garrett's heart rate kicked up a notch at the sight of a pretty woman, her red-gold hair flowing around her shoulders as she exited a vehicle. The Palmers must have seen Jodi walking into town and picked her up.

Which was another thing nagging at him.

Last night he'd said he hoped to see her at church, but although grateful for her taking on the project and aware she didn't have transportation, he hadn't offered any.

The church where he'd done a semester's internship had strict guidelines on staff interactions with members of the opposite sex, and he'd instinctively maintained those standards as much as possible when he'd come to Hunter Ridge—even if their rules were more lenient. Which is why he hadn't accepted Jodi's invitation to join her inside for cocoa. But he could have at least drummed up a ride for her.

She looked amazing this morning, her fair cheeks rosy from the cold and a bright smile rivaling the warmth of the morning's welcome sun. Then there was that eye-catching, begging-to-be-touched long hair that as a kid her folks kept cropped up by her ears. Not for the first time, he whispered a silent prayer of thanks that she wouldn't be in town long. Although many times a partner in his schemes when they were kids, she'd increasingly balked when he took his risk-taking tendencies to the extreme. No doubt she'd be unsurprised that those inclinations had finally caught up with him—and he was paying the price.

"Garrett? I said—"

"That's Jodi Thorpe," Garrett quickly responded, his face warming at Luke's curious look. Had anyone else noticed him gaping at the newcomer? Not recommended ministerial manners. "She used to spend summers up here. Sometimes Thanksgiving or Christmas. You may not remember her. She'd have only been about seven or eight when you left for the military."

"Thanks for the reminder of my old age." Although still on the sunny side of forty with a wife ten years his junior, Luke gave him a mild look of reprimand. "I don't remember a Jodi, but I do remember the last name. Grandma Jo was good friends with a Nadene Thorpe. This is a granddaughter?"

"Right. Hey, look, I'll talk to you later, okay?" Maybe he could make amends for not arranging transportation for Jodi. "I'm going to welcome her to Christ's Church."

Luke leaned in. "You do that, *flirt master*, but don't forget you have a million eyes on you right now. Until you hear otherwise, you're still in the running for a full-time position here. Don't blow it."

Luke's warning was unnecessary. Not only did he have God looking over his shoulder, but he was acutely conscious of how closely a single pastor was watched—and judged. Good impressions were especially important right now, even though, unknown to those around him, he had no intention of staying in Hunter Ridge, job offer or no job offer.

"No worries," he assured Luke as his gaze drifted back to the subject in question. "As a kid, that gal over there could shinny up a tree faster than lightning and nail a can with a slingshot better than I could. She once caught me off guard and pinned me down, too. Filled my mouth with a handful of dirt. Believe me, recollections like that kinda put a damper on any flirting business."

Or they would, anyway, if he could forget how sweet it had been to kiss her.

Chapter Three

Jodi had barely drawn back from giving a big thank-you hug to Marisela Palmer—one of her grandma's dear friends—when Garrett approached.

Or rather, *Pastor* McCrae.

Unbelievable.

It was with a sense of relief, though, that the guy she'd known since the summer before first grade hadn't let himself be shoehorned into a suit for his Sunday morning duties. Rather, he had on a pair of neatly pressed gray trousers, a white collared shirt, and a gray pullover sweater. No outer jacket despite the chilly morning.

She couldn't resist firing the first volley. "What happened to your tie, Pastor?"

His hand flew to his neck as he looked frantically on the ground around him. "It was there a minute ago."

"I think Jodi's teasing you, Garrett. Just like old times." Marisela, a petite black woman who looked at least a decade younger than Jodi knew her to be, looped her arm through his as she gazed up at him with affection. "I spied her coming out of Nadene's cabin this morning—a delightful surprise—and we gave her a ride. She tells me she had no idea until last night that you've been our minister this past year."

He patted Marisela's hand, but his amused gaze held Jodi's. "It looks as if she sufficiently recovered from the shock since she managed to get herself here on time this morning."

Garrett *would* have to remember that Grandma practically had to dynamite her out of bed, and often she'd dragged herself to the breakfast table still in her pajamas.

Before Jodi could make a snappy response, a pretty brunette with two small children in tow paused next to Garrett. Bundled against the cold, the faux fur–trimmed hood of the woman's burgundy coat framed a heart-shaped face and long-lashed dark eyes. She looked up at him expectantly, as if assuming introductions would be made.

Jodi's heart jolted. His wife and kids? Right before turning off the bedside lamp last night, she'd realized Garrett hadn't clarified a marital status. But a quick glance at both his and the woman's ungloved—and ringless—hands put the question to rest. So Garrett *was* single and still playing the field, although aspects of that part of his life would certainly have made a U-turn, as well.

His gaze flickered to the newcomer. "Sofia, you know Marisela. But I'd like you to meet Jodi Thorpe. Our grandmothers were good friends. Jodi, this is Sofia Ramos and her daughter Tiana."

He placed a hand affectionately on the head of the black-haired little girl next to him. "Her little brother is Leon."

While early grade schooler Tiana smiled shyly, Leon,

appearing to be about three, paid Jodi no attention as he tugged at his mother's coat, eager to be on his way.

"It's good to meet you." Jodi shook Sofia's offered hand.

"Are you visiting for the holidays, Jodi?"

"My folks are selling my grandparents' cabin, so I'm here to get it ready to put on the market." That response seemed to satisfy everyone.

"Such a shame to sell the place." Marisela shook her head. "But while they keep the utilities turned on and things in good repair, your folks haven't been up here at all this year."

Garrett looked down at his watch and made a face.

"Oops. Showtime. Children's choir has the opening number." He held out a hand to each child. "Kiddos? Let's get you in there for your moment in the spotlight— all set for your mama's ever-ready camera if she can sneak off the piano bench for a few shots."

Both giggling children willingly grasped a hand and trotted up the front steps beside him, evidently comfortable in the man's presence. Which again made Jodi wonder about his relationship with their mother.

Mr. and Mrs. Palmer invited her to sit with them, and it was with a mix of nostalgia and a sense of time too quickly passing that she spied a few now-older yet familiar faces—including Garrett's spunky Grandma Jo, who came over to warmly welcome her.

Much of the service was a blur as youthful memories assailed. Sunshine streaming through the stained glass windows illuminated the red velvet bows on each pew, and the familiar scent of furniture oil tickled memories. Remembrances of squirming on a hard pew at her grandmother's side vividly filled her mind, as did later instances of covertly watching a restless, teenage Garrett sitting with his buddies.

It all blended together with Sofia's lovely piano renditions in the background, that is until Garrett stood to deliver the morning's message. As if he had a direct hotline to her troubled soul, his words regarding right and wrong choices—how split-second decisions could make a lasting impact—unexpectedly hit their fragile target.

It was all she could do to maintain her composure as a montage of uncomfortable images flashed through her mind. Her life was such a muddled mess right now, mostly due to choices made. God had forgiven her. She believed that, not because she *felt* forgiven, but because that's what He promised. But hadn't she also paid for her mistakes in the worst possible way?

Now she'd very likely lose her job, too, through no fault of her own. Was it any wonder her faith was tottering? She took a steadying breath as a too-familiar suffocating sensation pressed in.

"Jodi? Would you like to join us?"

Jerked back to the present, she realized the service had concluded. She'd zoned out through the closing hymn, people were milling in the aisles, and Marisela was standing beside her, smiling uncertainly.

She gave an apologetic laugh as she stood to slip back into her jacket. "I'm sorry, I didn't catch that. Join you where?"

"Al and Dolly Lovell have invited us to lunch. You remember Dolly, don't you? Another of your grandmother's friends? You're invited, too—or we'd be happy to drop you off at the cabin if you'd prefer."

"Oh, do come." Another older woman, her fair hair cut in a chin-length bob, placed a hand on her arm.

"You remember me, don't you? Georgia Gates. I was your vacation Bible school teacher in third and fourth grades. Your grandma was such a dear friend. We miss her so much."

"Of course, I remember you." But for a fleeting moment, surrounded by those who knew and loved Nadene Thorpe, she couldn't help but wonder why Grandma couldn't still be there among them, too.

While she'd prefer to return to the seclusion of the cabin, she didn't want to be rude to her grandma's friends. If she got through the expected socializing today, she could then oversee the Christmas project as quickly and efficiently as possible. After that, she'd be free to withdraw from human contact for the remainder of her time in Hunter Ridge. "I'd be delighted to come as long as I won't be intruding."

"Of course you won't be," Georgia said, giving her arm a squeeze. "We'd love to catch up on your life and that of your folks and sisters."

Thankfully, they could all reminisce about Grandma, too, and there was plenty she could fill them in on regarding family members—marriages, kids, travels. She should be able to keep the attention off herself for the most part.

She'd started down the main aisle when she caught a glimpse of a familiar-looking young man in a wheelchair making his way toward a nearby side door she knew led to an outside ramp. She paused as her grandmother's friends continued toward the back of the church.

Drew Everton?

He'd been one of her friends from church and a longtime buddy of Garrett's. Top-notch student. Athlete extraordinaire. But she didn't see any sign of a cast or elevated leg, so what had…? He glanced up and caught her eye, an ear-to-ear grin illuminating his face. Then he expertly spun the wheelchair in her direction.

"Well, look who's here." His eyes smiled as he rolled up to her. "My mom said she thought she saw you, but I didn't believe her."

"Moms are always to be believed. It's me."

"You look great, Jodi." His dark-eyed gaze warmed as he looked her over. "Better than great."

"Thanks. You do, too." A lock of sand-colored hair dipping over his forehead, he was even better-looking than she remembered from the last time she'd seen him when he was a senior in high school. He'd sometimes joined her and Garrett in their youthful escapades, but he didn't have that wild streak Garrett had been known for. He'd been more cautious, a look-before-you-leap sort, a steadying influence that probably kept Garrett out of more serious trouble. "How *are* you, Drew?"

He gave a self-deprecating laugh and motioned to his legs. "I do all right, considering I can no longer chase after cute little gals like you and can't outrun their boyfriends should I attempt to steal a kiss."

She smiled uncertainly. "What happened?"

He shrugged. "A little accident. You think you're in control of your life and the next thing you know, you get your legs knocked out from under you. In my case, literally."

"This is…permanent?"

"It's been my reality for several years, but who's to say? Strides are being made in medical science, and God can always choose to step in. So I'm not giving up hope."

"I admire your attitude, but I'm sorry, Drew. This can't be easy."

A shadow flickered through his eyes. "Far from that."

His attention was caught by something behind her and his expression brightened. "Hey, you! Get on over here before I make off with your pretty little buddy."

She turned as Garrett approached. He nodded to her, and the two men shook hands.

"Did you know Jodi was in town?" Drew studied his friend intently. "You kept that to yourself."

Garrett raised his hands in a gesture of innocence. "I only found out last night. Ran into her by accident."

Drew squinted one eye. "That true, Jodi?"

"One hundred percent." It seemed surreal to be standing here talking to these two grown men she'd known when they were boys, and again she felt that faint sensation of suffocation. Disorientation. "I'll be in town long enough to take care of family business related to Grandma and Grandpa's cabin and then right back out again."

"Maybe we can—"

"Wish I could let you two catch up on old times." Garrett gave them a regretful look. "But Marisela Palmer sent me in here to retrieve Jodi, and I don't want her to come looking for the both of us."

"Scaredy-cat," Drew taunted.

"Guilty as charged." He tilted his head toward Jodi. "Marisela's in the car and waiting."

She and Drew said their goodbyes, then she impulsively leaned over to give him a quick hug.

"Talk about a shock," she whispered to Garrett as

they stepped into the noontime sun and still-crisp air. "I feel so bad for Drew."

Garrett's jaw hardened as he nodded, but he didn't meet her gaze. "Me, too."

"How did you con this poor girl into taking on the Christmas project, Garrett? Shame on you for burdening a visitor with church responsibilities." Georgia Gates clucked her tongue as she gazed at him from across the Lovells' dining table. "When we heard Melody headed off to Texas, we thought for sure you'd recruit Sofia."

Here we go again.

Garrett reluctantly looked up from his half-eaten apple pie to focus his attention on the older woman. Aware that all eyes at the Sunday lunch table were on him—including Jodi's—he placed his fork on his plate and carefully schooled his features to what he hoped was a pastor-like demeanor.

The ink had barely dried on his church contract when it seemed a not-too-subtle campaign commenced to set him up with Sofia Ramos. Is that why all the church ladies he'd talked to yesterday turned down his plea for assistance? They thought if none of them stepped up he'd be forced to call on the attractive single mom?

But they didn't know Sofia's whole story, and it wasn't his to tell.

"I think Sofia's hands are plenty full right now, don't you, Georgia? She's working full-time, and there are Leon's health issues to consider."

"I've always heard," Georgia persisted, with an emphatic nod to the others, "that if you need something done, give it to the person who is already successfully juggling a million things and they'll get it done, too. That's our Sofia."

"It's the holidays, though." Garrett again picked up his fork. "Let's show her a little mercy, shall we?"

Jodi gave him a pointed look as if to convey he hadn't let *her* off the hook for the holidays. But Sofia was the widow of a volunteer fireman who'd been killed on an icy winter road two years ago. She had enough on her shoulders as it was.

"The issue's been settled, Georgia," Dolly chimed in, coming to his rescue. "Thanks to Jodi, who has a big heart like her dear grandma."

Marisela smiled at Jodi fondly. "You probably wouldn't remember—you were only here a few days at Christmas some years—but your grandmother had so much fun helping Melody make deliveries. She loved holding the babies."

"So, then, young lady—" Good-natured Bert Palmer, Marisela's balding, rotund husband, leaned a forearm on the table. "Christmas is two weeks away. What's the plan?"

Startled—and looking prettier in that emerald-green turtleneck sweater than a woman had a right to look— Jodi's gaze flew to Garrett. "I assumed that at some point that's what someone would tell *me*."

"She accepted the role last night, Bert." Garrett set his fork down again with an inward sigh. Forget the pie. "I picked up Melody's notes and checklist from the office this morning, so we need time to sort it out."

"You'll need volunteers. I can help." Georgia smiled encouragingly at Jodi. Then, apparently realizing she'd been asked to volunteer yesterday and turned him down flat, she cut a sheepish look in Garrett's direction. "I can help, Pastor. But I can't take on the whole thing right now. Getting ready for grandkids coming next week, you know."

"I can assist, too." Marisela nodded in Jodi's direction. "I've helped in past years but, like Georgia, I couldn't assume responsibility for it all."

Dolly cut another slice of pie and slid it onto her husband's offered plate. "You can count on me, too, sweetheart. Let me know what I need to do. The young unwed mothers are so appreciative of any assistance they get, and we always come through for them. Baby food. Diapers. Maternity and infant wear. All topped off by a generous helping of things intended to pamper them a bit. I love seeing their faces when they open the packages."

Jodi's gaze, unexpectedly bleak, met Garrett's.

Guilt stabbed. Had he, in trying to get the project off his own overloaded plate, asked her to take on too much?

Unwed mothers.

She still couldn't believe she'd signed on to immerse herself in the world of young women with babies and no husbands. That was a situation she could all too vividly relate to. But she'd given Garrett her word, and Grandma's friends were looking at her as if she were Grandma come back to life.

But Garrett now appeared rather uncertain. Was he having second thoughts about her ability to take it on, thinking she'd let him and the church down?

Despite the initial shock last night, she could handle this. There was no reason she had to spend time *with* unwed mothers and their infants, was there? She'd sit in the overseer's chair and delegate. Her grandmother's friends promised support, as, she assumed, would others. They could be the ones making any required personal contacts.

Holding the babies.

Feeling the phone vibrating in the purse nestled by her feet, she excused herself from the table. In the hallway outside the dining room, she checked the caller ID. Her sister, Star.

"Aunt Jodi?" The giggling voice of her sister's five-year-old, Bethany, came through the earpiece.

"Hi, sweetie."

"Is it true you're a Grinch?" A peal of childish laughter ensued, and Jodi could hear Star whispering something to her daughter as she took possession of the phone.

"Funny, Star."

"I didn't coach her to say that, Jodi. Honest."

"Maybe not. But she overheard that somewhere, and I doubt the source is your ever-lovin' husband."

"Well, if the shoe fits…"

"It doesn't."

"The kids are disappointed that you aren't coming here for Christmas. They were looking forward to you taking them to see the holiday lights at the Phoenix Zoo again this year."

She'd miss that, too. The zoo put on a display of almost four million lights, special shows and rides to delight kids of all ages. Even grown-up ones.

"The thing is, things are really up in the air right now with my job and other stuff, and I told Mom and Dad I'd get the cabin in shape to put on the market while they're in Mexico."

"Which brings me to the reason I called. We're not going to let you spend Christmas all by yourself. Ronda and I and the kids are coming up a couple of days before Christmas."

Her heart sank.

"Isn't that a great idea?" Her sister's voice rose in excited anticipation. "Our hubbies will join us Christmas Eve."

This could not be happening. Not now. Not when she needed time alone. Time to ask God some hard questions and, hopefully, get her life back on track.

"Star, this isn't a good idea. I'm here a limited amount of time to get the cabin in shape. I can't do that with a houseful of kids underfoot." While Star's Bethany could be counted on to behave herself, little sister Savannah was only three and would be at that better-watch-her-every-minute stage. Then there was sister Ronda's four-year-old, Henry, who, from what she'd been told, was still a rambunctious handful.

"We can help," Star continued. "The kids will play outside most of the time, especially if it snows. You do have snow already, don't you? I think I saw that on the news."

"Yes, there's snow, but—"

"Perfect. They can go sledding and build snowmen like we used to do. And what was that game we played with the paths made in the snow? Fox and geese or something like that?"

"Yes, but—"

"Ronda and I were reminiscing last night about all the wonderful times we had at our grandparents' place up there. Amazing summers and fun-filled Christmases. Stringing popcorn for the big tree. Opening grab-bag presents. Finding baby Jesus in the manger on Christmas morning. Remember?" She sighed happily. "We were so fortunate to experience that—something our kids have never gotten to enjoy. Something that they'll never have the opportunity to experience when the cabin sells."

"Star—"

"This is it, Jodi, our last chance." Her sister's voice now openly pleaded. "I know you can pull something amazing together for the kids' sake. Our last big Christmas together at the cabin. One like Grandma and Grandpa used to give us."

Would kids that young actually make any lasting memories from a family get-together at the cabin—or was this a front for her sisters' own nostalgic journey?

Still trying to take in all her sister was saying, Jodi stared blankly down the hallway, then caught movement out of the corner of her eye—Garrett, who'd stepped to the dining room door, his eyes filled with concern.

"Everything okay?" he mouthed.

Oh, sure. Everything was fine. *Just fine.*

Chapter Four

"Thanks again, Garrett, for the loan of the pickup."

Jodi's words warmed him as he sat across from her in a cozy corner of his book-lined church office Monday morning, the soft strains of "Joy to the World" wafting from the open door that led to his now-absent assistant's work area, manned today by Dolly.

The grateful smile of his childhood friend was enough to tempt even the most determined man to re-think his priorities. But being tempted and following through on temptation were two different matters. He'd committed to a plan for his future, and not even Jodi reappearing in his life could stop him now.

Besides, undoubtedly she still thought of him as a big brother. She had no idea how he couldn't get her out of his mind for months after that amazing kiss he'd recklessly drawn her into. How he'd tried to shrug it off. Joke it off. Run other guys off. He'd never forget, either, the shock in her eyes. Big brothers didn't kiss little sisters like that. He'd broken a trust.

Did she think, by his asking her to help on the church project, that he still had designs on her? If so, no wonder she'd looked dazed after he'd all but twisted her arm to "volunteer."

"Rio's more than happy to lend you her truck since she's out of town until Christmas." Having Jodi on foot would have been problematic, but driving her around town and to neighboring communities could only lead to being targets of gossip. So he'd gotten in touch with his cousin Rio—Grady and Luke's little sister—and found a solution.

Jodi shook her head as if in wonder, the burgundy shade of a cable-knit sweater lending an attractive glow to her fair skin. "It's so funny to think Rio's all grown up now. I remember when she was competing at the county fair kids' barrel-racing division in elementary school."

"Twenty-one next spring and still barrel racing."

"Makes me feel old." A shadow that troubled him flickered momentarily through her eyes as she shifted in the wingback chair to look out the window beside them. Rio's red pickup, parked in the gravel back lot next to his SUV, already sported a light layer of snow. It looked like the lingering effects of an El Niño weather pattern were going to make themselves known this winter.

She again turned her attention to him, holding up the compact spiral notebook in which she'd been writing as they'd talked. "It sounds as though there's still a lot to be done."

In the past hour, they'd gone over the budget and checklist, and brainstormed strategies—over which they had opposing ideas—to meet the looming deadline. Not counting today, there were only eleven days until everything had to be delivered before Christmas Eve.

Had his powerhouse office assistant actually thought it could be pulled together in such a short time?

Now he'd unintentionally dumped his own headache on Jodi.

"I apologize for that. Melody's usually on top of things. One of the most organized people I know, and she keeps me organized, too. But with her mother passing away last spring and then trying to keep tabs on her father's welfare from a distance, I don't think her focus was on the project as it usually is much of the year."

"There's a lot of solicitation yet to be done for both monetary and physical item donation. Then supplementary purchases to be made. And distribution."

"That sums it up." He ran his hand through his hair. "You know, though, Jodi, like I said yesterday when you told me about your family coming, you don't have to do this. It's certainly a worthwhile project to help out unwed moms in the area, but Georgia was right. This isn't your responsibility. Church members need to pick up the ball and run with it."

Or *he'd* have to.

He couldn't risk a dark blot on his performance evaluation right here at the end of the year should the annual Christmas project flop. But he'd do all he could not to call on Sofia. Neither of them needed to encourage the matchmakers.

"Grandma's friends said they'd help." Jodi's chin lifted as she offered a determined smile, reminiscent of childhood days when she'd set her mind to something. "I'll make getting funding and donation commitments a priority this week, then leave it to the others if it comes down to that."

He squinted one eye. "From what you shared with

me this morning, though, this is the first real vacation you've had all year. Maybe in several years."

"I'm good with it." She tapped the notebook now on her lap. "I have Melody's cell number, checklist and contact numbers of past donors. I can take it from here."

It sounded as if she wanted him to stay out of the way. Why should that disappoint him? Wasn't that what he wanted—someone else to take over the project and free up his time for other demands?

"Okay, then, if you're sure." He stood to look down at her, noticing how her hair glinted softly in the lamp-light. "Did you want to take a look at the storeroom? See what has already come in?"

"Good idea."

She'd just risen to her feet, standing what some might consider a shade too close, when Sofia appeared in the doorway, a plate of cookies clutched in her hands.

"Oh, I'm sorry." Her dark-lashed eyes widened slightly. "I didn't know you had someone with you. Whoever is covering for Melody today must have stepped away."

She motioned apologetically to the work area behind her.

"We're finishing up." He took a step back, putting more distance between him and Jodi. "I'm going to show Jodi the storeroom where we keep donations for the unwed mothers project. She's going to manage it while Melody's away."

"Oh, really? When I heard yesterday that Melody had to leave town abruptly, I thought for sure I'd hear from you with a plea for assistance." Sofia thrust the plate of cookies into his hands—pumpkin spice, his favorite—then focused a curious gaze on Jodi. "That's very…nice of you, especially considering you're only in town for a short time."

"Blackmailed," Jodi whispered in a deliberately audible aside. "Believe me, someone who has known you since you were a first grader has loads of ammunition to work with."

She cut a playful look at him.

"Come on now, don't give Sofia the impression I railroaded you into this."

"You didn't?"

He had. Sort of. But he'd given her the opportunity to back out, hadn't he? "You said you could handle it."

"And I can." She leaned toward Sofia, mischief still in her eyes. "Garrett and I don't quite see eye to eye on some of the details, so you'd be doing me a great service if you could keep him out from underfoot."

"I think that can be arranged." Sofia's own gaze now teased as she looked up at him.

"Well, then—" Suddenly feeling compelled to escape the confines of the small office, he set the cookies on his desk, then motioned them both toward the door. "Please join us, Sofia."

No way did he want anyone stumbling across him alone in a storage room with Jodi. Where was Dolly when he needed her?

Together they made their way to the wing of the church that housed classrooms and a fellowship hall. In a side hallway, he unlocked a door with a smiling paper snowman taped to it. Then, holding it open to reveal a shadowed, eight-by-twelve shelved space, he flipped on the light.

It was all he could do not to gasp aloud.

Viewing the sole package of disposable diapers sitting on the floor, Sofia looked at him doubtfully. "The cupboard looks pretty bare, Garrett."

Where did everything go?

"Melody took some stuff to the crisis pregnancy center in Canyon Springs earlier in the fall, but it looks as if it hasn't been replenished." As pastor of the church, he should have been more attuned, not let it fall through the cracks. But he'd trusted his office assistant. Last December when he'd started here, the room had been overflowing with holiday baby bounty even before the final push for donations.

"We'll get this room filled," Jodi said matter-of-factly as she stepped away from the door, but not meeting his likely guilt-filled gaze. She probably wanted to throttle him. But he'd always been able to count on her to come through for him when they were kids. Covering for him. Saving him from the repercussions of his own misdeeds and shortcomings.

Apparently, despite the rough-and-tumble tomboy's transformation in many other ways, that invaluable attribute hadn't changed.

He took a relieved breath.

God rest ye merry gentlemen, let nothing you dismay...

"I'm sorry to hear that, Mr. Bealer."

Jodi stared blankly across the room at the cabin's stone fireplace, the phone pressed to her ear. Pete Bealer was the seventh person on Melody's contact list that she'd called following the "enlightening" meeting with Garrett. At the rate things were going, she'd consider herself fortunate to have a single baby rattle to split among the unwed mothers next week. Oh, and that package of disposable diapers sitting in the otherwise empty storage room.

"Wish I could help out but, yeah, it's been a rough year," the owner of the local ice-cream shop continued. "As much as I'd like to, I can't even blame all those artists in town for this one. According to the Chamber of Commerce's findings, they actually drew even more business to Hunter Ridge last summer than the one before. Go figure."

He chuckled. It was nice he could find humor in the fact that his outgo had nearly exceeded his income.

"I heard it was unusually cool late in the summer," she commiserated.

"It was, it was. Near-record rainfall, too. So folks were looking for something to warm them up rather than cool them down. I hear eateries with a fireplace or woodstove did a booming business."

"Well, thank you for your time. I hope things go better for you next year."

She returned the cell phone to her purse, then surveyed the knotty pine–walled, open-plan space—living room, kitchen, dining area—remembering it as much bigger than it was in actuality. Yes, there were two small bedrooms and an attic room that stretched the length of the cabin, but how had Grandma and Grandpa packed them all in here when Mom and Dad, her sisters, and other friends and relatives gathered for a weekend or longer?

It had been a comfy, kid-friendly retreat, with two sofas and several rockers. Folding card tables leaned against the wall for playing games at night. A bookcase filled with classics had welcomed them on a rainy day. And next week the now-silent rooms would be filled once again. But how did her sisters expect her to replicate for their children the delightful Christmases they remembered?

She wasn't Grandma.

A touch of melancholy permeated as she moved to the front window to watch snow flurries dancing through the early-afternoon air. Maybe her sisters were right. She *was* becoming a Grinch. And so much for the phone calls she'd made, trying to drum up a bit of Christmas spirit among potential donors—and within herself. An hour's worth of effort down the drain when she had too many other things to attend to.

"Where," she mumbled aloud, "is all the good cheer and generosity characteristic of the season?" No doubt she'd have had more success with her calls two weeks ago, before credit card bills from Black Friday purchases started rolling in.

She glanced over at the stack of Christmas decoration boxes she'd dragged out of the attic last night, but hadn't the heart to open. It hadn't been her intention to decorate during the brief time she was in town, but with her nieces and nephew coming next week and her sisters anticipating a nostalgic sojourn to the good old days, they clearly expected a little effort on her part.

Maybe if she wasn't trying to manage the church project, clean the cabin *and* prayerfully sort through her tumultuous life, she could handle a little holiday festivity for the kids. Maybe. Playing hostess wasn't one of her God-given gifts.

"How did I get myself into this?" Her voice reverberated through the raftered, wood-floored space.

No thundering voice from Heaven responded to her plaintive query. But then she already knew the answer to how she'd gotten saddled with the Christmas project—and unwed mothers of all things. It came down to the unfortunate fact that she was still infatuated with Garrett McCrae. Dumb. Dumb. Dumb. She was too old for crushes, especially on someone who'd made it clear that kissing her had been the worst mistake of his life.

Are you kidding me? Kissing Jodi would be about as thrilling as kissing our Labrador retriever. And she'd probably double up her fist and belt the first guy who tried.

Her breath caught at the still-vivid memory. After a heart-soaring kiss only a short while earlier, she'd overheard him joking with his buddies later that same night, after the Christmas Eve service. One of them—Richard?—had mumbled something she didn't catch, and Garrett's mocking response brought a round of laughter that she could still hear. Could still feel the hot waves of humiliation that had coursed through her.

Thankfully, neither Garrett nor any of the others had seen her, and shaking all the way to her core, she'd slipped silently away. But it cut deep, making it the worst Christmas of her whole life. The worst, that is, until she lost a baby to miscarriage four years ago this very month.

Looking back now, she recognized that she'd allowed overhearing Garrett and the laughter of the other boys to set her up for a fall when, not too many years later, Kel O'Connor blarneyed her—and her rickety self-image—right into his arms and into his bed.

Jodi clenched her fists. She was *not* going to think about Kel right now. Or Garrett. Not even Anton, although he was an innocent party in all of this.

As she took a step away from the window, she

glimpsed an SUV making its way up the pine-lined lane to the cabin. Garrett. What was he doing here? He hadn't said anything about stopping by.

There was someone in the seat beside him, too. Sofia? No, thankfully it was Dolly. Sofia, although seemingly as sweet as could be, was one of those women who made her overly aware of her own shortcomings in the domesticity department. Those cookies she'd delivered while Jodi was at the church hadn't looked store-bought, but what exactly was her relationship with Garrett that she was stopping by his office in the middle of the morning? Hadn't he mentioned on Sunday that she worked someplace full-time?

"This is a surprise," Jodi said as she ushered her guests in from the cold.

"I told Dolly about the bargain I'd made with you." Garrett unlooped what looked to be a hand-crocheted scarf from around his neck—Sofia's work?—and hung it on the coatrack by the door. His jacket joined it. "You know, how if you helped with the Christmas project, I'd see that you got assistance cleaning this place."

"He bullied you into cleaning, Dolly?" Jodi gave Garrett a look of reprimand as he helped the older woman off with her coat. He'd said earlier that he'd have high schoolers pitch in, not drag one of her grandma's friends into it.

"In case you haven't noticed, he's more of a sweet-talker than a bully. Which is why we've been delighted to have him heading up Christ's Church's ministry." His landlady smiled at him with affection in her eyes. "I told him I'd be happy to help, and he suggested we find out firsthand exactly what you need to have done."

"Well…" Jodi looked around the space somewhat

helplessly. A housekeeper came in once a week in Philly while she was at work, so she wasn't certain what all might be involved in that vaguely mysterious process. Kind of like the baffling nuances of home cooking— that's what delis and restaurant takeout were for, right? "Mom and Dad haven't been here this year, so everything's dusty. And they said they haven't done deep cleaning in years. I've found more than a few cobwebs."

Which she was *not* touching.

"Cobwebs?" Garrett's eyes gleamed. "That must have made your day."

"Funny." She gave him a smirk, then offered an explanation to Dolly. "When we were kids Garrett talked me into going first when we were exploring one of the attic spaces under the eaves, knowing full well spiders had strung their sticky webs across our intended path."

She shuddered at the memory, and Garrett laughed.

"That's our Garrett." Dolly shook her head in amusement. "Is it okay, Jodi, if I take a look around? That will give me an idea of what type of cleaning supplies I need to bring."

"Look to your heart's content. And I'll pay for any supplies."

Dolly disappeared in the direction of the bedrooms and bath. *One* bathroom. How on earth would her family get through next week in a packed house?

Garrett clapped his hands together. "So, how's it going with the project? Have you drummed up any donations?"

Jodi rubbed her hands up and down her sweatered arms to warm herself up. Another thing she'd need to get—firewood. "I made a few calls with little to show for it."

As in nothing.

"I plan to hit it hard this afternoon," she continued, unwilling to admit defeat. "But I may call Melody first. See if she has any tips."

"I remember her saying that some years she'd get more of one thing than another and had to fill in for what came up short."

This year might take a *lot* of supplementing if the results of the initial phone calls were an accurate gauge.

"I'll keep that in mind."

His attention abruptly focused across the room. "Hey, what's all this? Christmas decorations?"

Before she could stop him, he covered the distance to the holiday-designed boxes, crouched down, and popped the lid off one. "Oh, wow. I remember this."

He carefully lifted out a rustic-looking wooden crèche, a good eighteen inches tall and a maybe two feet wide. "This sat on the console table over there, didn't it? And baby Jesus never put in an appearance in the manger until Christmas morning."

"You have a good memory."

She moved to stand beside him as he continued to rummage, reaching in for the Bubble-Wrapped wooden figurines and freeing them from their plastic-encased confines one at a time.

"Remember the year we nearly ransacked this place trying to find where your grandma hid baby Jesus so we could kidnap him?"

"You thought Grandma would pay the ransom in chocolate chip cookies."

"Brats, weren't we?" He lifted up a black-bearded wooden figurine, a wise man cloaked in a turquoise robe. "This guy, he was my favorite. Remember how we'd march them around, making them talk about the star and going in search of baby Jesus?"

"And got them into *Star Wars* battles along the way." She knelt down beside him and picked up one of the sheep. She hadn't seen this nativity set since she left for college. Since before they stopped coming to Hunter Ridge for Christmas when Grandma's health deteriorated.

Frowning, Garrett pawed through the plastic.

She placed the sheep down next to the other pieces. "What are you looking for?"

He dug around a bit more, then sat back on his heels, a solemn look on his face. "Sorry you lost your baby, Jodi."

Her breath caught, a wave of cold flooding her body as her gaze flew to his. How did he—

"Hey, Jode, don't look so distraught." He patted her arm in consolation. "I'm sure baby Jesus will turn up by Christmas Day. He always did, didn't He?"

Chapter Five

❧

"Hey, isn't that Jodi over there, coming out of Dix's Woodland Warehouse?"

At his friend Drew Everton's words, Garrett's attention jerked from the menu at Camilla's Café in nearby Canyon Springs, and he turned to stare out the snowflake-decorated window by their table. It was Jodi all right, bundled against the cold in what looked to be a new turquoise jacket. New knee-high boots, too, which complemented her shapely, jeans-clad legs. As always, that long red-gold hair was an identity giveaway.

"Yeah. That's her." He once again studied the menu in his hands, unwilling to analyze why his heart rate had picked up a notch.

Inching his wheelchair forward, Drew reached across the table to flatten Garrett's menu on the table with the palm of his hand.

Startled, Garrett looked into the amused expression of his longtime friend. "What?"

"You are such a loser."

"What do you mean?" He pried the menu out from under Drew's fingers.

"Jodi. She's back in town after all these years, and you're determined to play it cool."

"There's nothing to play it cool about. Jodi and I are friends. Nothing more."

"Only because you're too dense to make it something more. The last time she came back to town when we were seniors in high school, she was a tomboy caterpillar that crawled out of its chrysalis as a beautiful butterfly. And don't tell me you didn't notice or I'll call you out as a liar, Pastor."

"Her transformation would have been a little hard not to notice," he conceded. "But Jodi and I've been pals since early grade school. I don't think either of us has ever seriously considered the other to be a romantic interest."

That wasn't a lie—as long as *seriously* was thrown in there.

Drew shook his head as he picked up his own menu. "You were so tied up in knots back then when the other guys caught a glimpse of her at the Christmas Eve service, it was laughable."

He had been. Richard was practically drooling and egging the rest of them on to see who could steal a kiss first. He'd had to do some quick thinking to remind them that Jodi was still Jodi—and likely still capable of defending herself. Not that she'd tried to defend herself from him earlier that night, although she probably wished she had.

"I was caught off guard, that's all. Don't tell me you weren't."

Drew snickered. "And you're still caught off guard? Is that the excuse you're going to give for letting her walk out of your life again?"

"I told you, Jodi and I—"

"Hey—" Drew nodded toward the window. "There she is again. Go catch her. Invite her to join us for lunch."

"I don't think—" He didn't relish the idea of her and Drew becoming reacquainted. Sooner or later the topic of how he'd sustained his life-altering injury would come up, and she'd realize her long-ago concerns about her childhood pal's bent toward high jinks and risk taking had sucked Drew into its whirlpool.

"Go get her, Garrett. You know I can't dash across the street." Drew leaned forward. "And if you won't do it for yourself, do it for me. Since you aren't interested in her, maybe I am."

Didn't Drew have enough gals fawning over him already? Enough that, as Garrett knew, it put one sweet little gal who had a serious interest in him at a disadvantage.

Irritated and not meeting his friend's gaze, he got up and stepped outside—coatless—then jogged across the street to the tune of a jolly holiday song played from strategically placed overhead speakers. He met up with Jodi as she reached Rio's truck.

"Garrett, what are you doing here? And where's your coat? It's freezing."

He wouldn't argue with that, but her smile, as always, warmed him.

"I'm having lunch with Drew. We get together every few weeks for guy talk. How about you? Shopping?"

"I am. How do you like the boots?" Gripping a colorful shopping bag in one hand and her purse in the other, she lifted her foot and turned her ankle this way and that to show them off. "Those old ones at the cabin weren't quite my style."

"Nice."

"Shopping is a sideline, though." The wind ruffled her hair, the red-gold glinting in the sunshine. "I actually came over to meet with my Canyon Springs Christian Church counterparts on the Christmas project—Kara Kenton and Meg Diaz, along with the pastor, who is Kara's brother-in-law. I felt a little nervous the whole time, though—Kara looks like her own expected baby could put in an appearance any minute now."

"Maybe she'll have a Christmas delivery." He rubbed his chilled hands together. "How's the project doing here?"

"Great. I have to admit I'm jealous. I made a few more calls yesterday after you and Dolly left, and several said they'd already donated baby stuff to the project not that long ago. I was under the impression it was significantly more than that package of diapers we found in the storeroom."

"Melody may have gotten an emergency call and felt it best not to hold back, thinking she could easily make it up with additional donations." His office assistant had a big heart and didn't like to see anyone in need. "Have you talked to her?"

"I left a message, but no, not yet."

"Well, don't worry too much about it. You're barely getting started." He glanced back toward the café where he knew Drew would be watching his every move. "Hey, I don't know what your plans are for the rest of your day, but Drew and I were wondering if you'd be our lunchtime guest. We'd just sat down when we spied you across the street."

At least his old buddy wouldn't talk about his injuries in front of Garrett. He could be counted on to dodge questions if Jodi asked him outright. Oddly, he and Drew seldom talked about the day they'd been goofing off along the river that had carved out the depths of the Grand Canyon. About how Garrett should have known better. Been more responsible. After all, he was the experienced river guide—one who'd badgered his buddy into a rafting trip.

"I still have a lot to do this afternoon, but that would be wonderful." Her smile widened as she stowed her bag in the truck. "I'd been hoping to touch base with Drew while I'm here."

She had? *Guess I'll play chaperone then. My good deed for the day.* But the thought didn't please him.

Inside the cheerfully decorated restaurant and out of the cold, he helped her off with her coat. She left her woolen scarf draped around her neck as he pulled out a chair for her between him and Drew.

"So what have you been doing with yourself since high school, Drew?" She smiled up at a waitress who handed her a menu.

"College first, then missions work around the globe—predominantly in the Middle East, a region I've long had a heart for. Emergency relief. Digging wells."

"Wow."

"Of course, that was before this." He rapped his knuckles on the arm of his wheelchair, and Garrett winced. "Now I'm active in missions support for quite a few ministries."

Jodi tilted her head in interest. "What's that involve?"

"Prayer, first off." Drew set aside his menu to give her his full attention. "Then constant communication.

Developing newsletters targeted to supporters, arranging travel, setting up sabbatical schedules and overseeing home-front things like financial assistance for missionary kids who are nearing college age."

"That would certainly keep you busy."

Drew grinned, obviously lapping up her attention. "Never a dull moment, that's for sure."

Fortunately, the waitress returned at that moment to take their orders, then the conversation drifted to how Canyon Springs, about thirty minutes from Hunter Ridge, had grown in recent years. A new equestrian center was drawing visitors to special events, the Lazy D Campground and RV Park had plans for expansion, and several new shops were popping up on Main Street. The annual regional charity fund-raising dinner was to take place here in town on Friday night. Garrett's cousin Grady and Grady's fiancée, Sunshine, would be representing the Hunter's Hideway clan this year.

As they ate lunch, the topic evolved into the good old days of growing up in their own small town. There was a great deal of laughter and poking fun as they reminisced, and Garrett felt himself relaxing despite Drew's challenge that if Garrett wasn't interested in Jodi, he himself might be.

His buddy was ribbing him, right?

"So, Jodi," Drew ventured as he poised to finish off his roast beef sandwich, "you said you're here to work on the cabin? That may be the line you're feeding folks, but I have a sneaking suspicion there's more to it than that."

Apparently Garrett wasn't the only one wondering where Drew was going with this, because Jodi raised a startled gaze to his friend.

* * *

Her throat suddenly dry, Jodi reached for her water glass.

"You know," Drew prodded, with a chuckle, "that you might actually have missed me and the good pastor here? That you couldn't wait to get back and renew our acquaintance?"

What was it with her? She had to stop reading things into simple conversation. She'd almost passed out yesterday when Garrett made that remark about her losing a baby. *Baby Jesus*, for crying out loud. She'd taken his words out of context. And being around the pregnant Kara Kenton that morning had filled her with regrets. Why was it all coming to the surface again? Because Garrett was a pastor now—official guardian of all things moral and good?

But jumping to the conclusion that Drew had zeroed in on her inner turmoil? She was losing it big-time. Nevertheless, she managed a laugh. "You caught me, Drew. I haven't had anyone around in years to give me anywhere as near a hard time as the two of you do."

She glanced at Garrett, who seemed to be watching her closely. Had he sensed she hadn't come clean in her glib response to his friend? Looking up at the clock on the wall, she placed her napkin to the side of her plate. "I'm sorry to dash off, but I have a busy afternoon ahead. Sorting to do and more phone calls to make."

Drew gave her a curious look. "Phone calls?"

"I'm soliciting donations for the church Christmas project."

"*Our* church Christmas project?"

She nodded, and Drew slowly turned to stare at Garrett. "I can see what you're getting out of this, buddy. But what's in it for her?"

"He's helping clean the cabin," Jodi said, for some reason compelled to jump to Garrett's defense.

Drew hiked a brow, his tone dry. "*He's* cleaning the cabin?"

"He's making arrangements for someone to," she clarified.

"Figures."

Garrett gave his friend an annoyed look. "I intend to help—delivering firewood and replacing smoke alarms and cleaning out the shed. But the reason she's organizing the project is that no one else at the church would volunteer to do it at this late date, and I have my hands full with other responsibilities."

Drew smirked, then turned again to Jodi. "You didn't have anything better to do with your time?"

"Call me sentimental. I'm told that when my grandma spent the holidays in town, she liked to be involved in this particular ministry."

Drew nailed Garrett with a frown. "You made that up, didn't you? To get Jodi to help."

She laughed. "No, he didn't. Grandma's friends assure me she enjoyed being a part of it. I want to honor her memory by filling in."

Maybe helping would somehow make amends to Grandma, too, for her own failings and unwed state of pregnancy. And win brownie points with Garrett? Good luck with that one.

"That's generous of you." Drew cut another look at Garrett. "But don't go letting this guy take advantage of the goodness of your heart. He may be a preacher now, and with the way God's been blessing the socks off his ministry here, we'll be stuck with him for a good long while. But that's not yet made him eligible for sainthood."

"Far from it," Garrett mumbled the admission.

"I promise I'll keep him in his place, Drew." Amused at Garrett's apparent discomfiture and Drew's obvious glee, she stood and Garrett instantly rose to help her into her coat. "I guess I'll see you two around."

"Guaranteed." Drew's comment was underlined with a smile, but she caught Garrett's unexpected frown.

Garrett lowered his voice as he walked her to the door. "Let's see about getting together tomorrow afternoon. Inventorying what's been donated so far."

Did he not feel that constant undercurrent running between them? That vibe of tension? No, of course he didn't. It was her own one-sided take on things. A pitiful hope that wouldn't die a merciful death. "I'll have to see what my schedule looks like."

Outside, the sun had once again disappeared behind gray-bottomed clouds. She'd enjoyed lunch with the comrades of her youth, but she felt like such a phony.

Drew was devoting his life to aiding ministries worldwide. Garrett was the pastor of a growing church, although she still had a hard time getting her head around *that* one. Both were men living life with faith-filled purpose. They weren't pretending to have it all together. Weren't hiding secrets that stained their soul. Nor were they masking doubts as to God's love or a bone-deep certainty that He was greatly disappointed in them.

She'd just climbed inside her loaner truck and shut the door when her cell phone chimed a tune.

"You've got to jump on this, Jodi." Her friend and

former coworker Brooke Calvetti's voice vibrated with excitement. "I heard today that they're posting two more openings here for project managers. Full-time positions with beaucoup benefits. All virtual. Working from home like I am from wherever you want to plunk down your bod."

Like Jodi, Brooke had worked at SmithSmith since college graduation. In fact, they'd first become acquainted at the company's new-employee orientation. But when a few months ago rumblings started about offshoring their positions, Brooke hadn't hesitated. She'd given notice and was now settling into life at a new company. Unfortunately, her abrupt departure had put more pressure on Jodi to accept a position to train and supervise the new overseas workers.

"It sounds as if you're liking the new job."

"Liking it? Are you kidding me? I love it. You've got to get your application in. Now. With the way the economy's been, people are going to pounce on this."

But where would she go to set up a home base? While she loved Philadelphia, it was a long way from family. She'd had sporadic experience working from home in Philly after starting at SmithSmith—the timing being such that she could conveniently keep her morning sickness under the radar. So she was familiar with the pros and cons of it. Both the freedom and the isolation.

It would be nice not to travel great distances at peak holiday seasons—she hadn't made it home for Thanksgiving in years. Missed some Christmases, too, when planes were grounded in a snowstorm. But even though working from home in the future would mean she might not have to deal with a commute in bumper-to-bumper traffic across the sprawling metropolis of Arizona's Valley of the Sun, the thought of baking-hot summers in Phoenix didn't appeal. She hated being trapped inside air-conditioned buildings, too.

Denver? San Diego, maybe?

"Have you looked at their website?" Brooke persisted. "This company is everything it claims and then more. You owe it to yourself to check it out."

"I'll take a look tonight. I promise." And she would. Sticking her head in the sand hoping that something would change at SmithSmith so she wouldn't have to make a decision would be foolish. As her mother always said, choosing not to make a decision was a decision in and of itself.

"Just think, Jodi, you can move wherever you want to and only have to fly to the corporate office maybe quarterly at most."

That sounded good. Maybe too good to be true. After all, the grass always looked greener on the other side, and Brooke had barely climbed over the fence.

Jodi gazed down Canyon Springs' main street, at the holiday decorations and the bustle of activity. Cities offered so much, but there was something appealing about a small town. At that moment, she spied Garrett and Drew coming out of Camilla's Café and regret tugged at her heart.

If only Garrett hadn't always seen her as his little sister.

If only she hadn't messed her life up when she'd moved to Philadelphia.

If only…she hadn't come back to Hunter Ridge.

Chapter Six

Still no answer. Pausing in the buffeting wind outside the Hunter Ridge Artists' Cooperative midmorning Wednesday, Garrett pocketed his cell phone. Every time he tried to touch base with his office assistant to get further direction on the Christmas project, Melody's number went to messaging. He sure hoped it wasn't because her father had taken a turn for the worse.

Maybe it was just as well, though, that he not be sticking his nose into something he'd relinquished to Jodi's oversight. She might not appreciate his interference. But yesterday she sounded stymied by the lack of progress, and while she told Drew she volunteered to honor her grandmother, she'd graciously refrained from admitting to his buddy that she'd been pressured by *him*.

Pulling open the wreath-decorated door to the Artists' Co-op, a bell chimed as he stepped inside. He was immediately greeted with a friendly wave by Sunshine Carston, his cousin Grady's fiancée, who managed the place and who, after the first of the year, would take a seat on the town council.

"How may I help you, Pastor McCrae?" Her brown

eyes sparkled as she brushed back a strand of shoulder-length jet-black hair. "Christmas shopping?"

"Sort of." He drew in the faint scent of oil paints and leather mingling with a holiday-ish pinch of cinnamon. "Actually, I'm trying to find a replacement piece for a nativity set. A baby Jesus, to be exact."

Just as a backup. Jodi's grandma's figurine would probably be found before Christmas Day. But although he'd teased her about how baby Jesus had always turned up in the past, for a flashing moment Jodi had appeared genuinely distressed when he told her he couldn't find the baby in the box with the other pieces.

"Is it broken? Maybe one of our artists can fix it for you."

"Missing."

"AWOL Jesus. Not good." Sunshine motioned him over to a display glass in the middle of the store. "Something like this?"

He leaned in to study several sets of figurines of the holy family. While striking, unfortunately all held a Southwestern-flavored simplicity rendered in terracotta and turquoise colors. Very unlike the traditional set belonging to Jodi's grandmother. The pieces here, too, were significantly smaller than those at the cabin. Mrs. Thorpe's Joseph was a good nine or ten inches tall. And carved from wood.

"Beautiful work, but not quite what I'm looking for."

Sunshine grimaced. "I hate to lose local business, but you might try an internet search."

"Last resort, but thanks for the suggestion."

He'd just stepped back outside when coming toward him with a determined step was Jodi, her coat hood pulled up against the cold. Their eyes met, and his spirits inexplicably lifted as she came to a halt next to him.

"What brings you out on this blustery day, Jodi?"

She let out a sigh. "I searched all over the cabin last night and still haven't found Grandma's baby Jesus. I can't have my nieces and nephew waking up to an empty manger. My sisters would never forgive me for that. Any ideas on where I might be able to find a replacement?"

He tipped his head toward the Artists' Co-op, but was reluctant to admit he was engaged in a similar pursuit. "You won't find what you're looking for in there."

"I never realized how unique Grandma's set is—and how large."

"Who will take possession of it once the cabin is sold?"

"We wouldn't want to split up the figurines. I guess…" A wrinkle furrowed her brow. "I guess if Mom and Dad don't want it at their place, it would go to Ronda or Star. You know, because they have children who will eventually inherit that piece of our grandparents' legacy."

She didn't look happy about that realization, though, and he wished he hadn't asked. Of the three girls, Jodi always seemed the most fascinated with the elaborate crèche scene even at an early age.

"I don't really have a place in my apartment to put something that big," she admitted. "And I certainly won't if I'm forced to accept an offer to transfer within the company I work for."

"You may be relocating?"

"I've been asked to take an overseas commitment. My company is offshoring a number of divisions, and as a primary project manager for one of those segments, I'm expected to be on-site as well. *India*."

"That's a big change."

"One I'm not real excited about. I've made trips there on business before and think it's a beautiful and diverse country. But living outside the US for any length of time isn't for me." She tucked a stray strand of red-gold hair back under her hood. "I'm one of the fortunate few who are being given an option to remain with the company. A lot of people are being laid off. But I'm beginning to rethink my options."

"I hope it works out."

A sudden gust of wind blew back Jodi's hood and, without thinking, he reached out both hands and pulled it up. Snugged it around her pretty face.

Her startled gaze met his, and lost in the beauty of her eyes, he slowly and self-consciously withdrew his hands. Stepped back. "Nippy out here."

"It is."

Conscious that anyone seeing them might wonder what they were doing standing outside staring at each other, he cleared his throat. "Things coming along on the cabin?"

"Slowly. Grandma's most personal things, of course, were removed years ago. But it's still slow going. Lots of memories to wade through."

"I imagine that's true. Good memories, fortunately."

"I'm blessed in that respect. A lot of families don't have that kind of foundation."

"Your grandma would be very proud of who you've become, Jodi."

She looked to him doubtfully as she braced herself against another blast of wind. "Why do you say that?"

"You're a fine young woman. Mature. Talented. You've worked hard to get where you are professionally, yet family—and God—still play a part in your life and influence your values and decisions."

She ducked her head slightly. Embarrassed at the praise? To avoid the wind? Or maybe he was coming across as too pastor-like, not her familiar childhood chum who'd have been more likely to tease her to tears than heap praises on her.

"I try," she admitted, thrusting her gloved hands into her jacket pockets.

"Will I be seeing you this afternoon?"

She gave him a blank look.

"Remember? Yesterday at lunch? I said I'd help you inventory the donations."

"Oh, right. But I know you're swamped with pastor stuff right now. That's the whole reason you asked me to help out, remember?"

He cracked a smile. "Maybe I'll be ready for a break."

But how wise was it to find excuses to spend time with Jodi? Was he secretly hoping for a glimmer of evidence that her sisterly feelings for him had shifted? But with him preparing to leave town shortly, what could possibly come of it? Too much water under the bridge.

She offered a smile of her own, albeit a slightly tight one. "Whatever works for you."

Maybe the way things ended when they were teenagers still made her uncomfortable. He wasn't enamored with the thought of apologizing at this point, though. That reminder of how he'd overstepped his bounds might make her even more ill at ease.

And if there was anything he didn't want right now, it was to make Jodi uncomfortable around him, brotherly feelings or not.

* * *

Grandma would be proud of her? Not likely.

Jodi carried a stack of baby blankets to one of the tables in the church's fellowship hall and set them down among the other accumulating donations. Grandma wouldn't have turned her back on her, but she'd have been deeply disappointed in her oldest granddaughter. Saddened and hurt that she'd so thoughtlessly distanced herself from her family values and the commitment she'd pledged to God in her early teens.

No, Garrett, Grandma would not be proud.

And what would Grandma now think of the fact that even after the humiliation Garrett had dealt her when she was sixteen, she couldn't get him out of her head a dozen years later? She felt skittish around him. Acted weird. He'd merely done something nice this morning in pulling her windblown hood back up, yet she'd frozen like a deer in the headlights. He'd probably helped her get her hood back on dozens of times when they were growing up. Of course, back then he'd have pulled it down over her face.

But it was ridiculous to be crushing on him at her age. And even if he did show interest, there was no way once he learned of her past, discovered the status of her faltering faith, that he'd remain interested. Besides, she still hadn't figured out where Sofia Ramos fit into the picture.

Jodi stepped back to survey the tables and clear her head. Where should she start? When she had arrived at the church after lunch, Dolly said Pastor McCrae was out of the office, so hopefully she could get this stuff sorted and inventoried before he put in an appearance.

"You're here already." Garrett strolled into the fellowship hall as he peeled out of a leather jacket, then draped it over the back of a folding chair next to her. He smelled enticingly of the fresh, cold outdoors.

Ah, well. Best-laid plans. "I wanted to get this done as quickly as possible so when I start making calls again, I can provide better suggestions for what's really needed."

He put his hands on his hips, his brows tenting. "When I recruited you, I genuinely thought it would be a slam dunk. Needing only to be tied up with a pretty bow."

"Well, we'll get to the pretty bow stuff eventually, but right now it looks like I have my work cut out for me." At his glum look, she hurried on. "I've worked on lots of other projects and it always seems you reach a plateau point. You know, where the goal looks to be entirely out of reach. Not going to happen. Then suddenly it all comes together."

With a little over a week before delivery time, though, they'd better start moving off the plateau soon.

"We do have a budget of sorts to supplement. There are members of the community—like Sawyer Banks, owner of the Echo Ridge Outpost—who don't know exactly what to buy and who've made cash contributions. Once we get this inventoried, we can do some shopping."

We? He intended to help inventory the donations and go shopping with her, too?

She'd brought her laptop and pointed to it. It was opened to a document with a boldly typed header: Christmas Project. The cursor blinked in silent anticipation. "Do you want to announce the items we've received as I type a list? Or vice versa?"

"Vice versa, I think." He pulled up a folding chair. "I'm not sure I'd know what half of these things even are."

And *she* would? Except when she'd all but been drafted into pitching in with her nieces and nephew when they were infants, she'd avoided tiny kids at all costs. Being around them only brought regret and heartache.

"Okay, then, you type. And we'll make an educated guess on the things we're not sure about."

He settled himself in front of the laptop, fingers poised over the keys, then shot her a heart-stopping grin. "Ready when you are."

As she went from table to table, naming off the items, bits and pieces of conversation of a more personal nature interspersed. He asked for an update on her folks—were they still teaching at the university? Taking mission trips during the summer and holidays? Yes to both.

He asked about her sisters—where they and their husbands lived and worked. How old their children were. In turn, she inquired about his family and received a rundown on the members of the extended Hunter's Hideaway clan, as well as a catch-up on his younger brother Marc and sister Jenna, now a single mother who'd only recently returned to town.

The conversation drifted comfortably along, a nostalgic reminder of times the two of them would shoot baskets or hang out on the front porch playing games or make improvements to their woodland fort. Back then they'd talk for hours on end about anything that popped into their heads. The conversation today likewise meandered.

Then, out of the blue, Garrett asked if she was seeing anyone, and the easy banter came to a halt. Was he hoping to set her up with one of his buddies? Drew, maybe? She held no delusions that he was asking on his own behalf.

She picked up one of the packages of baby bibs and inspected it, although it was an item she'd already called off to him. "Not at the moment."

She cringed inwardly, realizing that response would give the impression she was available for whomever he had in mind.

"I haven't dated for some time." Although that was an admission she'd have preferred not to make, she plunged on. "But that's by choice. I'd previously been seeing a man—a missionary to Mexico—through my church in Philly."

It was a church that she should have gotten involved with when she'd first moved there. If she'd surrounded herself with other believers from the very beginning, maybe none of the things that had shaken her world down to its foundations would have happened. But she'd already been drifting away during college, and afterward she'd been so busy acclimating to city life and her new job—and then she'd met Kel O'Connor...

"Anton and I corresponded and got together whenever he was back in the States. His family lived in Philadelphia, too."

"That didn't work out?"

Because of her. She'd met Anton a year after Kel and the baby, when she'd in desperation begun going to church again. And although he was a wonderful guy in so many ways, she'd dragged her feet when he expressed an interest. The following year when he was in

Philly, she'd been forced to turn him away when he'd wanted to marry her.

How could she have married him without telling him the truth about herself? About the baby? About her still-flatlined faith even though she warmed a pew each week?

"No, it didn't work out. It was for the best for both of us. But then…then he died last month." Two years after she'd sent him away, but his sister had provided the details. "There was a medical emergency in the remote village his team was working in and he volunteered to hitchhike out to bring help. But those who picked him up robbed, beat and murdered him. All for the few pesos in his pocket."

His empty, discarded wallet, she'd been told, held a photo of the two of them.

"Oh, man, Jodi." Garrett rose and came to her side to place a comforting hand on her arm. "I'm sorry."

She took a ragged breath, turning the package of baby bibs mindlessly in her hands. "Here was a man who served God so faithfully, who was endeavoring to be God's hands and feet in a place most wouldn't choose to set foot in. I've asked so many times—where was God that day?"

"I know how hard things like this are to understand." A distinct sadness filled his eyes. Compassion for her, or a wound of his own? "This isn't how God intended His creation to be. Granting mankind free will to love Him—or not—has come at a high cost. But it doesn't mean He's abandoned us."

"But why lose one of the good guys? It seems so senseless."

"It does. But we can't allow circumstances to dictate to us what *appears* to be a truth about God. We *can*, though, choose to believe what God tells us is the truth about circumstances. That He will never leave us or forsake us. That Christ *is* coming back. That's a fact. And one day He'll make everything right again."

"I wish I had your faith."

He gave her arm a reassuring squeeze. "It only takes belief the size of a mustard seed to please God, Jodi. Belief that He exists and that He's a rewarder of those who seek Him. I think your…friend…had that kind of faith."

"He did. And more. Anton was happy doing what he believed God wanted him to do." But if she'd agreed to marry him, might he have chosen a less dangerous mission in which to serve? Might he still be alive today if she'd been courageous enough to risk telling him about her shadowed past? "At least it's comforting to know he died doing what he wanted to do. And lived his life with passion and purpose."

"But it doesn't take the pain away, does it? Or the questions."

She shook her head. "No."

"I'm sorry for your loss, Jode. Even though you said things hadn't worked out between the two of you, I know this hurts."

"It does. In fact, it's one of the main reasons I came to Hunter Ridge. To have time to work through things. The job. Anton. Not just to fix up the cabin to sell."

"Then I saddled you with this." He motioned to the tables. "I'd be happy to check around again for another volunteer."

"Please don't. I think it's actually helped to have something else to think about occasionally."

He looked at her doubtfully. "You're sure?"

She nodded. Then tossed the package of baby bibs to the table. "Let's finish things up here so I can get back to the cabin and start making more phone calls."

"Or…" A smile tugged at the corners of Garrett's mouth. "We *could* go shopping."

Chapter Seven

Heading out of town to the discount warehouse in Canyon Springs, it felt a little odd having Jodi in the passenger seat beside him and Dolly in the back acting as guardian of his reputation. Although Jodi offered her the front seat, Dolly waved a paperback at them and insisted she didn't want to stop reading. If she sat in the front, she'd feel obligated to join the conversation, and she *had* to find out "whodunit."

That was Dolly for you. Come rain or shine—or a snowy day like today—this past year she'd been ungrudgingly willing to serve as chaperone as needed, even if it wasn't personally convenient. But, while appreciated, the need for one had become increasingly stifling—and doubly so since Jodi's return. More like he had a warden.

At least the roads were good today, although the roadside and forest floor were layered in white. Snowflakes danced in the air as another squall passed through. Interspersed with brief bouts of blue sky and sunshine that warmed the blacktopped surface, days like this made winter a bit easier to bear.

He glanced in the rearview mirror at Dolly engrossed in her book, then at Jodi who was quietly gazing out the side window at the passing snowy world.

He didn't know why he suggested they go shopping for the Christmas project this afternoon. Shopping would be better done next week when they had a true handle on what was still needed. But while he was only somewhat concerned that they wouldn't meet their collection goal for the project, Jodi seemed especially troubled by her lack of progress. He didn't like the thought, either, of her retreating to an empty cabin to make phone calls while the memories he'd stirred up about the loss of a former love were fresh in her mind.

When telling him about her job, how it was being relocated overseas, she'd stated that she didn't want to live outside the country. Had that played a role in keeping the two apart?

"Oh, look! An elk." Jodi's face brightened as she pointed out the window, and sure enough, through the tall-trunked pines he glimpsed a male elk with an impressive set of antlers moving among the trees. "There were two deer behind the cabin this morning. I hope they come back while my sisters' kids are here."

"I never tire of seeing them myself," Dolly chimed in before disappearing once again into her mystery.

Garrett and Jodi exchanged a smile, and a sense of contentment burrowed into his soul as they continued to talk about wildlife, the beauty of the Arizona mountains, the blessings they'd shared growing up—if only part-time for Jodi—in Hunter Ridge. Funny, but for a long time he hadn't seen the town—or his return to it—as much of a blessing. But somehow that perspective seemed easier to embrace as the months in his new position passed by. As he chatted with Jodi about it, re-lived memories, a deep sense of thankfulness took hold.

She peeped over at the SUV's speedometer and grinned. "I see you're still lead-footed, Pastor."

He eased off the gas pedal, enjoying the sound of her laughter. "Remember when I first got my license when I turned sixteen and took you for a drive?"

"I do. You already had a reputation for drag racing, and I think Grandma was down on her knees in prayer the whole time we were gone."

He chuckled. Having Jodi around these past few days had been good for him. Like now, they often fell into old patterns of talking about anything that they felt like talking about. Teasing each other. Challenging each other. It was an easiness he hadn't often felt except when around family members once he'd walked through the formal gates of pastoring a church. With Jodi, though, he could let down his guard and be himself, something he had to be cautious about with church and community members—especially single women.

He tried to live a transparent life, not to put on a fake pastor-y persona, but with Jodi's return, he could now see how much he'd come to subconsciously weigh each word, each action. Of course, there were those who clearly thought he could work a little harder at being "pastor-like," unable to recognize how much he'd already reined in his naturally exuberant personality.

When they arrived at the discount warehouse, Dolly pried herself away from her book to join them, but quickly disappeared into the cavernous space with her own oversize shopping cart.

As he and Jodi strolled down the wide aisles with merchandise of every assortment towering high above their heads, an unfamiliar sense of domesticity thrummed through him. People passing by, seeing them each at the helm of a cart and hearing their discussion as they filled the baskets, might easily take them for a couple. A married couple.

He shook the thought from his head as Jodi held up a package of—what did she call them? Onesies? Infant wear, they looked to be.

"Some of these?"

He nodded. "What do you think? Ten packages? Twelve?"

"Twelve. We didn't have many of these among the donations." She counted them out and put them in her cart, then checked them off their list.

And so they proceeded among the display tables and racks, filling her oversize cart with clothing items for newborns through toddlers. Then stops to load up on baby wipes, lotions and other assorted paraphernalia soon filled his.

It was fun—and kind of funny, actually, as neither had a clue as to what a baby might need if it hadn't been for Melody's checklist.

Laughing as they rounded a corner in search of Dolly, a firm voice halted them in their tracks.

"Well, *Pastor.* You two look to be having a high old time."

Randall Moppert, accompanied by his wife, Leona, swept a disapproving gaze from Garrett to Jodi and back again.

"We are indeed, Randall. Almost as much fun as the night I TP'd your house." Now where'd that smart-aleck response come from?

Curly-haired Leona giggled, then abruptly halted

when her husband, his graying mustache twitching, sent her a squelching glance. But her eyes still smiled. The woman had to be a saint to have lived with Randall all these years.

"Serving as a minister of God requires a certain level of decorum, Mr. McCrae. You'd do well to remember that." Randall's beady eyes narrowed as he motioned dismissively to their laden carts. "And what's all this anyway?"

"The church's Christmas project," Jodi inserted, not caring for the man's tone of voice as he reprimanded Garrett. She'd encountered him at church a number of times, usually when he was complaining about something. "Gifts for unwed mothers."

His smirk and the arrogant raising of his thick brows did nothing to endear him to her. "I've never approved of that annual effort myself—rewarding promiscuous young women for getting themselves in a family way."

His words pierced, and Jodi lifted her chin slightly to meet his condemning gaze. "They didn't get that way all by themselves."

He snorted. "Nevertheless—"

"We're supporting them, Randall, not rewarding them," Garrett said evenly. "They've chosen to honor the sanctity of life and not have an abortion. And we reach out to them because that's what Jesus would have done."

"I think it's a nice thing to do," the man's wife said softly, ignoring her husband's shriveling glare.

The man leveled a look at Garrett and Jodi. "Which doesn't, however, explain why the two of you are gallivanting off by yourselves in a neighboring town. A single pastor and a single woman."

"They aren't gallivanting off by themselves, Randy." Coming into view as she pushed a filled cart around the corner, Dolly smiled benignly at the old curmudgeon. "They brought me with them so I could shop while they attend to church business."

While Garrett's insistence on not being alone with her had irked Jodi, now she could see the wisdom of it.

Looking somewhat taken aback—his hopes obviously thwarted from laying a misdeed on the doorstep of his pastor—the man tightened his grip on his shopping cart. "I guess we have *something* to be grateful for, then."

Dolly nodded. "We can always find something to be thankful for when we take the time to look for it."

Apparently not quite sure how to take her comment, he glanced at his wife. "Let's get on with this shopping. It's already taken too much of our afternoon."

When the couple departed, Jodi exchanged a glance with Garrett and Dolly, but none of them said any of the words they were no doubt thinking. How miserable that man must be, scrutinizing every innocent nook and cranny around him for evidence of questionable behavior. And his poor wife…

It was only when they were back in Hunter Ridge unloading Garrett's SUV in the church parking lot, the sun now sinking behind the towering ponderosas, that she reopened the topic.

"That Randall person had no business behaving so disrespectfully to you."

To her surprise, Garrett chuckled as he lifted two oversize bags from the back and handed them to her, not appearing the least bothered by the other man's disparaging remarks. "Randall Moppert is one of the church members who can't get beyond who I was as a teenager."

"From your comment to him, I take it you targeted his house for TP-ing?"

"By accident."

"Randy needs to let that go." Dolly took one of her own shopping bags from Garrett. "You've more than proven yourself to anyone who's allowed God to open their eyes and soften their hearts."

"Thanks, Dolly. But coming from a woman who's all but adopted me, you're probably a little biased."

"I know a good thing when I see it. This church has a future as long as you're at the helm."

A flash of uncertainty flickered through Garrett's eyes, then he ducked his head slightly. Uncomfortable with the praise?

"I appreciate your appreciation, Dolly."

He hauled out three more bags, then motioned for the ladies to precede him to the door leading to the fellowship hall. While she and Dolly arranged the purchases in the storeroom, Garrett made several more trips out to his SUV.

"Looks like that about does it." He looked on approvingly as they accepted the last of the bags and added the contents to the growing stacks of items. The storeroom still wasn't full by any means, but they were getting there. "Did you want me to drop you off home now, Dolly?"

"No, I've called Al. He's going to pick me up, then we'll go out to eat since I wasn't home this afternoon to prepare anything. I'll wait inside until he gets here."

Garrett stuffed his gloves in his pockets. "Tell him I owe him. Big-time. A man who sacrifices his supper so his wife can babysit their pastor has a special place in Heaven."

"You know I'm more than happy to do it." She patted the bags sitting on the floor beside her. "I finished up my own holiday shopping and got a few things for Christmas dinner to boot."

"Well, there you go."

Jodi liked the way Garrett returned the older woman's smile with genuine affection.

Dolly tilted her head to look up at him. "You could walk Jodi to *her* car if you want to make yourself useful. It's almost dark."

"Oh, I'm fine," Jodi piped up. She'd need to brush off the snow that had accumulated while she'd been gone and didn't want Garrett to feel obligated to help with that when he had other things to see to. On the return trip, he'd mentioned conducting a marital counseling session early that evening for his cousin and his fiancée. He said that although Grady had originally balked at having his *single* relative instruct him, Sunshine had confidence in Garrett's ability to share the truths of God's word, and she'd proved quite persuasive in getting Grady signed up.

"I'm more than happy to do that." Garrett gave a nod to Dolly as he pulled on his gloves again.

Faint light lingered in the west, silhouetting the tree branches overhead as they stepped into the parking lot. The temperature had dropped considerably since leaving town earlier that afternoon, and Jodi tugged at her hood to snug it more closely around her face.

"Brr!"

"Brr is right," Garrett agreed as he turned up his own collar and gave her a lopsided grin. "You'd think this was the middle of December or something, wouldn't you?"

She laughed.

He shared a smile, then motioned to the truck as they approached it. "Rio has a snow brush or ice scraper, I take it?"

"She does, but you don't have to—"

"Pop on in there and get the heater going while I make short work of the snow."

Another gust of wind came out of the north, so it didn't take much to persuade her. She handed the combo brush and scraper to Garrett, then he slammed the door shut and she started up the truck. Flipped the defroster on full blast.

He worked quickly, brushing the snow off the hood and headlights, then made his way around to the taillights. It took a bit longer, though, even with the help of the defroster, to clean the windshield and back and side windows. To the rhythm of the scraper, she held her hands out to the heating vents and watched him in the dim light as he expertly sliced away the frozen snow that had almost melded itself to the glass.

She felt special, having someone like Garrett help her on a night like this. He was a good man. One any woman would be fortunate to have in her life. But dreams like that were for people who had time on their side. Time to get to know each other. To build bonds. For people who shared a mutual affection for each other—not a one-sided infatuation.

A wave of melancholy filled her heart as she continued to watch him, her mind drifting back in time.

Back to that night when she thought, for a single, bliss-ful moment, that maybe he felt something for her, too.

Abruptly, Garrett rapped on the driver's-side win-dow, startling her from her reverie. He'd finished clean-ing the windows and was motioning for her to roll hers down.

Cold from the open window swept into the cab. "Thanks, Garrett. Now you'd better get yourself in-side before you turn into an ice cube."

"Actually, I was wondering...do you have plans for dinner?"

Her heart stilled. "Tonight, you mean?"

"Right now. I have to eat earlier than usual so I can get back to the church. Do you already have plans?"

"Not really. I thought maybe I'd warm a can of soup."

"Then join me. How's the Log Cabin Café sound? Or Rusty's Grill?"

"We can do that?"

A crease formed between his brows. "What do you mean?"

"I mean, *you* can do that? Go out to eat with me with-out Dolly riding shotgun?"

He laughed. "I can—*if* we walk. You know, if we're out in the open where people can keep an eye us. Are you up to that? It's only a few blocks, but it is bitter cold out here."

What would it hurt? It wasn't like it was a date or anything. They both had to eat, right? And if he didn't think showing up with her at a local dining establish-ment would sully his reputation, well, who was she to argue?

"Actually, my stomach's still on Eastern Time, so I'm starving."

"Then let's do it."

He handed her the scraper, then let her roll the window back up and turn off the truck before swinging the door open.

Once outside, he guided her to the sidewalk in front of the church, and they headed toward the main road through town. The steadily falling snow by turns danced, then whipped, around them depending on if they were walking in the open or alongside a building or sheltering stand of pines.

Except for the occasional gust of wind, it was a quiet evening, most people with any sense having decided to stay close to hearth and home. But this was kind of fun, too, walking beside Garrett as the snow crunched under their boots, a snow glow overhead and halos encircling the streetlights.

If only she could stop shaking.

Not from the cold, but from nervousness. Excitement. How silly. She'd enjoyed visiting with Garrett on the drive to and from Canyon Springs. They'd indulged in quiet moments and a fun-filled time of renewing their acquaintance as they refreshed memories. But she wasn't sixteen anymore. This wasn't a date. They were just two old friends grabbing a bite to eat. Nothing more.

Garrett jogged her elbow. "So does Rusty's sound good to you?"

"Perfect. I haven't had his barbecue since the last time we—"

Abruptly her mind flashed back a dozen years. After a morning's hike on snowy trails, they'd eaten there for lunch on Christmas Eve. Her. Garrett. Drew. She'd had no idea that not too many hours from then, Garrett would back her into a corner of Grandma's cabin mudroom and kiss her almost senseless.

Had *he* known? Planned it? Maybe even plotted it with Drew or any number of his other buddies looking for a good laugh at her expense? She glanced toward Garrett, but he was focused ahead as they neared the little restaurant.

"—not since you, Drew and I ate there," she finished, the shaking anticipation now replaced by an unexpected heaviness in her chest.

"That's right. Christmas Eve." He smiled at her. "I'd forgotten we had lunch together that time you were in town."

That time she was in town…and the last time she'd let herself hope that Garrett might return her feelings.

Chapter Eight

Although he'd eaten at Rusty's Grill plenty of times in the last twelve years, it hadn't changed much since Jodi would have last been here. Its labyrinth of rustic, beamed-ceiling spaces made for a homey atmosphere, with flickering lanterns anchored to beadboard-paneled walls and woven plaid tablecloths accenting the stoneware dishes.

From where they sat at a small table near one of the fireplaces, Garrett leaned forward to get Jodi's attention.

"How's your barbecue?"

She glanced up from toying with her mason jar water glass. "Delicious."

But for a woman who'd claimed to be starving, she hadn't eaten a whole lot of her sandwich or sweet potato fries. His were long gone. "Are you feeling better about the Christmas project now? I mean, after we did that shopping today?"

"Yes, thank you. Those added items take some of the pressure off."

"I don't want you to feel pressured, Jodi." Without thinking, he slid his hand across the table to cover hers.

She lifted startled eyes and drew her hand from his. "I didn't mean it like that. I just meant it's good to know we have our bases covered. Somewhat, anyway."

He pulled his hand back as well and quickly glanced around the room at the other diners. Had anyone seen him reach out to her? But there weren't many people this early in the evening, and no one seemed to be paying them any attention. "We still have over a week. It will all come together."

"And next year Melody will be back and you'll be off the hook." She offered a smile as she pushed her unfinished plate slightly away from her.

He nodded to it. "Are you going to eat the rest of that, or would you like a to-go box?"

She glanced down, looking almost surprised to see over half of one of the best pulled-pork barbecue sandwiches in the state still sitting in front of her.

"It's very good," she said quickly, as though she needed to reassure him. As if not eating it might have hurt his feelings. "Yes, a box would be great. Thanks."

"Sure you don't want dessert? This place makes a mean pumpkin cheesecake, remember?"

She laughed, and the tension in his shoulders eased. He still wasn't quite sure how the comfortable atmosphere that lingered after the trip to Canyon Springs had become stiff and stilted by the time they'd settled in at Rusty's. Maybe she'd started thinking about that Anton guy again?

She shook her head at him, intimating he was as dense as a rock. "How could I forget Rusty's signature holiday cheesecake? I ordered one and you and Drew pulled out forks and proceeded to devour most of it when I had to slip off to the ladies' room."

"Then I owe you one."

He reached for the dessert menu, but with another shake of her head, she clasped her hand to her stomach. "Thanks, but I'm going to pass this time. There are already too many sweet temptations this time of year."

And speaking of sweet temptations…it was time he let this one get on home so he wouldn't be late to Grady and Sunshine's counseling session. He'd looked forward to extending his time with Jodi after the shopping trip, inexplicably happy that she'd agreed to go to dinner with him. But maybe it had been a bit too much togetherness? When you've exhausted your repertoire of shared memories, maybe you discover that's all you had?

He placed his napkin on the table. "Ready to go?"

She nodded, but before either could rise, a firm hand clapped him on the back.

"Well, look who's here."

Garrett turned to see a grinning Travis Hunter, cousin Luke's son, looking down at him as if he'd been let in on a big secret.

How old was he now? Sixteen? Seventeen? A good-looking kid, the unruly layers of hair brushing his shoulders always bringing a smile to Garrett. The boy's ex-military father had thrown in the towel on haircuts to keep the peace, just as Garrett's dad had been forced to do.

Garrett nodded to his young cousin, who was with his longtime girlfriend. A petite brunette with a pixie haircut and an abundance of eyeliner, she was a sweet, down-home gal despite her trendy looks.

"I can't believe you're still hanging around with this dude, Scottie."

Her smile widened as Travis gazed down at her. *Young love.* Had he looked at Jodi like that twelve years ago? So transparent? So...*goofy*?

He quickly made introductions, making sure he emphasized *old friends* so Travis wouldn't get the wrong idea and go running back to the family with what he might think was a scoop. It was bad enough having the teenager stand there grinning at them, his gaze bouncing from Jodi to Garrett and back again.

Garrett caught Jodi's eye, and they both stood.

Travis frowned. "You're leaving?"

"I have an early-evening counseling session with your Uncle Grady and his bride-to-be."

Travis laughed. "Sunshine's a quick learner, but you might have to schedule some remedial classes for him."

"I'll keep that in mind."

Eager to escape Travis's too-observant eye, Garrett motioned to Jodi, who preceded him to the front of the restaurant. Fortunately, she'd stepped around a corner before Travis gave him an exaggerated wink and a thumbs-up. No doubt he'd have some explaining to do at the next family dinner.

He settled the bill, fending off Jodi's insistence they split it as a thanks for her help. In the lobby, he assisted Jodi with her coat, then held the door open as they stepped into the still-frigid night.

"Look, Garrett. Isn't that beautiful?"

His gaze followed the trajectory of hers upward, where the clouds had parted to reveal a dark window of sky. There, a single star glittered.

Without thinking, he leaned in to whisper in her ear. "Star light, star bright…"

Surprised, she turned to him, her eyes questioning.

He pulled abruptly back and pushed his hands into his jacket pockets as they started down the street. "Don't you remember that? How we'd sit out at night, competing to see who'd spy the first star?"

Maybe he could get her reminiscing again. Back to a comfortable conversation such as they'd shared earlier.

She rolled her eyes. "Get your story straight, mister. That was the first *shooting* star."

"Oh, yeah. That's right."

They walked on in silence for some time, snow crunching under their boots. The wind had died down while they were in Rusty's, so it wasn't a half-bad walk back to the church.

He stopped and turned to her. "Do you remember… naw, you wouldn't."

He moved off again, and she had to hurry to keep up.

"What?" She punched him lightly in the arm. "What wouldn't I remember?"

"You know, that afternoon we charged our sisters a quarter each for a cup of lemonade from the pitcher we'd sneaked out of your grandma's refrigerator."

She laughed. "Of course I remember that, silly. When word got back to Grandma, the next day at lunch she charged us a quarter for a sandwich, a quarter for chips and a quarter for a glass of milk."

"Lesson learned the hard way, huh?"

"We learned a lot of our lessons the hard way," she agreed.

He sure knew he had.

They entered the parking lot all too soon, and at her

truck he waited for her to click the key she fished out of her pocket. The headlights flashed, then he opened the door. "Your coach awaits, madam."

With an almost shy smile, she curtsied, then climbed into the vehicle. The wind, fortunately, had served its purpose, keeping the windshield clear of snowfall since his earlier scraping.

He stood at the door, looking in at her. She was beautiful in the faint overhead snow glow, her hair spilling loosely around her shoulders. "I had a good time today, Jodi."

She gave him an uncertain look, as though not sure if she could agree or not. "I…did, too."

"You know you'll be the talk of the breakfast table at Hunter's Hideaway tomorrow morning, don't you?"

"Travis, you mean?"

"Guaranteed." Realizing he'd leaned a bit too close, he took a step back. "Guess I'll be seeing you tomorrow."

"Tomorrow?"

"Or maybe the next day. I said I'd clean out that shed for you, right?"

"If you have time."

"I'll make time."

He slammed the door, then moved away as she started the truck. The headlights came on, and with a parting wave, she backed out of the parking place and headed home.

He stood there in the dark for a full minute, then strode toward the church. Yeah, he'd make time.

"Thank you, Mrs. Garver. I'll be by to pick them up this afternoon." Thursday already. A week from tomorrow they'd make the delivery, so every donation counted.

Jodi checked another name off the list, but her happy dance around the room was soon interrupted by a knock at the side door. She turned down the CD player and hurried through the mudroom, then opened the door to Dolly.

"Come in, come in. Good news! The manager of the discount store donated three car seats. Diamond Grocery has promised formula. And Garrett's Grandma Jo is pitching in *again* with a few infant carriers that she ordered online. They should be here tomorrow."

"You're making headway."

Not as much as she'd like, but it was a start.

She helped Dolly with her coat, hung it up, and then followed her into the kitchen.

"How'd you get here, anyway?" Jodi asked. Dolly didn't like driving on icy roads if she could help it.

"Garrett."

"He's here?" She hadn't heard a vehicle, but after that last phone call she'd cranked up the volume on the Christmas music. "Is he here to clean out the shed? He'd mentioned yesterday that he might be over to do that."

"He brought a ladder, so I think he intends to clean the gutters. Those things fill with pine needles faster than you can blink an eye. Al bought us those covered ones last year. Worth every dime."

Jodi cast an anxious glance toward the refrigerator. "I'm not sure I have anything here that will make him a decent lunch. The two of us can have yogurt and fresh fruit, but that's not very substantial for a man."

"He's not staying long. He has to get back to the church. But either he or Al will pick me up later."

A twinge of disappointment that Garrett couldn't stay long caught her by surprise. He'd told her last night that he'd had a good time yesterday. He hadn't elaborated, though, so it might not mean anything more than he enjoyed a chance to get out of town. Or got his kicks shopping for baby stuff.

She'd had a good time, too, until the past intruded on her thoughts as they neared Rusty's. That uncomfortable meal was her fault. But the reminder of the last one they'd shared there offered a precautionary prelude to the evening—*guard your heart, girl.*

"So where should we start, Dolly? Bedrooms?"

"Let's turn the mattresses and pull everything out of the closets to sort through. Then if there's time, we can clean the floors. In the meantime, let's throw in a few loads of bedding for your visitors. Wash up the curtains, too."

"I think the flannel sheets are in the hall closet. Grandma kept those as a special treat for us in the wintertime. There was nothing more wonderful than cuddling into their toasty warmth."

They'd barely gotten started when she heard the back door open, the sound of boots stomping on the floor mat and the voice of an approaching Garrett echoing down the hall.

"Jodi, do you have any—hey!" He stood in the doorway, sock-footed but still bundled against the cold. "Let me do that. Neither of you should be manhandling a mattress."

He shooed them out of the way, then maneuvered into the room to make short work of flipping the mattress.

Dolly clasped her hands and brought them to her heart. "Our hero."

A grinning Garrett posed in a classic bodybuilder stance.

"Show-off." Jodi playfully poked him in the stomach, and he pretended to double over. "We could use your talents in the room next door, too, Mr. Muscle."

Eyes still smiling, he straightened up. "Lead on."

After turning the mattress in the adjacent room, he joined her in the hallway. "Do you have any garbage bags? You know, the big kind for yard work."

"I think I can accommodate that request. This way."

In the mudroom she opened a lower cabinet door, pulled out a box and handed it to him. "Voilà!"

"Exactly what I was looking for."

"Dolly says you're cleaning the gutters?"

"Yeah, and I want to get a replacement section for one of the downspouts. It's fairly beat-up. Looks, too, as if a few shingles need to be replaced."

She made a face. "The cabin's falling apart."

He laughed. "No, it's not. This is just a standard part of home maintenance. It's all good."

"I'm glad you know what you're doing. I sure wouldn't. You're a pastor of many talents."

"Bible College 101. Ark maintenance."

She folded her arms and leaned her hip against the counter. "Sometime, I want to hear about that. You know, how it all came about."

He quirked a smile. "God called. I came."

"Surely there was more to it than that." If she didn't know better, she'd think he was being evasive. But why would a minister be evasive about what led him to his Lord?

"Thanks, again." He lifted up the lawn bag box in acknowledgment, then moved to the door where he pulled on his boots.

"Garrett?"

"Yeah?" He looked at her, an almost wariness in his eyes.

That had to be nothing more than her imagination. He had a lot to get done in a short amount of time and probably didn't want to pause for a long conversation.

She'd halted him in his tracks, delayed his departure, but did she really have anything worthwhile to say to him? Or was she being stupid again? Once more forgetting this was the guy who'd broken her heart. Who'd be disappointed in her if he ever discovered her secrets.

"We got more donations."

Did she also imagine the relief in his eyes?

"Awesome. I told you things would pick up, didn't I?"

"You did. But we still have a long way to go. I'm securing a few car seats this afternoon, but we don't have many of the other big-ticket items like high chairs. Or strollers. Or portable cribs."

She wished she didn't sound like such a Debbie Downer. He'd put her in charge so he wouldn't have to deal with the details. But he'd also told her if she didn't want to do this, he'd find another volunteer. Is that what she wanted him to do?

No. He was helping her get the cabin ready to sell, and she'd keep her part of the bargain.

She squared her shoulders. "I'll make more phone calls throughout the day today and will do my best to emphasize the need for some of those items."

"Sounds like a plan." He gave her a thumbs-up, then once more turned toward the door.

"Garrett?"

He paused again, and it was all she could do not to flat-out ask him what had drawn him away from the river. From the passion that had possessed him since he was a teenager. Had there been a woman involved?

"What's up?"

"I—just want to thank you again for all you're doing to help me with the cabin."

"You're welcome."

He winked. And was out the door.

Chapter Nine

"I'd forgotten your grandparents had so much kid stuff." Garrett, standing inside the small metal shed in back of the Thorpe cabin early Friday afternoon, surveyed the shelves while Jodi peered in from the doorway. He spied a wooden swing Jodi's grandpa made that used to hang from a big oak's limb. A basketball, football, kickball, baseball and bat. Toboggans. He'd agreed to sort out the stuff for Goodwill from the stuff that had seen better days. He'd need to air up a few balls and test for slow leaks.

Jodi smiled. "They loved being surrounded by their grandkids and the children of friends—like you. They'd have been so happy to know that great-grandchildren will be spending time here at the holidays."

Putting the cabin on the market was no doubt on her mind. He knew it weighed on his, and it didn't even belong to his family. If he hadn't had other pressing plans, if the church had wanted to keep him on a permanent basis, maybe he'd buy it himself. Keep it in the family, so to speak. But there was no point in mentioning something that wasn't to be.

On impulse, he grabbed the bright red toboggan that Jodi had been pulling the night he'd discovered her alongside the road. Then he reached for a blue one and stepped out of the shed.

"What do you say we give these babies a test run? Make sure they're still safe for your nieces and nephew?"

"I'll leave that adventure up to you."

"Come on now. The Jodi I knew as a kid would have knocked me into the snow to be the one to make the first run. At least come with me. If I break my neck, I want someone to call 911."

"I can do that."

Together they hiked through the snow up a gentle series of rises behind the cabin. When they finally reached the top of their favorite sledding spot of bygone days, Garrett dropped the toboggans to the ground. Sunshine earlier in the morning had melted the surface snow somewhat, then as the temperature dropped again it refroze into a crusty layer. Not an easy run for beginners, but then they weren't beginners.

"Red or blue?"

"Excuse me? I'm here as a first responder only, remember?"

"We both know you're backing out because you don't think you can beat me down this hill."

She huffed her disagreement. "You think so, do you?"

He straightened both toboggans to face downhill, then lowered himself onto the blue one. "I know so."

She kicked a spray of snow at him, and he ducked. Then, laughing, he adjusted his stocking cap and made himself comfortable, readying for the flight downward.

"You're already a poor loser, and you don't even have the guts to give it a shot."

"I don't have anything to prove." She folded her arms as she looked down at him, determined to stand her ground. "I don't want to risk ruining my new coat."

"Sissy."

"Say whatever you want. I'm not doing this."

"Chicken." He made soft clucking sounds, his grin deliberately taunting. That pushed her over the edge.

"Okay, smarty-pants." She grabbed the red toboggan and pulled it a safe distance away from him, then climbed aboard. "We'll see who's laughing hardest when I beat you by a mile."

"Oh, yeah?" He gripped the steering cord as she settled on her toboggan. "Well, Jode, what do you say we make this competition worthwhile. Whoever loses has to eat three pieces of Old Mrs. Bartholomew's fruitcake—without drinking any water."

Jodi made a face. "No way."

"Afraid you'll lose?"

She slanted him a derisive look as her hands tightened on the cord. "You're on."

Satisfied, he grinned again, loving it when the competitive tomboy in Jodi surfaced. "So you're ready?"

"Ready."

"Then…one. Two. Three. Go!"

It took them both a moment to push off, then the toboggans quickly began their descent, picking up speed. He was the heavier of the two, which might have worked to his advantage. But a quick glance in Jodi's direction—at her determined face as she leaned forward and attempted to shift her weight to keep the toboggan on a straight course—told him he wouldn't be coasting over the finish line first if she had anything to say about it.

"Woo-hoo!"

He laughed at her cry of delight as the ponderosas flashed past them in a blur. That icy crust on the snow had them flying now. And it was harder to steer. The wind whipped off his knit cap, chilling his ears, and her hood fell back, freeing her hair to fly behind her in a silky curtain.

Beautiful. But a bump drew his attention back to manning the toboggan beneath him, his gaze focused ahead on the path running by a lightning-struck ponderosa that had always marked the finish line. When from the corner of his peripheral vision, he detected she was losing ground to him, he let out a whoop of triumph—only seconds before Jodi cried out.

"Oh, no!"

He shot a look in her direction, where a slight rise in the course had apparently shifted the trajectory of her toboggan as they neared the homestretch.

She was coming right at him.

Before he could maneuver to escape the inevitable, she plowed into him with enough impact to topple them both into the snow, a jumble of arms and legs.

With snow melting down the back of his neck, he managed to sit up and reach out to Jodi, who'd collapsed across his legs. "You okay, Jodi?"

"I'm sorry, Garrett." Her words came unevenly as she fought to regain her breath. "I hit a bump and a patch of ice and I couldn't stop it."

"But you're okay?"

His heart hitched as she turned to him, eyes radiant and cheeks flushed, her hair sparkling with snow as if with glittering stardust. She looked more than okay to him.

"Yeah. How about you?"

"It takes more than a pretty woman knocking me off my feet to keep me down." At the uncertain look in her eyes, he jerked his transfixed gaze away. Dumb thing to say. Brothers didn't make a habit of telling sisters they were pretty. Or at least he hadn't told his own sister that much. Not until recently when he knew she could use a boost. "Let's see if we can get ourselves untangled here."

It took several attempts, but with his assistance she was finally able to lift herself off his legs and, freed, he regained his footing, then reached down to clasp her outstretched hand.

"Easy there. Slick here."

She'd barely made it to a standing position when her footing gave way and she pitched forward into his chest, her arms flying around him to stay upright. He managed to remain standing, his hands gripping her upper arms to hold her steady.

And then she looked up at him, eyes wide, her face mere inches from his.

"I'm sorry…Garrett." To her dismay, her words came out a breathy whisper as she looked at him. Up close, the depths of his stormy gray eyes were even more amazing than she'd remembered.

For a long moment they stared at each other. Was his breath as ragged as hers, his heart pounding a little faster, too? She hadn't been this close to him since she was sixteen. Since that night when…

"Jodi?" he whispered, his head lowering slightly.

Heartbeat accelerating, her gaze dropped to his mouth, then back to his eyes as the moment stretched unbearably. Was he going to kiss her again? Right now? *And then what?*

Go tell his buddies like he'd done before, that kissing her was akin to kissing the old family dog? With every ounce of strength she could muster, she pulled abruptly from his arms and stepped back, feeling as dazed as he looked.

"I think I have my footing now. Thanks."

"Uh, sure."

She deliberately looked away, searching for the toboggans where they'd skimmed a number of yards farther down the slope. "So was it a tie? Or are you going to claim victory on grounds of interference?"

Her voice sounded halfway normal. The challenging words of her tomboy self emerging despite feelings far to the contrary of those long-ago days.

Garrett rolled his shoulders as he stuck his gloved fingers down the back of his coat collar and pulled out a fistful of snow. "I was unfairly assaulted in the homestretch. A win was as good as in my pocket, so I hope you enjoy the fruitcake Mrs. B's already delivered to my folks."

"Get real." She trudged toward her toboggan, careful of where she placed her feet. She didn't dare risk him trying to help her up again, even though it had to have been her imagination that he was about to kiss her. Garrett wasn't the type to make the same mistake twice. He'd made it quite clear that kissing her the first time had been a major one.

How dumb was she, anyway?

He jogged a ways up the slope to retrieve his cap,

then made his way to his own overturned toboggan. "I suppose we could call it a tie. Or—" He jerked his head in the uphill direction from which they'd come, his gaze challenging. "We could have a rematch."

"In your dreams." She picked up her toboggan. "I'm freezing. You're not the only one who got a collar full of snow. And chicken clucks won't hold any weight this time, so you can keep those to yourself."

He chuckled as he hefted his own toboggan. "Guess we'd better get back to work, then, before Dolly calls out a search-and-rescue team."

"Don't feel obligated. I'm sure you have more than enough to do this close to Christmas. Shut-ins to visit, counseling to do and a Sunday message to prepare."

He popped himself lightly on the forehead with the heel of his hand, then started down the slope, avoiding her gaze. "Thanks for the reminder. I need to give my all to those while I can. They'll soon be a thing of the past."

Struck by the abruptness of his words, she hurried as best she could across the snowy expanse to keep up with him. "What do you mean, a thing of the past?"

"When my contract concludes at the end of the month, I'll be moving on."

Her heart stilled. Dolly and Drew seemed to think Garrett's position was a permanent one. In fact everyone talked as if that was a given. "But I thought—"

"I haven't wanted to say much about it…" He cut her an uncertain glance.

"Are you saying you've turned down a contract? Or do you mean the church isn't extending you one?"

"No contract extension has been offered."

Were the board members crazy? From what she'd

seen, Garrett was the best thing that had happened to this church, to the town, in years.

He forced a smile. "It wouldn't matter if they offered one anyway. I came here knowing it was a temporary position, a layover while I prepared for my next phase of ministry. I'd been against coming here in the first place, but my Grandma Jo can be very persuasive."

Why hadn't he said something about this earlier? And why was he telling her now? Because he suspected she'd wanted him to kiss her and had to set things straight? "What are you going to do?"

"Mission work."

She halted, her breath catching as Anton's face flashed through her mind. Then she scurried to again catch up with him as he neared the pine that would have marked the finish line. She tugged on his sleeve and he paused to turn to her. "Outside the country?"

His gaze darkened, as if suspecting she might not approve. "Middle East."

A wave of nausea coursed through her. A dangerous—not a *potentially* dangerous—destination.

"It's been in my heart for years," he continued, "since I first gave my life to God. Now it's time to do something about it."

Now? Right when she hadn't seen him in twelve years and still found herself foolishly harboring a secret hope that maybe they'd both shown up in town at the same time for a reason?

"I'm…happy for you." Was she? Really? The ache in her heart said otherwise. "But I'm shocked your contract isn't being extended. You're so right for this church. From what I hear, you've made a difference in so many lives, bringing young people into active participation and injecting a new energy into the church's ministry."

"Thanks. I'd like to think the past twelve months haven't been in vain."

"They weren't. Which leaves me puzzled as to why you're being let go."

He grinned. "Believe me, Jodi, it's no mystery to me. There's a lot that's gone on behind the scenes that you know nothing about. Not all can look beyond my teen years—the drinking, the pranks, the attitude."

"Randall Moppert?"

"Among others. But for my part, coming under leadership authority has been a struggle at times. I'm learning, but admit I do have a mind of my own. I haven't always done things by the book. Haven't exactly been a poster-child pastor. It hasn't come as a surprise that there's been no talk of a contract renewal."

"But I think a lot of people are expecting you to stay on."

"Which is all the more reason, if you wouldn't mind, to keep this to yourself for the time being. I don't want this parting of ways to cause a division in the church between those who might want me to stay and those who can't get rid of me fast enough. I haven't mentioned it to many, and right now I'd like to focus on what lies ahead and not look back."

"I understand."

All too well, in fact. God had a plan for Garrett's life that clearly didn't include her.

Each lost in thought, they crossed the snowy ground leading to the old shed and put away the toboggans. Then she left Garrett to weed out the sports equipment as she headed back to the cabin and Dolly, her heart heavy.

What if she took Brooke's advice, though, and sought out a position with a new company, decided to work from home—could she perhaps work from Grandma's cabin in Hunter Ridge? There would be no worries about Garrett being her pastor. No reason to confess her relationship with Kel or about the pregnancy or her waffling faith. While Garrett wouldn't hold the former two issues against her, what would a minister do with an old friend whose faith had long ago hiked into the sunset?

Back in his office late that afternoon, Garrett stared out the window at the lightly falling snowflakes, unable to focus on his Sunday message preparation.

He'd almost kissed Jodi.

But this time she'd seen it coming and gotten herself out of the way. What was wrong with him? Jodi didn't want her "big brother" kissing her. She hadn't twelve years ago, and she didn't now. Which is why he'd blurted out his plans to leave Hunter Ridge to set her fears at rest.

She seemed taken aback by that news, but it eased the tension-filled atmosphere and diverted his thoughts from how good it had felt to hold her for those brief moments. To gaze into the depths of her eyes, remembering their first kiss and wanting from the very depths of his being to bring about a second.

Fortunately, Jodi's brain had still been functioning even if his hadn't been.

"Hey, Garrett, have a minute?"

He looked up to see Sofia standing in the open

doorway, Tiana and Leon in the background crowded around Melody's desk, which was currently occupied by Marisela Palmer.

"Come on in." He rose and moved to the seating area, motioning her to sit down. "What's on your mind?"

"I need a man's point of view," she said, lowering her voice as she glanced almost furtively in the direction of Marisela and the kids.

"What's up?"

"Drew."

"Ah." With Sofia, it always had something to do with Drew. He eased himself down into the chair opposite her.

"I learned from Mel Benito, who sometimes serves as an aide to Drew, that Drew's parents will be in Hawaii of all places on Christmas Day. It's a spur-of-the-moment thing—his mom's well-to-do best friend from college lives there now and sent them airline tickets."

"And?"

"I'd like to invite Drew to my folks' place for Christmas dinner." She took a deep breath, then rushed on. "Has your family already invited him?"

"At Hunter's Hideaway, it will be business as usual in the inn's main dining room midday and enjoying a more private affair in the evening. You'd both be welcome to come to that."

"I'm not saying your family needs to invite him. Or me. I was merely wondering if—"

"If he already has plans? His folks being gone is news to me, but I know they're his only family hereabouts since his brother and sister moved away. So all I can say, Sofia, is if you'd like to invite him to your parents' place, do it. Now. Once word gets out that he's on his own for the holiday, he'll be inundated with invitations."

"I know." Her mouth took a downward turn. "Every unmarried woman within miles will be calling him. Their mothers and grandmothers, too."

"Make yourself one of them, then. The first."

Her forehead creased. "But what if he says yes to my invitation, then someone he'd rather spend the day with calls later? He'd be stuck with me."

Garrett frowned. "Sofia Ramos, no man in his right mind would consider spending time with you as being stuck. Trust me on this."

"I don't want to look pushy like a few of the other women."

"He won't think it's pushy. I imagine he'll appreciate joining a family for the day. I've seen him around your kids, and he seems to enjoy them."

She rose to her feet, a determined look on her face. "Okay, then, I'll do it."

"Don't delay."

When she and her children departed, he moved again to stare out the window. *Open Drew's eyes, Lord.* When had his buddy gotten so thickheaded about women that he couldn't see what was right in front of him?

Of course, he should talk. Except for a short-lived relationship with river-running cohort Bena Darden that ended disappointingly when she couldn't deal with the U-turn his life took after Drew's accident, few women he'd dated since the night he'd kissed Jodi measured up. He'd gotten himself stuck, for whatever reason, in some teenage time warp. Probably, just like Drew, he'd obliviously passed up a dozen women who'd have made exceptional life partners.

After coming close to kissing Jodi today, it was definitely time to get a grip and move on.

Chapter Ten

"**Y**our family arrives when, Jodi?" At the conclusion of Sunday's worship service, Marisela rose from the pew beside her. "Christmas Eve?"

"Actually, the day before that, although my sisters' husbands will drive up on Christmas Eve."

"I know you're looking forward to seeing all of them."

She was—and she wasn't.

She'd been in Hunter Ridge a week now, and she'd accomplished so little that she'd intended to get done. Even with Dolly pitching in and with Garrett's occasional assistance, the place was in no way ready to put on the market. This week, too, she needed to make further headway on the Christmas project, submit an online application to Brooke's new company, and somehow get the house readied for a family gathering—one that would make a lasting memory for her nieces and nephew.

"It's been a year since I've seen them," Jodi couldn't help adding wistfully. "It's a good thing my sisters send photos or I probably wouldn't even recognize the kids."

"Your grandmother certainly would have loved that you're all getting together. Just like old times."

"She would."

Marisela nodded toward the front of the church as chatting people secured coats and headed toward the doors, eager to get to a noontime meal. "Wasn't Garrett's message good this morning? That young man is exactly what this stagnating congregation needed. I foresee a bright future for Christ's Church."

Obviously it hadn't crossed her mind that church leaders were thinking otherwise.

"Yes, a very good message." And it had been. Given that he hadn't even started on it when he'd left following their toboggan run, it was especially amazing. Another clear indicator to her that Garrett's God-given gifts were being put to good use here. But who was she to say God didn't have a plan for him elsewhere?

Marisela's husband, Bert, leaned in. "Would you like to join some of us for lunch again? We'll be heading to the Log Cabin Café."

"Thanks. I'd love to, but there are quite a few things I need to see to. Time is flying by so quickly."

"Don't drive yourself too hard. That's one of the dangers of our modern holiday season. No time to stop and smell the Christmas tree. You don't want to overdo and come down with one of those colds that are going around."

She sure couldn't afford to get sick. Although, if she came down with a cold, that might keep her sisters and their offspring at bay...

When she stepped out into the bright sunshine, amazed at how quickly the snow was melting from the sidewalks and parking lot, she couldn't help but notice the chatting cluster of people surrounding Garrett. His cousin Grady with a woman Jodi presumed to be his fiancée, Sunshine. A couple she remembered as his Uncle Dave and Aunt Elaine, the latter whom she'd heard was battling breast cancer. Drew, too. And *Sofia*, of course.

It seemed every time she turned around, a smiling Sofia was at Garrett's side. Which made her imaginings of Garrett's intention to kiss her a few days ago seem even more absurd. Of course he hadn't been about to kiss her after they'd collided on the snowy slope. Why would he settle for his tomboy childhood playmate when a perfect pastor's—or missionary's—wife always appeared to be hovering at his elbow?

Petite. Feminine. Soft-spoken. She was a musically gifted and culinarily talented woman with two sweet children who would tug at any man's heartstrings.

Jodi altered her course to give the grouping a wide berth, but had just reached her pickup when Garrett jogged up.

"Hey, Jode. Have a minute?"

She held up an index finger. "One."

"Then let me make good use of it."

He glanced back at family and friends who were still visiting with each other, and Jodi caught Sofia's lingering look in their direction before she turned again to Drew.

"What's up?"

"That load of wood I promised? Sorry I haven't gotten back with it yet. My sermon prep wasn't coming easy yesterday and time got away from me. I figured you wouldn't appreciate me banging around out back at eleven o'clock at night."

"No, I wouldn't have. But the time you took for the morning's message paid off. So no complaints here."

"You liked it?"

"I did." But once again, the words of his message had hit their unintended target. Or at least unintended by Garrett. God might have had a hand in hitting the bull's-eye painted on her heart, though. Why was it so hard to believe, as Garrett had shared, that God wanted His children to forgive themselves, just as He had forgiven them?

"Anyway," Garrett continued, "if it's okay with you, I'll swing by this afternoon and drop off the firewood."

"Whatever's convenient, but you may want to bring someone along to help unload and stack." *Sofia, maybe?* "I'll be out most of the afternoon."

He raised a brow in query, but she didn't feel inclined to explain her planned run to Canyon Springs while the roads were clear. She'd thoroughly explored Hunter Ridge last week, trying to find a replacement for Grandma's missing baby Jesus, but to no avail. A few phone calls to the neighboring town, however, turned up a possibility at a little gift shop that was part of a hotel and restaurant there. Kit's Lodge.

"I can do that." He scuffed the toe of his shoe in a crusty patch of snow. "So…do you have your tom all picked out?"

"Tom?"

"Tom turkey. For Christmas dinner. Grandma always says one day of refrigerator thawing for every four pounds, so keep that in mind. A twenty or twenty-five pounder for that crew you're expecting could take five or six days—or more."

She laughed. Who did he think he was talking with

here, Rachael Ray? "I'm not cooking a turkey. You know me better than that."

He clasped his hand to his heart. "I thought you were supposed to be delivering a Christmas just like your grandma used to give you and your sisters."

"I did come across her roasted butternut squash recipe. One for corn-bread dressing, too. And ginger apple cranberry sauce. But if I'm not messing with a home-cooked turkey, I don't see any point in burning the kitchen down trying to make side dishes or risk an ER run for family-wide food poisoning. My sisters can live with catering from Diamond's grocery store. After all, when I was back for Christmas last year, we all went out to a nice restaurant. The kids won't know the difference."

"Are you kidding me? That kind of substitution borders on sacrilegious."

She shrugged. No doubt Sofia could fix a turkey with one hand tied behind her back. Probably home-made rolls, too. And mashed potatoes without lumps. "Christmas dinner is all about people, right? And Jesus, of course. You know what the Bible has to say about those whose god is their stomach. Road to destruction and all that."

"I think you're taking that out of context."

"So sue me." She opened the driver's-side door and slid in behind the steering wheel.

"This isn't over, Jodi. You owe it to those kids to give them a real taste of old-fashioned Christmas."

"Not. Going. To. Happen." She pulled the door closed and started up the engine, unable to keep a straight face at Garrett's look of dismay. With a cheerful wave, she backed out of the parking space and headed off for lunch and a bit of shopping in Canyon Springs.

But she couldn't help but look in her rearview mirror as he stood there starting after her, then abruptly turned away and strode back to Drew…and Sofia.

Jodi was having Christmas dinner catered.

Garrett stacked a final armful of split, seasoned wood in an iron rack located not too far from the back porch of her grandparents' place. Close enough to bring a few logs inside as needed, but not close enough to harbor bugs and critters that might like to slip inside the cozy cabin.

Catered. That was almost blasphemous in small-town America, wasn't it? She'd made reference to a kitchen burning and food poisoning, but surely she was underrating her culinary skills. She'd been living on her own for years back in Philly. Surely she hadn't existed solely on cream cheese, pretzels and cheesesteak.

Jodi was messing with him. That's all.

He returned to the back of his SUV a few more times, hauling the remaining armfuls of wood to the side porch to get things started when Jodi's family arrived. Generously donated by his folks, the entire load was a bit more than needed for the following week. He covered the larger stacked pile with a canvas tarp to keep the wood dry, then, back at the SUV, he shook wood chips out of the heavy plastic sheet with which he'd lined the back interior, rearranged things neatly, and secured the tailgate.

He glanced at his watch. Four thirty. Not too much longer and the sun would set, but no sign of Jodi. Where'd she gotten off to? Not that it was any of his business. But the temperature was dropping, and from the looks of the sky, another snow system might be moving in. Big brothers had to look out for little sisters.

He bit back a groan. Little sister. Right.

As he opened the driver's-side door, he glanced back at the cabin. A lot of good memories had been made here. He could see why Star and Ronda wanted to share them with their kids before the place sold. Why they counted on Aunt Jodi to make it happen.

Yeah, Jodi was just messing with him with all that talk of catering Christmas dinner. She had every intention of pulling out all the stops for her nieces and nephew but, Jodi-like, was giving him a hard time.

Shaking his head, he climbed into his vehicle and fastened his seat belt, unable to suppress a grin at how she'd had him going.

But just in case it wasn't all talk, he'd better come up with a backup plan…

Jodi came home empty-handed.

The baby Jesus of a size similar to her grandma's set sold out before she got there. When she'd called on Saturday, the person she'd talked to hadn't been inclined to sell any of the nativity pieces separately. After all, what other customer would want to purchase a crèche without the star of the show? She'd have had to buy the entire set, which she'd been prepared to do. But with three still in stock, she hadn't had the foresight to ask them to hold one for her.

At least Kit's Lodge offered a fabulous Sunday menu and, when a very pregnant Kara Kenton and her husband, Trey, saw her coming out of the adjoining gift shop, they invited her to join them for lunch. Kara said their church was still receiving generous donations, so hopefully—even if Christ's Church fell short—there would be more than enough when they combined their projects.

But now on Monday morning, Jodi was back to searching the cabin for the missing baby Jesus. She couldn't have the kids racing down the stairs on Christmas Day to an empty manger. That would give them a memorable Christmas, all right. Jesus a no-show.

But where had He gotten off to?

Once again she emptied out the box that held the crèche and figurines, the pieces now arranged on the console table, but with no success. Maybe she'd find Him in one of the other decoration boxes. But even though she and Dolly had thoroughly cleaned the bedrooms and main room, she wasn't ready to drag out all the holiday trappings to look. She didn't even have a Christmas tree for the kids yet. Star and Ronda wanted a live tree like Grandma always had—one with a root ball that could be planted on the property in the spring, which meant a trip to the local landscape nursery.

Wandering into the kitchen, she looked down at her lengthy to-do list on the countertop and shook her head. She'd known she'd be busy getting the cabin ready to put on the market, but where were the hours she'd hoped to fill with quiet contemplation? Time to weigh the pros and cons of relocating overseas or leaving SmithSmith altogether. Time to finally come to terms with the impact Kel, Anton and her unborn child were having on her life.

Time to get right with God.

In all honesty, though, despite the initial confusion that had dogged her on the flight to Phoenix and the shuttle ride up the mountain, the choice to leave the company she'd worked for the past five years now seemed like a no-brainer. Submitting that application to the new company tonight would be one decision off her mental checklist. Only one hundred more to go.

If she worked hard and stayed focused, maybe she could get the project donations finalized and things ready by Wednesday evening for her family's arrival. Thursday afternoon would be spent with volunteers to wrap the donations, but she'd have Thursday morning mostly to herself. A long walk in the woods appealed, or maybe time in front of a crackling fire with a cup of hot cocoa. She needed time to catch her breath before her family descended on her.

At the sound of a familiar tune, she reached for her cell phone. Garrett. One more thing she hadn't bargained on when returning to town—renewing a teenage heartbreak.

"Hey, Jodi. Did you see I got the firewood delivered yesterday?"

"I did. I was going to call and thank you." Just not right away. She needed to put more distance between them. "I have someone coming to inspect and clean the fireplace chimney today. Then I'll bring in the logs and have it all ready to light when my family walks through the door on Friday."

"Good deal." There was a long pause, which she didn't rush to fill. "Will you be coming in to the church today? A few folks dropped off baby stuff after yesterday's worship service. They set it just inside the door of my office, but I can move it to the storeroom if you'd like."

"Thanks." She couldn't avoid Garrett forever, but the

fewer one-on-one encounters they had, the better her aching heart would feel.

"When do you plan to get your volunteers together to wrap and label the packages?"

"Thursday afternoon. Then delivery to Canyon Springs Christian on Friday morning."

"I may ride along with you ladies. I can do any heavy lifting, and there are a few things I'd like to talk over with the pastor there. Jason Kenton's served as a mentor of sorts since I took on this interim position."

Jason was also a young man holding a responsible church leadership role in a town in which she understood he'd spent his teen years and who had probably dealt with challenges similar to Garrett's. Undoubtedly Garrett had shared his plan for mission work with Jason, just as he would have with Drew.

She'd need to show more interest in that. Ask more questions. But not now. She wanted to get off the phone and back to her never-ending list. Find a tree. Shop for more grab-bag gifts and a gender-neutral present to be drawn by one of the adults. Place the Christmas dinner order at Diamond's grocery.

And that was just the bare beginnings of what stretched ahead of her before she'd be ready for Christmas Day.

"Jodi? You there?" Garrett's voice drew her back to the present.

"Yeah. I'm here. Just have a lot on my mind—and my to-do list."

"Well, then, I'd better let you get back to it. I still need to stop by, though, to replace those old smoke alarms. When did you say the chimney guy is coming? I could time my visit for when he's there."

"She. Chimney gal. And I'm not sure when she'll be arriving. We kind of left it open-ended for when she can work me into her schedule."

"Okay… I'll see what I can figure out."

Poor Garrett. Jumping through hoops not to be in the company of a lone woman. Maybe that's why things hadn't progressed more rapidly with Sofia? How *did* a single pastor get one-on-one time with a potential mate, anyway? While she'd rather not have him drop by today, she took mercy on him. "I can call you when she lets me know she's on her way."

"You'd do that?" The relief in his voice was evident. "I have the new alarms and a stepladder, so I'm all ready to go."

"Don't forget to bring me the receipt so I can reimburse you."

"Yes, ma'am!"

No doubt had she been able to see him, she'd have caught a brisk salute. "See you later, then."

"You, too."

But for a long moment, neither hung up, the silence between them stretching uncomfortably. It was as though he wanted to say something more—and she was expecting him to.

"Bye," he finally offered.

"Bye."

Then the line went dead.

Chapter Eleven

Garrett secured a new smoke detector in the ceiling of the second bedroom, thankful he'd thought to check them out earlier. Timing this chore with the chimney sweep's visit had worked out well.

"How's it going?"

He glanced down at Jodi standing in the doorway, and his heart did a betraying tap dance. In a pair of fitted bib overalls and a long-sleeved emerald T-shirt, her hair pulled back in a long braid, she looked bright and perky this afternoon. She'd made herself scarce since his arrival. Whether avoiding him or attending to other more pressing matters, he couldn't be sure. If it was the former, though, he had only himself to blame for that near-miss kiss. No wonder she seemed skittish around him.

He descended the ladder. "Just about done."

"Kriss is coming along with the chimney, too. It's taking longer than she thought it would. I guess it's been quite a few years since the folks had it cleaned out."

"Good to get it attended to, then. All safe for your family's arrival."

She nodded, then started to turn away.

"Jodi?"

She paused. "Yeah?"

What could he say to her that would ease the awkwardness between them? He sure couldn't tell her how he felt about her. How he'd felt about her since he was eighteen. Not a cool confession coming from someone she thought of as a big brother. Blurting that out would only further distance her.

"Um, never mind."

Something akin to disappointment flickered through her eyes. What had she hoped he'd say? That he valued her in the same way he did his younger sister? That everything was exactly as it had been between them as kids?

But he wasn't about to lie.

Which left him with nothing to say.

She nodded, then disappeared down the hallway to return to the main rooms. He carefully folded the stepladder, gathered up his tools and tossed the decrepit smoke alarm into the box with the others. When he'd made a few trips out to his SUV to secure his equipment, he returned to the cabin where Jodi was sorting through items she'd pulled from the cabinets and drawers and spread out on the kitchen counter.

Her nose wrinkling, she held up one item and waved it at him. A blue plastic device with a handle on one end and an oval-shaped opening on the other. "I don't even know what this is."

He approached to take it from her, unable to suppress a smile as he turned it over in his hands. Then he reached for an unopened glass container of jelly. "This, my dear girl, is a jar opener. You place the little lip under the rim of the lid like this, then lift it up like that and—" A soft popping sound confirmed the seal had been broken. "Voilà!"

He easily unscrewed and lifted the lid.

Her expression brightened. "Grandma was a sucker for those gizmo catalogs and kitchen shops."

He surveyed the items on the countertop. "It does seem she has a showroom's worth of gadgets right here."

"You're getting ready to leave?"

"Need to be on my way."

"Do you think I could get your help with one more thing?" She made a hopeful little face. "I don't want to take advantage of your time, but when I was up in the attic where the kids will be sleeping, I noticed it's really cold up there. Outside air seems to be creeping in around the windows."

"Let's take a look."

"Kriss?" Jodi called to the woman who was barely visible in the fireplace's yawning opening. "I'll be right back."

A muffled response indicated her announcement had been heard, then they headed to the narrow staircase that led to the space above.

"See what I mean?" Jodi briskly rubbed her hands up and down her arms when they reached the top. The space was in reality a finished room extending the length of the cabin, where it was possible to stand upright and dormer windows let in adequate light and fresh air, but her grandparents had always called it the attic because of the slanting ceilings. "Even in sleeping bags on cots, I can't put the kids up here with the wind whistling in around the windows like that."

"It is a tad on the chilly side." He moved to one of

the dormer window recessions to inspect it, surprised at the force of the cold air squeezing in around the edges of the window when he held his hands out to it.

"Pretty bad, isn't it?" Jodi slipped in beside him, her hands outstretched to the window as well. "There isn't enough time to get it replaced, is there?"

As her arm brushed his, the fresh scent of her shampoo filling his senses, he pulled slightly away. "Maybe not, but I think I can do a temporary fix for you."

"Would you?"

Still a little too close, he stepped back from the dormer nook, not wanting a repeat performance of last week's temptation, then moved to the other window. She followed behind him.

It was the same story on the draft at that window. "I may have something in my vehicle that will do the trick. I helped Dolly and Al with winterizing their place."

So why was he standing there looking at her instead of hustling off to get the needed supplies? A slant of afternoon sunlight reflected off the polished hardwood floor, illuminating her with a golden glow. Every fiber of his body cried out to take her in his arms, to tell her how he felt about her.

"Is something wrong?"

"We've been friends a long time, Jodi."

Her forehead wrinkled at that out-of-the-blue statement. "Yes, we have."

"So maybe you should get someone else to fix the windows." Oh, wow, that made a lot of sense.

She gave him a look that confirmed she was doubting his sanity. "Okaaay."

"It's just that—"

What good would it do to try to explain? Anything he

said would only make her more uncomfortable around him. And he sure didn't want her to feel sorry for him. But maybe she needed to understand why he'd be pulling back as soon as he got these windows taken care of, that while it was great to see her again, he wasn't feeling especially brotherly toward her right now. But a confession like that would be sure to send her running for the hills.

"Something's wrong. Talk to me, Garrett."

He drew in a breath, determined to make something up and get out of the house as fast as he could. That is, until she stepped forward to place her hand on his arm and his gaze melted into hers.

"I don't want to make you uncomfortable, Jodi, but—" He placed his hand atop hers where it still rested on his arm. "I know you've always thought of me as a big brother. And I know I offended you years ago when I cornered you in the mudroom that night and, well, didn't treat you as a big brother should."

He heard her quick intake of breath at his confession as her gaze remained locked on his.

"I...wasn't offended."

"Maybe *offended* is too strong of a word. But you were caught off guard. Embarrassed at your grandma walking in on us. Upset at my betrayal of our friendship enough to avoid me at church that night." She was looking at him as if he'd lost what was left of his mind. But he plunged on, determined to clear the air. "I should have asked your forgiveness when you first arrived here last week, gotten this out in the open. But there didn't seem to be an appropriate time."

Here goes, Lord. "What I'm trying to say is... I'm apologizing now so that you can understand why I—"

* * *

Jodi tightened her grip on his arm, cutting him off. "I didn't avoid you at the Christmas Eve service, Garrett."

"No? When I looked for you afterward, started to approach you in the parking lot where you were heading to your grandma's car, you looked straight through me like I didn't exist. Just kept on walking. You clearly didn't want to speak to me."

He'd come after her even after saying those hurtful things to his friends? Why? But she hadn't seen him looking for her in the parking lot. Maybe she'd been in shock.

"Then you never contacted me again," he continued, "even though I'd given you my email address earlier in the day. I didn't blame you for not feeling the same way about me as I'd come to feel about you. But I felt awful that I'd overstepped the bounds of a friendship that meant a lot to me."

He was claiming he'd had romantic feelings for her? Feelings he didn't think she reciprocated? No, he was putting a spin on it that flew in the face of what really happened. Her jaw hardened as she stepped away from him.

"Kissing Jodi," she recited quietly, "would be about as thrilling as kissing our Labrador retriever."

He stared at her as realization dawned. Realization that his selective memory of that night—attempting now to convince her that the kiss they'd shared had meant something to him—wasn't going to fly.

"Yes," she continued, "I overheard you sharing that tender sentiment with your buddies. It elicited the laughs I'm sure you were looking for."

"Jodi, I—" He shook his head slowly as he reached for her hand.

She pulled away as the memories of that long-ago night slammed into her with surprising force. But she wouldn't cry. She'd shed those silent tears into her pillow years ago, hiding them from her family.

"Please don't say anything more, Garrett. That evening is one I don't care to relive." She turned toward the door, but he moved to block her way.

"Hear me out. Please?"

"Then have the decency to be honest, Garrett. Stop with the spin. It's not becoming for a man of God."

"I wasn't spinning, Jodi. When you came back to town that Christmas, my let's-be-buddies conviction crumbled. It scared me to death. But without giving you any warning, I acted on my feelings when the opportunity presented itself. That's when I kissed you."

"Please don't try to convince me it meant anything to you."

"But it did. It *did*."

"And the Labrador thing?"

He drew in a breath, his eyes pleading. "The guys were all noticing you. Richard was even wagering on who could steal a kiss first. I couldn't let that happen." He reached for her hand again and this time captured it. "Believe me, the kiss we shared meant something to me. It still does."

The kiss had meant something to her once, too. Before it had been overshadowed by her grandma's scolding and Garrett's callous words to his friends.

"But I immediately realized," he continued, his hand tightening on hers, "that you weren't in the same place I was. You were only sixteen and still thinking of me as your pal. A big brother. So I didn't attempt to contact you."

"Brother?" She gave him an incredulous look. "I'd had the world's biggest crush on you for years. Do you think I'd return your kiss the way I did if I thought of you as my *brother*? Think again."

"But you looked so shocked. And then afterward—"

"I *was* shocked—as in surprised. Stunned. Dazed. And Grandma barging in on us was embarrassing. But I wasn't offended or upset—until by your own words you made it clear that the kiss meant nothing to you. That it was a big joke."

"I had no idea you'd overheard that." His eyes filled with what appeared to be genuine remorse. "It was a dumb thing to say. A desperate attempt to run the other guys off. I'm sorry."

"You expect me to believe after all this time that you didn't regret kissing me?"

"I did regret it, Jodi." He gently tugged on her hand to draw her closer, but his words cut deep as they confirmed her long-held belief. "I regretted it—but only because I'd betrayed your trust in me. And—" his words came softly, his gaze intent "—I regretted that I'd never be given the opportunity to kiss you again."

"Garrett—" This was too much, too fast. Her head was spinning as she tried to comprehend what he was telling her.

Before she could protest, he cupped her face in his hands. "So unless you have any objections, claiming that second kiss is exactly what I'm going to do."

She stared into his eyes—so full of hope. Garrett had cared for her? Cared for her more than as a little sister? But she shouldn't let him kiss her now. Too much time had passed. Too many unshared secrets darkened her heart. And he was leaving soon for a dangerous destination. A kiss now would be unwise. Complicate things.

And yet…slowly she shook her head, unable to voice a coherent objection. That's all the encouragement he needed, for he closed his eyes and leaned in to gently touch his lips to hers.

Garrett. Deliberately shoving away the nagging concerns, her own eyes closed as she drank in the amazing sensation of his mouth on hers. Felt his fingers lightly caress her jaw. Breathed in the faint scent of his aftershave. The chill of the room and the whistling of the wind coming in around the windows faded in the warmth of his touch.

Surely *this* kiss meant something to him.

His hands moved to her waist, and she slipped her arms around his neck, drawing even closer as if neither ever wanted the moment to end. A murmur of hope bubbled up in her spirit as his mouth again captured hers. Was she really being held in Garrett's arms, the future taking on an unexpected brilliance as new doors opened?

"Jodi," Garrett murmured against her ear. "I—"

A loud, merry tune abruptly shattered the quiet, startling her. The cell phone in her pocket.

Garrett grazed his lips along her cheek, then reluctantly stepped back.

With his arms no longer around her, the room's chill once again pierced and, dazed from the unexpected turn of events, she pulled out her phone. Star.

"I'd better take this. It's my sister. Keep your fingers crossed that they've changed their minds about coming."

He nodded, and she longed to reach out to him, but he moved away to again inspect a dormer window.

She forced a cheery note into her voice. "Hey, Star, what's up?"

"I wanted to let you know there's been a change in plans."

Jodi's spirits soared. "That's too bad."

"No, it's not. Ronda and I will be bringing the kids up on Wednesday instead of Friday. That way we can all have more time to relax and visit, and the kids will get more snow time. The weather forecast looks promising for additional white stuff."

Jodi's skyrocketing hopes deflated. There went any hoped-for time alone—and time to spend with Garrett to come to terms with what had just happened between them. "There's no way I can be ready for you by Wednesday."

"Don't worry about it. Ronda and I'll be there to help now, so don't knock yourself out. We got to thinking that we're dumping a lot on you. Expecting you to make all this happen for our kids, and that's not exactly fair."

No it wasn't, but… "I don't even have a tree yet."

The porch rails had to be wrapped in fresh greenery and fairy lights, too. An order for Christmas dinner needed to be placed, groceries bought. More gifts purchased. Activities planned.

Baby Jesus found.

"Star, I'm not nearly done clearing things out and boxing them up for keeping or a drop-off at Goodwill."

"Since we're coming early," Star said cheerfully, obviously thinking they'd hit on the ideal solution with an early arrival, "we can help with all that. And we won't take no for an answer. We'll pick up fried chicken or subs when we get to town, so don't plan anything for lunch, okay?"

Jodi glanced toward Garrett, who was watching her with sympathy in his eyes, obviously getting the gist of the conversation. What choice did she have but to agree with her sisters' plans? "Okay. Guess I'll see you then."

"Count on it."

When her sister hung up, Jodi re-pocketed her cell phone.

"Not what you wanted to hear, was it?" Garrett moved to stand beside her.

"No. As I'm sure you could tell from my side of the conversation, my sisters and their kids are coming early. So I have until noon Wednesday to get everything done that I have to get done."

"I'll help as much as I can. And I'll start with these windows."

"Thanks." But the heaviness in her heart didn't dissipate despite the opportunity to spend more time with Garrett. "I really needed—"

Time alone with God.

"We'll get 'er done, Jodi." He reached for her hand and lifted it to his lips for quick kiss. "And while we're working together—"

"We have things we need to talk about," she finished.

"Right."

But she wasn't sure she wanted to talk about them. To dissect and pull apart the blissful moments she'd just spent in Garrett's arms. To come back down to a world of reality—Garrett's imminent departure and her secrets that would have to be shared if things were to move ahead between them.

"Or maybe," she ventured, "we just live with knowing that we were stupid teenagers and that God knew what He was doing back then when He kept us apart. Not try to make something happen outside of His will that He has no intention of placing His blessing on."

Chapter Twelve

Garrett flinched inwardly at her words as he thoughtfully stroked her hand with his thumb. Was she right? Were the kisses they'd shared only a few moments ago merely a rebound from their teenage years, holding no substance? "Is that what you want? To set aside what just happened between us?"

"A lot of years have passed. We're different people than we were back then."

"True. We're now adults who are fully capable of honestly discussing our feelings. Capable of listening to each other and listening to God." He gently squeezed her hand. "I know the timing stinks with me readying to leave town, and I can't tell you what the future will bring. I can't tell you what God's plans are for my life, let alone yours. But I do know I'm open to whatever time He needs to share with us His direction. Are you?"

"I—" Her eyes searched his uncertainly. Searching—for what? A guarantee? A promise he couldn't make at this time? "I...am."

He softly released a pent-up breath he didn't know he'd been holding.

"But—" she hurried on before he could speak, "there are things you don't know about me, Garrett. Things that will make you feel much differently about me. Things that will open your eyes to the fact that maybe God has already cast His vote against any future for us."

What was she talking about? "Sometimes we let things get bigger in our minds than they really are, forgetting there's nothing that God can't make right."

"He can't take me back in time to make better choices."

"No, but—"

"I got pregnant, Garrett," she blurted, pulling her hands away from his and taking a step back. "About a year after I moved to Philadelphia, I had a relationship with a man I wasn't married to. And… I got pregnant."

A muscle tightened in his throat.

Anton? Or some other guy? But he couldn't point accusing fingers at her extramarital relationship. He, too, was guilty as charged. But she didn't have a child now…did she? Was she trying to tell him she'd had an abortion? "So…you have a child?"

She shook her head, and his gut tightened.

"No. Not a full-term baby. I miscarried him—or her—at three months. Four years ago this very month."

Grateful she hadn't made a decision to end a life, but not relieved when he saw the raw pain in her eyes, he again took her hand in both of his. "I'm sorry."

"And you know what's even worse? What still eats me alive at times?" She blinked back tears. "For most of those three months once I suspected I was pregnant, I woke up every single morning and went to bed every single night wishing that baby away. Wishing from the depths of my soul that I'd dreamed the nightmare it had become during my every waking moment. Shaking my fist at God because He'd allowed it to happen."

Chin trembling, she hung her head.

"I didn't want that baby, Garrett. Not…not until only a few days before I lost him. I'd just begun to come to terms with my reality, with the fact that I carried a precious *life* within me when, suddenly, something went wrong."

She looked at him again, her dark eyes filled with anguish.

"Did God," she continued, "answer my prayers to put that baby out of my life? I don't know, but I'll always wonder. Wonder what impact on the world that life might have had if I'd carried him to full term. I mean, even though the situations are quite different, what if Mary, the mother of Jesus, had panicked and rejected him the way I rejected my own child? Prayed his little unborn life away?"

Staring into her pleading eyes, his mind flashed to her reaction when they'd first discovered her grandma's nativity set was missing baby Jesus. How he'd unknowingly persuaded her to work on a project for unwed mothers.

"Oh, Jodi." His heart breaking, he gently tugged her forward.

She came willingly, slipping her arms around his waist to press the side of her face against his chest. To cling to him as though somehow she could draw strength from him as her tears flowed quietly, her body trembling in his arms.

His sweet, sweet Jodi had made a wrong choice— and borne so much pain as a result. He closed his eyes and laid his head against hers. *Please, God, hold her tighter than I can. Heal her heart. Fill her with your peace. Give me the words of comfort she needs to hear.*

The cold coming in around the windows seemed to intensify, the silence around them broken only by the sound of Jodi's muffled grief. Had the chimney sweep finished up by now? Left already? He'd gladly bear any consequences should someone take an exception to him being here alone with Jodi. She needed him, and he wouldn't turn her away.

Right now he only wanted to comfort and protect—for a lifetime—the woman he held so closely. A woman he'd so swiftly grown to care for—to love? Plans for the mission field threatened to fade into the background. But he'd made a commitment. To God, if not to a missions team itself yet. A commitment he still had every intention of fulfilling. But was it his Heavenly Father's plan to wrench this woman from his heart—or to somehow work things out between them?

He tightened his arms around her. How long they remained standing in the upstairs room, entwined in each other's arms, he couldn't have told. Time stood still. But eventually, Jodi pulled slightly back and looked up at him, lashes starred with tears. "Thank you, Garrett."

He leaned in to kiss her forehead. "You're forgiven, Jodi. You know God's already done that, don't you? From the moment you first cried out to Him."

She nodded, wiping away a tear, and he handed her his handkerchief. "But it's hard for me to forgive myself."

"At the risk of sounding blunt, being unwilling to forgive yourself is kind of like taking Jesus's sacrificial gift and tossing it in the trash."

"But I've harbored such a deep-seated anger toward

God about all of it. Anger because He didn't stop me from getting involved with Kel. Anger because I lost my baby. Anger because of Anton's death."

"Is that why things didn't work out between the two of you? You told him about the baby and he couldn't accept it?"

"No. Even though he wanted to marry me, I couldn't bring myself to tell him. I couldn't even tell the baby's father. Nobody knew except me, my doctor and the medical staff. Not even my family."

She'd borne her grief alone.

"But—but can't you see, Garrett, that I'm not exactly front-runner material for you, as a pastor, to be getting involved with? You may be able to forgive my past mistakes, but you can't partner with someone who's held a grudge against God, whose faith is still as wobbly as a sapling in the wind."

He gently cupped her face in his hand. "We're called believers for a reason, Jodi. Believers in God. Believers that He loves us and has good plans for us. Start believing now, this very moment, putting your confidence and trust in Him again. Let this be a turning point in your life that you'll look back on and be thankful for."

"You make it sound so simple."

"We make it more complicated than it is. I know you've often heard that without faith it's impossible to please God. We have to believe He exists and recognize He rewards those of us who seek Him." He smiled encouragingly. "And when you decide to believe—it's a *choice*, Jodi—it's been my experience that your eyes will be opened to how God has been with you all along. And you'll begin to see evidence of His continued presence reinforced, even in the midst of the worst of heart-aches."

Hadn't God found him when he was wallowing in the lowest moments of his life following Drew's injury?

"So what do you say, Jodi?" He had no right to ask her this, not with his future up in the air. But he couldn't stop himself. "Are you willing to join me in not only renewing your belief in Him, but believing He'll provide us answers to where He wants our friendship to go?"

Her eyes searched his. "Kinda scary, isn't it? I mean, what if He says no?"

"If he does, then we can know He has our best in mind and have peace with that." He could say that glibly enough, but deep down he knew what he wanted. Knew he'd be deeply disappointed if God permanently closed the door. "So… I'll ask you again. Are you willing to step out with me to see what He has in mind?"

A multitude of thoughts were obviously racing through her head. Then she swallowed. Nodded. "I am."

Joy bolted through him. But he'd just leaned in, hoping for a kiss to seal their pact, when from somewhere above their heads came a loud thump. Then a scrambling, scraping sound.

Jodi's eyes widened. "What's that?"

"Up on the housetop, reindeer pause…?" he couldn't help but sing softly.

She gently punched his arm. "Oh, you."

He laughed. "I think our chimney sweep has moved to the roof. Should we go out and make sure she's okay?"

"Maybe we'd better."

Hand-in-hand they headed to the stairs, his heart

filled with hope. But uncertainty lingered under the surface for, as Jodi had put it, how would God cast His vote?

For the remainder of the day and all through the next, Jodi's heart sang as she went about her chores. Praise songs bubbled up within. Old hymns surfaced from childhood that she'd long forgotten. And deep down inside, a peace she hadn't had in years flooded her soul. No, there were no guarantees that God had a plan for her and Garrett as a couple, but her joy went much deeper than the glimmering hope she held for that.

Today, all on her own, she'd made a gift delivery to Kimmy, a local fifteen-year-old girl seven months pregnant, who'd recently been kicked out of her home. An elderly great-aunt getting by on Social Security had taken her in, so the two were struggling even though determined to give the baby up to a family who would love and care for it. Jodi had found herself encouraged by the girl's resolve not to allow a mistake to become an even deeper, more permanent tragedy. And to her surprise, for the first time ever, when accusing fingers began to point at Jodi in her imagination, she'd prayerfully pushed them aside. Somehow, she hadn't come away from an encounter with the pregnant young woman with self-condemnation filling her *own* heart.

She'd never before confessed to anyone the full nature of her relationship with Kel or the loss of her unborn child. There had never before been an opportunity to be held in comforting arms as the grief of regrets and loss poured out freely. Never had she confessed her carefully hidden doubts as to God's love for her. Until Garrett.

It was long overdue. She could see that now.

And to audibly hear Garrett pronounce with such assurance that God had forgiven her? It had been as if a dam inside her soul broke open, and for the first time in ever so long, she was no longer held hostage to her doubts and fears.

O come all ye faithful...!

"We're making progress." Not long before sunset on Tuesday, Garrett stepped back to admire the fairy lights he'd finished wrapping around the greenery on the porch railings.

From the open cabin doorway, Dolly nodded her approval. "Picture-perfect, don't you think, Jodi?"

"So festive," she agreed. The tiny lights sparkling in the twilight reflected the glow in her heart—and the telltale shine in Garrett's eyes when he looked at her.

"If you have everything done out here," his landlady said as she motioned to the interior of the cabin behind her, "there's tomato soup and grilled cheese sandwiches awaiting you. Better get in there before Al eats more than his fair share."

Once inside, Jodi was again filled with a deep sense of satisfaction at the transformation of the cabin. With Dolly and Al generously offering to chaperone, they and Garrett had helped her with final preparations for her family's arrival tomorrow.

A brightly lit evergreen—straight from the local landscape nursery—now stood in a corner near the front window. She would let the kids decorate it when they arrived, just as she and her sisters used to do. Swags of greenery wrapped around support posts, and the nativity set—sans baby Jesus—stretched across the console table against the wall where it would be less likely to be knocked off by younger members of the family. Battery-lit candles flickered in the windows and on the mantel above a crackling fire, and the air held the subtle scent of pine and burning oak.

Garrett pulled out a chair for her at the big dining table. "Looks like something out of a magazine, doesn't it, Jodi?"

"Thanks to all of you."

"Your grandma would be so pleased with what you're doing for your nieces and nephew." Al reached out for Jodi's hand on one side and that of his wife on the other, preparing for the prayer. He nodded pointedly at her to take Garrett's hand on her other side, so she self-consciously slipped hers into Garrett's big, warm one and bowed her head.

Did Al and Dolly sense any difference in their interactions? Catch the furtive glances, the quick smiles, the lingering looks?

"Father God," Al began, "we thank You for this special season of remembering the most amazing gift You've bestowed on mankind, Your son, Jesus Christ. We thank You that on that day in history, hope was given birth, a bridge so generously established between You and your prone-to-wander creation. We are, indeed, a people blessed. Thank You for this food and our time together this evening. In Your son's name, amen."

Garrett gently squeezed her hand as amens echoed around the table.

"Looks like you're ready to welcome your family. Around lunchtime you said?" Dolly opened a tall metal tin and pulled out a packet of saltines.

"Yes, they'll be driving up in the morning. Today's fresh snow should please the kids, but I think the roads should be mostly clear by tomorrow. I'm not sure, though, if anyone is really ready to open the doors to Henry."

"He's the four-year-old?"

"Lovable and huggable." She tucked her napkin across her lap. "But sometimes a real handful. He keeps Ronda on her toes every minute of the day just to prevent him from doing himself permanent injury. Right from the beginning he was one of those kids who refused to stay in his crib, always climbing up and out when no one was looking."

Dolly crushed a cracker into her soup as she slid an amused look in Garrett's direction. "Reminds me of someone I used to know."

"Hey, what can I say?" Garrett shrugged, not looking the least bit repentant. "Henry sounds like my kind of guy. Some of us are born to adventure."

Like river-running—and a dangerous missions field?

She'd always loved sports. The outdoors. But she'd never been much of a risk taker—unless egged on by Garrett. They weren't to the point of discussing anything that smacked of a possible permanent union. But if things worked out between them, would he expect her to accompany him to the Middle East? Could the fledgling renewal of her faith lead her in that direction? Given a choice, she didn't even want to relocate overseas with her current job. But if that's where this relationship led, well, she'd support Garrett in his calling any way she could. She just needed to trust God would work things out as was best for both of them.

"If you and Henry are so simpatico," Jodi said, leveling a teasing look at Garrett, "I'm sure my sister would be happy to put you in charge of the little guy while he's here. She says she and her hubby feel God's given them a ministry to singles who think they want to be married and start a family. By the time they and Henry depart, singlehood is much more palatable."

Dolly cringed. "Oh, my."

A grinning Garrett reached for his spoon. "Bring him on."

The dinnertime conversation ebbed and flowed comfortably, and laughter often erupted. Al and Dolly appeared to feel perfectly at ease with her and Garrett. Of course, they'd known both of them since the two friends were little, and they'd housed Garrett this past year. No wonder she felt so comfortable, almost as if among family.

Not surprisingly, a twinge of disappointment burst her contented little bubble when Al inquired how the Christmas project was going. Due to all the preparations for her family's arrival and the fun flirtation with Garrett taking center stage, with the exception of a visit to Kimmy she'd let the project slide to the back burner of her mind. But with delivery only a few days away, she had limited time to pull it all together.

"Now, don't badger the girl." Dolly gave her husband a chastising look.

"I'm not badgering. Just showing interest."

And he probably was. But what about others who remembered the volume of donations in past years? Even though she'd been a part of the project barely over a week, would blame for a comparatively skimpy number of gifts be placed at her doorstep?

Would that, in turn, reflect poorly on Garrett?

He already felt there were those in the congregation who believed he fell short of their expectations. Even though he didn't think fondly of the project, Randall Moppert, for one, would no doubt gleefully add this poor holiday showing to his growing list of pastoral shortcomings.

"The project's coming along," Jodi said lightly, then bit into one of Dolly's molasses cookies.

"We still have a few days left," Garrett encouraged. "Someone I know, who has overseen a lot of projects in the past, recently told me that you often hit a plateau on these kinds of things. Then suddenly it all falls into place."

Al nodded thoughtfully. "That so?"

"Makes sense to me." Dolly helped herself to a cookie. "You know, the old saying that it's always darkest before the dawn."

"True." Al broke his own cookie in quarters and popped a piece of it in his mouth.

Jodi cast Garrett a grateful look, and he winked.

Her face warmed. "Now that things are pretty much ready for my family and they won't arrive until midday tomorrow, I'll have time to make more phone calls. I'm thinking, too, that my time might be well spent making personal visits to businesses around town."

Al clapped his hands together. "Now you're talking, gal. Get right in their faces."

"It might not hurt." Dolly dusted the cookie crumbs from her fingers onto her plate. "It might be harder for someone to say no if you're standing there looking right at them."

Al placed his forearms on the table and leaned in Jodi's direction. "It's my guess that if you bat those big brown eyes of yours at them, you'll double your donations."

Dolly poked her husband's arm, but Al waved her off, turning his attention to Garrett. "Don't ya think so, Pastor McCrae?"

Garrett's eyes locked with hers as he placed his napkin on the table, a smile twitching at his lips. "I wouldn't be the least bit surprised, Al."

Al slapped the tabletop. "See? What did I tell you?"

"Now you two stop your teasin'." Dolly rose to clear away her and Al's plates. "You're making our poor Jodi blush."

"Just makes her all the prettier, right, Garrett?" The look Al shot in Garrett's direction was a little too knowing. Even if Dolly hadn't sensed a shift in Garrett's relationship with her, her husband had obviously caught on.

"You won't hear any arguments from me." Garrett, too, rose to gather both his and Jodi's plates, his eyes twinkling.

"Well, then," Al announced as he slid a mischievous look in Jodi's direction, "that eye-batting strategy sounds like a plan to me. One that I fully expect in the very near future to show...welcome results."

Chapter Thirteen

Sitting in a big wingback chair in front of the cabin's fireplace Wednesday evening, Garrett laughed as a freshly scrubbed and flannel-pajamaed Henry crawled into his lap, a picture book in hand.

Garrett had stopped by in the afternoon to join in building a snow fort—and just in time to rescue Jodi's intrepid nephew from where he'd climbed on the porch railing and shinnied up a support post to dangle precariously from the gutter. And that was only the first rescue of several before they'd all been called in for supper—and an evening of stringing popcorn, making paper-linked garlands and cutting out snowflakes for the tree.

In the two days since he and Jodi agreed to seek God's direction, they'd shared hours of fun and laughter, serious discussion, and catching each other up on their lives. In so many ways it was as if there had never been a dozen years between that first kiss and the one that had only recently been shared. They had so many values in common. Felt strongly about the bonds of family. Wanted to be used by God. Hour by hour, minute by minute, the connection between them deepened.

And yet…he still hadn't brought himself to tell her about the role he'd played in Drew's injuries, the instrumental turning point in his relationship with God.

Why was that? He trusted her. He did. She wouldn't reject him because of his past mistakes any more than he'd reject her because of hers. But he couldn't bear to see the disappointment in him that was certain to reflect in her beautiful eyes.

He looked over at Jodi on the sofa, occupied with a book and her two nieces. She glanced up. He winked, and she smiled back, relaxed, happy and the light in her eyes clearly communicating her contentment.

If only he could relax into that same God confidence she seemed to be growing into. But uncertainty nagged. Not about how he felt about Jodi, but about how they could work things out for a future together given his plans for the Middle East. No way would he take her there, even if she'd be willing to go.

And what about his sister and her two kids, who'd recently returned to town? They were shooting up so fast that if he blinked twice they'd be all grown up. He'd like to think their Uncle Garrett's presence these past few weeks had filled a need for a male role model if even in a small way. And then there was Grandma Jo—how many more years would she be around to enjoy? And what if Aunt Elaine's health took a turn for the worse?

He'd invested a lot of time and prayer in the church and community, as well. Would his labor continue to bear fruit after he was gone? Would someone else pick up where he left off, or would the ball get dropped and roll off into the shadows?

Henry, paging through the book, cuddled closer, and Garrett gave him a hug.

Those things hadn't troubled him until Jodi's return. Previously he'd been able to shut them out at their first nagging glimmer. But not now. Which didn't exactly make him a cheerful holiday elf deep down inside, although he was doing his best to put on a good front.

Today he'd relished watching Jodi with the kids. Although she claimed not to have much experience with children, no one let that fact form a barrier between them and their Aunt Jodi.

And he, despite laughing protests, had been dubbed Uncle Garrett. He had to admit he liked the sound of that, and it seemed to amuse Star and Ronda. Both had a good laugh at their sister's expense, too, when he admitted he had a turkey thawing at his place in case they wanted to put the kibosh on Jodi's plans for a catered Christmas dinner. They took him up on his offer immediately and, thankfully, Jodi hadn't yet gotten around to placing an order.

It was obvious they sensed something between him and Jodi that they hadn't expected to see when they'd arrived. Something of which, from all appearances, they wholeheartedly approved. If he wasn't mistaken, Al and Dolly had also caught on to the shift between him and Jodi and were pleased.

Lord, it would be so easy to let myself love her. To love her family. But I know that may be something on down the road. Not for now.

Until Jodi had come back into his life, he'd assumed he'd be overseas for the long haul. But now his focus had shifted. More and more he found his thoughts drifting to Jodi. To his family. To the souls in Hunter Ridge. Now that he'd spoken up about his mission plans and admitted to an interest in Jodi, well, it didn't seem as if reconciling the two directions was as easily resolved as he'd first led himself to believe.

"*Read*, Uncle Garrett." Henry firmly patted the open book.

Garrett glanced again at Jodi, Bethany and Savannah cuddled on either side of her. But the warming of his heart only somewhat overrode the uncertainties dwelling there. Although he'd boldly talked of God's timing, of waiting for His leading, he'd need to make a decision soon about if—and how—he could work Jodi into his life. Although the thought of losing her left an ache in his heart, he didn't want to lead her on.

Would God have brought her back into his life only to ask him to give her up?

She'd had it rough since leaving Hunter Ridge. Thankfully, he'd been present tonight at dinner when Ronda announced her latest pregnancy, and he was able to unobtrusively slip his hand around Jodi's and give it a squeeze. While she'd earlier claimed to be struggling in her faith, though, he sensed a growing peacefulness in her these past few days. The peacefulness of this holy season that he longed to share.

He gave himself a mental shake and wrapped his arms more tightly around Henry. Then, opening the colorfully illustrated book to the first page, he cleared his throat and started reading aloud.

With the sun attempting to peep between layers of clouds, Jodi pulled into the church parking lot Thursday morning, hoping to use plans to prepare a gift-wrapping center for donations as an excuse to pop in and say hello to Garrett before paying visits to business owners. In addition to a boatload of wrapping paper, tape, ribbon and bows, with Garrett assuring her that he and Sofia had never taken an interest in each other, she'd even brought cookies just as Sofia had been known to do.

Not that she'd baked them herself.

Star had supplemented a college scholarship by working at a grocery store's bakery, and her acquired skills were out of this world. Jodi didn't think Garrett would mind that she hadn't assisted in their preparation—except to lick a spoon.

Her spirits rose at the prospect of making the delivery and a chance to visit with him this morning. She'd sensed that something was troubling him, that he wasn't sharing the same hopeful feelings of the holiday that she'd been flooded with the past few days. When he left last night, she'd stepped out on the porch to ask him if everything was all right. But he'd responded with a typical Garrett smile, reassuring her that it was merely a busy time of year and apologizing for being distracted.

Maybe that was all it was. Or maybe not.

Plastic wrap–covered cookie plate in hand, she'd just slammed the truck's door when she spied Drew's van in the parking lot and noticed him outside the fellowship hall. He struggled to hold the door open as he balanced a large cardboard box on his lap.

She was at his side in a flash. "Could you use some help?"

"Hey, there, Jodi! Great timing. The automatic door doesn't want to stay open long enough for me to get myself inside."

"Let me hold it." She stepped around his wheelchair

to grasp the handle. "I'll mention to Dolly to get some-one in to take a look at it."

"Thanks." He angled his motorized chair and slipped inside. When she entered, he spun the chair to face her, his eyes holding a speculative gleam as he spied the cookies. "You're looking pretty chipper this morning. Anything special going on in your life?"

Garrett. Garrett. Garrett.

But it was too premature to mention that to Drew. "There's a team coming to wrap presents for the Christmas project this afternoon. I'm here to get things set up, and that puts me in the holiday spirit."

He gave her a somewhat skeptical look, but didn't probe further. "So how's that going? Did you get the donations you'd hoped for?"

"Not as many as I'd like, but people are being as generous as they can."

He patted the side of the cardboard box. "Well, maybe this will help."

Touched that Drew would think to donate some-thing to aid unwed mothers, she set the cookie plate on a nearby table, then stepped forward as he lifted the lid. She peered inside the box, filled with stuffed toys of every imaginable kind. Bears. Puppies. Kittens. Whales. Turtles.

"Ohhh, Drew! Thank you." She leaned over to give him a hug, then reached in to pull out a silky soft pen-guin and cuddled it close. "Where on earth did you find these?"

"As usual, I let my credit card do all the walking—online. These were delivered last night."

She placed the penguin back in the box and lifted

out a zebra. "These are adorable. You are such a sweetheart."

"And speaking of sweethearts… I'm especially curious seeing those cookies over there. How's my old buddy treating you? I'd have to be blind not to notice there's something going on between the two of you since you came back."

Her face warmed as she focused her attention on the black-and-white-striped critter in her hands. Was it that obvious? "You know we're good friends."

"Tell me another one. Garrett's acting kind of secretive, too. So what's up?"

She couldn't tell a bold-faced lie. But she was limited in what she could say. While hopes abounded, there wasn't anything concrete yet. They'd talked of being open to God's leading, but neither had uttered the word *love* or made any promises, although she knew, for her part anyway, that was the state of her own heart.

"I think…we're exploring how we feel about each other."

Drew raised a brow. "Exploring?"

"Prayerfully," she quickly added, "asking God to show us if He wants us to move beyond friends."

"I may be mistaken, but it appears to me it's already gone beyond that."

"We don't want to get ahead of ourselves—or God. There are a number of things yet to be worked through, some potential roadblocks, including Garrett's plans for the future."

Drew chuckled. "Garrett has plans for the future? You mean beyond the next five minutes?"

"Going into missions is a big step."

Drew raised his hand. "Whoa, whoa. Stop right there.

Missions? Garrett has plans to be a missionary? Since when?"

A muscle in Jodi's stomach tightened. *Drew didn't know?*

Had she let something slip that Garrett didn't want shared with his longtime friend? Her mind raced frantically, recalling earlier conversations. He'd said, when he told her of his plans, that he hadn't shared his intentions with many. But surely the ones he'd told would have included the minister in Canyon Springs and Drew, wouldn't they? Especially since Drew had such a heart for those in the Middle East. Garrett would want his support, his assistance, his prayers.

"He didn't—?"

"Tell me? You'd think he would have, wouldn't you? But this is the first I'm hearing of this." Drew's brows lowered and his jaw hardened, suddenly a formidable-looking man. "He wouldn't be planning on a destination in the Middle East, would he?"

Jodi stared at him as his gaze pierced into hers. She'd unintentionally stirred up a hornet's nest. "I shouldn't be discussing this. You need to talk to Garrett."

He slammed his fist on the arm of his wheelchair, startling her. "He is, isn't he? That's where he's going. Don't you get it? He's going to the very place I was headed before *this* happened."

He roughly motioned to his legs.

Now she understood his anger. Garrett was taking over his dream, doing something Drew long had a stake in, but his damaged body would no longer permit him to fulfill the requirements.

"I'm sure he didn't intend to hurt you. That's probably why he didn't say anything about his plans and his destination. He didn't want to make you feel bad that you couldn't go, too."

Drew shook his head. "No, no, no. Don't you get it? My feelings aren't hurt. But I *am* mad. He's doing this out of guilt."

"Guilt for what?"

"He somehow has it all messed up in his mind that he can somehow pay God—and me—back for the misguided responsibility he's assuming for my accident."

Jodi tensed. Garrett was involved in Drew's accident?

"He blames himself because we were on a rafting trip on the Colorado. One he'd badgered me to go on before I headed back out on another missions trip. We'd hiked into a side canyon early one evening to do some swimming. Got clowning around just like we often did. Thinking to evade Garrett, I... I dived into the water— and didn't clear a slab of stone lurking under the surface."

With a soft gasp, she pressed her fingers momentarily to her lips. "Oh, Drew."

"He dived in and kept me from drowning. Got me air vacced out of there to Flagstaff. But he's had a hard time letting go of the possibility that moving me, pulling me out, is what really caused the injury."

"But if he hadn't taken action, you'd—"

"Be dead. Guaranteed. But he still feels responsible since he was one of the crew. He said he'd never have allowed any of the other guests on the trip to do what we were doing."

"So you think he's going to the Middle East..."

"Because *I* can't. I'm certain of it." Drew smacked the palm of his hand on the arm of his wheelchair. "God used the accident to get his attention. But in all these five years, I had no idea he harbored an intent to do missions work in the Middle East. Never." Drew fisted his fingers. "And when I get my hands around his throat—"

"But you don't know what God—"

"This is God's doing? We both know Garrett can hands-down physically deal with the rigors of a commitment like that. But what I can't see is that his heart is in it." Drew's frown deepened. "I lived and breathed my devotion to the people of that part of the world. I studied the languages, the cultures, the political and religious and economic issues. I openly immersed myself in prayer for that region. Still do. But Garrett's kept his intent a secret from everyone. Doesn't that strike you as odd?"

"Maybe he knew he'd get pushback from you. From others."

"I'm not buying that it's his calling. In the twelve short months that he's been back in Hunter Ridge, he's been instrumental in reviving this church. In drawing local and regional churches together to cooperate for God's goal of meeting spiritual and physical needs. You've only been here a short time, but that's got to be apparent to you, too. This is where his gifts lie. His calling. How can he not see that?"

In spite of his protests that some in the church would be happy to see him go, Garrett seemed ideally suited to the ministry he'd been given here. From all evidence, he was making a difference. Who was to say, though, that God might not call him elsewhere? But Drew's concerns were also legitimate. Had Garrett's intended destination been anywhere but the Middle East…

Drew grasped Jodi's arm. "If he thinks he can slip

out of town without looking me square in the eye and telling me he's not doing this out of a guilty conscience, he's got another think coming."

With that, Drew released her and spun his wheelchair around, smacked his hands against the bar on the exit door and pushed his way out of the building.

Shaken, Jodi stared after him until the door slammed closed. Why had Garrett never shared any of this about the accident with her? She'd poured out her heart to him regarding her own regrets. Had allowed him to hold her, comfort her. Yet he'd harbored a deep wound of his own, never allowing her the opportunity to reciprocate.

Hurt, her gaze swept the open space where not many days ago they'd inventoried the donations—then beyond to the hallway that led to his office. She had to get the wrapping supplies brought in and the workstations set up. If she hurried, though, there would be time enough to have a word with him before she met the others at lunch. She needed to explain to him in person how she'd inadvertently brought his plans to the attention of Drew.

Could Garrett's friend be right? Was he doing this for all the wrong reasons? And how might questioning his motives impact their newly fledged relationship?

Chapter Fourteen

"Get off my case, Drew."

Irritation rising, Garrett held the cell phone to his ear as he paced the living room floor of the Lovells' house, grateful that the older couple had gone to see friends that morning and he'd had the place to himself to work on his Christmas Eve message.

"You've been holding out on me, buddy. Until Jodi let it slip, I had no idea you intended to set sail for the same destination I'd mapped out."

Jodi had betrayed his confidence?

"So you think," Drew continued, his tone harsh, "that you can make up for what happened that day on the river?"

"Nothing will ever make up for that day on the river. Don't talk crazy."

"I don't think it's me talking crazy here. Why'd you keep this a secret? Is it a done deal? You've signed on the dotted line?"

"Not yet, but I will. Soon." He'd originally applied right out of college and been turned down, but now he had a year's worth of ministry experience under his belt and, hopefully, would be receiving a strong enough recommendation from church leadership to get him in the door.

Drew's voice raised a notch. "This is nuts. You've never said a peep about being into foreign missions, let alone something like the Middle East."

"You don't think I can handle it?" He'd done his best to stay in top shape since leaving the demands of river rafting.

"The physical rigors, you mean? That's not the issue here. I'm talking about following what God's put in your heart. Honing what He's gifted you to do."

Garrett ran his hand roughly through his hair. "I may not have made a public service announcement at the time, but this dream has long been in my heart. It's what pulled me from the river and into Bible college."

"Your dream—or mine? You used to tell me I was out of my mind to trek all over the globe, risking my neck to tell people about Jesus who'd just as soon kill me as look at me. You said I had a death wish, remember?"

"Think back, Drew. That was before God recruited me to His team."

"Which happened, I will remind you, after the river incident."

"I wish you and everyone else would stop calling that an incident. It makes it sound as if you'd done nothing more than stubbed your toe."

Garrett heard his friend draw a labored breath and braced himself for another verbal assault. But it didn't come. Instead, Drew's tone quieted.

"We've been friends a long time, Garrett."

"Yeah, we have."

"As a friend, as one who walks by your side on God's path, I'm asking you to step back and reevaluate this."

"Listen, Drew—"

"No, *you* listen. I don't like being wheelchair-bound. I don't like being kept off the mission fields while they are ripe for harvest. But don't you think if God had wanted me back out there, that He could have prevented what happened from happening? That He could have had me dive in just a few inches from that submerged rock? Don't you think God's big enough, in control enough, that He could have done that?"

Garrett gripped the phone more tightly. "You're not saying God *made* this happen, are you? That He would—"

"No! But things happen. Accidents. Our souls are housed in a temporary, sometimes-fragile physical home that often takes a beating. I pray for God's healing daily, but I've accepted where I am. Accepted that God can still use me for a good purpose. But *you've* let my situation eat at you for the past five years and have somehow gotten things all twisted up in your mind."

Garrett grimaced. "Thanks for the vote of confidence."

"You know what I mean. You're so gifted, so God-empowered for a ministry like the one you're growing at Christ's Church. You're reaching people I could never have reached while off in the Middle East—people I'm not even reaching now that I'm right back here in our hometown. But *you* are."

At the sound of a slamming car door, Garrett's attention was drawn to the window. Rio's truck out by the curb. Which meant… A moment later the doorbell rang.

"I've got to go, Drew. Someone's at the door."

"You don't owe me or God a single thing, bud. Promise me you'll rethink this. Pray about it."

"Look, I've got to go."

"Right." For a moment he thought Drew would continue, but he abruptly disconnected.

Garrett stuffed his cell phone back in his pocket. Jodi was here, and with his SUV sitting in the gravel area next to the driveway, he couldn't pretend not to be home.

He hurt not only from Drew's verbal thrashing, but from the fact that Jodi had shared his plans with his friend. Had she done it intentionally? Hoping Drew would try to dissuade him from following through? No, he refused to believe that.

Lord, please let me respond to her as a man of God should.

He pulled the door open to face Jodi, her gaze faltering as she offered a smile and held out a plate of cookies. A peace offering?

"Hey, Garrett."

"Hey."

"Have a minute? Marisela was at the church office and said you were working from home. There's something I need to talk to you about."

He held open the storm door, and she slipped in past him, out of the cold, to set the cookies on a nearby table.

"I think I made a mistake." She looked at him uncertainly. "I didn't know you hadn't told one of your best friends about your missions plans. And I didn't know your destination had been *his* plan before the accident. He wasn't happy, so I think you'll be hearing from him."

"Already have."

She winced. "I'm sorry. I tried to get here as fast as I could to tell you, but I had to—"

"It's okay. He was bound to find out sooner or later."

"It wasn't my intention to say something I shouldn't have. But in some ways, it helps to understand things better."

"Like what?"

"Why you're driven to an especially dangerous type of missions work." She hesitated, her eyes searching his. "Drew believes you're trying to make up to him—and God—the fact that he can no longer actively participate in field work."

"He told you about the part I played in his injuries, did he?" He knew she'd eventually find out, he just didn't think the time would come so soon. "I'm sorry, Jodi. You should have heard it from me."

"I don't fault you for that. I know it must be hard to talk about. But please don't be mad at Drew for telling me. He thinks the world of you and is concerned that you're giving up your position in Hunter Ridge. Both of us can see what an amazing difference you're making in this town."

"You forget, Jodi, there is no position to give up. I haven't been offered a contract extension."

She grimaced. "I still don't understand that, but we believe God's gifted you in so many ways for small-town ministry. I'm sure other churches in little towns are looking for someone just like you."

"Gifted for small-town ministry, but not to touch the lives of those elsewhere?"

"That's not what we're saying. It's just that—"

"It's not about where I'm most gifted, is it?" he said gently, an ache forming in his heart. He didn't like where this conversation might be leading. Surely God wouldn't...

Jodi had lost a love on the mission field. It was only natural she'd hesitate to face the possibility of reliving something like that again. He should have recognized that earlier. They'd talked tentatively of a future together. No promises. No timelines. Yet clearly moving in that direction. But he wasn't being fair to her. "You don't want me to go, do you?"

"I— It's not that I don't want you to go if that's where God is leading you. It's that I want you to be sure. Drew wants you to be sure."

"I'm certain, Jodi. God put this on my heart years ago when He called me away from a job I loved. He gave me a purpose. His purpose."

"Or a means to pay Him back because you took one of His most valuable players out of the game?" He flinched inwardly, and apparently startled by her own words, Jodi reached out to grasp his arm. "I'm sorry, Garrett. I shouldn't have said it like that."

God, please don't take this where I think you're taking it. Don't ask me to— "I know you mean well, Jode, but—"

"You and I've been friends since we were kids, and in these weeks since I came back to town, I believe those bonds have greatly strengthened." Her grip tightened on his arm, her eyes pleading just as his heart was now pleading before God. "We know each other well, maybe as well or better than anyone else knows us."

Before he could open his mouth to respond, she rushed on. "I can't pretend that I understand what you feel is the direction that God is asking you to go. But I wouldn't be a true friend if I didn't point out that this direction rings of taking up Drew's dream—and not God's will."

He drew a breath, the ache inside growing heavier. *Jodi, his sweet Jodi*. The woman he'd only days ago come to believe might be the choice of God's heart for him, doubted him. Doubted he'd heard from God.

Amid the heady feelings he and Jodi had cautiously expressed to each other, hadn't doubts as to how things could work out still lingered on his part? Had God been trying to tell him that despite being head over heels for Jodi, that's not the direction He wanted them to go? Had he, in his growing love, ventured too far from God's intended purpose for his life when he'd allowed himself to reconnect with her?

She didn't support him, *couldn't* support him in this venture. And it was wrong of him to ask her to. To expect her to put her life on hold while he invested his in a dangerous corner of the world. To force her to live in fear of something happening to him just as had happened to her Anton.

But could he bring himself to sacrifice everything that he'd hoped and prayed for between the two of them? As much as he hated it, as much as it felt as if the chest that housed his heart was cracking, splintering, he had to.

For Jodi's sake.

He reached for her hands, grateful that his weren't shaking. "I believe…we've come to a crossroads."

"What do you mean?"

Please, please, not what I think he means.

She tightened her grip on his hands, attempting to draw from them a strength she knew she didn't possess. Not if, from the sorrowful look in his eyes, he was about to say what she feared he was preparing to say.

"We've been friends a long time, Jodi. Good friends." His thumbs gently stroked the backs of her hands. "But as much as we might have recently hoped for something more, I'm now—very sadly—recognizing that friendship is all God wants us to share."

Please, no.

Heart crumbling, she stared into Garrett's unwavering gaze as she tried to form a response. But no words came. In her effort to help him, she'd pushed him too far. Right out of her life.

Although his eyes remained bleak, he offered a tentative smile. "Friendship isn't a bad thing, Jode. Not an inferior thing, as some might believe. True friendships, like ours, stand the test of time. Far too many romantic ones often falter and fail."

She ducked her head, not wanting him to see the pricking tears.

"I know this is catching you off guard. Believe me, it's caught me off guard, too. I'd hoped—" He glanced away, then took a slow breath.

"Is it because I told Drew about your plans? Because I—"

"No, Jodi. It's not anything you did or didn't do. It's about us. About listening to God. Being willing to obey when He shows us where to go. Only a few days ago, we agreed to that, remember? To put our trust in Him? But I have to admit, I didn't expect an answer—*this* answer—to come so swiftly."

She lifted her head. "We can't…go in the same direction?"

He gave her hands a gentle squeeze as he looked down at her, his eyes filled with compassion. "I think you know the answer to that. You understand, don't you, where I'm coming from?"

She swallowed. And nodded. She knew what he was saying. But understand?

I will not cry.

Gently pulling her hands away from his, she turned away, afraid he'd see the trembling of her lower lip. "I'd better get going."

He caught her arm, his eyes alarmed. "Talk to me, Jodi. Don't rush off. I didn't mean for you to—"

"I'm not rushing off, but if I don't go now, I'll be late." She paused to catch her breath in an effort to keep her voice from cracking. "I'm treating the project volunteers to lunch. Then we're having a gift-wrapping party."

As if she were in the mood for that now? *Please, Lord, don't let him invite himself along.*

"It sounds like you have a busy afternoon planned." He almost sounded hurt that she had plans that didn't include him. But did he honestly think she'd want to hang out with him after what he'd just said?

With ice-cold fingers, she secured her scarf around her neck and turned to the door.

"If you want to, Jodi, we can talk about this more later." He looked at her uncertainly, as if it finally dawned on him that something he'd obviously been giving considerable thought had come as a complete surprise to her. "I *will* be seeing you around, right? Before you leave town?"

She forced what she trusted would pass as a genuine smile. A good old tomboy-Jodi version as she fisted her hand and popped him lightly on the shoulder as she would have done when teasing him as a twelve-year-old. "Sure."

Looking somewhat bewildered, he held the door open for her. She stepped outside to jog across the snowy yard with what she hoped looked like a carefree lope. But by the time she reached the truck, her hands were shaking so badly she could barely insert the key into the ignition. Pressing her lips tightly together, still holding back tears as she pulled away, she managed a cheery wave to where he stood watching from the doorway.

She didn't drive immediately to the Log Cabin Café to meet her friends. Although she'd used it as an excuse to escape Garrett, she had a little time to spare. With her family at the cabin, she couldn't go there, so she quickly found herself on a Forest Service road. Not far enough in to get her in any kind of trouble, but out of sight of the main road.

And there she parked and turned off the ignition.

She didn't dare allow herself to cry, or the volunteers meeting her for lunch would pick up on it. While she might be able to pass it off as a sentimental day with memories of her grandparents, that would be a lie.

Just like the lie she'd told Garrett—or rather, what Garrett assumed from her nod of agreement when he asked if she understood where he was coming from.

Oh, yes, she understood. Too clearly. Although only days ago he'd claimed otherwise—and that kiss, too, testified otherwise—he still couldn't get beyond his childhood memories of her. Jodi his pal. His buddy. His tomboy partner in crime.

She'd spoken to him bluntly about his mission

plans—as friend to friend. Not lover to lover. That had been her downfall.

For the second time in her life, she'd allowed Garrett McCrae to raise her romantic hopes to crazy, dreamed-of heights, only to drop her crashing to the ground as he walked away, his own heart unscathed.

"How could I have let this happen again, Lord?" She stared up into the gray heavens, blinking hard to hold back the tears. "And how could *You* have let this happen to me?"

The accusation hung in the chilly air, the silence of the forest surrounding her pressing in close. Then she humbly bowed her head and fell into her Heavenly Father's comforting arms.

Chapter Fifteen

"We haven't seen you in a while." Grandma Jo placed her hands on her trousers-clad hips, looking Garrett over with a critical eye as he walked in the entryway door to his folks' cabin that evening.

He'd hoped that dinner with his parents, sister and her kids might get his mind off his last encounter with Jodi. It didn't take any genius to figure out he'd upset her. And when she hurt, he hurt. This isn't how either of them anticipated things would turn out between them. But given a little time, she'd see the wisdom in his decision, wouldn't she? See that he'd made it for her. Not because he didn't care, but because…he loved her.

An evening with his family was just what the doctor ordered. But he hadn't counted on Grandma Jo being here, too.

Garrett pulled off his jacket and hung it on a wall peg next to the others. "It's a busy time of year."

"And from what I'm hearing, you're even busier renewing your friendship with Jodi Thorpe."

Friendship. That's all. He'd made sure of that. But

where was the promised peace that was to come with making a right decision? "What is it you're hearing?"

"A little Travis bird mentioned seeing the two of you at dinner one night." A twinkle lit her eyes. "And you wouldn't believe the number of people who've reported that they've seen your SUV over at the cabin since she returned."

Little towns. A weariness settled into his heart.

"Don't worry, Grandma—we're always chaperoned." Except for the short interlude that morning at the Lovells' house. Could that land him in hot water? "Either Dolly or Jodi's sisters or somebody else I've dragged along."

"I'm not worried. Not about that, anyway."

It wasn't like Grandma Jo, usually a straight shooter, to beat around the bush. No way, though, could it have gotten around town already that he wouldn't be here much longer. Drew would respect his privacy even if he didn't agree with him. Jodi wouldn't have said anything to anyone, either—at least he didn't think she would.

"But I take it you *are* worried about something having to do with me?"

"*Concerned* might be a better word. Have you heard from church leadership regarding your future at Christ's Church?"

He couldn't keep hiding his plans from Grandma much longer. Pretty soon everyone in town would know, and she shouldn't be the last. "No, I haven't."

"I was under the impression—" She abruptly cut herself off.

"That they'd have the courtesy to let me know by now that my contract won't be renewed? I came into this interim position a year ago knowing it wasn't permanent, that it was merely a refueling stop between college and what I really planned to do."

Her brows raised slightly. "You've made other plans?"

"I walked into this job with other plans. If all works out, not long after the first of the year I hope to be in language and culture training. And eventually in foreign missions."

She stared at him. "Where?"

"Middle East. Wherever I'm needed to meet the practical and spiritual needs of war torn countries. Wherever God sends me."

"Why there?" Her gaze was as sharp as her words. "That's where Drew intended to go, isn't it?"

"God handed off the baton."

"Are you certain, Garrett?"

"Grandma, I know you've wanted me to minister here in Hunter Ridge ever since I told you I'd decided to go to Bible college. But that's not where my focus is. It's not where it's ever been."

"Do your parents know?"

"Not yet. I'm sorry I didn't tell you sooner. I felt it was better kept to myself until my year here was over."

Or had he been hoping God would change His mind?

She frowned. "What does Jodi think of this? Is she going to let you carry her off with you into those dangerous regions?"

"Jodi and I are friends. Nothing more. I hadn't seen or spoken to her in twelve years. Sure, we were best buds as kids, but people grow up. Change. She's here until just after Christmas, and I won't be here much longer than that."

For the first time in his remembrance since Grandpa

had passed away, Grandma Jo looked lost. "I don't know what to think of all this."

"Be happy for me, Grandma. And pray for my safety and that I'll be a blessing wherever one is needed most. That's all I ask."

She nodded, but her gaze remained troubled. Which did nothing, as he slipped past her in search of the rest of his family, to usher in that peace he'd been praying for.

"It was totally amazing what we accomplished this afternoon," Jodi called to her sisters as she removed her boots and peeled out of her jacket. She hung the latter on a peg, then joined her siblings in the kitchen where she further boosted a happy lilt to her voice that she didn't feel. "I don't think I've ever seen that many wrapped and beribboned packages in one place in my whole life. All neatly labeled for easy identification and distribution. It was so much fun."

But she'd hoped for more donations and hadn't had time to make many of the face-to-face visits that Al was certain would bring more rolling in. She feared, when hearing the other women describe the carloads of presents delivered in the past, that she'd fallen far short of Melody's legacy.

And Garrett's expectations.

As the children's chatter carried from the living room area, Star pulled a stack of bowls from one of the cabinets and handed them to her. "You're delivering tomorrow, right?"

"Right. Most of it will be taken to the church in Canyon Springs, where volunteers will group the packages for the regional pregnancy centers and those with four-wheel drives will see that gifts get out even to the more remote areas. Like the reservation. I delivered a few packages on my way back here, too." She couldn't resist stopping by to see Kimmy. "That's why I'm running late. Thanks for holding supper for me. It smells delicious."

Tonight's treat was beanless beef chili, the kind served on top of a fluffy bed of rice and finished off with a dollop of sour cream and grated cheddar.

"Is Garrett joining us?" Ronda rummaged in the silverware drawer, searching for enough spoons. "He used to love Grandma's chili."

A knot tightened in Jodi's stomach as she paused in placing the bowls around the table. "Actually...he has things to take care of this evening. Christmas is a busy time for him."

"A preacher's work is never done, I guess. At least we can put some aside in the freezer and give it to him the next time he pops in."

She didn't have the heart to tell her sister he wouldn't be popping in. Ever.

A cheery ringtone alerted her that she had an incoming call, and reaching into the pocket of her knit vest, she retrieved it. Melody Lenter, at long last. With the family noisily congregating in the main room, she quickly moved into the hallway near the bedrooms for privacy.

A tingle of apprehension touched the back of her neck. Would the other woman be disappointed when she learned donations weren't up to that of past years? So many people said they'd already donated. And although she'd explained that apparently emergency needs had come up that required raiding the intended Christmas gifts, some were sincerely unable to contribute further.

She caught the call on its final ring. "Melody! We meet at last."

"I'm so sorry, Jodi." A lilting Southern drawl carried through the ear piece. "I kept thinkin' I'd have me some time to get back to you, but Daddy's been in and out of the hospital. And now his oldest sister and her husband have come down with the flu and I'm running back and forth between the two households, trying to keep everybody fed and watered. It's just one thing after another."

"Sounds exhausting."

"When you talk to our good pastor, please let him know I'll do my best to be back right after the first of the year. No promises. But after the holidays my sister will be in town and can spell me for a while." Melody paused to draw a breath. "So how are things going with the Christmas project? Fun, isn't it, honey?"

"It has been." She could be honest about that. For the most part, anyway. After she'd better come to terms with past issues that had held her hostage for way too long, she'd actually enjoyed it.

"Have y'all made the deliveries? Christmas is only a few days away."

"We're teaming up with Canyon Springs Christian to get that taken care of tomorrow."

"Perfect. It sounds as if everything's under control."

"I hope you won't be too disappointed with the outcome of leaving the project in the hands of a stranger. I understand you've faithfully overseen it for quite a few years."

"Now, why would I be disappointed? I trust Garrett to have found someone capable of handling it. I'm sure you've done a fine job."

"I can't help but wish, though, that we could have filled the storeroom to overflowing."

"That shouldn't have been *too* hard to do. It was three-quarters full already."

Obviously, the stress of being a full-time caregiver had rattled the woman's memory. "When Garrett first showed me the storeroom, it was all but empty."

Jody cringed as the woman laughed, not taking her revelation seriously.

"You must have looked in the wrong storage room."

"Little snowman on the door?"

Melody gasped.

"There was a single package of disposable diapers, to be exact," Jodi added.

"No way. No way." She was obviously in denial. "There were stacks of those. And maternity and baby clothes. Cases of baby wipes and formula, bottles, you name it. It was like a baby warehouse."

"None of that."

"Someone must have broken in and—" The woman went abruptly silent. Had she fainted from shock?

"Melody?"

Then came a giggle. A giggle that immediately erupted into a full-fledged belly laugh. Had the poor woman lost her mind?

"Melody?"

"Oh my goodness." The words came between raspy gasps. Half laugh, half wheezing for air. "Oh, my. Oh, my. Oh, my."

"Are you okay?"

"The exterminator." She broke out in laughter again. She'd gone off the deep end. Garrett had mentioned she could sometimes be a bit flighty, but hadn't mentioned anything to this extreme.

"You've lost me, Melody." She didn't want to push her, but surely something more lucid would come forth if she was encouraged to explain.

"The exterminator. The bug guy, honey." Melody laughed again. "He was scheduled for his quarterly visit and no way did I want him prowling around squirting his little chemicals in the nooks and crannies of that storeroom. They claim that stuff is harmless, but I didn't want to risk pregnant mamas or little ones being exposed to anything dangerous. So the weekend before he was to come, Ralph and I—Ralph's my husband— hauled all the donations over to our house."

"Are you saying there are *more* gifts somewhere?"

"Tons, honey, tons. In our guest room. The day after we moved them out of the church, I got the call about Daddy. So Ralph and I took off. I didn't give it a second thought that we'd temporarily moved everything off the premises. I remembered to call Garrett and tell him we were leaving town, but that's about it." She gave another laugh. "Poor Pastor McCrae, I bet he just about fell through the floor when he opened that door to an empty room."

"Close to it."

"Well, honey, you just apologize to him for me. And if you knock on Sissy Taylor's door, my neighbor to the north, she can lend you my house key and get you right in there. Will that give you time to wrap everything and make deliveries?"

Did she have any choice? But her relief at being able to meet everyone's expectations was so immense she wouldn't have cared if she personally had to stay up all night long and wrap every single item all by herself.

"It's doable."

"I'm so glad we could finally connect tonight." Melody giggled again. "And that you reminded me of what I'd done with all those donations I've been collecting since early summer."

"Garrett remembered the storeroom being fuller a few months ago, but thought there had been some maternity-related emergencies."

"I dipped into it a time or two. But not in a major way." A happy sigh carried over the phone. "Well, all's well that ends well, right? I've got to run. Hear Daddy calling for me. But honey, I do wish you the best of Christmases. And you give our favorite pastor a big holiday hug from me, will you?"

"I—"

"Take care now."

Jodi remained standing in the hallway for a long moment, stunned at this unexpected turn of events. Then, like Melody, she couldn't help but laugh as she again joined her sisters in the kitchen, her mind overcome with wonder. "Wow."

"Wow, what?" Star demanded.

"From that smile on your face—" Ronda cut her a mischievous look as she stirred the chili "—I'm guessing that was a call from Garrett."

Jodi's high spirits faltered, but she made a funny face at her sister. "Nooo. Remember how I said donations for the Christmas project weren't up to previous years? How I felt I'd let everyone down? Well, that was Melody, who has headed up the project for years. And guess what?"

Ronda placed her hands on her hips. "I'm not going to guess, Jodi. Just tell us."

"She'd forgotten that before she made an emergency trip out of town that she'd taken a storage space full of donations to her house for safekeeping"

Both sisters squealed.

"This is fantastic." Ronda's face almost glowed, then her eyes widened with alarm. "Are they already wrapped or will you have to do that before making deliveries tomorrow?"

"Unwrapped." But she didn't care. "I'll make some phone calls—get Melody's house key and round up volunteers to come in early to transfer the gifts to the church."

"Let us know if there's anything we can do to help."

Thank you, thank you, Lord. After supper she'd call around for a wrapping crew and a few more cars and drivers. It was a last-minute job she wouldn't mind doing in the least, and she imagined the others would be happy to pitch in again, too. Garrett would be delighted.

At the thought of Garrett, a queasy feeling rolled over in her stomach. Should she call him, too, and let him in on the good news?

Chapter Sixteen

"Do you have time for a quick chat, Pastor McCrae?"

From where he sat at his desk early Friday morning, typing up notes for Sunday's Christmas message, Garrett looked up at church board members Bert Palmer and Julian Gonzales standing in his open office doorway.

He'd been expecting this "chat" for weeks. While it wouldn't be comfortable hearing them deliver the expected message, at least he'd had other plans all along.

"Sure, come on in." Garrett stood, motioning them to the seating area. Julian closed the door to give them privacy, and the three settled into the wingback chairs.

"Hard to believe, isn't it?" Julian ventured. "A whole year has gone by since you signed on to pastor Christ's Church. You've probably been wondering why we haven't come to see you sooner. You know, about your future here."

"I admit I thought I might hear from you earlier."

"We apologize for that," Julian continued as the two board members exchanged a glance. "It wasn't our intention to leave you hanging. But there have been issues involved that required input and resolution."

"Understandable." They probably had members lined up out the door, eager to share lamentations on the performance of their interim pastor. A few of the complainants might even have been his own extended family members. Hadn't Luke been known to scold him for not following protocol?

"But before you continue, though—" Garrett wanted to smooth the path for the pair he'd come to highly respect this past year. "I'd like to say that working with you and the other church members has been an experience that I'm deeply thankful for. It's been a growing time. A stretching time. A time of blessing. I don't regret having taken on this filler role until you could find a permanent replacement."

The men exchanged glances again.

"Fire away, then, gentlemen. And don't hold anything back. I can take my lumps like a man."

Bert frowned. "Lumps?"

"I mean, you don't have to sugarcoat anything. I'm well aware of my shortcomings and the areas in which I still need to grow. I know that at times I haven't met expectations and have probably let you down."

Julian shifted in his chair. "I can't say we agree with your self-evaluation, Garrett. At least not the way you've worded it. Quite frankly, we've been delighted that you *haven't* met our original expectations."

"Or rather, our concerns," Bert clarified. "As you probably guessed, we had our doubts when your grandma approached us about you after yet another pastor pulled out to leave us sitting high and dry. You'd left behind a pretty wild legacy when you headed out of town after high school. And after that, Drew Everton's accident."

Bert looked uncomfortable at having to bring that up.

"Again, I fully understand." At least he hadn't disappointed them entirely. "And in spite of your reservations, thank you for the opportunity you've given me to take part in ministering to my hometown."

Julian grinned. "Sounds to me, then, that you're willing to take us on for the duration."

Was this a roundabout way of asking if he could fill in a little longer? Tide them over to the next minister? "What duration are we talking about? A month? Two?"

Bert gave him an odd look. "However long God leads you to stay on as our permanent pastor."

Garrett straightened in his chair. "You're asking me—?"

"We're muddling this all up, Garrett," Bert apologized. "Julian and I are here on behalf of the church board to offer you a permanent pastorship for as long as you want to be here or until God leads you elsewhere. Complete with a raise, health insurance and a retirement program."

Garrett blinked. They were offering him a job?

"That's what took us so long to make this offer," Julian added. "We didn't want to commit to benefits we couldn't deliver, but that's been taken care of now. Offerings are up since you came on board, and we've now worked out the paperwork and legalities involved."

"We wish we could offer you a parsonage, though." Bert gave him a regretful look. "You know, so you wouldn't have to keep boarding with the Lovells. We had to sell off our parsonage to make ends meet after the last economic downturn."

Garrett could only stare at them, trying in vain to process all that they were saying.

Julian chuckled. "You know, Bert, I think we've left Garrett speechless for the first time in his life."

Bert smiled, too. "So what do you say, Pastor Mc-Crae? When you originally interviewed, you'd mentioned furthering your education. We can be flexible—maybe even assist financially as you pursue an advanced degree."

They wanted him to *stay*? Offering a raise? Assistance with his education?

"I am," he said slowly, "as Julian pointed out, entirely speechless."

Stunned, to be exact. This new direction was out of the blue. He hadn't considered it as an option. All along he thought Old Man Moppert and a few long-entrenched, hard-to-please others would ensure he'd be out of here by year's end.

Bert leaned forward. "Are you willing to take us on?"

"To be quite honest, I don't know what to say. This offer is, to say the least, unexpected."

Bert gave Julian an I-told-you-so look. "Our wives said we should discuss this with you early on, even if we didn't have all the details worked out. That you might be making other plans. You haven't, have you?"

"Actually, I have.

"That big-city church you interned at wants you back, right?"

"No, but I have another venture under consideration."

"So have we lost out? A day late and a dollar short?" Julian's shoulders slumped. "Oh, man, Marisela and Staci aren't going to be happy with us."

Suddenly uncomfortable, Garrett rose and moved to stand behind his chair, gripping the padded back.

"I'm afraid I've long had my heart set on mission work, gentlemen."

Then why did this unexpected offer fill him with such an incredible joy, tug so insistently at his spirit? Had Drew been right? This was his calling? Or did the fact that he'd instantly thought of how staying in Hunter Ridge might enable a future with Jodi prove this was yet another test to be passed, to prove his mettle and strengthen his resolve? Mission work in remote areas of the world wasn't for the indecisive. God had to know He could count on you.

Julian perked up. "We can provide opportunities for you in hands-on missions work if that's what you're looking for. Like building homes in Mexico or doing projects on the Arizona reservations. We might even be able to foot the bill for a short-term overseas trip on down the road. You know, with one of those ministries Drew's so involved in."

These guys were *serious*. They sincerely wanted to keep him here. But did God want him to turn them down flat? Close the door on temptation and settle it right now, once and for all?

Bert raised a brow. "If you haven't made a final decision on anything, would you at least agree to pray about it? Give God a chance to weigh in? Maybe give us a word of hope to take back to the board—and our wives?"

What would it sound like to these fine men if a minister bluntly said no, he wasn't willing to pray about it? They had him over a barrel. And he could hardly say he'd pray about it and then *not* pray about it, even if he thought he already had a good idea how God felt about this one.

He gripped the back of the chair more tightly. "I'd be willing to do that."

Both men stood, and Bert thrust out his hand for a shake. "No hurry. No pressure. Take all the time you need."

Still overwhelmed, Garrett also shook Julian's hand. "I thank you both for your support."

"Not just us, Pastor. The whole board. And, except for a few members who shall remain nameless—although a man with your spiritual discernment can probably guess the outliers—the membership will welcome you with open arms."

"I'm sincerely humbled."

"We're grateful you'll give our offer your prayerful consideration." Bert gave him a quick nod. "We'd love to keep you, Pastor McCrae, but we want you to be firm in God's will should you decide to accept."

When they departed, Garrett closed the door, then dropped into the chair behind his desk, overwhelmed. He'd had it in his head for so long that God called him to fill the role Drew had been forced to abandon. Despite denials to Drew, Jodi and Grandma Jo, he'd harbored a certainty that in some small way he could make up for the part he'd played in the tragedy that robbed his friend of a long-held dream.

Then Jodi had unexpectedly reappeared on his doorstep—the girl, now a woman, he'd never quite gotten over. He was more drawn to her these past two weeks than ever before. She knew him like no one else did—the good and the bad.

And he'd turned her away.

He'd pushed her away because of a commitment to what he'd been so sure he'd been called to. Was this job offer at Christ's Church a test from God? A temptation of the enemy to lure him away from God's best? Or an answer to the prayers of a lonely man who deeply desired to follow his Heavenly Father's leading?

He leaned back in the chair and closed his eyes. He had a lot of hours of prayer and scripture meditation ahead of him.

He *had* to get this one right.

"Garrett's going to be amazed when he finds out what happened," a smiling Sofia said as she, Jodi and nine other ladies from the church finished loading— to the gills—six vehicles parked outside the church.

Garrett *would* be amazed, that is, if he joined them on their trek. He'd originally planned to come along this morning—but that was before he'd made a U-turn in their relationship. Jodi wasn't ready to face him.

"The mothers are going to be thrilled with all of this." Sunshine Carston waved her hand toward the SUV next to her, an early wedding gift from her husband-to-be. "And the volunteers at Canyon Springs Christian should be able to beat the Pacific storm front that's supposed to push in tonight."

"You've done a great job on this project, Jodi," Delaney Hunter called to her. "Even without last night's unexpected boon, it would still be a respectable Merry Christmas for gals who need to know they're loved."

"I can't accept all the credit." Jodi secured the canvas tarp covering the pickup bed's contents. "Like the saying goes, it takes a village."

"That it does," a male voice chimed in from where Garrett was helping a bundled-up Dolly out a side door of the church. The ladies cheered as their much-loved pastor put in an appearance.

In spite of herself, Jodi's heart gave a happy leap, which she immediately tamped down. Now that she was considering a move to Hunter Ridge, it was just as well that Garrett wouldn't be ministering at the church here. How could she bear to see him on a regular basis?

Perhaps today, though, she'd have an opportunity to apologize. To find a few minutes to again ask his forgiveness for betraying a confidence and to assure him it had never been her intention to draw him away from God's plan for his life. Not that another apology would change anything between them. He'd made his decision. But maybe it would ease the ache in her heart.

Marisela put her hands on her hips. "We thought you might be skipping out on us, Pastor."

"You know me better than that." Garrett wagged a playful finger at her, then surveyed the cars, SUVs and pickups. "So everything's loaded? You don't need my Explorer?"

Delaney shook her head at her cousin-in-law. "Nope, this does it, even with last night's surprise bonanza."

"A surprise?"

He focused a curious look on Jodi. Was he wondering why she hadn't called to share the news with him? Quickly she filled him in on her phone call with Melody.

He chuckled at the end of the tale. "So it was at her house this whole time?"

She nodded, enjoying the dumbfounded look on Garrett's face.

He laughed. "Does God work in mysterious ways, or what?"

"He does."

"Amazing. So, then, ladies—" His merry gaze now embraced the others. "Since my SUV isn't needed, the least I can do is drive one of the vehicles." He held out his hand to Jodi. "Keys, please."

He was going to drive hers? Was she expected to ride along with him, or ride with one of the other volunteers?

"You go in the middle, Jodi." Dolly gave her a push toward Rio's truck. "I want to be where I can grip the armrest in case Garrett takes a curve too fast. That boy still doesn't understand what a brake pedal is for."

The others laughed and moved toward their respective vehicles, but Jodi hesitated—until Garrett jerked his head in the direction of the truck to indicate she was to go before him.

How awkward. But she'd be squeezing three into the front seat of any of the other vehicles, too, and it might draw unwanted attention if she refused to ride with Garrett and Dolly in her own truck.

When he'd opened the passenger-side door, she reluctantly climbed inside, then searched for her seat belt as he helped Dolly aboard.

"All in?" He slammed the side door and strode around the front of the truck to climb in. Then he squinted up at the lowering clouds. "Good thing we can get this done this morning."

Jodi nodded, uncomfortably conscious of Garrett's jacketed arm brushing hers as he buckled his seat belt. She could smell the leather of his jacket and the clean fresh scent of his aftershave—and scooted a tiny bit in Dolly's direction.

The older woman patted her arm. "I imagine you're enjoying your family."

"I am. It's been fun. My two brothers-in-law will

be coming this afternoon instead of tomorrow, hoping to get in ahead of the snow. So the more the merrier. Although I wasn't originally sold on the idea, I'm glad that my sisters insisted we do this."

"Your grandmother certainly loved having you all here for the summers and holidays."

Jodi nodded, conscious of Garrett's listening ears. Grandma had loved it when he and his Grandma Jo visited, too. Except for that last time, of course, when she'd caught him teaching her granddaughter the fine art of kissing.

She shoved aside the memory. "It was a dream world that most kids don't get to enjoy now. So much more freedom. I'm thankful for the time I got to spend up here."

"As much as I once wanted to get away from this town," Garrett joined in as he took the caravan's lead out of the parking lot, "I can't imagine growing up anywhere else."

He might say that, but once again he could hardly wait to put the little community behind him. At least, though, he wasn't like so many who wandered aimlessly, who spent the majority of their lives trying to find a purpose.

The trip to Canyon Springs went quickly, with Garrett and Dolly doing most of the talking, only occasionally encouraging her to join in. Did Garrett find this as awkward as she did? Thankfully, not many knew that only a few days ago it appeared God might be drawing them together. How rapidly things had changed. If Dolly noticed anything out of kilter about their interactions today, she didn't let on.

Despite their falling-out, Garrett was still so, well,

so *Garrett*. Bursting into song when the radio channel they'd been listening to piped up with an especially jazzy rendition of a Christmas carol, he elbowed her until he got her to join in. Even Dolly found herself nodding along with the beat. Just like old times, fun followed Garrett wherever he went.

Which left her feeling a little sad. Did he feel nothing, not even a twinge of downheartedness at having closed the door to her?

When they pulled into the parking lot at Canyon Springs Christian, Dolly gasped. "This looks just like a Christmas card, doesn't it?"

It did. The native stone building, set back in a stand of ponderosa pines, featured a cross atop its bell tower and a snow-covered roof that resembled that of an icing-topped gingerbread house.

With snow flurries now dancing in the air, Meg Diaz and other volunteers from the church joined those from Hunter Ridge in hauling in the gifts to be divvied up for distribution that afternoon.

Jodi caught up with Meg. "Where's Kara?"

Meg linked the fingers of both her hands and held them out in front of her like a rounded belly. "Her husband didn't want her out today for fear she'd slip and fall. For once Kara wasn't stubborn about it, so you can imagine how she's feeling right about now."

Not long ago, envy would have stabbed—and guilt would have gnawed. But today Jodi felt free. Clean. And filled with compassion for Kara's discomfort.

She glanced in Garrett's direction to find him watching her as he lifted a box from the back of the pickup. He dipped his head slightly and winked, almost as if he understood.

We would have made a good team, Lord.

But she wasn't going there today. No gloom fests. Today was about helping single moms, young women who were likely just as scared as she'd once been. Feeling just as stupid. Just as alone. Just as ashamed. Maybe even angry.

Among them would be young women like Kimmy who'd been kicked out when their family couldn't deal with the reality of their situation. At least Jodi knew with all her heart that her own family would never have kicked her out of their home.

Could she ever bring herself to tell them the truth of that difficult time in her life? Maybe. Someday. She'd certainly discuss it with her nieces if she suspected either was being pressured by a boy who claimed to love her. It might be, too, that she'd one day be called on to have a heart-to-heart with a teenage Henry.

As she carried another bag into the church, she couldn't help but glance in Garrett's direction as he hauled in one of the heavier items. On the drive over, he'd acted as if he didn't have a care in the world. But that wasn't true.

She still suspected that, like her, he needed to be set free from the chains of guilt that bound him. But to do that, wouldn't he first need to admit that there were any chains at all?

Chapter Seventeen

No doubt about it, he was proud of Jodi.

With a Christmas tune playing quietly in the background on their return trip to Hunter Ridge, the gentle notes of a saxophone the perfect backdrop for the now steadily falling snow, he glanced over at Jodi who was chatting with Dolly about the best way to cook a turkey. He'd had Al drop it off at the Thorpe cabin yesterday, to her sisters' delight.

He wouldn't say anything to her about those proud feelings, of course. But she'd proven today how big the strides were that she'd made in the way she'd dealt with the unexpected arrival of a seventeen-year-old single mother with her infant and a very pregnant teenage mom-to-be. In fact, she'd gravitated to them, the peace now in her heart reflecting in her expression as she'd placed an arm around one of the girls. She'd even reached out to cradle the baby in her arms.

It would take time. There would undoubtedly be setbacks. More healing for God to do. But she was going to be okay. Someday God would send her a man worthy of her, a man who would be a father to *her* children. Drew? Man, as much as he loved his buddy, he sure hoped not.

Adjusting the windshield wiper speed, he refocused his thoughts, although not on anything any more comforting. He'd been up a good deal of the night, but still had no clear lead as to what he was to do. How could he be certain if leaving—or staying—was the right decision? His thoughts were muddled, that's for sure, but he knew God wasn't a God of confusion. He had to be patient, not rush in one direction or the other. Julian and Bert said to take his time. He needed to trust that God would find a way to clearly hammer home His preference.

"What's *your* preference, Garrett?"

Startled as the background conversation intruded on his thoughts, he turned to Dolly, her gaze fixed intently on him.

"Pardon?"

"What's your preference? Corn-bread dressing or cranberry-walnut stuffing?"

"Yes."

Jodi laughed, and his heart hummed at the sound. Dolly merely shook her head.

"Well, you asked, didn't you? I assumed you wanted an honest answer." He couldn't help but smile. He'd miss Dolly when—if—he left. She'd put up with a lot from him this past year. He'd forever treasure his time with her and her husband. Fifty years of marriage. Three kids. Seven grandkids. It was a joy to hang around couples who'd weathered the good times and the bad. People who knew how to put someone's best interests before their own, to love richer or poorer, in sickness and in health. Maybe some of their wisdom would rub off on him.

But could he honestly say, fully believe, that he'd ever be capable of meeting someone else's needs before his own? Or had he done that when he'd given Jodi back to God?

He glanced again at Jodi, who was gazing almost pensively out the side window. *Penny for your thoughts, pretty lady.*

Dolly had asked him, although unrelated to the thoughts drifting through his mind, what his preferences were. He couldn't deny he was beginning to have a few very distinct ones.

But he had to be sure.

"I thought Garrett would stop by today." The corners of Star's mouth turned downward as she dropped one-third of a cup of pancake batter into the hot nonstick pan. "The kids had so much fun building a snow fort with him the other day. I even felt like a kid again myself. And today—building snowmen, playing fox and geese and all the inside games. Those would have been even more fun if he'd have joined us, don't you think?"

Jodi smiled despite a melancholy tug at her heart as she glanced at the children crowded around the nativity scene, each holding a king or shepherd figurine as they journeyed them in their imaginations to Bethlehem. Just like she and Garrett used to do. "Life's always more fun when Garrett's around."

Star sighed as she lifted the edge of the pancake with a spatula and flipped it over. Nice and golden. "I don't see how he could resist the promise of pumpkin pancakes this evening—he has to eat sometime, doesn't he?

And how could that obviously smitten man miss out on another opportunity to see *you*?"

She wasn't ready to tell the family that a romantic relationship that had sprung to life so quickly had already withered and died. Ironically, her visit to Hunter Ridge had originally been motivated by not wanting to put a damper on her family's holiday. Now this.

"Come on, Star. It's Christmas Eve. I imagine today's been packed for him. I had no illusions that we'd see him beyond a glimpse in the pulpit tonight."

Jodi dipped into the batter bowl and poured a dollop into her own heated pan. Pumpkin pancakes before the Christmas Eve service was a tradition at the cabin, and it took teamwork to prepare enough for the hungry household. Then after the service, they'd return for a family time around the tree—reading the Christmas story, singing favorite songs, and sharing a bedtime snack of chocolate chip cookies and hot chocolate.

Oh, and each opening one present.

She'd already slipped one away that she'd earlier placed under the tree for Garrett. Maybe she'd mail the gloves once his plans were firm. Even desert regions could be bitterly cold.

"Tomorrow, then." Star gave a conclusive nod as she slid a pancake onto the almost-filled platter, then again dipped the measuring cup into the batter.

"Don't count on it."

Star frowned. "Why not?"

"You forget, sis, he has family here in town, and they have their own gatherings and traditions."

"Oh, pooh. Doesn't the Bible say a man shall leave his mother—"

Star had already assumed that there was something of a more lasting nature between her and Garrett. She'd obviously seen *something* there. At least Jodi could take consolation that she hadn't imagined it—although that was a pretty sorry solace.

"Mmm. This smells incredible." Star's husband Mac joined them to lean in and snatch a piece of crisp bacon off the warming tray, then kissed his wife's cheek.

Star all but purred at the attention. "We're almost ready to eat. Where are Ronda and Jon?"

Mac lowered his voice. "I think they're trying to get the you-know-what assembled."

"Well, tell them to get on in here and take care of that later. Jodi already has the table set. Doesn't it look great? Just like Grandma used to do."

He stepped back to inspect the festive arrangements. The sun had already dipped behind the silhouetted ponderosas, the fat candles in the lanterns lending a homey glow to the mismatched china, cloth napkins, and red-and-green plaid tablecloth. "Sure wish I could have experienced a bit of your childhood. My grandma thought holidays were an excuse to eat out or cater in."

Jodi cringed. If not for Garrett, that's exactly what they'd be doing.

Star cast her an impish look, then slid her final pancake onto the waiting stack, and Jodi did the same. She wasn't looking forward to tonight's Christmas Eve service, but there was no way to get out of it without drawing her family's unwanted attention to the disappointing outcome of a relationship that had such a short time ago seemed so promising.

Happy holidays, everyone.

How could she bear seeing Garrett up front tonight, all the while knowing that he didn't have room in his big heart for her?

* * *

What a day.

His cell phone pressed to his ear, Garrett gathered his Bible from the dresser top as he prepared to head off to the church. He was running late. Again.

"You're more than welcome, Dick. Gotta keep those kids of yours toasty warm. And Merry Christmas to you, too."

He pocketed his cell phone with a smile. While he'd have preferred the utility company hadn't mentioned his name, making arrangements for overdue bill payment for a couple who had fallen on hard times was an expense he was more than happy to cover.

He'd just opened the door to the coat closet in the living room when his cell phone rang again. He placed his Bible on a nearby chair and jerked his jacket off a hanger, still managing to answer on the third ring.

"Mr. McCrae?" a youthful male voice asked tentatively.

"You got him."

"Me and my friends—we got home before dark. Our folks thought we should let you know. Thanks for stopping to help us."

On his way back from Canyon Springs, having dropped off an elderly church member who feared driving on bad roads but wanted to spend Christmas with his sister and her family, he'd spotted a carload of teenagers at the side of the road. Out of gas.

"You're welcome. Jake, was it? I'm glad to hear you made it safe and sound."

"We hope you have a Merry Christmas."

"I'm counting on it. Merry Christmas to all of you, too."

He again shoved his phone into his pocket, then glanced at his watch and groaned. It was a little hard to sneak in late when you sat at the front of the church. He'd spent much of the day, though, putting out fires, so to speak. Usually with the arrival of Christmas Eve day, the hectic aspects of the holidays settled down. But not this year.

Nor had today been spent as he'd originally envisioned only a few days ago. He couldn't count the times his thoughts turned to Jodi and her family. Wondering what they were doing, if the kids had missed him as they made another snowman—and how those pumpkin pancakes they always had on Christmas Eve would have tasted.

But he had only himself to blame for being left out.

He'd taken his eyes off the ball, so to speak, allowed himself to get sidetracked when Jodi arrived in town. He should have thought it through better before getting carried away and suggesting they give God a chance to see where He wanted them to go. *He'd* already been told, hadn't he? Nevertheless, he'd let himself play with fire. Got his hopes up—and probably Jodi's—about finding a way for him to manipulate God's plans.

He slipped his arms into his jacket sleeves and adjusted the collar. Now another unexpected twist threatened to derail him. He'd promised Bert and Julian he'd take the offer under prayerful consideration. But nothing had changed since yesterday, had it? Not really. He was still a man with a purpose—one that didn't include Jodi or a local pastorship. God hadn't changed His mind, and neither should he.

So why didn't he feel at peace with that?

And had he, truly, ever felt a peace about it? He'd

long told himself the restlessness, the underlying disquiet, would go away. That peace would come after he got through Bible college. Got through this interim pastorship.

It would come once he was released from here and on the mission field, right? That confirmation?

Leaning into the closet, he pulled his guitar case from the back. He hadn't played in a while and should probably have carved out some time to practice today. Too late now, though.

"Don't you look handsome." In her coat, boots and gloves, Dolly paused in the living room doorway to gaze at him with a smile. While he wasn't in a suit, he'd topped the forest-green cashmere sweater his folks had given him as an early Christmas present with a tan corduroy sports jacket. And a tie. "You should dress up more often. I imagine Jodi would agree wholeheartedly."

Was Dolly feeling him out? Sensing that something had subtly changed since only a handful of nights ago when she and Al had helped him and Jodi decorate the cabin? But he didn't want to talk about Jodi.

"Thanks for the vote of approval." He zipped the jacket up to his neck, then pulled his gloves from his pockets. "Are you sure you and Al don't want a ride? It's getting kind of nasty out there."

"He's warming up the car, and we'll be right behind you."

With a quick kiss to her cheek, he headed out the door, Bible and guitar in hand. When he arrived at the church, he paused before exiting his vehicle to take in the Kinkade-like scene. Stained glass windows glowed through the steadily falling snow, and a troupe of faithful worker bees, shovels in hand, were busy keeping the sidewalks and steps cleared for those arriving.

Unless the Heavenly referee blew His whistle before Garrett turned down the church's offer at the conclusion of tonight's service, this would be his last Christmas in Hunter Ridge for who knew how long. Maybe forever. When he'd returned to town a year ago, not particularly happy about it but determined to yield to God's—and Grandma Jo's—will, he hadn't expected to feel a tug at his heart as he prepared to leave.

Assuming she came to this service and tomorrow's as well, tonight would be one of his final glimpses of Jodi, too. But he wasn't surprised at the heart tug accompanying that realization.

"There you are." Marisela called with a smile as he stepped inside the main door. She and her husband, whom she nudged with her elbow, were greeters tonight. "Bert here was afraid he might have to get out his harmonica, so we're both glad to see you here—and with that guitar of yours."

"Can you play 'Silent Night' on that harmonica, Bert?"

The older man's smile widened. "You betcha."

"Plan on it, then. We'll close with a duet."

Bert's eyebrows rose, but Garrett patted him on the back and headed into the dimly lit church. Good folks, the Palmers.

Once settled on the platform, though, his heart momentarily stalled when he spied Jodi—beautiful in the soft candlelight—sitting near the front next to Drew, with her family members filling the pew on her other side.

You're not making this easy on me, Lord.

As Sofia's gifted fingers on the piano keys filled the hallowed space with the sweet notes of "O Come, O Come Emmanuel," he momentarily closed his eyes. Drawing in the faint scent of pine from the beribboned swags of evergreen branches, he endeavored to focus his thoughts on this holy time of year. On the gift of God's son.

Julian Gonzales, not only a church board member but a talented vocalist, followed Garrett's opening prayer with a moving solo of "What Child Is This?"—then led the congregation in song after worshipful song. A cluster of giggling grade school children followed, crowding onto the platform to recite "pieces" he'd memorized himself when their age, and then it was his turn to speak.

In spite of good intentions, he hadn't much time to prepare the message. The past several days had been filled with activity. With prayer.

As he gripped the edges of the lectern, he gazed out over the congregation. His Grandma Jo was over there with his sister's two kids on one side and cousin Luke's little Chloe on the other. And seated next to the little girl, Luke's Travis and his girlfriend. Travis's oldest sister, Anna, too, who, like Jodi, was shedding her tomboyish ways.

Newlyweds Luke and Delaney smiled back at him, and Grady had his arm comfortably around his fiancée's shoulders, Sunshine's kindergarten-aged daughter Tessa snuggled in at his other side. Then close by, Sunshine's best friend, Tori Janner, who was almost a part of the little family that would unite in an upcoming Valentine's Day wedding.

Uncle Dave and a somewhat frail-looking Aunt

Elaine, a sparkling turban on her head, looked into each other's eyes, savoring each day together that God granted them. His gaze slowly passed over other uncles and aunts. Cousins. His own folks. A sanctuary full of people, many of whom he'd known since childhood. People he'd come to love this past year.

He'd miss them all.

Even Randall Moppert.

With a smile tugging, he cleared his throat and bowed his head. "Please join me in prayer."

He couldn't have told anyone afterward exactly what he'd said to God during that prayer—or in the message that followed. But he spoke from the depths of his heart during both, filled with a deep thankfulness. His message was of God's love for His creation, a message of the redeeming miracle of Jesus's birth and ultimate sacrifice on the cross, a message of the hope yet to come at His promised return.

God willing, his words would continue to impact hearts here long after he'd moved on from this pastorship.

At the conclusion of his message, he reached for his guitar and motioned to Bert to join him on the platform. As the delicate opening notes of "Silent Night" whispered to the farthest corner of the hushed sanctuary, he again looked out on the people of this church. Christ's Church.

"Silent night, holy night…"

Now standing, the congregation joined him, softly at first, then with an increasing power that echoed through the candlelit space.

"All is calm, all is bright…"

He drew in a breath, his heart weighing heavy with an unknown future stretching before him.

"Round yon virgin, mother and child. Holy infant so tender and mild…"

He swallowed as his eyes drank in the faces of those before him. His folks. Drew. The beautiful Jodi…

The people of Christ's Church.

His church. *His* community.

In that moment, as he quietly picked the strings of his guitar, a tingling sensation curled up the nape of his neck. And peace—that precious, promised peace that passes all understanding—finally pushed its way in to settle into his heart, the beacon he'd long awaited to guide him.

Tears pricked his eyes, but he blinked them away. God had spoken, and this time he was listening.

"Sleep in heavenly peace…"

Chapter Eighteen

It was getting late.

It was already ten thirty, the cabin having finally settled down for the night with giggling kids tucked in their sleeping bags on cots in the attic room above and the couples having slipped off to their own rooms.

She'd be on the sofa again, not bothering to pull out its folding mattress and make up the bed. At least that morning at the grocery store she'd finally found a baby Jesus to substitute for the one she hadn't yet found. Granted, it was a cheap plastic version and only half the size it should have been, but maybe it wouldn't matter to the kids?

As silence descended on the cabin that held so many happy memories—new ones made tonight—she finished cleaning up in the kitchen. Her nieces and nephew had loved the grab-bag gifts. Silly, inexpensive little items, but you'd have thought she'd spent a fortune based on the delight they'd been greeted with. And not a single electronic item among them!

They'd shared warm cookies and cocoa before gathering once again around the brightly lit Christmas tree, taking turns to select a song that would be sung next. The evening wrapped up with Mac reading the Christmas story to sleepy-eyed children—and bedtime hugs and kisses.

Although she'd felt God close throughout this family-filled day, when the couples, hand in hand, had gone off to their own rooms, she struggled to hold back the sense of aloneness that assailed her.

Grabbing a dampened dishcloth, she vigorously wiped down the countertop. *I will not have a pity party tonight.*

But how could she stop thinking of Garrett? Her heart had ached when he'd stepped to the lectern this evening, looking sharp in a green sweater and sports jacket—and tie. She'd had to smother a smile at the memory of a ponytailed teenager who'd cruised around town on a motorcycle that her grandma had forbidden her to ride.

What Grandma didn't know, though, hadn't hurt her…right?

Again an unbidden smile tugged as she put away the silverware and wiped down the dish drainer. At least if she landed that job Brooke had told her about, she could live right here in this much-loved cabin. And with Garrett no longer the local pastor, she could fit comfortably into her new church home, too.

But I'd thought for sure, Lord…

At the sound of soft tapping, she paused to listen. Had one of the kids decided to sneak back downstairs? Then the sound came again—more persistent—and this time she pinpointed it. The back door of the mudroom.

Drying off her hands, she slipped into the adjoining room and drew back the curtain to peep out.

Garrett?

Her heart gave a happy leap, but she quickly tamped down rising hope. He probably wanted to make things right between them. To tie up any loose ends of misunderstanding before he left town. Saying a silent prayer for wisdom, she opened the door.

"Hey, Jodi."

He sounded so casual, his words no different from the many times she'd opened this door to him throughout their growing-up years.

"Hey, Garrett."

"I know it's late." His words came softly, no doubt noting the darkened cabin when he'd approached. "But I was hoping you'd still be up."

"I'm winding down." Her own words were whispered. "Just straightening things in the kitchen so all will be ready for tomorrow."

"I'm sorry I couldn't get here earlier." He glanced off into the snowy night, then back at her. "If this isn't a good time, I can—"

"No, no, this is fine." She stepped back to motion him inside. She may as well get this over with. Perhaps offer the apology that she'd never had the opportunity to make—to assure him she'd never intended to challenge his calling, to stand in the way of God's leading. "Everyone's tucked in for the night."

"That must have been quite a feat settling down the troops." He shut the door behind him. "Especially Henry. That kid has energy to burn."

Just like his "Uncle" Garrett?

"I think we wore them out today, then let them stay up a bit later than usual. My sisters are so set on making lasting memories for them of the cabin. But no matter how much we try, it's not quite the same without Grandma and Grandpa."

"No, it wouldn't be. But there are times, you know, to cherish the past, yet make way for the future."

Was he alluding to *their* past? That they needed to treasure it for what it was—the good times of their childhood—and not mourn what could never be?

"I thought you might like to know," he continued, "that right after tonight's service, Trey Kenton texted that Kara had their little girl."

"Ahh. A Christmas Eve baby."

"And speaking of babies…" He pulled off his gloves and placed them on the countertop, then reached into his pocket to pull out a little gift bag. "I bought you something and wanted to make sure you got it tonight."

He emptied the bag into the palm of his hand.

A tiny plastic Jesus.

"Garrett, thank you. I still haven't found Grandma's." She took the infant from his hand, identical to the one she'd found and tucked away for morning. But she wouldn't tell him that. His thoughtfulness touched her too deeply to spoil his gift.

"I looked all over for something more substantial." He gazed down at the holy child almost self-consciously. "You know, sized to match your grandma's, but…"

"No, this is perfect. The crib won't be empty. Thank you." But her heart ached as she cradled the child in her hand.

He glanced at the open door from which the Christmas tree lights illuminated the small mudroom. Then he gave it a push to slightly close it, apparently not intending for the whole house to hear what he had to say.

"I also came to apologize, Jodi."

She shook her head. She hadn't expected that. "No, Garrett, I owe *you* an apology."

His brow crinkled. "How do you figure?"

"Because it was never my intention to hold you back from where God has told you He wants you to go. That wasn't Drew's intention, either. He didn't want you driven by guilt, and I only saw what an amazing impact you're having on this church and community. But neither of us spent years in prayer, listening to God about it as you have. We had no right to an opinion. No right to challenge you."

"I…disagree."

"No, you were right. We were wrong."

"What I mean, Jodi, is as longtime friends you and Drew had every right under the sun to challenge me. To keep me from moving blindly forward. Not that God couldn't have used me on a foreign mission field. I know He would have. He could take it and bless it even if I'd gone for all the wrong reasons."

A tingle of disquiet rippled through her. "You're talking past tense, Garrett."

And thoroughly confusing her.

"Tonight God showed me that in my blind determination to go to the Middle East, I'd been running away from His good and perfect will. Not toward it."

"I don't understand."

The corners of his mouth lifted as he looked intently into her eyes. "I've been offered a full-time ministry position at Christ's Church, Jode. And I've accepted it."

Her breath caught. "Are you certain, Garrett? You're not just letting Drew's and my all-too-human doubts influence you?"

He shook his head. "At first, I thought you both were

flat-out wrong. That God was testing me to see if I'd turn aside at the first opposition. I was determined not to let that happen. I took offense at what I perceived as your and Drew's interference. So I apologize. I'm sorry if I hurt you."

"Don't apologize. We may have grown up as best friends, but too many years have passed to give me the right to insert myself into your decision-making after having only recently become reacquainted."

"But in many ways, it's been an amazing reacquaintance, hasn't it?" He tilted his head in question.

"It has." Or at least it had until their falling out.

"So to answer your question, yes, I'm certain about committing to the church. To Hunter Ridge. Everywhere I turned the past two days God's confronted me with people not only in need, but people who need *me*. As hard as I tried at first to shut out the implications of that, tonight it was as if God opened my eyes to see what you and Drew had seen. That my life, as impossible as it seems, is making a difference right here in my old hometown."

"He's confirmed the direction you're to take?"

"Rock solid." He placed his hand over his heart. "He's given me that elusive piece to the puzzle that I'd longed for. The piece I thought would fall into place once I escaped this town, once I got away from the reminder of Drew's accident and off on a mission field. I thought that then, somehow, some way, I'd be absolved for the part I played in his injuries."

"Drew said it wasn't your fault."

"Maybe not my fault in that it wasn't a premeditated attempt to injure him. But I should have been more cautious."

"Drew said you *both* got carried away, were goofing off."

"And which of us, do you think, has the longest track record of that?"

"He accepts the responsibility. You didn't make him jump into the water."

"No, but—"

"Let it go, Garrett. I know from my own experience that the hardest thing in the world is to forgive ourselves even when God and others already have. Didn't I hear a very recent Sunday message on this very topic? And someone wise once told me that being unwilling to forgive myself was akin to taking Jesus's sacrificial gift and tossing it in the trash."

Garrett flinched. "Someone wise told you that, did he?"

"Yep."

"You think I should take his advice?"

"I would."

He paused to think a moment—pray?—and she could hear the cabin walls creak. A window rattle. The wind had picked up.

"So you have peace about staying, Garrett?" She had to be sure. Sure that she hadn't aborted God's plan for his life.

"An amazing peace. It hit me during the Christmas Eve service tonight as I looked out across the sea of faces. My family. Yours. Drew. Members and visitors. My heart swelled with a love so powerful, a peace and sense of purpose so overwhelming, I can't even describe it to you. I know that feelings ebb and flow, but I'll always remember this night. Will commemorate it in my heart. I've prayed for this peace, this confirmation of my calling for five years…and now tonight God sent it. Until He tells me differently, this is where I want to invest my life."

A ripple of joy coursed through her. And yet…

"I'm happy for you, Garrett. You will make—are already making—a difference in this town."

"It won't be easy, though."

"God doesn't always call us to do easy, does He?"

"Seldom. But God also revealed to me tonight one thing that would make it a significantly less painful journey." He gently took the baby Jesus from her and placed it next to his gloves. Then as he looked deeply into her eyes, he took her hand in his. "Marry me, Jodi. Marry the new pastor of Christ's Church of Hunter Ridge."

Her eyes widened as all the doubts she'd soothed herself with the past few days—reasons she'd never make a good minister's wife and how God knew that all along—assailed her.

"I… I can't play the piano."

He laughed, his hand tightening on hers. "Or cook? Keep house? Or teach little kids in Sunday school?"

"None of those things. Not very well, anyway."

"To be perfectly honest, Jodi, I'm a pretty good cook, if I do say so myself. Enjoy it actually—if you'd do the cleanup. Sofia's got the piano playing covered. Marisela's backup. And all the Sunday school slots are currently filled. So even if you'd want to, you'd have to wait awhile to get your foot in the door."

"But—"

"Jodi, I love you. I think I've loved you ever since we were kids. Loved you even when you literally gave me a kick in the seat of the pants that sent me sprawling into the dust. I just… I can't imagine life without you in it."

Words she'd only dreamed of hearing.

"I've loved you for as long as I can remember, Garrett. I never dreamed until earlier this week that you might feel the same about me."

"Then it looks like, Jodi, you owe me an answer to my question."

"You posed a question? It was worded more like an order."

"I'm a desperate man, besotted with the woman I love—and scared to death she'll walk away and never look back." He tugged her closer. "So *will* you marry me? We could buy this cabin from your folks and settle in for a happily-ever-after. I even promise to be on my best behavior, too."

She clucked her tongue. "I'm not so sure about that."

"I will. I promise."

"What I mean is, I like you just the way you are." She looked disapprovingly at the uncharacteristic presence of his tie. "I don't want to wake up some morning next to a stranger."

"So is that a yes? Or do I need to get down on my knees and beg?" He dropped to one knee, again clasping her hand. "Will you marry me, Jodi?"

"I will."

Slowly he rose to his feet, his eyes not leaving hers. It didn't take coaxing on his part for Jodi to step into his open arms. But Garrett's lips had barely touched hers when something behind her crashed to the floor with a startling clatter. She spun to see an old tin that Grandma kept on the mudroom shelf, its lid popped off to expose cotton batting stuffed inside.

She pulled away from Garrett and knelt to pull out a cotton-wrapped object. The moment she held it in her hands, her suspicions were confirmed. "You're not going to believe this, Garrett."

She carefully unfolded the cotton. Then, cradling its precious contents in the palm of her hand, she stood and turned to her husband-to-be. "Baby Jesus."

Garrett reverently touched the tiny wooden figurine. The one they'd searched so long and hard for. His eyes then narrowed as he glanced suspiciously at the open shelf behind her. "How did that tin work its way to the edge of the shelf to fall off *right now*?"

She gazed in wonder at the baby in her hand. "It's tempting to think Grandma's given us a seal of approval, isn't it?"

"I'd be more inclined to suspect," Garrett said, shaking his head with a smile, "that she requested a diversion before things got too hot to handle in here."

"You think?"

He gently took baby Jesus and laid Him and the cotton batting next to the plastic one. Then he reached for her hand and tugged her close to gaze into her eyes. Gave a sigh of resignation.

"I love you, Jodi. And as much as I'd like to see how fast we could steam up those windows, out of respect for your grandma, I'd better get going."

"But you just got here." She wasn't ready to let him go. Not yet. Not ever.

His eyes twinkled as he released her hand and reached for his gloves. "It's late—and there's plenty of time in our future for steamy."

She laughed. He was right.

A lifetime.

Her heart dancing in anticipation, Jodi kissed him on the cheek. "But let it be known that I cast my vote for a *short* engagement."

Epilogue

Jodi nestled into the warmth of her sleeping bag, staring into the darkness from her nest on one of the living room couches.

Wide-awake on Christmas morning.

She was worse than a kid—all eyes and ears long before the sun would get around to crawling up over the horizon.

Garrett said he'd see her today. *But when?*

It had been all she could do last night not to bang on closed doors and announce to all what had taken place between her and Garrett. But before he'd stepped into the snowy night, he'd said he wanted to be there when she shared the news. Thankfully, everyone had already gone to bed or she couldn't have managed it. Her glowing face would have been a dead giveaway.

Smiling, she snuggled down deeper in her warm cocoon, relishing the pungent scent of the shadowed Christmas tree, the hint of wood smoke from the banked fire.

After Garrett had departed last night, she'd slipped baby Jesus into his manger. There she'd knelt for quite some time, the radiance from the Christmas tree lights reflecting the praise and wonder that overflowed from her heart. With reluctance, she'd finally unplugged the lights and crept into her makeshift bed. But she'd lain awake for who knows how long, savoring Garrett's words and treasuring the moments he'd held her in his arms.

He wants to marry me.

His tomboy childhood pal. A buddy who'd punched him and kicked him, competed with him, and shared more adventures than she could count. A friend who'd loved him to pieces with her little-kid heart. A woman who'd later made so many mistakes and harbored doubts as to God's love for much too long.

A sound from outside caught Jodi's ears and she tensed, straining to hear. Gravel on the driveway?

Instantly, she was on her feet, wrapping the sleeping bag around her sweatsuit-clad shoulders and thankful for the cozy socks the kids had given her last night. Heading to the front window, she peeped into the wintry night where a softly illuminating snow glow reflected off the lowered clouds.

Her heart leaped at the sight of Garrett's SUV, headlights off, creeping as silently as possible up the drive.

He'd come, just as promised.

She spun away from the window, then abruptly halted. Reindeer-faced socks and a velour sweatsuit. No makeup. Hair mussed from a restless, almost sleepless night. What a scary sight to greet her future husband.

Husband. She liked the sound of that.

Heart racing, she tossed the sleeping bag on the sofa and quietly hurried to the bathroom to finger-comb her hair and swish around a capful of mouthwash. Pinched her cheeks to add a bit of color. She reached the mud-room door and opened it just as Garrett stepped up on the porch.

"You came." Her words weren't but a breathless whisper as the frosty air swirled in around her ankles.

He slipped silently inside and closed the door behind him, then in the dim light drew her close to touch his warm lips to hers.

She nearly melted on the spot. *Last night hadn't been a dream.*

When he finally pulled back slightly, she could hear the smile in his voice. "Merry Christmas, Jodi Thorpe."

"Merry Christmas, Garrett McCrae."

"I didn't sleep a wink. How about you?"

"Well, maybe one. Or two."

He chuckled. "We're quite a pair, aren't we? I apologize for getting here so early, but I—"

She placed a silencing finger momentarily to his mouth. Then gave him a playful kiss. "I thought you'd never get here."

His hands tightened on her waist, his tone suddenly serious. "You know, I got to thinking after I left here. I sort of sprang all this on you last night. Out of the blue. I didn't even bring a ring. Or consider your career plans. If you need more time to think about it…"

Jodi tensed. Surely after the breathtaking greeting he'd just given her, he wasn't having second thoughts, was he? Getting cold feet? She grasped the lapels of his jacket and tugged lightly. "I'm already taking steps to obtain a work-from-home job, so if you're thinking of weaseling out of this, it's too late, Pastor."

She felt the rumble of silent laughter under her hands.

"No weaseling going on here. I wanted to make sure

you're good with this. I can be pushy sometimes. I've always liked to get my own way."

"No foolin'." He wasn't telling her anything she didn't already know.

He was silent for a long moment, and overhead she could hear the creak of the attic floor. He tilted his head to listen as well.

"Sounds as if the troops may be stirring." He took one of her hands in his. "Are you ready to announce our engagement to your family?"

With her free hand, she poked him in the chest. "Just try to stop me."

"No way. I seem to recall a time when that got me wrestled to the ground and my mouth filled with dirt."

Jodi winced. What a brat she'd been. "I did do that, didn't I? I'm sorry."

"Now don't you start apologizing or we'll be standing here all day while I confess my own youthful sins."

The glow of Christmas tree lights suddenly illuminated the mudroom as the strains of "Joy to the World" from Grandma's old Mitch Miller Christmas sing-along CD filled the air.

"My sisters are up." Tears unexpectedly pricked her eyes. "That music was always the signal for us that it was okay to come down the stairs and open presents."

Garrett gently brushed away a tear trickling down her cheek. "You miss your grandma. I do, too."

She took a steadying breath and looked toward the adjoining room, the sound of childish laughter and the pounding of feet on the stairs echoing through the cabin. "I wish she could still be here to enjoy her great-grandchildren."

"Your sisters' kids, you mean?" His words came softly as he cupped her face in his hands. "Or *ours*?"

Startled, she gazed into his love-filled eyes.

"Oh, *yes*, ours, too."

He nodded, satisfied, and then once again captured her mouth with his.

She giggled.

Blame it on the mudroom. Clearly, there would be a slight delay in making that engagement announcement.

* * * * *

**WE HOPE YOU ENJOYED
THIS BOOK FROM**

LOVE INSPIRED

INSPIRATIONAL ROMANCE

Uplifting stories of faith, forgiveness and hope.

Fall in love with stories where faith helps
guide you through life's challenges, and discover
the promise of a new beginning.

6 NEW BOOKS AVAILABLE EVERY MONTH!

LOVE INSPIRED

Stories to uplift and inspire

Fall in love with Love Inspired—
inspirational and uplifting stories of faith
and hope. Find strength and comfort in
the bonds of friendship and community.
Revel in the warmth of possibility and the
promise of new beginnings.

Sign up for the Love Inspired newsletter
at **LoveInspired.com** to be the first
to find out about upcoming titles,
special promotions and exclusive content.

CONNECT WITH US AT:

 Facebook.com/LoveInspiredBooks

Twitter.com/LoveInspiredBks